THE CHAMBER OF TEN

A NOVEL OF THE HIDDEN CITIES

D1313407

CHRISTOPHER GOLDEN & TIM LEBBON

DIVERSION
BOOKS

The Hidden Cities Series
The Map of Moments
Mind the Gap
The Chamber of Ten
The Shadow Men

Diversion Books
A Division of Diversion Publishing Corp.
443 Park Avenue South, Suite 1004
New York, NY 10016
www.diversionbooks.com

For more information, email info@diversion.com

First Diversion Books edition December 2018
Print ISBN: 978-1-63576-393-5
eBook ISBN: 978-1-63576-392-8

LSIDB/1812

In memory of Bonnie Moore

Therefore I tell my sorrows to the stones;
Who, though they cannot answer my distress,
Yet in some sort they are better than the tribunes,
For that they will not intercept my tale:
When I do weep, they humbly at my feet
Receive my tears and seem to weep with me.

—WILLIAM SHAKESPEARE,
Titus Andronicus, Act 3, Scene 1

CHAPTER 1

GEENA HODGE STOOD ON THE BOW OF THE WATER TAXI AS IT chugged toward San Marco, the colors of the Doge's Palace brought to life by the sun, and wondered how much longer Venice would survive before it crumbled into the sea. Though the Italian government had committed to a seven-billion-dollar project to install a complex system of flood gates to hold back storm surges and seasonal high tides, it was already over budget and behind schedule. Sometimes it seemed hopeless.

But even the most optimistic Venetians were fooling themselves. The city had been built on top of wooden pilings sunk into a salt marsh, with sediment and clay beneath that, which was little better than raising palaces on top of a sponge. Venice bore down, squeezing a little more water out of its foundations every year, and sinking just a bit farther. Between that and the rising global sea level, Venice was screwed. Maybe the new tidal gate system, MOSE, would work well enough—fouling up the Venetian lagoon's ecosystem in the meantime—and maybe it wouldn't. Even with the best-case scenario, they would only manage to buy themselves a century.

La Serenissima, they called it—the most serene—and Venice remained a city of serenity and beauty. She was still Queen of the Adriatic, steeped in history and scholarship and art, unique in all the world. There was nowhere like it, and the world would never see its like again. But much of the population had fled the routine flooding and the absurd tourism-driven cost of living in the city, and those who remained were like the curators of a living museum.

Geena's own project, approved by the Italian and Venetian authorities, was evidence that some people in the city understood that ruin could be slowed but not prevented.

"As lovely as ever," said the man beside her. "She's a gem, Venice." Howard Finch, a television producer from the BBC, had come to her in search of a story. And though she had one to give him—as extraordinary a story of archaeology and history as he was ever likely to encounter—she wished he would go away. Reporters were bad enough, always armed with just enough research to get the story wrong. But producers could be much worse. They didn't even *try* to convince you they weren't full of shit.

"Haven't been here in nearly twenty years," Finch continued. "Hard to believe some of the things I've heard."

"Such as?" Geena asked, and immediately regretted it.

He puffed himself up in that way that was universal among the very pompous and very rich in every culture. Geena had been born and raised in the Park Slope neighborhood of Brooklyn, New York. She had met plenty of arrogant men in her thirty-six years, but as bad as Americans could be, the Brits had had much more time to perfect the art of pompousness. Pomposity. Whatever.

"Talked to a bloke last week who said nobody lives on the ground floor at all anymore. Got all the windows bricked up, just letting it go to ruin. Surrendering. And those walkways in the Piazza San Marco—"

"*Passarelle.*"

"They're out all the time now, so people can get through when the canal water floods in."

The water taxi's engine shifted from a purr to a groan as it began to slow, gliding toward a dock not far from the trees of the Giardini ex Reali. They still had an excellent view of the Doge's Palace, but behind his façade Finch seemed uninterested in anything except the sound of his own voice.

Geena smiled at him. She had pulled her hair back in a neat blond ponytail and had actually put on makeup this morning, asked pleadingly by Tonio Schiavo, the head of the archaeology department at Ca' Foscari University, to "come smart." The smile had been part of her marching orders as well. Usually Geena did not have to be told to smile—most days she loved her life—but she wanted to be working, getting her hands dirty, not playing tour guide.

"Mr. Finch, not too long ago the low-lying areas of the city flooded maybe eight or ten times in a year. Now that number averages closer to one hundred. A third of the time, the Piazza San Marco is full of water from the canals, which includes raw sewage, among other unpleasant things. Everyone has Wellington boots in Venice, or they wrap plastic around their shoes, even to use the walkways put out for just that purpose."

Finch nodded in fascination. "Christ, it's like something out of one of those crap sci-fi apocalypse films, isn't it?" he asked, without looking to her for confirmation. "But they've really abandoned the ground floors?"

"Sadly, yes. The bricks are wearing away on the outside. On the inside—what would you do if your first floor was flooded four months out of the year? They're sealed off, left to the water."

"And then what? It keeps rising, they move up another floor?"

"I've wondered the same thing myself," she admitted, but didn't dare comment further. *Nothing negative*, Tonio had instructed, and Geena had no wish to jeopardize her stewardship of this project.

Besides, they had other things to talk about.

Finch had come to Venice on a scouting trip to find out if the Biblioteca project might be worth some air time on the BBC, or if the whole thing would amount to as much hot air as Geraldo Rivera opening Al Capone's vault. Geena didn't mind the idea of a film crew coming in to do a short documentary on the Biblioteca, especially if it would mean some attention would be paid to the broader aspects of her project.

As Venice sank, history was being sucked down into the lagoon. Even the oldest buildings in the city were built on top of the foundations of more ancient structures. The sinking was nothing new. Once upon a time, Venetians had simply raised the ground floors of their buildings every so often to combat the rising water. But with every inch that the weight of Venice dragged it down, and every inch that the sea level rose, more of that ancient architecture was being lost forever.

There were frescoes on walls, secret chambers, and artifacts in long-abandoned rooms and buildings across the city that were being eroded away by salt and sewage and prolonged exposure to the water. Her team—which for a time had mainly been herself and a group of graduate students—had been rescuing what they could and documenting whatever they couldn't in some of the oldest buildings in the city. And then one day, tearing away a crumbling brick and mortar wall in a semi-hidden alcove at the back of the Biblioteca Nazionale Marciana—the National Library of St. Mark's—Geena herself had noticed that the salt from constant flooding had worn tracks in the original wall. But the tracks weren't consistent, and upon closer inspection, she discovered that they marked the seams around a secret door, long since sealed but now being undone by salt and time.

Behind the door, they had found a hidden staircase. Some of the graduate students had been amazed, but Geena had taken it in stride. In centuries past—perhaps in Italy more than anywhere else in the world—secrecy, betrayal, and paranoia had been the order of the day, and hidden passages and chambers had been commonplace. The trope of the secret room existed in fiction because it had so many real-life examples. But people loved that crap, and if it helped to continue to get her work funded, Geena was all for having the media make a big deal out of the city's secret history and mysteries.

The water taxi pulled up to the dock and they waited while a crewman hauled the boat snug against the bumpers before disembarking. Normally Geena used the *vaporetti*—the boats that functioned as buses in this streetless city—but the university would reimburse her for the additional cost of the taxi.

They set off along a tree-lined path toward the wide cobblestoned entrance to the Piazza San Marco. Small waves from passing boats rolled up onto the stones, but the plaza was not flooded today. The Doge's Palace loomed ahead. Over the tops of buildings she could see just the tip of one of the domes of St. Mark's Basilica. But they did not have even that far to walk.

"Before we get there," Finch said, "I must ask . . . do you really believe what you've found is Petrarch's library?"

They walked alongside the Biblioteca, its wall visible through the trees. When they reached the cobblestones, Geena turned left and pulled Finch along in her wake. On such a perfect day the Piazza San Marco was breathtakingly beautiful, the sun making it all seem almost pristine. An illusion, Geena knew, but a lovely one.

She stopped twenty feet from the Biblioteca's front door.

"How much of the history do you know, Mr. Finch?"

He smiled, and a flicker of hidden intelligence shone in his eyes. "Call me Howard," he said. "And I've done my research, Dr. Hodge. Petrarch had what was essentially a circus train of wagons that traveled around with him so he could keep his library close at all times. But eventually he realized how impractical that was. Inspired by ancient stories of public libraries like the one at Alexandria, he arranged to set one up in Venice. In—what was the year?— 1362, I think, the poet moved his entire library here, hundreds of volumes of writing, much of it from antiquity, detailing philosophies and histories and the lives of the ancients, not to mention poetry, of course. Priceless works, many of which modern scholars consider lost, or even pure myth. The Venetians set him up with a posh house—"

"Palazzo Molina," Geena put in.

Finch waved away the interruption, nodding. "Time goes by, he has a falling-out with the city and pisses off to Padua—a major slap in the face to Venice. A few of the items turn up later in the Vatican Library and other places. Some are in the Doge's Palace. But the bulk of them were lost or ruined. The only thing most scholars have agreed on is that when Petrarch left Venice, his library left with him."

By now, Geena found herself smiling. Finch might not know a hell of a lot about the current state of the high-water crisis in Venice, but he had certainly done his homework where Petrarch's library was concerned.

"Something funny?" Finch asked, apparently irritated by her smile.

"No, no. Sorry. I'm just glad I don't have to go through the whole backstory for you."

"Fair enough. But you still haven't answered my question."

"Well, Professor Schiavo showed you some of the best preserved examples of the books we've already taken from the chamber. We've recovered hundreds of pieces."

"And they are impressive, no doubt, and their antiquity is not in question. But how can you be certain of their origin? You're convinced that all those scholars were wrong—that Petrarch never removed his library from Venice after all and instead just moved it into this secret chamber of yours?"

"We've found ample evidence," she told him. "Records that include a catalog of all of the works collected in the library, some written in Petrarch's own hand and noted as such. My assistant, Nico Lombardi, will give you access to all of that and run it down for you. Those records are evidence enough, but the architectural details support the finding as well."

Finch smiled and opened his hands. "Let's pretend I know nothing about architecture."

Geena could not help smiling in return. Finch might be pompous, but he wasn't utterly lacking in charm.

"While we walk?" she said.

"By all means."

"Like most cities," she said as they approached the library's front doors, "Venice is far older than what you can see, going back the better part of a thousand years. Scholars have been frustrated for centuries by the lack of any written record of the city's origins, but most agree that the bulk of its original settlers came here fleeing the constant invasions of Roman-era cities by barbarians and Huns."

They reached the door and, though the Biblioteca was her province, Finch opened it for her. The quiet from within seemed to reach out and draw them in, and Geena lowered her voice as she entered.

"The Doge's Palace was constructed over a period that spanned most of the 14th century and beyond, on top of what remained of much older fortified buildings that we know very little about. The years that Petrarch lived in Venice fall squarely within that period."

A woman behind a desk glanced up and smiled at her, and Geena waved as she guided Finch through the foyer and into the vastness of the Biblioteca. They made their way to a room that had once been more a shrine to books than a library. Several people sat at long tables, studying or reading in silence, but the books they were perusing had come from the stacks upstairs. None of the books were shelved or stored on the ground floor anymore.

"This building is not the original library," she whispered as they passed through the room. "It dates only from the 16th century. But the staircase we found and the chamber below it are much older. They had been completely sealed, and Petrarch's collection extraordinarily well preserved. We've found documents that indicate the existence of the room was a closely guarded secret."

"And no water damage? No evidence of flooding?"

"None." Geena led him through a narrow corridor. "At some point, we theorize that all of those who knew of the chamber died and the secret of its existence died with them."

The corridor ended at the double-doored entrance to another room that had once housed books. Two large staircases inside the vaulted room led up to the second floor. The corridor turned to the right just in front of those doors, but to the left was a little jog in the corridor, and it was through this fragment of labyrinth that Geena led Finch. There lay the small alcove room where she had discovered the hidden door.

Finch glanced around the room—the ruined fresco on the south wall, the Murano glass window that looked as though it would have been more at home in a Gaudi church than in this little corner of a Venetian library, and the carved old-wood shelves that had surrendered to rot. He paid little attention to the most interesting characteristic of the room—the remains of the early 17th century brick wall, and the ordinary stone wall behind it that dated from three hundred years earlier.

She would not be able to impress him with the ingenuity of the hidden door, for it stood open. Geena always felt a bit melancholy at the idea that something that had been so secret and had remained sealed in silence for so long now hung perpetually open and exposed, but she consoled herself that they weren't grave robbers. Their motives were pure.

Lights had been strung through the open door and down the stairs into the chamber. Even from the alcove, she could hear the chatter of voices echoing up from below, where preservation efforts were still under way.

And then the back of her neck prickled with a once-strange sensation that had now become quite familiar. *Hello, sweetheart.*

Nico had felt her arrive, and now he reached out to touch her with his thoughts. From the moment they had first met, she had sensed something different about him, had felt a kind of intimacy that had seemed unlikely and inadvisable for her to share with one of her grad students. But only when they had made love for the first time and she sensed his thoughts in her head, shared what he felt and desired in a way she could never have imagined before, had she really understood.

After that, of course, he could no longer hide it from her. It wasn't telepathy, exactly—not mind-reading in the simple pop-culture sense—but Nico could touch the minds of others with his own and share images, memories, and thoughts. Such things were not concrete, but rather a sense of what she felt, an understanding of what she was thinking without a need for words.

Like their relationship, his touch could not be hidden completely from others. He knew whenever anyone was about to enter the chamber—knew who it was—and the other members of their team often looked at him oddly. But, again like their relationship, Nico's touch was treated with a respectful silence. And perhaps also with confusion. Their co-workers might gossip about them after hours, but such things went unspoken in their company.

"Dr. Hodge?" Finch prompted. "Are we going down?"

Geena smiled. "You didn't come all the way to Venice to see an open door."

But as she started down the stone steps, she was distracted by a kind of giddiness that swept over her. She felt as though she might laugh out loud, and it took a moment to realize that the emotion flooding her belonged not to her, but to Nico. And it was not merely her arrival that had filled him with such joy.

She felt the touch of his mind, her name in his thoughts, and she picked up her pace. Finch hurried to keep up, muttering about caution and the lack of a handrail, but Geena did not slow. Nico had found something major, but she had no idea what could have excited him so much.

The stairs curved to the right and she trailed her hand across the cold, dry wall. They had yet to figure out exactly how the chamber's architects had sealed it off so completely, making it airtight and moisture-free. Even with the door opened there was no humidity here, and no evidence of water past or present, despite the depth of the chamber and its proximity to the Grand Canal.

At the bottom of the steps another old door stood open, and she stepped through into a warren of plastic sheeting illuminated by work lights and the glow of laptop screens. A preservation tent had been set up in the far corner of the large chamber, and members of her team carefully prepared manuscripts for transport to a room at Ca'Foscari University that had been specially built for the care of ancient documents.

"Dr. Hodge?" Finch called behind her.

But Geena was drawn through the anthill industriousness of the recovery team by the giddy urgency she felt in Nico's mind. Several members of the team tried to speak with her as she passed, but she waved them off with a tight smile. This was not the way she had imagined Finch experiencing the size and delicacy and historical significance of the Biblioteca project, but she could not stop herself. Nico did not get this excited about just anything.

Plastic curtains covered an archway that separated the two wings of the chamber. As Geena rushed forward, Nico pushed through, and she saw the smile that she'd felt in her mind. His olive skin shone in the glare of the work lights. Mischief and glee danced in his dark eyes.

"Dr. Hodge!" Finch called from behind her.

Geena stared at Nico. "What is it?" she said, the words almost a sigh.

"We found another door," he said, reaching for her hand. And then he was tugging her along in his wake, back through the plastic curtains, Howard Finch forgotten, and they were rushing into an area of the chamber they had barely begun to catalog.

"You opened it?" she asked.

"Of course!" Nico said, but she could feel the touch of his mind and knew he was toying with her.

"You didn't go in," she said.

He cast her a sidelong glance. "This is your project, Geena. We opened the door just a few minutes ago, but you should be the first to enter. I will spoil this much of the surprise, though. There are stairs, and they go deeper."

◈

Geena swung the beam of the heavy-duty Maglite side to side, studying each step as she made her cautious descent. Nico came right behind her, shining his own industrial flashlight over her shoulder, illuminating the darkness ahead. What fascinated her most was how dry the air remained. A subterranean chamber beneath Venice ought to be seeping with ground water, but she saw no sign of weeping between the stones in the stairwell walls.

The stairs curved to the left. If her sense of direction served her well, they were closer than ever to the canal. She ran her free hand along the wall as she took each step—eighteen, by the time they reached the door at the bottom—wondering the entire time why anyone would need a hidden room beneath a hidden room, and whether they would find yet another hidden room below that.

Her imagination ran with that question as she swept the Maglite's beam over the door. The wood looked petrified, the iron strapping across it dull but otherwise untouched by time. It had no lock, only a heavy metal latch. And at the center of the uppermost of the iron straps across the door, a large X had been engraved.

X marks the spot, she thought, but knew that was foolishness.

"Ten," she said.

"Ten what?" Nico asked.

Geena traced the number with a finger. "Let's find out." Her breath caught in her throat, an almost sexual excitement filling her. The base of her brain buzzed with Nico's anticipation; he felt it, too. These were the moments that they both lived for. Discovery. Dispersing the ghosts of the past like so many cobwebs and stepping back through time.

She turned to grin up at him, and at the others gathered on the steps behind him. Silver-haired Domenic, their expert on ancient texts; tall, grimly beautiful Sabrina, camera recording it all; and Ramus, the Croatian grad student she had promoted to site manager only three days before. She put a hand up to block the worst of the glare from their flashlights and could see one final dark silhouette on the stairs above her. Howard Finch. He had asked to be a part of the initial foray and she had agreed, knowing that if they found anything of import, BBC funding would flow.

"No one has been here in at least five hundred years," Geena said. "It's exciting, I know. My heart is pounding. But remember our purpose. Preservation of the site is important above all else."

This received a round of nods and murmurs of assent. Geena took a moment to run down a mental checklist. Plastic sheeting had been hung to cover the door they had used to access these stairs. A preservation team waited in Petrarch's library for a signal, in case their entry into this new subterranean level caused rapid deterioration of anything they might discover. Sabrina was filming.

She opened the door.

Maglite beams illuminated the room beyond. Her heart thundered in her chest and her face felt flushed. With Nico so near she felt his excitement, and it added to her own in a manner not much different from the way they shared arousal during lovemaking.

Yet as she scanned this new chamber with her torchlight, she could not help but feel a momentary disappointment. Aside from three thin marble columns at its center, it had no trace of architectural style, nor any visible art. Unless there were passages into connecting rooms, the chamber measured only forty feet or less in diameter. It had nothing of beauty or adornment about it, and reminded her more of a dungeon than of the intricate stonework of Petrarch's library above them.

"What is this place?" Nico asked.

Geena led them in and the small exploratory group fanned out. A number of vertical stone obelisks were spaced at what appeared to be equal intervals around the chamber, which she now realized was round. That facet in itself was interesting. Why go to the trouble of building a perfectly circular room without making some effort toward aesthetics?

"How many of these obelisks are there?" she called out.

To her surprise, it was Finch who answered first. "Ten."

She shone her light at the nearest one and saw that the black stone was engraved with the same Roman numeral as they had encountered on the door to the chamber.

"Do they all have the same number on them?" she asked, sweeping the light around, picking up glimpses of obelisks and the faces of her team. "Or are they different?"

"This one is the same," Domenic called from across the chamber.

"Do you think—" Geena began.

But Domenic beat her to it. "It could be some kind of secret meeting place for the Council of Ten."

Geena nodded, though she doubted anyone saw her. From the early 14th century, Venice had been primarily controlled by a secretive group of ten men, from whose number the next Doge would always be chosen. The group had been created to oversee the security of the Republic and protect the government from corruption or rebellion, but grew in power until, by the mid-15th century, the Council of Ten had total control over Venice.

But there had been many members of the Ten over the centuries, and many of their burial places were well recorded. If these obelisks were the tombs of Council members, the obvious question was, why *these* ten?

A ripple of sharp curiosity ran up the back of her neck, but it was not her own. Nico had found something. She turned, searching for him with her light. The others' Maglite beams strobed the dark chamber.

"You're not going to believe this," Domenic said, his flashlight illuminating a section of the stone floor.

As Geena approached, she saw what had made such an impact on him. In the space between two of the obelisks, an almost perfectly round disk of granite had been set into the stone floor. Whether by design or over the ages, it had sunk slightly so that it sat an inch or two below the level of the rest of the floor.

"It's almost like a cork," Finch said, coming up behind her.

"Precisely what I was thinking," Domenic said.

Geena glanced at them and then stared down at the granite disk, her mind racing. She knelt and ran her fingers along the edges of the stones surrounding it. They had been carefully hewn to create a circular space to fit the disk.

"How did they accomplish it?" she muttered to herself.

"What?" Finch asked.

She looked up at him, then turned to Sabrina, who was filming just behind her. "I hope you're getting this." She stood and gestured around the room. "I have no idea how the architects of this room kept it dry, but that's not the biggest mystery here." She pointed at the granite disk. "It may turn out that this is nothing more than some kind of decoration, but it certainly looks like some sort of plug."

"To a drain, do you think?" Domenic asked.

"Either that," Geena said, glancing again at the camera, "or there's yet another chamber beneath this one."

"Geena," Nico said.

For a moment she'd nearly forgotten him. Even the comforting touch of his mind seemed to have withdrawn. She turned and found him with the beam of her light.

Nico stood halfway across the room, shining his Maglite between two of the central columns. They were too close together to have all been intended as support for the ceiling; some kind of artistic whim had been at work here. But whatever had piqued Nico's curiosity was hidden amongst those columns.

"Coming," Geena said, although she needn't have said it aloud.

Nico did not look up. She shone her beam on his face and a flicker of concern went through her. He looked almost mesmerized, and had turned strangely pale in spite of his dark complexion, as though he might be sick.

When Geena reached the three marble columns, she expected to find something horrific hidden in the shadows in their midst— some ancient mummified corpse or torture device. Nico's silence had spoken volumes. She tried to silence her own thoughts to see if he might be sending her some of his thoughts or impressions, but that familiar feeling, his touch, had left her.

Careful not to touch the marble surface, she leaned between two of the columns and shone her Maglite into the space between them. A stone jar stood on a round table carved of the same marble as the columns around it. It had been sealed with thick red wax that remained intact but otherwise was as plain as the room that surrounded it. And given its place at the very center of the room, almost guarded by the columns, there seemed no doubt that the jar was the locus of the chamber.

Ramus poked his head through the last remaining space between the columns, but then withdrew, his eyes replaced by Sabrina's camera.

"What do you make of it, Nico?" she asked.

Nico did not reply. She flashed the beam of her Maglite up to his face and saw that his expression had gone slack. He seemed so entranced that when he spoke, it startled her.

"Do you hear it?" he asked. "Like there's electricity in the walls."

But Geena heard nothing of the kind.

"What's he talking about?" Finch said, appearing just behind Nico, rising up on his toes to try to get a look at what had drawn all of their attention.

Nico slipped between the columns. Before Geena could speak, he reached out—eyes glazed with fascination—and lifted the jar off of the marble table.

"What are you—" she began.

He shook the jar like a child trying to figure out what a gift-wrapped present might contain. That alone might have destroyed whatever was inside.

Sabrina swore.

"Nico, no!" Geena cried, pushing between the columns.

She reached for the jar with her free hand, but never laid a finger on it. Nico went suddenly rigid, eyes wide, and he began to shake as if in seizure. His hands spasmed and both the jar and his flashlight fell, crashing to the stone floor. The jar shattered, shards flying, and Geena caught a glimpse of something gray and damp spilling out.

Nico's mind touched hers. It began with that familiar prickle at the back of her neck, but then a spike of pain thrust into her head and she screamed, jerked back, and cracked her skull against a marble column.

And she *saw* . . .

This very chamber, illuminated by a ring of sconces high on the circular walls. A circle of heavy wooden chairs surrounds the three marble columns at the center of the room—ten, of course. Upon each chair sits a dark-robed man. They are not dressed identically; this is no cult. Some have jackets beneath their robes, checkered in combinations of black, red, tan, or green, while others appear far more severe, even monastic. The robes vary in length and cut, but they are all black, as are the hats the men wear, for none has a bare head.

One of them speaks in an old Venetian dialect. This is . . .

What is that final word? Something like "foolish." No, not that. "Unwise."

She sees not through her own eyes, but the eyes of another. She— he—is standing in the midst of the three stone columns at the center of the chamber, in the shifting pattern that the intrusive candlelight pushes into the shadows around her. She can feel his body, tall and thin and male. Unlike the others, his robe is stylishly slit in various places to reveal crimson cloth beneath and he wears no hat to cover his thick hair. He fixes the man who had spoken with a withering stare.

This is for Venice, *he says.* The Doge must be banished. And if you think it unwise, consider your fate should he ever return.

The one who had questioned his wisdom falls silent. Satisfied, he vanishes back into the shadows of the columns and begins to sing. His voice rises in what might be song, or chant, or ritual. Light begins to radiate from an empty space amongst the columns—in the exact center of the room. It is dim at the start but glows more and more brightly until it obviates the need for candlelight.

At some signal amidst that song, the Ten draw small identical blades from within their robes. Glancing anxiously at one another, each makes a cut on the palm of his left hand, la sinestra, *and then makes a fist, squeezing drops of blood onto the floor.*

The light emanating from within the columns is washed in pink, and then deepens to bloody scarlet.

The chamber goes dark.

Geena collapsed, spilling out from between two columns and onto the floor of the round chamber. She blinked away the vision that had filled her mind and the pain that accompanied it. Someone called her name. The light from Sabrina's camera blinded her and she winced. Closing her eyes tightly, she felt a torrent of images sweep over her—Nico's blank expression, the stone jar shattering on the floor, the dark-robed men slicing the flesh of their palms, drops of blood falling.

Feedback, she thought. Nico's touch made him what, in times gone by, some had referred to as a sensitive. He'd had some kind of psychic—no, *"psychometric," that's the word*—episode. And their rapport, the intimacy of their minds, had caused it to spill over to her.

Christ, it had hurt.

"Nico?" she said, starting to rise.

She spotted her torch, frowning as her ears picked up a new sound in the circular chamber. A trickling of water. That made no sense. The room had been sealed for centuries, dry as a bone, despite the proximity of the Grand Canal and the spongelike foundations of the city.

But as she reached for her Maglite, her eyes followed its beam to the chamber wall and she saw glistening tracks of water drizzling over the stone. It bubbled from pockets of ancient air.

"What do we do?" Sabrina asked, sweeping the camera around, trying to get it all on film.

"Son of a bitch," Geena whispered, snatching up the light and shining it along the base of the wall. The beam found a chink in the stone where water gushed in, sliding over the floor in a rapidly widening pool.

Geena?

It was Nico, but he had not spoken aloud. His voice was in her head. And it was afraid.

Howard Finch loomed in front of her, a ghost-man with wide, panic-stricken eyes. "What are you waiting for? We've got to get out of here!"

Only then did the real danger occur to her. But by then it was too late.

A section of wall gave way and the water rushed in.

CHAPTER 2

FOR A MOMENT AS THEY WERE FROZEN IN SHOCK, GEENA'S gaze settled on Nico. His expression was pale and twisted with fear, but not of the water. His eyes looked beyond those ancient walls, perhaps lingering in the vision they'd just shared, wondering whose eyes he had been looking through.

Then someone grabbed her shoulder and pulled, and the room erupted into chaos.

A voice shouted in Italian, so fast that she lost track of what it was saying. Something about *steps* and *cold* and *black*, but she could not place the words in order or context. Water washed around her feet and splashed up at her ankles and shins, cold and thick with slime. The chamber filled with the rumble of tumbled stones and the roar of gushing water. The shouts and cries of her friends echoed strangely around the round room.

"Dr. Hodge!" Ramus shouted, grabbing her shoulder again, but she tore herself away to focus on Nico.

What's he seeing? she thought, and then she saw Nico turn and trip over something on the floor. She grimaced against the flash of sensation she expected from him—

Pain, that must have hurt, and I'm sure I heard him cry out.

—but none came. Nico was on his hands and knees, feeling around under the rapidly rising water as if he'd lost something valuable.

"Nico!" Domenic shouted, hauling at the old wooden door with the X stamped on the metal bracings. "Geena! All of you, come here and *help!*" He pulled harder, but the water was up to their knees now and rising quickly. It was not only the weight of the water against the door that kept it closed, but the force of the flow. Finch went to help, grabbing the wooden jamb and prizing at the door.

Geena thought of all the submarine suspense films she'd ever seen, every one of which featured a scene when a heroic submariner would sacrifice himself to save the rest of the crew. She let out a burst of terrified laughter, and Ramus grabbed her arm and hauled her toward the door.

"Nico!" she shouted.

He was still scrabbling about on the floor, dipping his head under the rising flood again and again. The water carried a rich, oily chemical smell, and beneath that was the rank odor of sewage. The darting flashlights could not pick out color, but she knew the waters would be almost black with filth and shit. "Nico, come *on!*"

He surfaced at last, standing, backing against one of the three central columns for support. He had something in his hands, a thick substance that slipped slowly through his fingers. *He's gone insane,* she thought briefly, opening her mind and urging him to touch her. But there was nothing there at all—no excitement or fear, no joy or confusion.

"Nico," she said, so quietly this time that she could hardly hear her own voice above the roar of water. He looked up and met her eyes, but he did not see her.

A higher, larger section of the curved wall fell, and the flow of water became a torrent.

"Help us!" someone screamed. As Geena turned she saw Domenic prop one foot against the wall and pull against the door. Finch helped, and Ramus, and old timbers crumbled and split. The door disintegrated, metal bracings dipping into the water, and Sabrina and her camera were ushered through first.

Ramus went next, standing with his back against the curving staircase wall and helping Finch after him. The producer disappeared, his jerky shadow thrown back by Sabrina's camera light.

Geena was leaning against the flow of water now, feeling almost solid things grabbing at her thighs, trying to pull her down. *Just the rush of water*, she thought, and she cursed her imagination as she felt long fingers, curved nails . . .

"Geena!" Domenic shouted from the open doorway. He was two or three steps up and leaning into the room, and seeing him there made her realize how high the water had already risen. She jumped for him and grabbed his hand, then tripped on something she was sure had not been there before. She'd lived in Venice for long enough to know to squeeze her mouth shut, not cry out, as she fell forward into the water.

Domenic's hand closed tight around her own as she went under, crunching her fingers together. She closed her eyes and exhaled through her nose, but still she tasted the rankness of the water, a slick touch across her tongue. Then she kicked, Domenic pulled, and she surfaced to fresh shouting, finding her footing on the staircase's first step.

Nico was pushing past her, reaching for purchase.

"Take my hand," she said, reaching out to him. But he forged on past the others and toward the flashlight beams waving frantically from above.

"Come on," Domenic shouted. "We have to save what we can from the library!"

The library, she thought, and the staggering weight of ages pressed down around her. This was just another moment in the endless history of this city, and in years to come no one would know of what had happened here. They might save much of Petrarch's library and find a moment of fame amongst the archaeological community, and perhaps even further afield. Or if the ceilings came down and the walls fell in, burying them and destroying the manuscripts, perhaps there would be a plaque with their names on it. Either way, the effects on the city would be minimal.

But screw that. The past was her passion, and she was here to make sure it was known.

They rushed up the curving staircase into the library room, panting, soaked and stinking, and she looked for Nico. Members of the team were bustling around, asking if they were okay, and then Ramus pointed across the chamber at the far wall. Beside where the preservation tent had been set up, several spurts of pressurized water were gushing against a polythene curtain.

"Get everything out!" Domenic shouted. "We're below sea level here. We've got to assume the chamber's going to flood."

"What happened down there?" someone asked.

"They disturbed something and the waters came in," Finch said, a hint of accusation in his voice.

"No, that's not what happened at all," Geena said, but Domenic and the others frowned at her, because it wasn't clear *what* had happened. *Disturbed something*, yes, she thought, *but none of us touched that wall.*

"Nico?" Ramus called. "Help me with . . ." But he looked around the chamber, and Nico was nowhere to be seen.

Geena turned back to the door into the lower chamber as Domenic was about to push it closed.

"No!" she shouted.

"It might hold the water back for a minute more," he said. "Geena, we have to save—"

"In case he went back down." Saying it made her feel sick. That stuff slicking between his fingers . . . She closed her eyes briefly and opened herself up to his touch, but there was nothing there at all. No fear or pain, for which she was glad. But no thoughts for her, either.

"Where the hell is he?" Ramus asked.

"I saw someone running a load of books up," Finch said. "It could have been him."

"Then let's get the rest of this stuff out of here." The archaeologist in Geena took over, and her mind settled around what needed to be done. Nico would have to wait. One crisis at a time.

She barked orders, and her team reacted. Confusion and fear had given way to a plan of action, and they appreciated that. She darted around the chamber, dodging between polythene sheets, shadows cast by the lights strung from the ceiling moving around her, bumping into people, loading her arms with manuscripts that should have been removed in airtight containers, moisture content measured, tests carried out for acidic contamination, and she could already see dampness from her clothes soaking into the old books.

She had instructed Sabrina to continue filming for as long as she could, concentrating on the several tables and old shelving units where so much material was stacked. But she also saw the girl aiming her camera at the chaos around them, the water now spewing in great gouts from the crumbling western wall, and the BBC man, Finch, following like her shadow. *He should be helping!* she thought, but she could see the stunned, hungry look on his face. It seemed that the BBC would have their documentary after all.

The door to the lower chamber drifted open and water from below gushed into the library. At the same time, the far wall crumbled and fell, a huge drift of rock and silt slumping across the chamber's floor. Water washed in farther, and Geena saw an old bookcase leaning forward as waterlogged sand built up behind it.

Ramus ran for the bookcase, and she saw in a blink what was going to happen.

"Ramus!" she screamed, but the noise filling the chamber stole her voice away. She grabbed a student dashing past with a heavy Hessian bag, dropped her armful of ancient, priceless texts into the bag, and sent him on his way to the surface. Then she splashed across the room, lifting her legs high to move faster.

Ramus was at the tilting bookcase, trying to select which books and rolled manuscripts to save. His eyes were wide and smarting from the stench . . . or perhaps he was crying.

Geena grabbed his arms and pulled him back.

"Dr. Hodge—" he shouted, but she pulled harder, tugging him

back past a polythene curtain as the bookcase fell and followed them through, a slick of silt rushing after it.

"We get our legs stuck in that and we'll drown!" she shouted.

Ramus nodded grimly. She pushed him on his way, then turned and shoved another curtain aside, looking desperately for any sign of Nico. *Not here*, she thought, rushing back toward the door to the lower chamber. To her left she saw Sabrina filming her, and behind her Finch stood with mouth open and eyes wide, perhaps assessing which prime-time slot this could fill. She waved them away.

"Go!" she shouted. Sabrina obeyed immediately, and for a moment Finch grabbed her arm and frowned, saying something unheard and gesturing to the flooding chamber. Sabrina pulled away and ran for the staircase leading up, and Geena thought, *Good girl.*

She pushed back toward the far end of the chamber, knowing how foolish she was being; the water was around her thighs now, pulling at her, the silt trying to suck her down. But she stood transfixed for a moment, looking at that doorway and trying to figure out just what the hell had happened down there. Thirty feet below sea level for hundreds of years, and it was as if their arrival had broken a seal.

Or a jar, she thought. When she closed her eyes to squeeze filthy water from them, she saw those men cutting their palms, and when she opened them again the water around her legs looked red.

"Nico!" she screamed. *"Nico!"* But there was no answer. If he *had* gone back down, there was nothing she could do for him now. *He'll be dead already*, she thought, and that unfamiliar blankness she felt from him—no sensation, no images—suddenly felt darker and more ominous than ever.

Then she turned and left the chamber, scooping up one last handful of books on the way. And started to cry for everything she knew was lost, and everything that might yet be.

They were gathered in the main library, carefully depositing all that they had rescued on one of the long tables there. The few readers were standing back in surprise, and the librarian was helping, laying each book and manuscript flat. An air of panic hung over the scene, and when they noticed Geena approaching she saw their eyes flit past her at the shadows. She turned, but there was no one behind her.

"Has anyone seen him?" she asked. Heads shook.

"I've called the police," Ramus said. "Told them what's happening. They'll bring the engineers."

"Divers," Domenic said, and the room fell silent. They all knew what divers would mean. *Air pocket*, Geena thought. *If he's anywhere down there, he might have found somewhere to breathe.* But it was a foolish thought. Nico had hardly seemed to know where he was the last time she had gotten a good look at him.

"Dr. Hodge," Finch said, his voice fraught with concern, "I was close to the staircase, and I'm fairly sure I saw . . ." He trailed off when he saw how everyone else looked at him.

"If he made it out of there, he'd be here with us," she said, and felt the shakes closing in. "He must have banged his head, something like that." But even as she spoke she was reliving those few strange moments before the wall had started to give way, and wasn't sure. The look in his eyes . . . he hadn't been himself.

"Did you see anything?" she asked the room, and was met with confused, uncertain frowns.

"After he dropped that jar, he fell," Ramus said. "Then you hit your head and said something."

"What?"

"I couldn't hear. Then the water."

Faintness washed over her and she closed her eyes, leaning on the table. Her hand touched the rough edge of an old manuscript and she looked down at its yellowed blank cover, wondering what incredible stories it might contain.

"He's not dead," she said, but no one answered. And in her voice was desperation rather than certainty. "He could be disoriented, right? Could have . . . gone home or something? I need to get home. He might go there."

"I'll go with you," Domenic volunteered. "And we should hurry. If we're still here when the police arrive, they might hold us up."

He held her arm and guided her from the library. Geena looked back at the others. They were all watching her leave. She hated the pity and hopelessness she saw in their eyes. Even Finch.

"Get this to the university," she said, waving vaguely at the little they had managed to save. But right then the tragedy of what they had lost could not touch her.

The sunlight hit them when they exited the library, as did the whipping of pigeons flapping overhead and the bustle of tourists going about their business, oblivious to what had been happening below their feet. Geena and Domenic approached the canal silently, attracting a few curious glances and wrinkled noses. She expected to see a stretch of canal boiling with bubbles from the tumult below, but there was no sign of any upset, only the gentle waves that lapped constantly over the pavement. She'd often wondered where these waves came from when there was no boat traffic, since they were far from the open sea, but Nico had told her it was Venice's heartbeat. She was glad that the waves were still there.

"Are we going to his apartment, or . . . ?" Domenic asked.

"Mine," she said. "It's closer." *And I think he's happy there*, she thought. Domenic smiled at her as they jumped down into the water taxi. None of her students or fellow lecturers had ever openly mentioned her relationship with Nico, though she'd known for a while that it was common knowledge. Secrecy seemed foolish now.

The journey took longer than it should have. They caught a water taxi south across the Grand Canal. Her gaze focused as it always did upon the white façade of San Giorgio Maggiore to the east, but then, as the water taxi approached the dock at Fondamenta de la Crosa, she spotted a gondola motionless across the waterway. A man argued with the gondolier, who was talking in a never-ending stream of fast Italian, waving his arms and looking at the heavy old buildings surrounding them, while a fat woman knelt and looked down into the water. She had one sleeve rolled up and was saying, "But, my phone, my phone. It has my pictures, all my pictures. My phone!"

Their driver honked his horn and gesticulated, and the gondolier redirected his stream of invective. Domenic shouted something to their driver and pointed toward the side of the canal. Their motor roared, and the taxi drifted in that direction.

"Shortcut," Domenic said. "I know a way."

Geena could see no way to exit the boat into the building, but she knew better than to question Domenic. As the boat stilled again he stepped into the water. Geena looked over the side and saw the small wooden dock just below the canal surface.

"Is it safe?" she asked, but Domenic grabbed her hand and urged her over the side without answering. He paid their driver then reached up to a pair of heavy wooden shutters, fiddling with the catch and sighing audibly when they fell open.

"I once loved someone here," he said, explaining before Geena asked. They ducked into the building, climbed some stairs, passed through two empty rooms whose uses were lost to history, then descended to exit onto a narrow alley between buildings.

Did Nico really come this way? Geena wondered. Ever since leaving the library she'd felt that she had also left Nico behind. She tried to shrug this idea away because it spoke of terrible things, but the air around her was empty of him, the sun beating down on streets no longer touched by his shadow. She sobbed once, and a fat man glanced at her with a look of disgust.

"What?" she snapped, and Domenic steered her away.

There was not enough room to run, yet they moved quickly. Perhaps it was their expressions that prompted people to step aside and let them pass, or maybe it was simply the stink rising from their clothes. As they reached the end of a narrow alley and emerged into a small square filled with trees, Geena felt some outside influence blossoming deep in her mind.

She paused and grinned, and thought, *Nico!* She caught a shimmer of other streets—how *he* saw them, not how *she* saw them. Venice was his home; he'd been born here, and everything was familiar.

But beneath that sensation was one of fear and pursuit, and she felt Nico's hairs prickling on the back of her neck.

"What is it?" Domenic asked. Geena could not answer. She waved him away, trying to make sense of what she sensed and felt, and trying to discern whether it was her pursuit of Nico that troubled him so. But already the contact was gone, leaving a dark void within her, and a terrible sense of doom.

She waited for another touch, but perhaps it had been wishful thinking.

Domenic guided her through the streets, steering her through the neighborhood like only a person who had lived here all his life could. When she would have gone left onto one of the main streets, he went right and they ducked through archways and courtyards, lost in a part of that amazing city where even the ever-inquisitive tourists rarely found themselves. She let him lead, but when she realized where they were she started running, heading for her building and trying to gasp out Nico's name. But she was too out of breath, and felt queasy from the filthy water she had swallowed.

He'll be in the apartment, in the shower, confused at what happened and apologetic for scaring us all so much. She dug out her keys as she ran, narrowly avoiding being run down by a boy on a scooter. She burst through the main doors and hurtled upstairs to the second floor, and Domenic was still behind her when she unlocked her own door and threw it open. *Nico wouldn't have locked it behind him*, she thought, and even before the emptiness of the flat became apparent she knew he was not there.

"I'll call Ramus," Domenic said quietly, because the people back at the library would need to know that they might be looking for a body.

Geena folded into her sofa and let the tears come, but when she shifted she started retching. Domenic was with her when she vomited, holding a towel and wiping her mouth afterward. She looked into the towel and all she could think of was that slick stuff dripping between Nico's fingers.

"What has he done?" she asked. But Domenic shook his head, because he did not, could not, understand.

❖

In Geena's dream, she relived that afternoon on a continuous loop. They arrived, Domenic made some food, she ate even though she thought she could not, and then he fetched a bottle of wine from the kitchen. Pouring, she knew she could not drink. Drinking, she knew she could never sleep. And finally falling asleep, she would find herself arriving at the flat's front door again, realizing its emptiness and knowing she could never eat, drink, or sleep until they had found Nico, one way or another. The dream was disturbing partly because it was so normal, and partly because she knew she was dreaming. Her life would be stuck in a loop until Nico was found, and her subconscious stated that most obviously whilst asleep. Each time she reached the drinking part and Domenic reached for the phone, her hopes would rise . . . but then she'd see his face when he answered, and recognize her friends' concern when he turned away to tell them how she was. *I'm not good*, she thought, downing another glass of wine and knowing she would never sleep.

I know I'm dreaming yet still I hope, and how cruel is that? She finished the bottle of wine and Domenic helped her into her bed, her body showered clean and filthy clothes replaced with a loose shirt and pair of sweatpants, and she fell asleep again, waiting for her arrival at the flat's front door with hope once more burning bright.

This time the door did not open. Darkness flooded her mind, and when she opened her eyes she saw the vague outline of the bedroom windows, curtains shifting slightly beneath the sea breeze.

"This is different," she whispered, and then she knew she was no longer dreaming. She sat up and breathed in deeply, ran a hand across her chest and felt the buttons of the clean shirt she'd put on. Nico's shirt. He liked seeing her dressed like this.

Then she turned and saw Nico's body lying on her bed.

Geena screamed. She couldn't help it, even when Nico sat upright and reached for her, muttering calming noises, tears glittering on his cheeks. She screamed because her dreams had convinced her there was no hope and that nothing changed, and here she was with Nico lying beside her as he had so many times before.

Domenic rushed into the room and snapped on the light, silver hair in disarray and eyes squinting from sleep.

"Nico!" he shouted, and the joy in his voice drove away the last of Geena's fear. She fell sideways with her arms out, and because Nico had already been coming for her they propped each other up, hugging and crying.

"I thought you were dead," she said with her face pressed into his neck. She felt his pulse against her cheek and that made her cry even harder. He stank, and she breathed in the stink because even below that she could smell his familiar scent.

"I thought I was lost," he said, sobbing into her neck.

"Nico, you crazy bastard!" Domenic said. He joined them on the bed and hugged them both, and Geena took so much comfort from the contact that she did not allow either man to let her go for some time.

"Tell me this isn't a dream," she said at last.

"Which part?" Domenic gushed. "Petrarch's library, almost drowning, or nearly losing this idiot?"

He laughed out loud, and beneath his laughter Geena heard her love whisper, "I can't tell you it's no dream."

She was too relieved for it to register. Later, she'd have cause to think back to that moment, go over what he had said again and again, and she would realize that Nico had lost the ability to discern the difference between reality and nightmare. *I thought I was lost . . . I can't tell you it's no dream.*

But right then all that mattered was the rising sun, the City of Bridges welcoming in another day, and that they were alive.

CHAPTER 3

I'M NOT USED TO BEING AWAY FROM YOU," SHE SAID. "BEING
so out of touch. I didn't like it one bit." *And it scared me,* she wanted
to say. But now was not the time, because being scared was connected to whatever had happened down there. Maybe later they
would talk about that, but not now. Nico looked so tired, so
drained, yet unprepared for sleep.

"Neither did I," he said. "I didn't do it on purpose, Geena. It
wasn't my . . ." *Had he been about to say* fault? *If not his, then whose?*
"Wasn't my intention," he finished.

"I don't blame you," she said. "I'm just glad to have you back."

They were sitting at the small tile-topped table in front of the
open French doors of her living room, daylight washing over them.
The balcony was so small that it housed only a couple of plant pots
containing herbs—rosemary, coriander, some garlic bulbs—but
she had the table placed so that it gave the impression of sitting
outside. At this time of the morning, sunlight streamed over the
rooftops of the facing buildings, splashing the table and warming
the room, offsetting the refreshing coolness of the retreating night.

Sometimes blinds clattered open across the narrow street from her, and she would always wave a polite greeting to anyone who glanced over instead of pretending to ignore them. She knew that was appreciated. There was the old man who lived with a dozen cats, the young professional couple with two delightful kids and a live-in nanny not much older than her charges, and the young single man who always made sure he looked her way. She indulged in an innocent flirtation with him, but not this morning. She saw his curtains drawn back and his own doors opening onto his tiny balcony, but she kept her eyes on Nico. He had so much to tell her, but she did not want to scare him off.

That was how he seemed this morning—scared. There was a fragility to him that she had never seen before, and he would not meet her gaze.

"Where did you go?" she asked. She wanted to say, *What happened down there, why did you pick up the stone jar, why did you scream, what did you see, why did you run?* But there was still a rawness to things, as if the previous day's events involved blood and death rather than water and worry.

The knives, the dripping blood . . .

"I wandered for a while," he said, picking at a plate of dried meats. He had not actually eaten anything yet, though he'd drunk three cups of coffee and was working on his fourth. "After I finished running, that is."

"But what were you running from?"

He dropped his gaze, unable or unwilling to respond.

She tried again. "Where did you go?"

"Nowhere," he said. "No destination, I mean. Through alleys and courtyards. Into places I didn't think I'd been before, but which I found myself remembering. And even the streets I travel every day had a familiarity about them . . ." He shook his head, draining the coffee and checking to see if there was more left in the pot. "But it was a strange feeling."

"Strange how?"

Nico thought for a moment before replying, and when he did,

he gazed into the middle distance as if he were trying to remember the answer to a riddle he'd first heard years before.

"You know how sometimes when something is removed from a familiar landscape—a line of trees, or a building, a fence of some sort—and at first you don't recognize exactly what is missing, but you know *something* is different? Absent?"

Geena nodded, buttering some bread.

"Like that, except all the way through the city. Every time I turned a corner into a place I knew, there was something not quite right. I still knew it, but not how it was."

He began to shake with growing frustration, gaze darting about the room as if searching for answers that would never be found within those walls.

"So what do you think—"

"Enough! I don't know," Nico said, standing abruptly and spilling coffee over the tablecloth.

A chill went through her. Christ, what had happened to him? "Nico?"

"Forget it," he said. "I'm fine, really. Just a bad day. My mind . . . I'm always picking up traces and echoes of this and that, and sometimes things . . . seep in."

"You never told me that," Geena said.

He stalked back into her bedroom, drawing the shades to block out the sunlight and hiding in the gloom. Geena followed and stood in the doorway, leaning against the jamb. He still stank of that rancid water; strange that she should only notice that now.

"You really need a shower," she said, and was delighted when he smiled.

"I just . . ." He stood, already unbuttoning his dirty shirt. "A scare. Panic. Excitement at what we'd found."

"I understand that," she said, and she did. But that did not account for the way he'd acted, nor for what she'd seen and sensed through him. *Does he even remember?* She still had the butter knife in one hand and she touched it to the other palm, casually, stroking it across the skin and feeling a slick of butter left behind.

Nico glanced at her hand—

—the splash of blood, light darkening from pink to red, a collective groan that echoed—

—and then turned quickly away, shaking as he unbuttoned his pants.

Geena gasped and held on to the door frame. She blinked away the flash of vision. Not even an image. Just a sensation. Then she looked down at her palm, certain that she'd cut herself. But there was only butter, already melting from the warmth of her skin.

Nico pulled down his trousers and boxers and stepped into the bathroom. Moments later she heard the water turn on, then the sound changing as he stepped beneath the spray. He sighed, groaned, and she heard the soft thud as he rested his head against the tiled wall.

Geena went back and cleared the breakfast table, trying to fill her mind with inanities rather than let it dwell on the image of blood. She scooped up the plates, piling them on top of each other, then carried the empty cups through to the small kitchen. Filling the coffee machine with water and fresh coffee, she leaned against the counter and smelled the gorgeous aroma of brewing coffee filling her flat once again.

For a moment I thought I'd lost him.

She and Nico had met two years before at a lecture she was giving, and the attraction had been instant and mutual. He'd persisted in asking her on a date, and it had taken three days for her faltering professional concerns to be cast aside. She knew that fraternizing with students was frowned upon, yet there had been something about him that drew her from that first moment. His good looks and youthful fitness didn't hurt, but his was also a mind that she perceived as an equal to hers. His eyes betrayed an intelligence and quirkiness that matched her own, and more than anything she'd sensed a passion in him about the past. For many, history was simply times gone by, but for Geena it was a more rounded, real, whole place than the present. The past was set and immutable; it had walls and boundaries, rules and certainty. The present was unreliable.

On their first date he had taken her to the Museo Archeologico, and that night they had made love in his small apartment, windows open, moonlight silvering their sweat-sheened skin, cool air flooding the bedroom. The next morning she had wandered naked into the bathroom, only to be startled by Nico emerging from the shower. His laughter at her shriek of surprise had melted her heart, just a little, and through the embarrassment she had found a smile.

He was twelve years her junior, and she loved him because he did not make her feel younger than her age.

The coffee machine was grumbling as the last of the coffee dribbled into the pot. She focused, trying to see if she could sense his mind reaching out to her, and felt only a warm, gentle satisfaction. She wished there were something more.

Geena pulled off her shirt and slid down her sweatpants. She crossed the small living room, glancing out the window but not caring if cat-man or the young flirter were looking. Steam billowed from the bathroom—he must have the heat turned high—and she stood in the doorway for a while, watching his shadow through the shower curtain. She frowned, trying to sort her confused emotions from those of his she might be feeling; frustration, anxiety? And she thought about what the dreams had been telling her last night—that Nico was gone, that she would never hold him in her arms again, never feel him smile and shudder against her neck as he came inside her. Never again argue with him about who was the greatest painter or sculptor.

She pulled the curtain aside and stepped into the bath. Nico still had his back to her, face turned up into the overhead shower and hands both clasping a tablet of soap. He was rubbing at his shoulders and chest, and his breath came in short gasps.

She stepped forward and reached around to his stomach.

Nico jumped and spun around, almost sending her sprawling. The shower reached her, and it was scalding hot across her face, shoulders, and chest. She gasped.

"I just can't get myself clean," he said, and for the first time since she had met him, he sounded like a child.

"I'll help you," she said. He nodded and smiled gratefully, and for the next half an hour as she scrubbed his skin pink, he projected only an unfamiliar, heartrending vulnerability.

Domenic returned mid-morning with a doctor, and although Nico protested, he let the doctor look him over. There were no injuries and no obvious indications of any head trauma. He sat through the whole examination looking vaguely befuddled, and when the doctor stood to leave, Nico walked him to the door.

"How is he?" Domenic whispered.

"I don't know," Geena said. "It's like he's been away a lot longer."

"How do you mean?"

She shrugged. How could she communicate to Domenic the subtle differences, the awkwardness between them that had never been there before? So instead she changed the subject. *Divert your mind and sometimes the answers will creep up on you*, her father used to tell her. He'd never given her a piece of advice that had failed her yet.

"Is Dr. Schiavo angry that we're not at the site?" she asked.

"Of course not. You two have had quite a trauma—"

Geena frowned. "Not more than anyone else who was down there when the wall gave way."

"Not true," Domenic said. "I didn't explain to Dr. Schiavo what had happened with you and Nico—that's not my business to explain to him—but I told him you'd both had a close call. Ramus is site manager and he's been there all day, talking with the city engineers about shoring up the canal wall, getting pumps in, all of it. You let us worry about all of that for today."

"Have you looked at the film yet?" she asked.

"No, but your BBC friend is all over us." Domenic rolled his eyes.

"Let's have a viewing here. Finch can come, too."

"You're sure?" He looked around uncertainly, and at first she thought he was still worried about Nico. But then she realized the source of his discomfort and smiled.

"Sure. I don't think we can pretend that Nico and I are a secret anymore, can we?"

"I suppose not," Domenic said, returning her smile. "I'll call the others and get them here for . . . two o'clock?"

"What's at two o'clock?" Nico said, entering from the hallway.

"We're going to watch the footage Sabrina shot," Geena said.

"Of course!" he said, and his eagerness was troubling. He pushed past them with a vague smile and started picking up books and magazines, clearing the sofa, tidying Geena's room in preparation for visitors. She watched him, wondering why she was unsettled, and it was only when Domenic touched her shoulder that it clicked.

"Geena? I said, do you want me to pick up some food?"

"Oh, yeah," she said, and she went into the kitchen to fetch her purse. *He still smells of the canal*, she thought. As Nico had passed her by, she'd caught a whiff of Venice's old, dirty water, even after all that scrubbing.

As if it were as ingrained in his skin as it was in the foundations of the city itself.

Domenic brought pizza and Finch arrived with two bottles of cheap wine, wearing a bemused expression at actually being invited. Geena welcomed him in and chatted inconsequentialities, and when he saw Nico standing by her living room window he nodded once.

"Glad to see you're well," he said.

Nico only smiled in response.

Ramus and Sabrina arrived around two p.m., hot and hassled from their dash through the city. The temperature had been rising all day, and now the air had grown motionless and heavy with humidity. Geena had opened all her windows and turned on the ceiling fan in her living room, but all these measures only seemed to push the hot air around rather than provide a cooling breeze. She'd chilled the red wine, much to Finch's consternation, and they drank from tall glasses filled with ice. She would happily forsake some of its subtler tastes to be refreshed.

With other people in the flat, Nico projected his normal self. There were familiar intimacies: his fingers playing across Geena's as she handed him a wineglass; the touch in the small of her back that always made her weak at the knees; his smile, dazzling and beautiful, the best part reserved for her. But there was still something different about him that went beyond the faint aroma beneath his aftershave and perspiration. She did her best to shut out the strange time spent in the shower in case lingering sexual frustration was clouding her thoughts. Even then, there was a distance between them that had not been there before. And she could think of no better way to describe it than how she had put it to Domenic.

It's like he's been away a lot longer.

She was glad when Ramus closed her blinds and Sabrina loaded up the DVD player.

"Burned this an hour ago," she said. "Dr. Schiavo wanted to see the footage first, so I left the camera in the lab, told him I had to get home for my grandmother's birthday. He's quite concerned."

"You told him we're all fine, though?" Geena said.

"Yes, yes," Sabrina said, then looked away sheepishly. "Actually, I meant he's concerned about Petrarch's library."

"Well," Geena said, letting the word hang for a while.

"Maybe we fucked up," Domenic said. No one answered, and for that Geena was grateful. This was her responsibility, and she usually had strong shoulders.

"I haven't even had time to check that it works," Sabrina said, slipping the disc into the machine.

"Now you tell us!" Ramus said.

"They usually work," she muttered defensively.

"Yeah, I've heard about you and your home movies," Domenic quipped.

"Make sure you've put the right one in!" Ramus seconded.

"Oh, you've seen them as well?"

The banter continued until Sabrina held up a hand, smiled as she made a gun with forefinger and thumb, and shot Ramus.

"Jealous boy," she purred, and then the screen blinked into life. She paused the picture on the title card, which contained the date, location, and time of the filming. She glanced around at Geena, then her eyes flickered briefly to Finch.

"I invited him here," Geena said. "Mr. Finch is more interested than ever."

"I am," Finch said. He sat at the small window table, wineglass already empty before him. He was sweating and uncomfortable, but there was an eagerness about him, too. "After what I saw, I'm certain this could be a fascinating documentary."

"We lost about half of what was still down there," Domenic said bitterly.

"And it's the recovery of what was saved that will make the program," Finch said slowly, talking down to him, though the silver-haired Domenic wasn't much younger than Finch himself. Geena was still unsure whether she liked the British man for his candidness, or hated him for his vacuous pomposity.

"Nothing to do with a fucking flood and half of us almost dying," Ramus muttered. The room fell silent for a few seconds, then Sabrina chuckled and pressed PLAY.

Nico tensed as soon as the first images appeared. Geena felt his thigh harden against hers, and another waft of dirty-water smell stung her nostrils. *Doesn't anyone else smell that?* she thought. Perhaps afterward she would ask Domenic. She glanced sidelong at Nico, but his face seemed calm, eyes flickering with the reflected TV picture.

Heads bobbed on the screen as Sabrina and her camera followed them down the curving staircase. They paused at the bottom, then Geena opened the door and stepped into the lower chamber.

I should have held back, Geena thought. *I was much too eager to see what was down there, and a lot of that came from Nico. I sensed his excitement. He projected it to me.* She glanced at him again but he seemed enrapt with the picture. *So why can't I feel anything from him now?*

She rested her hand on his knee—an intimate gesture that she had performed a thousand times before when they'd been sitting beside each other. But this time felt like the first, and he flinched before settling back against her. She gasped softly, confused, and his awkwardness bristled the small hairs at the nape of her neck.

"Get your hair cut!" Domenic said to Ramus. The younger man's flowing mane filled the screen for a few seconds, and sitting on Geena's floor he ran both hands through his hair.

"No way," he said. "Gives me my sexual power."

Nico shifted a little, but Geena did not move her arm.

On the screen, flashlights were shone around the chamber. She concentrated, trying to see anything they'd missed down there before. In their excitement there might have been obvious features that eluded them, or which the dancing lights had skimmed across too fast to see. She knew that a camera saw things differently.

"Strange columns," Ramus muttered. "Why have three for support when one would do the job?"

"It's a hiding place," Geena said, thinking of how the man had stood within those columns, in his elaborate robes.

"Hiding what?" Sabrina said.

"None of us saw the urn until Nico touched it," Finch said, and Geena started. It was the first time anyone had called it an urn, and the first she'd thought of it as such.

On screen they circled the room, examining the obelisks and then the granite disk in the stone floor of the chamber. Their voices coming from the TV sounded tinny and distorted.

"What is that?" Nico asked, nodding toward the screen.

Geena frowned. He'd only been twenty feet away while they'd been looking at the granite disk. He must have overheard them. But when she glanced at his face, she realized he had not. His entire focus had been on the stone jar hidden amidst those three columns.

"Some kind of plug, we think," Domenic offered.

"Plug?" Nico echoed. "Covering what?"

"A drain or a well?" Geena suggested. "Or a sub-chamber."

"Is that even possible?" Nico asked.

But no one replied. None of them knew how to answer that, and now the plug was submerged under water in a room whose structural integrity was uncertain. It would have to be a question for another day.

It was strange seeing herself on the television, and stranger still seeing Nico. Geena concentrated on his image, on the way his eyes had widened and he seemed drawn to the shadowy space amongst those columns. She should have noticed something off about him, even then.

"What's wrong with you?" she whispered, and the screen flickered and blurred.

"Damn it!" Sabrina said, picking up the remote control. The image paused, jerked up and down a little, then started again.

"Dirt on the disc?" Ramus asked.

"No," Sabrina said, grinning. "I put the right one in."

On-screen, Nico was standing close to the three columns now, looking into where their shadows met. Geena watched herself approach him, shining her flashlight into his face, then leaning over to see what he was seeing.

Ramus' head filled the screen, then Sabrina's hand appeared before the camera, picture shaking, and she pulled him aside. The jar—

—*Urn*, Geena thought, *maybe that* is *what it was*—

—filled the screen, and then Nico's voice rustled through the speakers, indistinct and yet clear to Geena. She remembered exactly what he'd said before everything changed.

"Do you hear it? Like there's electricity in the walls."

Finch appeared on-screen behind Nico, muttering something as Geena's lover leaned in and grabbed the jar. The picture flickered again. Lines crossed the screen, snow made nonsense of the images. And behind the crackle and hiss, something more definable: a hum of potential.

When the picture resolved again, the jar was already broken on the floor. Nico stood with his head back and his hands fisted at his sides, and Geena saw herself slumping slowly down against the nearest of the three central columns, one hand reaching for the back of her head. She was muttering something.

"What's that I'm saying?" she asked, leaning forward on the sofa.

"Don't know," Sabrina said.

Nico was talking on the screen as well, and his voice seemed louder and more insistent, clearer and yet no easier to understand.

"That's a very old dialect you're speaking there, Nico," Domenic said, his voice level, though his eyes were full of questions and mystery.

Geena could read and translate some of the old Venetian dialects easily enough, and her students all had differing abilities to do the same. But the last time she'd heard anyone actually talking like this was Domenic, and even he had to refer to carefully prepared pages to do so.

On the screen, Nico seemed to be standing straighter, his voice filled with confidence, and he raised one shadowy hand to point around the edges of the room. The old words still tumbled from his mouth, but his voice had deepened. His shadow, thrown against one of the obelisks by the camera light, seemed to grow taller, though Nico himself was not moving. Then he held both hands out in front of him and shouted.

"Huh?" Sabrina said, sitting on the rug before the TV.

"That's weird," Ramus said. "Don't remember that at all."

Geena did not remember it, either. Those few seconds . . . they all seemed mystified by the moments unfolding on-screen. They had all been there, but none of them seemed to recall what the camera had captured.

"How do you know that dialect, Nico?" Domenic asked.

Nico said nothing, only stared at the screen, and now it was as if the interference from the TV had transferred into his eyes. They looked *different*. She held her breath and reached for him, glancing around because no one else seemed to have noticed, and then she hesitated.

Who am I about to touch?

She grabbed his shoulder and shook gently.

As Nico turned, the TV went blank again, and this time the picture seemed to have vanished for good.

"Nico?"

A tear streaked from his right eye and ran down his cheek. He did not speak. His face was Nico, and so were his eyes, but for a beat there seemed to be something else inside him.

"What is it, Nico?" she asked softly.

"That's it," Sabrina said. "There's no more. All the filming I did after that. . ."

"Maybe it'll still be on the camera?" Finch asked, standing from the small table.

"Maybe."

Nico glanced around at everyone, then looked back to Geena. For a moment he seemed to be imploring her to do or see something—eyes widening, leaning toward her as if for an embrace—but he said nothing, and the moment passed. He leaned back in the sofa and closed his eyes.

"I'm so tired," he said. "I'm going to rest." He stood slowly and walked from the room, and Geena watched him all the way.

"So where's the rest of the footage?" Finch asked. "And what the hell was he doing down there? He didn't look like much of an archaeologist to me, not when—"

"Just shut up!" Geena shouted, turning on Finch. He looked away, embarrassed, and stood beside the window staring out.

"Geena, I think you were saying the same," Domenic said.

"What?" She frowned at him, confused, angry at everyone speaking at once when all she wanted to do was go after Nico, hold him, find out what was wrong.

"On the film. I couldn't quite hear what you were speaking, but it didn't interrupt Nico's words. It flowed with them." He frowned as if struggling to verbalize his thoughts. "It's like . . . you were repeating what he said."

"But I . . ." *I don't know that language*, she wanted to say. But then she recalled the vision she'd had, broadcast to her from Nico, of those men in the chamber so long ago. The words they were speaking, and how she had understood every one.

"I need to go to Nico." She stood and left the room, and it was a relief. Glancing back once before entering the bedroom, she saw that all eyes were on her.

Domenic was the last to leave. Ramus had guided Finch from the flat with the promise of a meal in one of Venice's better restaurants—on the BBC's expense account, of course—and as Geena heard the two men leave she knew that Finch was in good hands. Ramus was gregarious but circumspect, and he'd leave Finch later that evening with nothing but an impending hangover. Sabrina went next, quiet and brooding. And then Domenic, sparing a glance into Geena's bedroom as he passed the open door. They locked eyes for a moment, and Geena offered a soft smile. Nico was asleep beside her. She didn't want to talk in case he woke up.

Domenic smiled back, feigned speaking into a phone—*Call me if you need me*—and left.

You were repeating what he said, Domenic had told her. She shivered and wondered what that meant.

"Cold?" Nico asked.

Geena jumped. She'd been certain that he was asleep. Nico turned on his side and rested one arm across her chest, hand cupping her left breast through her shirt.

"Just worried," she said. "I didn't know where you'd gone, and for a while today I thought . . ." She shook her head and gasped, trying to hold back the tears. She hated crying. It took her back to that long period of grief following the death of her mother, after which she had vowed to live well in tribute to her mother's memory. Tears wasted time that could be happy.

"I'm sorry, Geena," he said. Nico's English was excellent, but he knew that she adored his accent. And she knew that he could speak English fluently, if he so desired. Usually he did not.

"Just don't do that again."

He caressed her breast slightly, then let go and sat up. Looking around the bedroom, he sighed with what sounded like contentment. But when he turned back to her, she realized that he'd been working himself up to saying something.

"For a while yesterday it was as if I was . . . somewhere else," he said. He spoke quietly, as always when he was serious, leaning down on one elbow and not quite meeting her eyes. He looked past her at the bedside table piled with books on history and archaeology, as if the truth of what had happened could be contained within them.

"What did you feel?" she asked. She could never quite get used to talking like this; his strange ability was always acknowledged between them, but rarely discussed.

"Everything was suddenly old. Not just that chamber and the things in it, but the air around us, the water pressing at the walls. The time that was passing us by. I was removed from everything, letting it all flow past. Like a stone in a stream. But everything that passed me left a taint. Old. All old."

"Something in the jar," she said, sitting up so that he had to look at her. "When the water burst through you were holding something. Feeling it."

Nico looked away, running a hand through his hair. He sniffed. Said nothing.

"I felt a lot of what you—"

"I know!" he snapped. "I can't help it."

"I wasn't *blaming* you." He was suddenly exuding disinterest—a palpable, almost offensive attitude that made her feel queasy. They'd spoken of love and even marriage, but right then he felt like a stranger. She shuffled behind him and put her arms around his chest, resting her chin on his shoulder. Hugged tight. He resisted for a few seconds, then softened into her embrace, leaning back against her and reaching around to stroke her thigh.

"Let's sleep on it," she said, mainly because she was exhausted thinking about it all. He was alive and back with her, and whatever had happened down there would fade with time. *Sleep makes every-*

thing better, her father had told her in the days and weeks following her mother's death. And though she knew that was not literally true, she had come to realize that the passage of time did make difficult things easier to cope with. They became history, which could be mused upon and recalled, instead of a painful, injurious present.

They stripped and lay down, Geena cautious about making advances in case that morning's episode in the shower was repeated. But later, when the sun had fully set and moonlight cast the silvery light of make-believe through the room, she woke to find Nico pressing against her. He was stroking her, hard against her leg, and passion rose from sleep with her, making her wet and receptive to his touch. She turned on her side and hooked a leg over his hip. As he entered her he sighed heavily, and she buried her face in his neck because his breath still carried the taint of Venice.

He took complete control, making love to her as if it were the first time in months. She welcomed the passion and opened her mind to him, seeking the mysterious union that made their loving so powerful. Her skin tingled, and as she closed her eyes she felt Nico's movements as if they were her own, felt her breath gasping against his neck, the feel of her breasts squeezed gently in his hands. It was always the most powerful sensation she had ever experienced, the sense of someone else enveloped in the open and frank throes of passion. She lost herself to it, tasting Nico's skin and tasting herself through his mouth, penetrated and penetrating, and she also experienced that brief moment of sheer delicious panic that this would be too much for her, this would drive her mad. But beyond that always lay the staggering impact of mutual climax, and she held him tight, embracing and embraced as they cried out together.

As Nico came he growled, then chuckled in a voice far too low to be his.

"Nico?" she said after she'd caught her breath. She was shaking. Their minds were suddenly parted, and when he lifted his head and looked down at her, his face was expressionless. "Nico?" He slid aside and lay on his back, one arm above his head. His eyes closed. Asleep.

But Geena lay awake for a long time. Her heart was thumping, but no longer with exertion. She wanted to rouse him, look into his eyes to see who she would see. The lovemaking had been as amazing as ever, but somewhere there at the end, hazed by passion, there had been an instant of utter dislocation . . . as if she were making love with a stranger.

She lay down beside him at last, but still she could not sleep. And with every intake of breath, she searched warily for the scent of that old flooded chamber.

There's a mist coming in from the sea. On the left is the Madonna dell'Orto church, its façade glittering with moisture from the mist. To the right, a canal leading out to open water. It's quiet—no motors, no voices, only the gentle wash of water against the shore. It's a very long time ago.

The man through whom she is viewing this memory—the same tall man from that flashback in the chamber, she is sure—walks beside the canal, heading for a boat moored against a wooden jetty. Several steps ahead of him walks another man, wearing wide trousers and tights, a narrow cloak, and a codpiece studded with fine jewels. He carries a sword, which remains in its scabbard. There's a grace about him, but when he glances back his face shows signs of illness. The left side droops, eye down-turned and opaque, mouth dipped.

There are several soldiers waiting in the boat, all of them heavily armed, each of them shifting nervously as they watch the approaching group.

Surrounding the droop-faced man are several more soldiers. They give him a wide berth, but their pikes are held horizontally, blocking any route through their ranks.

The tall man who owns this memory is chanting, and dark droplets spatter the cobbles behind him. In this pale, gloomy morning they have no color, but they splash like blood.

The canal beside them does have color. It is red.

They reach the waterfront and the soldiers in the boat stand to atten-tion. They blink quickly, breath pluming from their mouths, and their fear is a palpable thing.

"So those cowards wouldn't come to see me on my way, Volpe?" the droop-faced man asks.

"On my advice, Giardino Caravello."

"You fear me."

"No," the tall Volpe says mildly, and Caravello's confidence seems to fade.

"You have no right—" he begins, but Volpe intercedes.

"I have every *right!" he roars. A flock of startled pigeons lifts off behind them, wings snapping at the air as they flee through the mist. "The safety of Venice is paramount in my mind and heart. You would seek to corrupt it.* Tear *it."*

"And you believe that you are incorruptible—"

"No! No more talking, Caravello. The Council of Ten has decreed that you be banished from the State of Venice forever, and if you return you will be executed." He steps forward, passing between the line of sol-diers until he is almost face-to-face with the other man. He smells gar-lic and wine on his breath. "Your death will be quiet and unobserved, in some dirty courtyard. Your body will be weighed down with rocks. Added to the foundations of the city."

Caravello tries to smile, but his illness turns it into a sneer. "You cannot frighten me."

"I have no wish to frighten you," Volpe says. "Just to kill you. Give thanks to the Council that you suffer only banishment."

He steps back and nods to the soldiers, and they move forward hes-itantly, none of them catching Caravello's eye as they herd him slowly toward the boat.

"Faster!" Volpe hisses. "The man is no longer Doge. He's lower than you all, and I'm already sick of the stench of him."

Caravello glares at each soldier as he boards the boat, and every one of them averts his eyes.

Volpe grins. "Enjoy your small victories. They will be your last." Then he presses both hands together before him, chanting, shoulders tensing, and Caravello falls onto his back in the boat. He shouts, but his voice sounds muted and pained. A hazy redness surrounds his face.

"Go well," Volpe says. He turns his back on the boat and walks toward the heart of the city, and as he passes by, the canal turns from red to black.

❖

Geena snapped awake, gasping into her pillow, reaching for Nico but finding only cool sheets. She sat up and scanned the gloom of her bedroom, but he was not there.

I knew everything they were saying, she thought, but already the vision seemed to be fading. Like any vivid dream, it seemed to be built on air and mist, and waking cast the first eddies that would disperse it.

"That was no dream," she said out loud, hoping to hear a reply. But her apartment was silent, empty of anyone but her. She sat there for a while, sore from the night before, wondering where Nico had gone and wishing for the safety of dawn.

CHAPTER 4

Nico Stood on the tiled courtyard in front of the church of Madonna dell'Orto, watching the rising sun lighten the brick façade from brown to rose to a pale peach. The arched windows of the bell tower were steeped in shadows, as though the night had barricaded itself inside to try to outlast the sun. The white stonework of the arches and the various statues in the façade all seemed to be emerging from shadows themselves, and gleamed like ivory as the morning light revealed them.

The Madonna dell'Orto at sunrise was a sight to behold. But Nico would have been better able to appreciate it if he could have remembered precisely how he had come to be there.

He swayed a little, then regained his balance. His thoughts were muzzy and he tried to shake the feeling. The morning seemed to be burning off the shadows in his mind just as it did those that had cloaked the city.

Think. You kissed Geena while she slept, got out of bed and dressed, careful not to wake her, and left her place.

That much he did recall, along with the confusion that had

roiled within him. His departure had been urgent and he had hurried through the maze of passages and bridges to the edge of the Grand Canal, with his pulse racing and the sense that some vital task must be accomplished. Paranoia made the small hairs stand up on the back of his neck and he had reached out with his thoughts, seeking the heightened emotions he could often sense. Fear had its own flavor. And malice. How many times had he escaped violence in a bar or club by departing just before things turned ugly?

But he had sensed no malice, no violent intentions, no one following him. Why he should think someone might be following him, Nico didn't know. It made no sense, but he could not escape that suspicion and had hurried onward, more frantic than ever to reach his destination . . .

. . . only he didn't know where he was going. Not at first. It felt to him as though some enormous hook had been set into his rib cage and was tugging him forward. He had hurried along the edge of the Grand Canal in vain hopes of discovering a water taxi running in the pre-dawn hours, knowing that crossing the water was the next step toward his destination.

His memory had holes in it. Blackouts, like some awful drunk.

He remembered sitting in a creaking *traghetto*, its small motor buzzing, echoing off black water below and black sky above. Somehow he had persuaded the man to take him across the Grand Canal from Guideca to San Marco. The fellow had looked exhausted; he'd probably been up all night ferrying revelers to various hotels and clubs. Nico had tried to pay him, but the man had gotten a pale, frightened look on his face and had shooed him away.

Only when he walked through the vast emptiness of St. Mark's Square at half past three in the morning, and then into the labyrinth of alleys and bridges and canals beyond, did it occur to him where he was headed. The destination had popped into his head the way a song title might once he had given up trying to remember it.

He had nearly turned around then. Geena had been soft and warm and in need of reassurance. Yet the compulsion had been impossible to resist, sending him out to wander Venice in the small hours of the morning with only the sounds of scurrying rats and the water lapping the sides of the canals to keep him company.

Now he found himself here, gazing up at the beautiful face of this church, and he could recall only about half of that journey. Portions of his memory, even of the path he had taken to get here, were blacked out.

In their place, other memories rushed in—vivid recollections of the sounds of construction, the stink of men working, the hoisting of statues into place, sculptors at work. . . . His hands trembled as he stared at the church.

"Impossible," he whispered, there in the light of the rising sun.

Yet if he closed his eyes he could practically see the workers constructing the church's façade, placing the pilasters, laying the brickwork around the enormous circular rose window that lit up now with the dawn's light.

"What the hell is happening to me?" he asked the sunrise.

A piece of paper skittered across the tiles in the breeze, eddied in a circle, then continued on its way. He ought to turn around and go back to Geena, spoon behind her and press his nose into her hair, breathing in the scent of her. That was what he wanted to do. But somehow the commands did not travel from his brain to his muscles, and his body did not obey him. He felt like a marionette.

Go in, he thought.

Or someone thought for him. That was exactly what it felt like. The ideas that kept bubbling to the surface of his mind did not feel like his. Sensitive to the thoughts and emotions of others, able to touch their minds with his own, he had spent his entire life learning to sort out the difference between his own internal voice and those of others, and he knew that this voice did not belong to him. Nico was afraid, and yet fascinated as well.

The stone jar, he thought. *The urn*. And he knew it had begun with that. Down in the strange subchamber beneath Petrarch's library, he had tapped into some enormous psychic repository from Venice's past. He could see and taste and smell things as they had been in centuries past. These sensations came in flashes and visions and in whispers in his mind.

As a boy, whenever he had changed schools and been surrounded by new people—even when he had first attended university—he had needed to take time to adjust to the tidal wave of new minds around him, to build up fresh walls. A day or two would be all he needed to sort himself out, to quiet the voices in his head and reassert his own thoughts. To be himself.

This would be the same, he felt certain. Somehow he had tapped into some kind of psychic reserve and now it echoed around inside of him, making him feel as though his thoughts were not his own. For now, that meant trying to shut out the rest of the world—even Geena—and focus on this opportunity. He could see the past as though his own eyes had witnessed it, feel the power of the man whose memories had seeped into his own . . . for certainly he had been powerful. And a psychic as well. He must have been, for Nico to pick up such powerful emotional residue from that chamber.

What are you thinking? You don't know what the hell you're talking about.

He mocked his own presumptions. True, he had never experienced anything like this, nor even heard of anything remotely resembling this turn of events in the research he had done about his own abilities. But what else could it be? It made a bizarre kind of sense. He thought about scientific theories concerning haunted houses, in which "ghosts" were explained as the resonance left behind by traumatic or otherwise emotional events. He wasn't sure how much of that he believed, but he knew what he felt right now, and "haunted" was as good a word as any.

A day or two and he'd be just fine. The blackout moments would go away, the compulsions would vanish, the voice and its memories would be gone. But while they were with him, he knew he had to use them, to glean what he could about the history of Venice from the information and the feelings suffusing his every thought. Most people would find it terrifying—and the compulsion to act did frighten him a little, as did the blackouts—but now as his thoughts regained some semblance of order, Nico realized that for an archae-ologist, this was the opportunity of a lifetime.

When he and Geena made love, and sometimes even just in quiet moments they spent together, he felt as though her thoughts were a part of him instead of some external thing he could tap into. This made that seem like nothing. He felt the presence of this "other" inside his every thought, there with him, and he even knew the name of the man whose psychic echoes were reverberating through his mind and had drawn him here.

Zanco Volpe.

Nico knew Geena had sensed some of this, though how much he could not be sure. He ought to have talked to her about it. She would have been fascinated, wanting to know every detail, and it would have been natural for him to share that with her. Yet he had found himself attempting to hide his thoughts from her, trying to put up barriers between them. It hurt and confused him to shut her out, and he could not really have said why he did it.

But some of the wild tumult of his mind had spilled out to her, he knew. Geena herself was not a sensitive, but over the course of their relationship they had built up a rapport so intimate, their minds so open to each other, that he could not shut her out completely.

Only now it occurred to him that it might not be him who was trying to shut her out. Not really.

He only wished he could control what parts of Volpe's psychic echo he could touch and see. As he had walked through the streets he had seen two images, the past superimposed over the present, and it had taken his breath away. No one alive had ever seen Venice the way it had been in ages past. Sixteenth century? Fifteenth? He wasn't quite sure.

Stray thoughts that had to be Volpe's swam up inside of him. And there was that hook in his chest that drew him onward and filled him with a sense of purpose. Perhaps Volpe had had some unfinished business when he'd died, and the echoes of his purpose filled Nico, overriding his own intentions.

He had been confused at first, fighting it, two sets of thoughts in conflict inside his head. But now he wanted to go along, to see where these psychic echoes would lead him before they diminished to nothing and then vanished altogether.

He took a breath, closed his eyes, then opened himself to Volpe's voice and the memories that stirred within him.

We're here, he thought. *What now?*

Nico felt an overwhelming compulsion to enter the church. He began walking, unnerved by the peculiar sensation that he was only along for the ride, a passenger in his own body. As an experiment, he tried to resist, to fight his forward momentum, and for a moment he could feel anger that was not his own flaring in the back of his mind.

Then he blacked out. His thoughts were extinguished like a snuffed candle flame. Yet even in his unconscious state, he remained vaguely aware that his legs had continued to move.

After she'd woken to find Nico gone from her bed, Geena had managed only a fitful, restless sleep. Deep slumber had proven elusive, and by the time the sky outside her bedroom window had turned from black to indigo to a powdery blue, and the gentle morning light had suffused the room with its warmth, she could not force herself to stay in bed a moment longer.

She'd been off-kilter ever since the ruin of Petrarch's library and Nico's brief disappearance, and she didn't like the feeling. As a little girl, she had been shy and unsure, and she had spent the entirety of her adult life refusing to allow that little girl to rule her. Half of her initial attraction to Nico—beyond the physical, at least— had been that he never questioned her ability to accomplish things for herself. Geena thought it must have something to do with him being so much younger, but whatever it was, she liked it. No second-guessing. No underestimating. No presumptions.

It was time to put the little girl away and be Dr. Geena Hodge again.

So what are my priorities here?

Nico. Petrarch's library. BBC co-financing. Making the boss happy. If she dealt with the second and third things on that list, the fourth would surely follow. Part of that was finding out what exactly had happened down in the subchamber. *The Chamber of Ten*, she thought, remembering the Roman numerals written on the door and on those obelisks, as well as the vision that had spilled out of Nico's mind and into her own. And what of the granite disk set into the stone floor? Could it really cover an entrance into an even deeper chamber?

All of these threads were intertwined. All pieces of some kind of puzzle that, for the moment, had only revealed its edges to her. And she had a feeling if she found the answers to the questions that were plaguing her, she would learn more about what was going on with Nico. If all was well, he would show up early today, either at the university or at the site.

The site. Her head hurt just thinking about it.

The director of the Biblioteca Nazionale Marciana—a petite, blue-eyed Roman named Adrianna Ricci—had no doubt been racing around in a fury for the past two days, trying to figure out who to blame. The water had poured in from the canal, filling Petrarch's library almost to the ceiling, but only the subterranean chambers had flooded. The Biblioteca itself had suffered no damage. Still, Adrianna would not be pleased with the equipment they were having to bring through in order to deal with the flooded rooms, or the potential damage being done to the building's foundations.

Geena would sic Howard Finch on Adrianna and he would undoubtedly throw a little BBC money her way, if it hadn't been done already. The university would show the video to city officials, who would see that the research team had done nothing that would affect the walls of the chamber and—if Geena knew her boss, Tonio, the way she thought she did—would persuade them to blame the Italian government. All of the canal disruptions caused by the MOSE project or any number of a dozen other factors, not least the gradual sinking of the city and rising of the sea level, would be blamed as contributing factors as Venice tried to get Rome to foot the bill for a levee wall beside the foundations of the Biblioteca.

The factor that might speed things up was that the hole in the canal wall was dangerous. It could grow and undermine the Biblioteca, causing the entire building to collapse. The effect on tourism alone—one of the landmarks of St. Mark's Square devastated—would be enough to get the city moving. They would already have engineers planning and a repair crew would be gathering.

Still, it could take days even for a temporary solution, such as pumping the chamber out, and Geena had no intention of waiting that long. If Tonio had not already put it in motion, she intended to send Sabrina and a team of divers down into the flooded chambers today. She wanted to know what those obelisks were, what might be in them—though she had an idea—and to see if there was anything else that they had missed.

But Nico had to be her first priority, and though she *hoped* that he would show up for work today, she feared otherwise.

The curtains billowed with a warm morning breeze as she hurried from her bedroom to the apartment's tiny bathroom. She ran the shower and then tied her hair back with a rubber band, not waiting for the water to get hot before she stepped under the spray. Her shower last night had been refreshing, but she did not want to take the time to wash her hair again, so she soaped up and rinsed off and then toweled dry, all in a matter of minutes.

Trying to distract herself.

Nico's my top priority.

She had responsibilities to the university and to her team. Tonio might have been worried about her after things went haywire and sympathetic in giving her time to recover yesterday, but today he would expect answers and action, and he had every right to that expectation. She had work to do. The public would be intrigued, the media would try to find some way to paint them all as incompetent, and scholars would scream for their heads. They had saved roughly eighty-five percent of the books and manuscripts from

Petrarch's library—most of which had already been removed before the incident—but some would no doubt shriek over the loss of fifteen percent and claim that those were the most valuable of the manuscripts.

All of these things had been rolling around in her mind over the course of the hours of darkness since she had woken to find Nico gone. She had slept and dreamed and then woken to thoughts about the project—who would handle the media inquiries, and whether or not she should expand her team once she had the BBC funding.

These were genuine responsibilities, real problems to be solved, but she focused on them in order to prevent herself from thinking about the thing that was really troubling her: the silence in her mind.

Other than the vision she'd had during the night, she had not felt the touch of Nico's mind since they had made love. And even during their lovemaking, there had been something cold and unfamiliar in him, as though she had touched the mind of a stranger.

Been touched by, she reminded herself. Her closeness to Nico sometimes made her forget that he was the sensitive, not her.

Now she moved about the kitchen, cracking two eggs into a frying pan and then shredding some cheese and strips of ham into the mix and scrambling the whole thing together. Two slices of toast. A glass of bitter orange juice—you couldn't get decent OJ in Italy—and a cup of coffee strong enough to make a lesser woman cry. And while she prepared her breakfast . . . and while she sat and ate it. . . and while she pulled on a clean pair of black jeans and a sleeveless white top, leaving her hair in the ponytail . . . she thought about Nico.

Not just about him, but *to* him. Geena kept her mind open, waiting for that familiar prickling of the skin at the back of her neck, the comforting caress of his thoughts against her own. When Nico was close by she felt it nearly all the time, often with images and words and emotions. But even when they were apart, as long as he was in the general vicinity she could get a sense of him—his moods, mostly. It had made her relationship with Nico the greatest of her life, not only because of the extraordinary way their thoughts mingled during sex, but because he kept himself so open to her. She had a freedom that she could never have had with another man— the freedom to love without reservation, knowing that if Nico stopped loving her, or fell for someone else, he would never be able to hide it from her. She hungered for him all the time, but more than that, she felt safe with him. At home.

Now, her thoughts wide open as though trying to lure him in, she could not sense him at all. For a short time after the incident yesterday it had been like this, with Geena so cut off that she had been certain he was dead. Now she knew that Nico was alive, and so this silence could mean only two things. Either he had left Venice completely, or he had gone silent purposefully.

She tossed back the last of her coffee and rose, scraped the remains of her breakfast into the trash, then left the dish in the sink for later.

It took her a minute to find her cell phone. She had no memory of bringing it into the bathroom with her, but there it was on the shelf above the toilet. The battery needed charging, but she refused to take the time for that now. There were half a dozen messages from Tonio and members of her team, but nothing more. Nothing from Nico.

She called him, waiting for the ring.

An ancient David Bowie song played somewhere in the apartment—Nico loved Bowie—and for half a second she let herself believe that her boyfriend had returned. Stupid, of course. Nico's phone was here, but that didn't mean he was.

Following David Bowie, she found the phone on the windowsill beside her television in the living room, but the song ended just as she reached for it. Her call went through to voice mail and she hung up. She would take the phone with her, and return it to Nico when she found him. She hated being out of touch.

Geena thought about writing a note but then didn't bother. Anything she might say in a note, he would already know.

"What the hell's happening to you?" she whispered into the

empty apartment, and she didn't know if she meant the question for Nico, or for herself.

Tucking her and Nico's phones into her pocket, she left, locking the door behind her. As she went down the stairs, she forced herself to be calm despite how weird it all was.

She would go to the university first—she needed to touch base with Tonio—and then she would head over to the Biblioteca. If she did not cross paths with Nico at either location, then she would have to go looking for him.

The church bells were silent this morning.

Nico frowned, staring not out one of the arched windows but into a corner of the square bell tower. The heavy bells loomed above him, their weight oppressive, as though they might tumble down at any moment. Plaster strips on the walls led up into the cell that surrounded the bells.

The bell tower had been constructed of brick in the waning days of the 15th century and the first few years of the 16th, but remained an elegant and impressive combination of styles, including the Byzantine dome at its peak. Yet it was the corner that drew his attention—ordinary brick, put together by Venetian masons, which was to say, the greatest in the world.

How the hell did I get up here?

A little ripple of fear went through him. The fascination and even excitement he had felt before now took a backseat to the unsettling nature of these blackouts. Somehow he had entered the church and found his way to whatever private stairs led up into the bell tower. Had doors not been locked to bar his path? Had no one attempted to stop him? And if someone had . . .

Did I hurt anyone?

He took a moment to survey his own body, searching for pain in his fists or elsewhere that might indicate a fight, but everything seemed perfectly fine, except for the fact that he had no memory between the moment he had started walking toward the church and seconds ago, when he had found himself staring into the brick corner of the bell tower.

Nico turned and looked up at the bells again. Not the original bells, he knew. Zanco Volpe had seen to the installation of the original bells of Madonna dell'Orto, and he had given very specific instructions to the workers, just as he had overseen every element of the casting of the bells themselves. He had done something to the metal in its liquid state, added some ingredient that seemed unclear in the midst of the psychic residue bouncing around in Nico's head. But Volpe had altered the metal in some way, in secret, with no one there to see him. He had engraved ancient sigils in the bells, so tiny that only a metal-smith would have noticed.

On the day that the bells had been rung for the first time, the men pulling the cords were his men, and they had practiced for days to get the sequence and timing exactly right. He remembered it as clearly as Volpe himself had at the time of his death, more than four hundred years earlier.

The bells had rung in perfect sequence, their emanations a harmony that sealed the spell into the metal, so that every time they were rung thereafter, on down the years, the enchantment had been reinforced. Centuries of spellcraft, all focused on this one location, for the protection of the single item that Volpe had hidden away here.

Until some unthinking fool had replaced the bells.

All of these thoughts were racing through Nico's mind. *Spellcraft? Enchantment?* He stared at the corner, where the bricks had deteriorated a little, sagging backward as though a void existed behind them—which he knew to be true. It seemed amazing that no one had noticed the way the wall had sunk in that corner, or attempted to fix it.

Not that long since the old bells were taken away, then, a voice whispered in Nico's head.

"Stop," he said, pounding his fists against his temples.

He wanted to know, wanted to see all of the pieces of history that lurked in his brain, but he did not want Volpe whispering in the back of his head in that archaic dialect. Until now, he hadn't even realized that the thoughts were not in his own modern Italian, but here he was thinking in a language he shouldn't even understand to begin with.

A century or less, Volpe thought.

"Stop!" Nico shouted.

But this time his hands didn't go to his temples. Instead he reached out for the bricks, digging his fingers into the crumbling mortar around them, scraping and prodding furiously, so that the pads of his fingertips were raw. His breath came fast. Several times the blackness swept in at the corners of his mind, only to retreat. He wanted to know what was hidden behind the wall in that brick corner, but it was not Nico doing the digging. He knew he ought to stop, or at least be more careful, but still he worked his fingers in, breaking up mortar, pulling chips of it out, loosening several bricks.

He stopped, breathing raggedly. His fingers burned with pain. He thought he ought to look at them, but seemed unable to lift his hands. He looked down and saw tiny drops of blood falling from his fingertips. He had to bind them. Get somewhere he could disinfect and bandage them.

Instead he thrust his fingers between two loose bricks. One of them tumbled into a space between the inner and outer walls, and then he began to tear others loose, pulling them out to thunk on the floor at his feet.

Damnable bells, he thought. He could have hidden it in the wall of the nave or in a crypt beneath the church, but he had thought his use of the bells ingenious . . .

Nico blinked, swaying on his feet. He breathed evenly, fighting off the darkness. *Not my thoughts. Those were not my thoughts. How can this just be psychic residue? It doesn't feel like echoes anymore.*

He paused to listen for anyone who might have been summoned by the sound of his excavation, but he heard no urgent footsteps, nor any cry of alarm. Perhaps the church had been locked and he had broken in. Or, if the doors had been open, perhaps the priest or caretaker who had unlocked them this morning lurked in some back room, thinking it too early for anyone to be in the building.

His hands pushed into the gap in the wall, reached down, and touched something solid. A smile spread across his face as his fingers clasped its edges and drew it out. A layer of grit silted off, showering to the floor. Gently he brushed dust from the cover, running his fingers over the leather, still impossibly supple after all these years, the pages stiff and yellow but not yet brittle. Five hundred years bricked up in a wall and the book looked little different than it had on the day he had placed it there, laying the last of the bricks himself.

The cover bore no letters in any language, no markings at all, but this was only right. The Frenchman from whom he had acquired the book had called it *Le Livre de l'Inconnu—The Book of the Nameless*. And rightly so, for it contained unspeakable things. It was the most important and most dangerous book that Petrarch had collected during the years of his voracious acquisition of knowledge, but possessing it had so troubled the poet that he had entrusted it to the abbot of a German monastery. In time, Volpe had managed to acquire it for himself, and return it to Venice. He had made good use of it, until his time had grown short and he had realized he had to hide it away so that it would not fall into the wrong hands.

Unable to control himself, Nico lifted the book and kissed the soft leather. But he did not open it, and would not do so in this holy place.

As he left the bell tower, hurrying down the steps, his thoughts strayed far ahead, already thinking about the next thing he would need to acquire if he was to restore the protections that had been shattered when he had dropped that jar . . . when his heart had been exposed to the air and the spell broken.

Nico froze two steps from the bottom.

His heart. The gray, withered thing in the urn had been the heart of Zanco Volpe.

Footsteps shuffled just ahead. His throat dry, his head aching, Nico looked up to see a priest with thinning white hair and a curved spine hobbling toward him. The old man stared at him.

"Who are you?" the priest asked, righteous ire reddening his face. "What do you think you're doing up there?"

Nico did not know the answers. Before he had entered the bell tower, the line between himself and Volpe had been distinct—one alive and one dead, one real and one an echo, one modern and one ancient. Now the two seemed more blurred. He did not know where he ended and Volpe began, whose will controlled his hands, whose soul gazed out from behind his eyes. Insane, for Volpe had been dead for centuries. He was nothing more than the smoke that lingered after the fire had burned out.

"Who *are* you?" the priest demanded again.

Nico tucked the book under one arm and fled, racing past the priest, through the nave, down an aisle, and out the door, with the old man shouting hoarsely after him.

CHAPTER 5

GEENA ARRIVED AT THE UNIVERSITY JUST A FEW MINUTES before eight o'clock in the morning. She strode down a corridor lined with faculty offices, her footfalls echoing loudly. In the summertime, the university always felt abandoned to her. There were still students and teachers around, but far fewer, and the usually bustling main building seemed like some old haunted mansion.

She had stopped by Nico's apartment on the way and used her key to let herself in. It would have given her peace of mind to find him asleep in his own bed, but she had known the moment she entered that the place was empty. Dust motes swirled in her wake as she passed through. He slept at her place nearly every night, and only retreated to his own when one of them had to focus on work that did not involve the other. Considering that they were both working on the Biblioteca project, that was rare.

If Nico needed to clear his head, Geena knew he was much more likely to go wandering around the city than to hide out in his apartment, but she had to check, just in case. There had been no sign he had ever come home after the incident two days before, not even to change his clothes. The shower was dry, no damp towels hung from the bathroom door, and the only dirty laundry was a sack that he had brought back from her place a few days earlier and not gotten around to doing yet.

Stalker, much? she thought.

But she knew she wasn't being a stalker. As much as she loved him and depended on him, this wasn't even about the security of their relationship. She was simply worried about him.

The university was her second stop. The Biblioteca project was her baby, and Dr. Schiavo would expect her to be on top of things. He had given her some breathing room the day before, and she appreciated that, especially because—officially—he had to pretend he did not know that she and Nico were sleeping together. But now, as far as anyone in the department knew, Nico was "back," and no one had drowned. Tonio would want her to get down to business.

Her keys jangled as she took them out of her pocket. A loud, buzzing electric hum came along the corridor, the familiar sound of one of the janitors buffing the floor. It eased her mind to know that, contrary to appearances, she was not alone here.

She knew before she opened the door that nobody would be inside. The frosted glass glowed warmly with the daylight, but the simple fact that the door was locked had told her that the office was empty. Now she stepped inside, greeted by the almost unnoticeable static of electricity in the air, both from the lights that she switched on and from the computers that continued to hum, fans running, screen savers drifting against black desktop backgrounds.

A light cotton jacket hung over the back of Domenic's chair. Had he worn it yesterday, or had he already been here this morning? No, that made no sense. If nobody on the team was here in the office, that meant they were all likely over at the Biblioteca.

Geena took a deep breath.

"Okay," she whispered, her voice sounding dull and flat in the empty office.

She checked her voice mail and saved all of the messages without writing them down. E-mail could wait. Going through papers on her desk, she found Howard Finch's business card and slipped it into her pocket. She could call him from her cell on the way to the Biblioteca. She'd have to call Tonio as well, and then catch up with her team on the status of the flooded chambers. If she timed the water bus right, she'd be arguing with Adrianna Ricci at the Biblioteca in forty-five minutes.

Geena shut the lights off and stepped back into the corridor, pulling the door shut behind her.

"Leaving again so soon?"

The voice startled her and she dropped her keys. Even as she turned, she realized it was Tonio and felt foolish for jumping. Tonio Schiavo was fifty-one years old, with a proud Italian nose, a slight paunch, and thinning hair, but he maintained a certain suave handsomeness. Charm could do wonders for a man. The department head smiled and stooped to pick up the keys for her, handing them over.

"I'm sorry," he said. "I didn't mean to frighten you."

Normally she would have bristled as the presumption that she had been scared and given him crap about being a chauvinist. Today she barely noticed.

"I'm a little jumpy," she said, locking the office door.

"After nearly dying on Monday, I'm not surprised," he said. His blue eyes softened with genuine concern. "You're okay?"

"Okay? No. I'm upset about the manuscripts we lost—"

Tonio smiled. "Be happy with what we'd already recovered. Your team did nothing wrong."

"You seem far calmer about this than I expected," Geena said, eyes narrowing. "Shall I assume the BBC is responsible for your good mood?"

"You should," Tonio replied. "Mr. Finch is at the site waiting for you. His camera crew ought to be here tomorrow."

Geena nodded. "Fine. It gives us a day to plan. I wanted to talk to you about sending divers down—"

"I agree," Tonio said immediately. "In fact, I spoke with Sabrina about it yesterday."

She paused, unhappy that they had been working around her absence, though she knew they had done it for her own benefit.

"So what's the plan?" Geena asked.

Tonio must have sensed her irritation, for he shook his head immediately.

"No, no, this is your project, Geena. One hundred percent. It isn't mine or the BBC's or anyone else's but yours. I'm just here to facilitate for you—"

"I know that," she assured him.

"Good. In any case, Sabrina is getting a team together. She knew she had to wait on you before sending them down. I want the whole thing on film, of course, and so does Finch. The BBC has asked that you wait until their camera crew can be ready as well. That might be tomorrow, or possibly Friday. How does that sit with you?"

"That's fine. It'll give us time to do at least a preliminary catalog of the materials we managed to save yesterday." She glanced back at the closed office door. "What are they doing over there now?"

"Cleaning up as best they can," Tonio said. "Making sure the Biblioteca staff will stay away. Ramus is going over plans with the city engineer. Domenic is—"

"Is Nico with them?"

Tonio arched an eyebrow. "I assumed he was with you."

He'd chosen his words carefully, as always, talking around the relationship without ever directly acknowledging it. And, as always, Geena would pay him the courtesy of doing the same.

"I haven't seen him this morning," she replied.

"Ah," Tonio said, nodding as though he understood. "Well, Sabrina didn't say whether or not he was at the site, but you could try her on her mobile."

Geena smiled, knowing it would come off as false but unable to stop herself. "That's all right. I'm headed over there now, anyway. I'm supposed to be running this show after all."

Tonio nodded. "All right. Keep me up-to-date."

They parted ways, Tonio's heavy footfalls marking his retreat even as Geena retraced her own steps along the corridor. She needed caffeine, and hoped that the little café she liked just off St. Mark's Square would be open. She would talk to her team, then drag Nico away for a coffee and a frank conversation about what the hell was going on in his head.

If he was there, of course.

Geena hurried toward the small dock where the water bus stopped every thirty minutes or so—though in Italy that might mean twenty or forty-five minutes instead of thirty, or not at all for hours.

She waited alone, the summer sun glinting off the dark water of the canal, the day quickly warming up. There'd been no opportunity for her to see any weather forecast, but so far it seemed to be shaping up to be what her father had always called "a scorcher."

Sighing and impatient, she pulled out her cell phone to check the time—8:36 a.m. Staring at the phone, she thought about calling Sabrina or Domenic to ask if Nico was there. It would be the simplest thing to do. But if he wasn't with them, she would be facing a serious problem. She had a job to do, people counting on her, and a multimillion-dollar project in her hands. But if Nico wasn't at the Biblioteca, the temptation to head off in search of him would be almost too much to resist.

Stop, she told herself. *He's a grown man. He can take care of himself.*

But she couldn't quite convince herself of that. Normally, yes. But whatever had happened in the Chamber of Ten the day before yesterday had . . . what? Scrambled his brain? Somehow he'd been blasted with memories that did not belong to him, and they were confusing him, even changing him. That scared her.

She put the phone away. To the Biblioteca first. Get things under control. If Nico wasn't there, she could go hunt him down after she made sure everything was on track for the arrival of Howard Finch's BBC colleagues the next day.

To the east, she saw the water bus churning in her direction across the canal. At least she wouldn't be waiting out here for—

❖

—the book feels warm in his hands. He caresses the supple leather of the cover and finds it unnervingly akin to human skin. But he can almost feel the dark promise that lies within its pages, so any hesitation is immediately dismissed. Forty-seven years he has been searching for The Book of the Nameless. *Petrarch had publicly claimed not to have a copy, but his private writings, found in his hidden library, had revealed the truth. He had briefly owned it, but given it to a trusted friend, a scholarly monk. Petrarch had not wanted the responsibility inherent in ownership of* The Book of the Nameless. *Always the humanist, he had been afraid to unleash its power, afraid to hold that kind of magic in his hands.*

Now he has acquired the very same copy that Petrarch had so foolishly given away, and he covets it even more than he had before it was his. Seconds in his possession, and already he guards it jealously. If half of the legends surrounding this book are true, his enemies—the would-be mages plotting against him—will not stand a chance. If they ever had.

"Monsieur?" the Frenchman says.

Volpe glances up, blinking. The Frenchman has just handed him the book but somehow he had nearly forgotten the man's presence. Lizotte, his name is. Henri Lizotte. He is a thief of the highest order, though he fancies himself a collector of antiquities. He dresses like a dandy and travels with a small boy all in frills and colors like some kind of harlequin or jester. Lizotte refers to the child as his valet, but Volpe suspects the Frenchman of using him for a different service entirely.

"It is as I promised, oui?" the Frenchman asks, stroking his thin mustache.

He agrees that the book is, indeed, as promised, and for several seconds considers the option of simply killing the Frenchman. The right gesture to the guards that surrounded them would have ended Lizotte's life, but the Frenchman must have known the peril into which he was placing himself by coming here, by agreeing to sell this book.

And how was he managing that feat? How could he part with it, when any fool could have felt its power?

With a flick of his wrist, Volpe gestures toward Lizotte. "Pay him. But get him out of here."

Away from the book. Volpe is its master now.

The Frenchman seems content. He casts one final, wary glance back at the book as though afraid it might follow him out of the room, then he happily leaves with the household servants to receive his payment.

"Well?" asks Il Conte di Tonetti. "Is that The Book of the Nameless *?"*

Volpe nods, sizing up the Count. "It is. You've done well, Alviso."

The man smiles. Il Conte Alviso Tonetti had been a member of the Council of Ten for less than a year, but had quickly become Volpe's most valuable ally and spy among the Council. The man's home, within view of the Rialto Bridge, might no longer be as opulent as it once was, and his family's reputation might have been tarnished by scandal a generation ago, but that only made Il Conte a more determined ally. He had something to prove.

Of late it has not been unusual for Volpe and Il Conte Tonetti to meet in secret at the Count's home. The ordinary council chambers are far too susceptible to spying, and the Chamber of Ten, below Petrarch's library, also seemed to have its share of spies of late. The Doge—Pietro Aretino—had been one of them only two years ago. He had seemed content to obey Volpe's secret edicts as a member of the Council of Ten. But once the prior Doge had died and the Council had voted him to replace the dead man, Aretino had grown jealous of Volpe's influence.

He dabbles in magic now, and that is Zanco Volpe's province.

Pietro Aretino wants to rule Venice in more than just name. And that, Volpe cannot allow. Worse still, in his dabbling, Aretino has discovered the presence of the dark power deep beneath the city. Like the gases of decay building up inside a bloated corpse, the evil of Akylis remains long after the ancient magician's death. Already the evil has tainted Aretino, and the Doge has begun to tap into that power to transform himself into more than a dabbler.

Volpe cannot allow it. The man's dark ambitions must be ended before they can blossom any further.

He glances around Tonetti's music room, admiring the harp and the lute and the violin upon their stands, but appalled by the ridiculously ornate piano, which is painted in such a way that it appears almost to be dripping gold. The rear wall of the room is a tile mosaic done in the Moorish style, which clashes dreadfully with the paintings in the room's entryway. Tonetti knows next to nothing about art, but he acquires it with vigor in order to impress other wealthy people. Still, it is a beautiful place, and each of the servants seems both obedient and happy—an unusual combination.

"How long, then?" Il Conte asks. "Now that you have the book, how long until we move against the Doge?"

"Days," Volpe says. "It will take me time to master these spells. I only hope that he does not grow brash and attempt to kill me first."

"He'll never reach you," Il Conte says. "You're too well protected."

Volpe thinks on this for a few moments, then narrows his eyes. "Are you certain only two of the Ten are his allies?"

Il Conte nods. "As certain as I can be. I believe the others are loyal, and those two—"

"Caiazzo and Soldagna."

"Caiazzo and Soldagna," Il Conte repeats, confirming. "They chafe at the bit. The Doge has promised them many things."

"I have promises to give them as well," Volpe says.

He smiles, again caressing the warm leather binding of the book, staring down at its featureless cover.

"Two days. The day after tomorrow, you and the others will turn on Caiazzo and Soldagna. Kill them in the Chamber. I want to show Aretino the evil fruit borne of his deceptions before he is banished from Venice forever. If the Council would not rebel against it, I would kill him as well, but they would turn on me in an instant, and that, I cannot afford. Without influence, I cannot control the city. Without control, I cannot protect her properly. No, the Council would never stand for me killing the Doge."

Volpe raises the book and presses his lips against the warm leather, in a gentle kiss.

"Fortunately, they are not so precious about their fellow Council members."

Geena blinked against the brightness of the sun, tasting blood on her lips. She felt hands on her arm and allowed herself to be helped up to a sitting position. The water bus swayed at the dock just a few feet away. The concerned man holding her arm—young, a student maybe—asked her several times if she was all right before she could focus enough to answer.

Her fingers flexed as though searching for the book they had held in the vision that had invaded her mind, spilling over from Nico, she felt sure. Where was he now? In an old mansion near the Rialto Bridge?

Maybe so.

And she had to find him. If these flashes were filling his thoughts constantly, she worried that Nico might well go mad.

If he wasn't already.

◆

Music played out in the street, a tinny melody that sounded like the sort of thing an organ grinder's monkey would dance to. Nico blinked, then shook himself and took a deep breath. He glanced around the room and found himself sitting in a chair in a rich man's kitchen.

Fuck. It had happened again.

"What now?" he asked aloud.

Instinctively his right hand reached out and touched the ancient book, which lay on the iron and glass kitchen table. Plants grew from hanging pots near one of the two tall windows. Some of them were herbs used for cooking, so whoever lived here took their culinary tasks very seriously.

A blink of his eyes and he saw it differently. A ghost-image lay over the whole room like some three-dimensional double-exposure photograph. He had been here before, a very long time ago. The building must have been cut up into luxury apartments, but once upon a time it had been the home of Count Alviso Tonetti. He sat now at a kitchen table in the 21st century, but his eyes saw Il Conte's music room as it had looked in the dawning years of the 15th, complete with the garish piano.

The room where Zanco Volpe had received *The Book of the Nameless* from the Frenchman. The very place where he had first opened it and begun to peruse the dark power in its words.

Nico understood now. He had been overcome by the impulse to return here—a safe and private place in which he could delve into the book again, away from prying eyes, and where whatever darkness might slip out of those pages would be easier to control.

He stared at the book. Where had that thought come from? How could darkness escape the pages of a book? No matter how ugly the intentions of its author, it was still nothing more than words on paper. And yet he felt somehow unclean now, as though some invisible stain had settled into his skin that could never be removed.

A tremor went through him. His right hand was stiff and ached with a deep, throbbing pain that he had not noticed immediately. Now he looked down at his hands and found that not all of the stains upon him were invisible. The knuckles of his right hand were swollen and bruised and blood smeared the back of his hand.

What did I do? he thought. Then he said it aloud, but it came out differently. "What did you do?"

Nico rushed to the window. If he cocked his head just right, he could see the Rialto Bridge. That tinny music came from the throng in the marketplace that ran alongside the canal. Tourists milled amongst carts laden with leather goods, T-shirts, pocketbooks, jewelry, and a million so-called souvenirs. On the canal, gondoliers shouted good-naturedly at one another as they poled their slim vessels through the sludgy water.

If the back of the building had that kind of view, and with this gleaming kitchen—the appliances alone probably cost more than he made in a year—he figured the rest of the place must be pretty swank as well.

So whose apartment was this, and where was the owner?

What the hell am I doing here?

He snatched the book off the table by pure instinct, not wanting to be parted from it, and went exploring. The apartment was not enormous, but whispers of money were everywhere. The high metal ceilings, expensive woodwork, and marble fireplace told him all he needed to know. Every room was so immaculate that he assumed the owner had a cleaning service. Odd that he had never connected cleanliness with wealth before, but the thread was there.

A small table near the apartment door had been overturned, spilling a picture frame, a stack of mail, and a dish of Murano glass made to look like pieces of candy across the floor. On the wall behind the table was a single streak of blood.

Nico held his breath, turning in a circle, trying to figure out where the struggle would have led him. Down a short hallway, he found two bedroom doors, but both rooms were empty, the beds neatly made and unrumpled. Which left the bathroom.

His hand shook as he reached out and gave the door a shove. Hinges creaked as the door swung inward.

At first he thought the man in the bathtub must be dead, and his throat tightened, his stomach roiling with nausea. Christ, if he'd done this . . .

Black electrical tape bound the man's ankles. His arms were behind his back, but Nico could only assume his wrists were similarly trussed. Layers of tape had been wound around his head, covering his mouth. He'd taken a beating, face swollen and bruised and bloody.

But then he saw the man's chest rising and falling, and he knew he wasn't a murderer. Relief flooded him and he sagged against the open door. As he did, the book nearly slipped from his grasp and he gripped it more tightly, then looked down at it. He had almost forgotten he was carrying it. The warm leather felt as though it might as well be a part of his own body.

Revulsion made him want to drop the book, to leave it there on the bathroom floor and get the hell away, but his hand would not obey. Nico backed into the hallway and hurried to the door. He opened it and glanced out to make sure no one would see him exiting the apartment, then he slipped through and hurried along the corridor, descending the stairs toward the first floor at perilous speed, the book clutched to his chest.

Geena, he thought. *Where are you?* He needed her, but even more so, he needed time to sit and think all of this out. On the street, he turned right, navigating alleys and bridges as fast as possible without breaking into a run. Before he could talk to Geena about what was happening to him, he had to try to make sense of it, not just go on intuition.

He hurried through a beautifully landscaped courtyard, its stone and brick foundations crested with an abundance of flowers in full bloom, their vivid colors bright in the summer sun, the heat of the day trapping the scents of a dozen varieties like a city hothouse. A black dog ran by in the opposite direction as if it was chasing something, or being chased, and Nico smiled humorlessly as he saw himself in the same situation.

He would head back to his own apartment, make himself a cup of coffee, and think. Though just holding that book made him uneasy, he knew he would have to open it if he was going to figure out what had happened to him. If Volpe's presence in his mind was more than psychic resonance, he wanted to know how to get it out of him. He needed to be able to think clearly again, without fearing a blackout.

As if summoned by the thought, the darkness began to edge in at the corners of his mind again. *No*, Nico thought, fighting to maintain control, to continue seeing out of his own eyes.

But as he crossed a narrow, crumbling bridge, with a gondolier poling a Japanese couple along the canal below, he could feel the presence that now lurked always behind the curtains of his mind. Words played across his thoughts, enchantments from the book he still held as close to his heart as a lover's secret journal, and he wondered how long he had sat in the unconscious man's kitchen reading that book before his own consciousness reached the surface of his mind again.

The presence inside of him—the spiritual remains of Zanco Volpe—had other things on his mind as well. He had the book, but there were other ingredients he needed to acquire if he hoped to be able to protect Venice.

Protect Venice?

He'd broken into an ancient church, a city landmark, and stolen a book that must be priceless. He had barged into some random man's apartment and beaten, bound, and gagged him. What the hell did any of that have to do with protecting Venice?

The spell must be recast before they try to return.

Nico staggered, caught his foot on a protruding stone, and fell headlong down the stone steps leading down from the bridge. The book flew from his hands. He banged his right knee and skinned his palms, hissing through his teeth at the stinging pain of it. But he'd gotten away easy. It could have been much worse. The voice in his head had taken him by surprise. But had it been an answer? Was the presence inside of him self-aware? Or was it just Nico's subconscious interpreting the things it had learned from the psychic backlash down in the chamber beneath Petrarch's library?

Regardless, he knew what else he needed for this spell, and it was a dreadful shopping list. Even now, the words echoed in his head and he could not tell if they were his thoughts, memories of what he must have read in the book, or the murmurings of a Venetian magician who'd been dead for centuries.

The hand of a soldier, the seal of the master of the city, the blood of a loved one.

"Fuck," he whispered, ignoring the stares of two old widows as he bent to retrieve the book.

Its cover seemed none the worse for wear. The blood on his palm soaked into the leather and it stuck to his hand, strangely rough on his skin.

He wondered if the blood would still be there when he looked again.

CHAPTER 6

GEENA DIDN'T BOTHER TO STOP AT THE BIBLIOTECA. SHE passed it by without giving the building so much as a glance, heels clacking on stone as she strode through St. Mark's Square, pigeons taking flight to clear her a path. More than one tourist turned to frown at her for disrupting their feeding of the birds, which Geena had always thought a disgusting tradition. One man, a bearded fool speaking German to his companions, had pigeons roosting on his head and outstretched arms, grinning for a photograph, with no thought given to what diseases the birds might be carrying.

As she entered an alley between two restaurants—a waiter serving outdoor tables shooting her a curious glance—she pulled out her cell phone and rang Domenic.

"Good morning," he said cheerily. "Are you two feeling any better?"

You two? She flinched at the words. Did they all think it was all right for her relationship with Nico to be public now that she had let them see how much she cared for him, feared for him, and loved him?

"Have you ever heard of a member of the Venetian government named Zanco Volpe?" she asked, unintentionally curt.

"I don't think so. Was he a senator or a member of the Ten?"

"I'm not sure. Maybe just an advisor of some kind. But he had a lot of power in the city."

Domenic knew more about Venetian history than anyone she had met since she had first come to work at the university, three years before. He knew Venice, its people and culture and politics— but he knew the history best of all.

"The name isn't familiar," Domenic admitted. "Why do you ask? Did you and Dr. Schiavo find something in the Petrarch manuscripts?"

Geena could not think of any way to explain it to him that would not have led to a thousand other questions, not to mention worries about her mental stability. Instead, she ignored the question and forged ahead.

"What about someone called Akylis—maybe some kind of magician or shaman or something?"

"I've never heard 'Akylis' used as a person's name before," Domenic said.

"But you've heard the word?"

"I don't know the etymology of it, but scholars have suggested the word as the root for the naming of ancient Aquileia, on the northern shore of the Adriatic. It was founded in the second century B.C.—"

"Count on you to know that," Geena said, her mood lightening for a fleeting moment.

"It's my job to know that," Domenic reminded her.

"What about a Doge named Pietro . . . shit, something, I can't remember the last name . . . and a count called Alviso Tonetti?"

She came to an alley too jammed with people and turned left, seeking an alternate route. Striding past a puppet shop where she always loved to stop and stare at the extraordinary marionettes in the window, she spared only a glance.

"That's an easy one," Domenic said. "The Doge was Pietro Aretino—"

"That's it, yeah."

"—and, according to the history books, Tonetti was his neme-sis. Records from the period say that the Doge plotted to dismiss the Great Council, Venice's equivalent to the Senate, as well as the Council of Ten and make himself some kind of emperor. Tonetti persuaded the Great Council to banish the Doge, and two of his conspirators—members of the Ten—were executed. Well, mur-dered, really, because it wasn't as though they were tried for crimes against the state or anything. They called Tonetti 'Il Conte Rosso' after that because of the bloodshed."

"Holy shit, it's real," Geena muttered.

"What?"

"Nothing, nothing," she said quickly. A glimpse into a shop win-dow filled with Carnival masks gave her a start. Too many faces watching her. Too many people around her.

"What year was that? With the 'Red Count'?" she asked.

"Early 1400s. Maybe 1415, 1417, around there."

Then she remembered the second of Nico's weird visions that had spilled over into her brain, of soldiers escorting another ban-ished Doge to the canal, forcing him to leave the city.

"There were other Doges banished, weren't there?"

"Two that I know of. Geena, what's this all about? Are you com-ing to the Biblioteca today, or what? We've got a lot of prep work to do before the BBC crew shows up tomorrow. And, honestly, I'm sick of the dirty looks I'm getting from Adrianna Ricci."

"I'll be there as soon as I can," she said, dodging around an elderly couple walking arm in arm past shop windows, taking up the entire alley. "Just trying to track down . . . I just have to meet Nico and then I'll be there."

"I thought he was with you?"

Geena cut through a cluster of people and crossed a wide, well-preserved bridge. The buildings along the narrow canal that flowed beneath it had beautiful façades and many windows were filled with flower boxes, but the first floors were crumbling and stained by past high tides.

"Who were the other two Doges?" she asked, ignoring his question.

"Giardino Caravello in the 1390s, and then the most famous, Francesco Foscari, in 1457."

"Foscari?"

"Yes. One of the subjects of Lord Byron's play *The Two Foscari*. The same family the university is named after. Actually, some of the research I've read suggests all three of the banished Doges were related—perhaps distant cousins. Caravello, the first of the three, was apparently banished because he wanted his relatives in all levels of Venetian government. And not just Venice. The family had spread out to other powerful Mediterranean cities, sort of insinuating themselves into government wherever they could. Caravello was much more interested in power for his family than the glory of Venice."

"And the other two, Aretino and Foscari, were related to him?" Geena asked.

"According to some sources," Domenic said, impatiently. "Now are you going to tell me what all of this is about?"

Geena emerged from an alley and turned right on Riva del Ferro, the Grand Canal on her left. It had always seemed strange to her that this stretch of water was considered part of the Grand Canal, as it was so much narrower than other segments, but it was still broad enough that water buses, taxis, and private boats purred in both directions. The Rialto Bridge was just ahead, with its series of arches forever enclosed to protect the many shops inside the bridge.

But Geena knew she wasn't going that far. In the flash of memory that Nico had blasted into her head, apparently unintentionally, she had known this place. She knew the house that had once belonged to Il Conte Tonetti.

A small crowd had formed in front of the once grand mansion. A police boat was moored at the edge of the canal and other officers had come on foot. Half a dozen of them clustered outside the front door, keeping people back from the old building.

From somewhere behind her, around the curve of the canal, she could hear the siren of a water ambulance. The noise echoed off the water and the bridge and the faces of the buildings, growing into a sound that was almost a scream.

Heart fluttering in her chest, imagining the worst, Geena shoved her way into the crowd. People snapped at her in Italian. Whatever tourists had been in the vicinity when the ugliness had begun had made themselves scarce. These were Venetians now, the people of the city. Neighbors and shopkeepers and even a couple of gondoliers, who she thought must have been having coffee in the café two doors down.

"What happened?" she asked. "Can someone tell me what happened?"

The frantic edge in her voice made her cringe, but it seemed to draw the right attention. A young man, no more than twenty, tossed his cigarette to the ground and stamped it out.

"A break-in at one of the apartments," the guy said. "I heard one of the cops say the owner was beaten badly. The weird thing—at least from what the police were saying—is that the apartment wasn't even robbed."

Ice trickled along Geena's spine. Flush with guilt by association and fear for Nico, she continued to forge her way through the crowd, searching for his face. But she knew in her heart that he had already gone. How long ago had he been there? An hour? Thirty minutes?

Retreating to the shadow of the Rialto Bridge, she pulled out her cell phone and called Domenic again.

"Are you on your way?" he asked upon answering.

"Dom, listen. You know everyone in Venice. You must know someone with the police, right?"

For just a second, Domenic was quiet. When he spoke again, his levity had vanished.

"What's wrong, Geena? What's going on?"

She hesitated, hand clutched tightly around the phone. If she let someone else into this craziness, what would happen? It already felt completely out of her control, but at least for the moment it was still between her and Nico. Intimate. Their problem and nobody else's.

But she knew that was a lie. Their intimacy had been shattered, turned into a twisted mirror of itself. Whatever they were sharing now, it wasn't natural, and it frightened her.

"It's Nico," she said. "He's gone missing again. I . . . I don't think he's in his right mind, Dom. I'm afraid something terrible is going to happen."

As she spoke the words, the water ambulance pulled up to the edge of the canal and two EMTs jumped out with their gear, hurrying toward the front door, the crowd clearing them a path.

"I'm afraid it may have happened already."

The hand of a soldier . . .

The very idea was abhorrent to Nico, and he'd been trying his best to turn his mind away from what it might mean. But he was finding it difficult to concentrate. His thoughts were scattered, darting here and there, calling up images and pushing down recollections that could not be his. As one thought seemed to coalesce, another would stalk in and rip it to shreds. His head ached, his eyes throbbed, and he felt more apart from this city than he ever had before.

The thing inside him, though—Zanco Volpe—that felt very much at home. And he had to accept now that the presence lurking in the shadowy corners of his mind was not merely an echo. Somehow, it had will and purpose. Volpe's ghost? Nico didn't know. But he knew for certain this was more than psychic residue.

Nico was being steered and directed, his movements dictated by the subtlest commands from deep inside. From Volpe himself. Sometimes he thought he heard a voice—deep, guttural, and cruel—and other times it was like walking through a waking dream. He *knew* he was dreaming, but he had no control over where this dream took him. Volpe could usurp Nico's consciousness, sometimes with only a thought or an urge, but other times blotting it out completely. Those were the blackouts, and they frightened Nico the most. Bad enough that Volpe could take him over, make him see through his own eyes without any control over his body, but the idea that he might come awake at any time to find himself having done something hideous made him sick.

What if he had killed the man in that apartment, where Il Conte Rosso had once lived? *Christ, how do I stop this?*

Leaving the old mansion he had struggled to fight against this loss of control, and for a while he had stumbled through the streets with the book clasped to his chest. He must have looked like a drunk, staggering into walls, talking to himself in a dialect he had only ever seen written in books. More than once he had come close to falling into a canal.

Maybe that would be for the best, he'd thought, and then that presence within had reared up and screamed, raging with anger at such a casual intimation of death. Nico had drawn back, terrified, and the landscape around him had changed, as if a panorama of yesterday was always just below the surface of his perception. For a time after that, Volpe had walked him through the city, and Nico had shivered in the dark, cool places of his mind.

Now it was Wednesday afternoon, and he was on his way to San Michele. Sitting in the small water taxi and watching the cemetery island draw closer, Nico could relax against Volpe's influence. The old Venetian seemed to have eased back a little—

Does he need rest, is that why? I have to remember that. Have to file it away somewhere deep, where even Volpe can't reach.

—which meant that Nico could close his eyes and try to rest as well. But only try. Because the darkness behind his eyelids was filled with the impact of fist against flesh, and flashes of terror in that man's eyes.

The boat rocked from swell to swell as it crossed the Canale delle Fondamente Nuove. The driver sat rigid in his seat, eyes focused on their destination, and he had never once turned around to try to enter into conversation. Nico had only vague memories of boarding the boat—Volpe had been at the fore then, aiming his flesh-and-bone host in the direction he wanted—but he sensed fear in the man's stance, and a nervous set to his shoulders. *What did I say to him?* he wondered, and almost laughed at the acceptance that had already settled in him. Acceptance that it was not only Nico in this body now, but someone else as well. Someone powerful and determined, whose aims were still clouded in mystery.

He rested the book on his knees. Sometime during the noon hour he'd entered a store and bought bottled water and sandwiches, and the book was now wrapped in the carrier bag. Its cover was unstained by the blood from his grazed hands, as if the bindings had absorbed the moisture after being so long hidden away. He had vague, flashing memories of huddling in doorways or beneath street lamps and trying to open the book, but each time that happened he'd woken somewhere else, with the book wrapped in the bag once again and Volpe's presence a smiling, excited warmth in his mind. *What else has he just found out?* Nico knew that the volume must be both terrible and amazing. It belonged back at the university, where Geena and he could examine and translate it with the others in their team, but even the merest thought of trying to transport it there—

My book, my hands hold it, my eyes read it, my talents use it. Volpe's voice was shockingly loud inside his head, and Nico gasped and stiffened against the fiberglass seat.

The boat's pilot pushed on the throttle, breaking speed limits and risking his license. They reached one of the many jetties and the driver swung the boat expertly against its edge. He remained staring straight ahead as Nico climbed out, unnerved or perhaps even afraid.

"A tip," Nico said, holding out a folded bill. He did not like having this effect on people.

Those thumps, that face filled with fear, the thunk! *as he fell into the bathtub . . .*

But buying forgiveness could never be that easy. The driver throttled away without taking the money, leaving a raging wash behind him as he aimed the boat back across the lagoon. Nico stood for a while watching him go, thinking of heaving the bagged book out over the water and letting it soak and sink, pages disintegrating, whatever arcane knowledge contained within—

Darkness struck like lightning.

He blinked, vision clearing, and found himself walking through the cemetery on the Island of the Dead. Bile rose in the back of his throat and an icy chill ran up his spine. Who the hell had Zanco Volpe been when he lived here in Venice? Who, and what? A psychic? A fucking magician?

No. Not magic. Nico wouldn't believe that. Telepathy was only science not yet fully understood, psychic abilities were facets of the mind. Somehow Volpe's mind had not died with his body, it still lingered, but that didn't make him a ghost.

Yet even as this certainty filled him, a low, chuffing laughter rippled through the hidden places of his mind, as though Volpe stood behind some curtain like the Great and Powerful Oz, pulling levers, so sure of his control.

Nico clapped his hands to the sides of his head. *Get out!* he screamed, inside his own skull.

But the presence growing like a tumor in his brain was silent for once.

No words were necessary. Nico's thoughts and Volpe's were intimately intertwined now. He knew what *was* necessary, and why Volpe had directed him here to the island of San Michele: *the hand of a soldier.*

He'd been here before many times, because a man with his interest in the past could not resist the melancholy air of a cemetery. It was an incredible location, a cemetery island in a city of islands, a burial place for two hundred years. Two islands originally, the canal that separated them was filled in the early 1800s, and since then bodies had been ferried to the island on funeral gondolas, buried for a decade, and then exhumed and kept in huge banks of ossuaries. Space restrictions meant that being put to rest on San Michele was never a permanent arrangement.

Nico had always loved cemeteries, partly for the fascinating array of tombs and memorial stones, but also because of their timeless atmosphere. They kept their history on view, and every grave told a different story. A couple of times Geena had come with him, and he remembered standing together before Stravinsky's tomb, holding her hand and leaning in so that their shoulders were touching. She'd told him . . .

I won't think of her, he thought. He closed his eyes and came to a standstill, reining in his thoughts, because he did not want Volpe to see Geena in his head, sense her, feel her . . . and he had no desire to share precious private memories. He would think of anything else; the Chamber of Ten, his parents' home, his old school friend Celso who liked to joke that—

He was holding her tight, breathing in her breath as they worked their hips in harmony. Her leg was stretched over his, allowing him entry and curling around to pull him in. She was worried that something was wrong, but for a while this took them away. Her eyes were hooded and heavy. She gasped into his mouth when she came, mixing their sighs as they merged their thoughts, and it was as delicious as ever before.

"Fuck off!" Nico shouted, full of rage and hatred. He had wanted to shield the precious parts of his memory from the intruder in his mind, but Volpe stripped away layers of thought with savage ease.

With an effort of will, Nico dropped the book and tried to run, to deny Volpe what he wanted—an ingredient required for the ritual he seemed desperate to perform—but his legs would not obey.

What is it, magician? Nico thought. *What's so important about your fucking ritual?* He did not even believe in magic.

But then what was this?

Nico dropped to his knees there amidst the tombs of the Venetian dead and placed his hand on the book, which had spilled from the bag. And he chuckled, in a voice that was not his own. "You're becoming troublesome, Signore Lombardi. So I shall have to take the reins from you. I am not your true enemy, but if you continue to fight against me, remember that the next time you are with your beloved, it will be my hands on her soft skin. The things I could do to her. I could give her pleasure or pain, but either would cause you torment. Now, behave."

Nico's rage turned to tears.

And his vision went dark again, a prisoner inside his own body.

Later, more time lost, more of his life spent knowing and sensing nothing, Nico found himself across the cemetery island in one of the mausoleum areas. All around him the huge stone structures housed hundreds of ossuaries, and the finely crafted façades were adorned with flowers, plaques, and sealed pictures of those interred. Cypress trees sprouted seemingly at random, but he knew that the cemetery had grown around them. He'd always liked the fact that this place of death paid such attention to burgeoning life.

The hand of a soldier, Nico thought, and Volpe exuded satisfaction.

Nico hugged the book to his chest and breathed deeply, trying to remain calm. He'd rather be at the fore and in control of his movements, even if doing so involved going through with Volpe's desires. He was trapped. The blackouts were horrible, and he was desperate to avoid them as much as he could. But even his thoughts were subject to hijack, his feeling of powerlessness and vulnerability encouraged by the presence that had so quickly changed him from the man he had been.

So he walked between the mausoleums, holding the book carefully, and trying to use the sensations immediate to him to distract him from thinking of Geena.

Hand of a soldier, he thought. *Look for a military grave, smash it open, steal the hand.* Nico blinked because those thoughts were not his own, but he did as instructed.

Several monks appeared around the corner of a mausoleum building, nodding and smiling at him, but then frowning uncertainly as they passed by. *I wonder what they see,* he thought, but Volpe seemed content to stay in the background.

He walked the paths, reading names and inscriptions until he found one that looked suitable. Nico paused and took a step back, quickly jarring to a halt as though he'd struck a wall, but there was nothing behind him. Volpe's influence, that was all.

"Leave me be, don't touch Geena, and I'll do this for you," Nico whispered. "Whoever you are. Whatever you are. You've got me, and I can't get rid of you, but if you keep hurting me like that—"

And then his voice changed, his whole throat seeming to twist out of shape as he lowered his head and uttered a final, awful sentence.

"I have yet to hurt you."

Nico gasped and leaned forward against the mausoleum. He heard footsteps, and glancing to one side he saw that one of the monks had returned. The old man paused for a moment, watching Nico, and then he bowed his head softly and left. *They think I'm mourning someone dead*, he thought, *when in fact I'm cursing them.* Volpe allowed him this thought, and then Nico felt control taken from him again.

He watched, but did not command. He moved, but did not instruct. The dead Venetian pulled his marionette strings, and Nico had no option but to obey.

He wandered some more, straying into an old part of the cemetery. Here he found a broken tomb, and as he lifted a triangle of jagged rock, several lizards darted across the stone. One of them seemed to freeze and bend to look up at him. Then it lowered to its stomach and flipped onto its back, dead.

Nico's body, Volpe's mind, carried the heavy shard of tombstone back to the mausoleums, glancing around to make sure no one was nearby. He set the book down between his feet and swung the stone at the tomb he had chosen.

The façade cracked, but it took several more strikes before it crumbled and fell away. He cut the back of his left hand against a sharp edge, and as the pain filtered through to Nico, Volpe opened his mouth and laughed. Birds, unconcerned at the impact of rock on stone, took startled flight at the laughter. He reached inside for the metal ossuary. It was strangely warm to the touch and Nico jerked his hand back as if stung . . . then reached forward again, hearing a sigh in his mind as his fingers closed around a rusted metal handle. As he pulled, metal scraping across stone, the sound of approaching footsteps startled him. He tugged harder and the container slid out, dropping to the ground, lid snapping open, contents spilling across the random stone paving.

Looking up, he saw the shadow first, and then the monk rounded the corner.

"What do you think you're doing?" the man said, aghast.

Help me, Nico wanted to say. But as he reached out his hands to plead, he felt Volpe rising again, both angry and excited, and so full of life for a man long dead.

CHAPTER 7

ON THURSDAY MORNING, GEENA SAT INSIDE A SMALL CAFÉ across the street from the Biblioteca. She had spoken to the police the previous afternoon and then spent time at the site with her team, but she had been totally consumed by thoughts of Nico. They had all noticed how preoccupied she was, but Domenic—always looking out for her—had done his best to divert any questions that weren't work related. They all meant well, she knew. Domenic had reassured her that Nico was probably just clearing his head, that he'd be back.

But Wednesday night had turned into Thursday morning without any word from Nico.

She ought to be at the Biblioteca right now. The BBC camera crew had arrived, including a specialist in underwater documentary footage and several divers. The rest of Howard Finch's production team would reach Venice in another day or two, but the dive was scheduled to begin within hours. Her team would be waiting for her. She ought to go in.

Instead, she sat watching the entrance to the Biblioteca from inside the café. She'd seen Finch arrive a few minutes earlier. Domenic had already texted her to say he was on his way and that Ramus, Sabrina, and Tonio were already inside. They were probably fending off the ire of Adrianna Ricci.

She ought to go in. It was her project.

But Domenic hadn't arrived yet, and she needed to speak with him without the others around. And all the while she bore a sinking feeling in her gut, knowing she was letting everyone down.

She had just ordered another coffee when Domenic hurried through the door.

"Geena!" he said. "What's wrong? Your messages had me worried."

"He still hasn't come back," she said. "He hasn't called and I've had these terrible feelings that . . ." She sobbed, once and loud, and it startled her so much that she gasped before the first tear came.

Domenic sat at her table and propped his bag against the chair legs, waved at a waitress, and generally did everything he could to avoid looking at her. *I can't blame him*, she thought, and she sniffed and wiped her eyes with a napkin.

"Sorry," she said. Domenic glanced at her and waved his hand— *Hey, don't mention it*—but still could not meet her eyes. "But it's just not *like* him!"

Domenic held both hands out, shoulders raised in a frozen shrug.

"I know." Geena sighed. "I know. Nico and I kept it to ourselves for so long. It's awkward."

"Not really awkward," he said. "Just . . ." The waitress came then, and they both ordered large cappuccinos with extra shots. When she left, Domenic sat quietly looking through the window at the library building across the street. He tapped his fingers on the tabletop.

"Just what?" Geena asked. *He really wants to be over there, not here with me. And I can't blame him for that. Will he blame me for not wishing the same?*

"Well, he's not a kid," he said. "A lot . . . you know . . . younger than you, but no kid. He can look after himself."

"What do you mean?" she asked, but she already knew. She'd

been so wrapped up in her own world that she hadn't taken time to try to view it from the outside.

"I mean, is Nico missing, or is he just not here? With you?"

"You think this is to do with things between me and him?" she asked. And yes, that was exactly what he meant. A flush of anger rose and receded again, and in its place was a sudden sense of how alone she was. This hit Geena sometimes, striking hard when she least expected—a feeling that no one else really understood her. Before Nico, she'd believed it stemmed from being so mixed up in history that the present was not the same place for her as it was for other people. Much of the time she spent thinking about the past, not the here and now, and some days she'd go home after a day at the university and spend the evening adjusting to the present. And then Nico came, touching her mind, and the reasons for her remoteness became wonderfully different.

"I'm just trying to look at it from all angles, Geena."

"I wasn't going to tell you what sort of trouble I thought he was in," she said. "That policeman you put me onto, I spoke with him on the phone yesterday, and I didn't tell him, either."

"Why not?"

"Because I think Nico beat someone half to death yesterday."

The waitress arrived with their drinks and placed them on the table quickly, sensing the awkward silence her presence had instilled. Geena held Domenic's gaze, trying to read his expression. Past the shock she saw concern for her, heartfelt and deep, and she reminded herself that she had friends.

"What do you mean?" he asked when the waitress left.

Geena looked up when the café door opened. Finch stood in the doorway. A smile was already slipping from his face when he saw them, one hand half raised in greeting.

"Howard," she said, waving him in. He was the last person she'd wanted to speak to, yet he'd arrived at an opportune moment. Had she really wanted to tell Domenic about the beaten man? And if she did, how the hell would she explain how she'd linked Nico with the assault?

She couldn't. No one would believe her, and besides, her bond with Nico was precious and personal. It was special and peculiar to them, and she had never mentioned it to another person.

"Am I, er, disturbing . . . ?" Howard asked.

"Not at all," Geena said. "Please." She pointed at the seat beside Domenic, and the producer sat down awkwardly. He coughed, rubbed his hands together, then shook his head when the waitress stood beside him.

"Ah, the film crew is prepping the cameras and getting into their dive kits," he said. "And, ah, as this is your project . . ." He trailed off, looking at Geena as if waiting for her to finish his sentence.

I can't be here, Geena thought. *He's out there somewhere, and I can't be here.* But of course, she had to be. She had responsibilities, and she had no idea where Nico might be. Rushing off and leaving all her responsibilities behind would not help her find him, and at least here she might feel grounded.

"Yes," Geena said, glancing at Domenic. He was frowning at her, and she knew that as soon as the two of them were alone again, he would grill her about what she'd said, and why she had not let him in on this the previous night. She'd called his police friend and told him simply that Nico was missing, and the response she'd received was just what she expected. *He's an adult. Unless you think he's hurt or in danger, there's little we can do.* And picturing the beaten man she'd seen carried from that old building, she had told the policeman that no, she had no reason to suspect either.

Yes, he's in danger, she'd been thinking. *And perhaps I am, too.* But she was not about to give Nico up to the police.

"Yes, my project. I was just sitting here tanking up on caffeine before facing Adrianna." She smiled, and Finch laughed politely, glancing sidelong at Domenic's stern expression. He knew there was something more going on here, but he was obviously unsure how to broach it.

"So, your whole team will be here for this?" he asked.

"Most of them," Domenic said. "Nico is resting; he's picked up a bug somewhere."

"Lot of it around," Finch said.

Geena drank some of her coffee and enjoyed the steam rising before her eyes, cutting her off from the two men for a moment. *I'm here when you need me,* she thought, wishing that Nico's strange touch could go both ways.

"So Tonio tells me Sabrina's footage from Monday's accident convinced your bosses to let you do a six-part series?" Geena said, and Finch seemed to visibly relax. They finished their coffees while Finch filled them in—his series would cover the sinking of Venice, Geena's original project attempting to salvage Venetian antiquity from the rising waters, Petrarch's library, the Chamber of Ten, and the recovery effort—but all the time Geena was aware of Domenic simmering gently beside her. She would have to tell him soon, she supposed. But she would give it until lunchtime. If she'd heard nothing from Nico by then, she thought, she would need the support.

As she crossed the street with Domenic to her left and Finch to her right, the morning sun broke across the Biblioteca's façade. A gentle breeze blew from deeper within the city, carrying a mix of the city's scent with it—coffee, baking bread, sewage, dirty water, cigarette smoke, and that indefinable aroma of water that always seemed untouched by whatever impurities the water might contain. A rush of optimism was blown in with the breeze, and Geena felt herself lifted. *Everything's going to be all right,* she thought. By midday, she would have cause to wonder where such foolish ideas might have originated.

They entered the Biblioteca and as they passed through the foyer, they could already hear the library director's voice raised in protest, echoing shrill and angry along the halls.

"Sounds like your camera team have met Adrianna," Domenic said as they entered the reading room.

"Yes, quite a lady," Finch agreed. "First she told us we'd come to the wrong place, then she claimed there were old Venetian laws forbidding filming in the library."

"She does like keeping the place quiet," Geena said.

"Sounds like she's the one making all the noise now," Domenic said, chuckling.

They walked back into the now cramped room where the secret door to Petrarch's library stood open. Sabrina, Ramus, and Adrianna were there, as well as several strangers—the BBC crew, she guessed—and two senior students she recognized from the university. These two had dived on many sites around Venice, sometimes on their own, and sometimes taking one of several other students or lecturers down with them. Sabrina was one; not yet fully trained as an archaeological diver, still she was well versed with all the technology, and she knew the dangers. They were already wearing dry-suits, and Sabrina was chatting with the BBC crew via an interpreter. They pointed at various pieces of camera technology arrayed on a table before them, and Geena guessed they were trying to decide whether they'd be able to patch Sabrina's camera images directly through to their laptops. One of the BBC crew was standing behind Sabrina, surreptitiously eyeing her shapely behind in the suit. *And it's the Italians who get the reputation as leches,* Geena thought.

Tonio emerged from the stairwell that led to the flooded chamber below—Petrarch's library—a look of concern on his face. He noticed Geena and brightened, and she saw his eyes flickering either side of her as he looked for Nico.

"Geena!" he called, holding out his arms. "We've been waiting."

She nodded at Tonio, then smiled at Ramus and Sabrina. She knew them well enough to know that they were uncomfortable, but she could not make out why. Was it the BBC crew and the sudden widening of attention surrounding their project? Or had Domenic told them something of her conversation with him last night?

Now was not the time to ask. *Everything's going to be all right,* she thought again, and maybe getting into some work would help her emerge on the other side with a clearer view of what was happening.

Perhaps it was not only Nico who had been affected strangely by their unsettling experience and near escape from the flooded chamber below Petrarch's, but her as well.

"Sorry I'm late," she said. "I just like to keep people waiting. So, when will we be ready to go?"

In the end, it was the BBC crew that held them up. After suffering several technical difficulties in linking their own equipment to the university's laptops and filming equipment, it seemed they had a small dispute amongst themselves. Finch took them to one side to mediate, throwing frequent apologetic glances Geena's way, and she smiled and shrugged. Meanwhile Sabrina and the two divers checked one another's diving gear again. As well as the dry-suits and breathing apparatus, they carried a length of thin rope each, powerful lights, and a reinforced plastic helmet that sat snugly against their heads, protecting them in confined spaces. They went through safety procedures, and Geena noticed that both divers were carrying two knives each. The flooded chambers would be extremely hazardous. As well as the poor visibility they expected, everything left down there when the flood struck would be floating at random, and there was plenty that might entangle them.

"So what are you going to do now?" Domenic asked her quietly.

"I don't know," she said. She was avoiding his gaze because she knew that she owed him some sort of an explanation.

"You talked with—?"

"Yes, thank you. But as I told you, as far as the police are concerned, Nico isn't missing." She expected some protest from Domenic, a comment about the police's ineptitude, but he only nodded grimly and looked down at his laptop, pretending to read the screen.

"But he *is*," she said. "He's lost, and I need to find him."

"After this is over, I'll help you."

"Thank you," she said, and felt tears welling up again. *Oh no. Not now. Don't start blubbering now!* she berated herself. She was stronger than that. But when one single tear did escape her left eye, she knew it was not all for Nico. It was because she did not understand what was going on, and that what she *had* seen of him was so wrong.

"I think we're ready!" Finch said.

"About time," Tonio muttered.

Geena touched Sabrina on the arm. "Be careful down there."

"Of course. I've got these two hunks to look out for me."

"Well, don't rely on two hunks. Look out for yourself." Geena smiled at the divers to let them know she meant nothing by it— she'd used them before several times, though for the life of her she could not remember their names. She could see the tension in their faces, and she viewed that as a good sign. They were worried, they were cautious, and that meant that they would be taking care.

"We'll want an all-around view of Petrarch's library first," Finch said, "starting with what's left of the manuscripts that were—"

"No," Geena said. "Straight down to the lower chamber."

An uncomfortable silence settled, but only for a moment.

"For the documentary, I really think we'll need—" Finch began carefully, but Geena cut him off again. His shock turned subtly toward anger.

"We need to see why the hell this all happened," she said. "We did nothing down there, and yet our presence caused the chamber wall to give way and flood. One of our divers is an expert in Venetian architecture and old structures built to withhold water. He'll see if there's still danger."

"How could there still be danger?" Finch asked. "The water's up to sea level."

"Mr. Finch," Tonio said, "Geena's correct." He blinked at Geena, his look saying, *We'll be having words later.* "And quite frankly, we are the experts here."

Finch bristled, his team fiddled with equipment or examined their fingernails, but then he offered Geena a soft smile. "I'm in your hands," he said, and she was certain he meant it. He was a strong man, but not harsh. And whatever his superiors back in London said, he was already becoming more than aware of the intricacies of this operation.

The hairs on her neck stood on end, she felt a rush of warmth as if the sun were touching her again, and when Geena blinked—

A square with tourists taking photographs and drifting this way and that, crumbs from breakfast still on their lips and breath heavy with morning coffee. Sunlight floods in over the roof of a hotel bounding one side of the square, a fountain is spanned with a mini-rainbow, pigeons take off in a wave from a far corner, and the world seems to be dragging her perception onward against her will, hauling her quickly across the square when the only way she wants to go is back. She tries to close her eyes—

"Geena!" Domenic said. "Are you all right?" He had hold of her forearm, and she had to blink several times to clear her eyes of the bright sunlight she'd seen in that moment of psychic connection. The library was dark by comparison. All eyes were on her.

"I . . . I'm sorry," she croaked, coughing to clear her throat. "Yes, time to go. Yes." Domenic would not let go, and she had to turn and walk away before he loosed his grip. She approached the divers, aware of Tonio watching her, feeling Finch's gaze on her back, and Sabrina paused in tightening equipment straps across her waist when Geena drew close.

"Geena, you look—"

"Don't take any risks," Geena said, louder than she needed to, echoing off the stone walls of the too-small room. "I was just thinking about those obelisks, wondering if they were even fixed to the walls." It was an offhand way to try to explain her brief flake-out, though she knew that Domenic at least would see right through her, but mentioning it now seemed a good piece of advice. "The water might have knocked them aside, or they might be ready to fall at any moment. Not to mention the stone disk in the floor—the one Domenic called a cork. If that's a seal of some kind, we should see if it remains intact."

"I wondered the same thing," Finch said behind her.

"This is just an initial look," Geena continued. "Don't disturb anything down there if you can help it." *But what have we already disturbed?* she thought. She'd recognized that square. It had been richer than a memory, and she knew what a touch from Nico felt like. She'd been seeing what he could see right now . . . and he'd been moving fast.

Sabrina and the divers worked their way through the narrow corridors leading to the first old staircase, and Geena followed. Domenic was behind her, and for a moment she was angry at him—*Can't I just have a moment on my own?*—but that anger was misdirected. She should really be angry at herself. *After this is all done,* she thought, *I can take time to sort things out.* She glanced back at Domenic, and in his uncertain expression she saw doubt.

They went down. Sabrina was between the two divers, her camera held in front of her, cable playing out behind. There were two BBC technicians at corners in the corridor, making sure the cable did not tangle and ensuring there was plenty of slack. She and Domenic watched until the diving lights had faded and the water's surface calmed again, and Geena could not help thinking they had been swallowed.

"Let's go back and see what's left," Domenic said, and Geena nodded. She noticed that he did not lead the way, though. He was following her like a parent keeping an eye on their unruly child.

Back in the empty reading room, Tonio and Ramus were gathered behind Finch and his team, all of them staring at one of the larger laptop screens. As Geena approached she heard Sabrina's muffled voice narrating her slow journey down into Petrarch's library. Even Adrianna had come to watch, steely-eyed yet obviously fascinated with whatever had been beneath her all these years. Geena and she exchanged smiles, and Geena looked over Tonio's shoulder.

The visibility was terrible. Virtually any dive they performed in and around Venice was marred by the filthy water—silt and shit, chemicals and refuse—but Geena had been hoping that the contained environment down there would have allowed the water to settle. It seemed it had not. Sabrina focused her camera and light on the back of the diver ahead of her as he led the way across the jumbled chamber, and the stark light picked him out like a ghost against the murk. Strange lighting effects gave him glittering wings—reflections from his equipment buckles and air tank, Geena guessed. There was no way of telling how far they had progressed other than Sabrina's commentary.

"Floor's pretty treacherous," she said. "Shelves fell and broke. Some of the books are still whole. Most are pulp."

Tonio sighed, and Geena placed a hand on his shoulder. *We got most of it*, she wanted to say. But what she *really* wanted to see was farther down. She wished the audio link wasn't just one-way—she wanted to tell Sabrina to hurry. An urgency was bearing down on her, though she could not discern its origins. Impatience made her shift from one foot to the other. Domenic was behind her, a warm presence, and suddenly she wanted his hand on her shoulder, the comfort of a human touch. Because something in that last vision had felt *in*human.

The divers moved on, Sabrina filming the mess on the floor, and then they paused when they reached the open doorway leading down.

"Go on," Geena whispered, and Tonio glanced back at her.

"Maybe it's too deep," Finch said. "Or too dangerous." Nobody replied, but Geena thought, *Is he feeling it, too?*

The lead diver started down the staircase.

"Here goes nothing," Sabrina's distorted voice said. One of the BBC technicians adjusted something on the laptop's sidebar, and Sabrina's breathing came in clearer and louder.

Geena's neck bristled. *No!* she thought. And she held Tonio's shoulder again, locking her knees and concentrating on standing upright as—

She's fighting the forward motion. People look at her. Sunlight blinds her, scorching eyes so used to darkness. The people who look appear unsettled, as if they're seeing someone they can't quite place. Through a narrow street where cafés hustle on either side, vying for trade and custom, she emerges onto a street she knows, running along-

side a canal and crossing a narrow bridge, heading toward the Piazza San Marco and the Biblioteca. More people see her, and they stand aside. She's struggling, fighting, exerting every ounce of her energy, and there's a desperation there that makes her feel—

Geena opened her eyes and swayed a little, then felt Domenic's hand on her shoulder.

"I think you need to leave," he whispered in her ear. "A doctor, or rest. I'll come with you."

She shook her head and shrugged his hand from her shoulder. *Nico's coming,* she wanted to say, but Domenic would only ask how she knew.

"We're heading down," Sabrina said. "The water down here . . . much colder. Strange." *Strange.* The picture was all shadow and movement, and there seemed to be no order to what Geena could see on the screen. They watched, none of them speaking, as the image opened out into one of greater shadow. Their powerful diving lights played around the chamber, barely piercing the murk, alighting on one toppled obelisk with a broken lid. Geena stretched forward, frowning to concentrate her vision.

"What *is* that?" Finch said. He turned and spoke directly at her. "You don't think there are still . . . ?" She could smell garlic on his breath, and stale wine, and for some reason she wondered where he had spent the night.

Zoom in, she thought, and Sabrina seemed to have the same idea.

"Concentrate your lights here," Sabrina said to the others, but neither of them did. "Hey, can't you—?" Her voice was cut off, and the image on the screen became confused again: blurs, shadows, flickering lights. The technician played with the sound levels.

"It's not that," Geena said. "I can still hear her breathing." And she could . . . slightly harsher than before, heavier, and when Sabrina's voice came again it suddenly seemed much louder.

"What *is* that?" The camera steadied and homed in on a tumbled section of wall, and glaring pale from the slump of rocks, silt and building blocks slewed across the chamber floor, things that looked like bones.

"My God," Finch said.

"I don't think so," Domenic said

Geena gasped. *They built those walls using. . .* And then everything faded again.

❖

Zanco Volpe waits outside the grand Biblioteca Nazionale Marciana, enjoying the sun on his face and the cool breeze blowing in across the lagoon. There is a hint of anticipation about him—something is coming, and it will change everything—but there is also a warm glow of satisfaction. He looks at his hands, feels a sense of pride and excitement at what they have done, and within him there lies a solid heart of magic. Black or white, it does not matter. The nature of magic is not dictated by its source, but by its user. And Volpe knows that his aims are pure.

He remains seated on the ornate stone bench even as he sees movement in the building's doorway. Il Conte Tonetti appears, still hidden by shadows but twitchy as a hunted bird. He lowers his head and walks from the building, down the steps and across to where Volpe is waiting. He only looks up when he approaches; people move out of his way. He's dressed in his best finery and is redder than usual.

"It is done," Il Conte says. "Caiazzo died quickly. Soldagna put up a fight."

"Good for him," Volpe says, and he feels the butterflies of excitement stroking his insides. It's almost done, *he thinks.* I'm almost free again.

As Volpe stands, Il Conte reaches out to take his hands, his own hands smeared with blood.

"Not on mine!" Volpe shouts, stepping back with his arms raised. He has no idea what effect another man's blood on his skin might have. The spells are delicate as yet, his talents still uncertain, and he will not risk them for an instant.

"I . . . I apologize," Il Conte says, and his face crumples.

"Be a man," Volpe says, his voice strong and deep. "You are Il Conte Rosso now. That's how you'll be known. And you helped save Venice today."

"Yes," the Count says, "of course." Though he cannot conceal his doubt.

"Tonight we move on Aretino." Volpe turns away from the Count and the building that hides the Chamber of Ten. The next time he sets eyes upon this place, the city will have a new Doge, and he will have moved on yet once more.

"I've never felt such power," he says. For the first time in a long while, he cannot feel his many decades weighing down upon him.

Outside, Geena thought. *That's all from outside.* She opened her eyes but still everything seemed dark. Someone was pulling her against their chest, arms around her waist—Domenic. Her legs felt weak, and she shifted position until she could feel herself supporting her own weight again.

"Geena," Domenic said, and she turned to look up at his face. The concern was almost heartbreaking, because she knew she had been shunning him. "I won't take no for an answer this time. We have to get you—"

"No," she said. "I'm not ill. I'm just. . ." *Seeing visions from the past? That was Il Conte Rosso, and I saw the fresh blood on his hands that gave him his name.* She could not just run now. If she did, she might miss Nico.

"You look like you've seen a—"

"I think he's outside," she said, and they both glanced through the arched door of the reading room and into the foyer of the main entrance. Sunlight, but no shadows.

"You mean Nico?" Domenic asked. Ramus was looking at them oddly, but the others—Finch, the BBC crew, and even Adrianna—had their attention riveted to the laptop screen.

"They filled the walls with bones," Finch said again, and it had the sound of someone trying to convince himself of what he saw.

"I've never seen anything like this," came Sabrina's muffled voice. She was breathing faster, and Geena sensed simmering panic.

"Tell her to calm down," she said, glancing back at the main doors again. *That was all from Nico*, she thought, *and he was approaching across the piazza, and then suddenly the flashback that wasn't* him. *It was Volpe.* She shivered, because even thinking the name gave her goosebumps.

If he had approached, he was holding back, waiting outside or something. Maybe he was just afraid to come in because that would mean facing her questions.

"One of the obelisks is open!" Sabrina said, and that snapped Geena's attention back to the laptop. She pushed her way past Finch, with Domenic still beside her, and knelt so that she could get a better view of the screen. Tonio placed one hand on her shoulder and she knew what that touch meant: *This is amazing!* Sabrina's crazy camera work settled at last, focusing on the broken lid of one of the obelisks and the thing it contained.

"They're tombs," Tonio said.

In her time working in Venice, Geena had been witness to the exhumation of dozens of bodies, all of them buried many hundreds of years ago. They never frightened her, but there was always something unsettling about setting eyes on a corpse that had been out of sight, alone, and at peace for so long. Though she was not a religious person, to Geena it felt intrusive and disrespectful, and she'd always had trouble identifying the line between recently buried and of archaeological interest.

"My God," Sabrina's voice hissed, "it's wearing . . ."

A hat, Geena thought. *A black hat and robe, covering less formal attire beneath.* And she thought of bleeding palms and the vague sense of ritual.

"Nico!" Ramus said. "Look everyone, it's Nico!"

For a moment Geena scanned the screen desperately, thinking that they'd seen his drowned body down there, and in the space of a heartbeat the idea that she'd imagined everything since the flood hit hard. But then she sensed those around her turning away from the table of equipment, and she, too, stood and turned.

She bit her lip against the wooziness that still shifted the world around her. Behind them Nico was standing just inside the entrance to the reading room.

"Nico!" she said, unable to keep the rush of relief and affection from her voice.

He seemed not to hear; his eyes were blank, his face expressionless. He carried a heavy-looking bag in one hand. Then he started walking toward them, and Geena cringed at the way he moved—a stiff, stilted walk as if he'd smashed bones in both of his legs.

"What's wrong with him?" Ramus asked.

Geena moved toward him. Domenic's grip tightened briefly on her arm before letting go, but she knew he was still behind her. *Don't be a fool*, she thought, *Nico would never hurt me.*

She smiled, vision blurring with tears that seemed to well up from nowhere.

Behind her the BBC team were still chattering excitedly about what they had seen, and Finch seemed to be talking into a cell phone. *Of course*, she thought. *They don't even know about Nico.*

"Where have you been?" she asked. Nico had paused. He looked dirty, tired, and sad, and she could already tell that he hadn't washed since leaving her apartment. "Nico, I've been so worried and . . ."

"No," he groaned. He sounded desperate and pained, as if talking was a strain. The sudden look in his eyes—burning and triumphant—did not match that voice.

"Nico?" *I saw what he did to that man*, she thought, but could she *really* suspect him of doing something so terrible?

No. Not him. Not Nico. *But someone else.*

"Run, Geena," Nico growled, low enough for only her to hear. Glancing back she could see others turning to watch them now, and one of the BBC men was pointing a small handheld camera their way. Domenic was approaching her, his eyes flitting from her to Nico and back again.

She turned back. "We're going to find out exactly what happened," she said.

"No! *Run!*" Nico repeated, louder this time. The terrible urgency in his voice gave her a frisson of fear.

He leaned forward, and then his walk turned into a headlong rush, a controlled fall that set his feet stumbling against each other. And for the first time she saw what he had in his other right hand. A knife.

"Come here, sweetness," Nico said. But the voice was no longer his own. Deep, guttural, harsh, she had heard it before in those strange flashes of a time long gone. And it carried a madness she could have never expected in someone she loved so much.

Just as Nico fell against her, Domenic pulled her back.

But the knife still did its work.

CHAPTER 8

STABBED ME STABBED ME NICO STABBED ME . . .

She felt hands ease her fall as she slumped to the cool tiled floor. Voices were raised, and somewhere in the distance pounding footsteps faded away, leaving only the taunting ghosts of their echoes. More than one pair of footsteps, too, and someone must be chasing him, and she thought, *Don't hurt anyone else.* Faces gathered above her and she did not recognize any of them. She felt for the pain, searched for the flash of agony that would show where the knife had punctured and how much damage it had done. She held her breath, terrified, and then gasped again in case she would never draw another.

Someone was holding her arm too tightly and she tried to twist it away, but there was no give. Her head rested on something soft—a leg, a hand, a bag, she didn't know—and then Domenic was above her, his strong features stark in the light that had suddenly become so clear and defined. *Shouldn't my vision be fading, not solidifying?* She'd read somewhere that hearing was always the last sense to go before death, and when she gasped again her ears seemed to pop and the confusion and panic roared in.

"Don't move her. Don't *move* her!"

"Ramus, stay away from him. He's still carrying the knife!"

"Call an ambulance—"

"Call the police—"

"I'll get the first aid kit."

And from a distance, "I'm going after him!" Ramus, running, pursuing Nico because he'd appeared here at the library and *stabbed* her.

"Oh shit," Geena groaned, and she looked up into Domenic's face as she probed for the injury. She drew breath without it bubbling, felt her heart thumping good and strong, and there was no rush of warmth in her stomach. And the person holding her left arm squeezed even tighter.

She turned her head slightly and there was the wound. A slice across her shoulder, a bloody tear in the fabric of her blouse. The wound pouted slightly, and though gruesome it was also strangely beautiful. Such vibrant colors. She worked in the faded stone- and dust-shades of history, and yet here was the true lifeblood of her, and it was as bright and alive as any color could be.

"Don't look," Finch said. She realized that he was kneeling on her left side, leaning over her and sheltering her from the bright sunlight streaming in the library's high windows. He touched her arm, turned it this way and that, then caught her eye for the first time. "It's not as bad as it looks," he said. "No artery hit. It'll bleed like a bugger and you'll need stitching, but you were lucky."

"He didn't get me anywhere else?" she asked, and her soft voice sounded surreal. *Am I really asking that? About Nico?*

"No," Finch said. "I've checked. That's the only place. And he was hardly here long enough for that. Here." He plucked the folded handkerchief from his jacket pocket, shook it open, folded it again, and placed it on the wound.

Geena hissed, her body stiffening.

"You press down on it," Finch said. "It'll hurt, but we need to stop the bleeding."

Geena nodded her silent thanks, then put her right hand over the material and pressed. The pressure hurt but there was also a comfort there as well. *Covering part of me that should never see daylight*, she thought.

"You seem to know what you're doing," Domenic said. She was leaning back against him, and he felt strong and secure. He was very much there, whereas Nico—

I have to help him, Geena thought. And she remembered his eyes, and what he'd said as he lunged for her.

"First Gulf War, and Bosnia," Finch said. "I was a reporter back then. Saw lots of nasty stuff, and went on all the first aid and self-defense courses I was offered."

Come here, sweetness, he'd said. Those eyes had not been his.

"I have to help him," Geena said.

"What?" Domenic sounded surprised, and angry.

"Nico. He's not . . . in his right mind."

"You're not fucking kidding," Finch said.

"Geena, he just walked in here and tried to kill you," Domenic said. "If I hadn't—"

"No," she said, sitting up, closing her eyes against a brief spell of wooziness. "Domenic, thank you. But no. He wasn't trying to kill me. Not Nico."

"I won't let you go looking," Domenic said. "That's the police's job now. They're on their way, and they'll want statements. This was assault, at the very least."

"Looked like attempted murder to me," Tonio said. He was breathless, sweating slightly, and his eyes were wide and shocked. The look did not suit his usually suave self. "He ran across the piazza and disappeared. Ramus went after him, but I saw him stop on the other side. I called him back, but he's pacing the square."

"He'll come in when the police arrive," Domenic said.

"What about Sabrina?" Geena said.

"Don't worry," Finch said. "My boys have signaled them to make their way back up. They'll help them out. There'll be plenty of time for more dives, but next time . . ."

"More security," Tonio said.

"Yeah," Finch agreed. He was still glancing across Geena's body, his eyes flitting again and again to her covered wound. *Looking after me*, she thought, and she felt an overwhelming rush of affection for this man she had until now thought of only as an intruder, an inconvenience.

"Thank you," she said, smiling at him. Finch nodded and smiled back, and she knew that her gratitude was appreciated.

Doors slammed open out in the foyer and then Ramus returned to the reading room. He was sweating and wide-eyed, excited more than afraid. He was an intelligent kid with a sharp mind for antiquities, but right then he looked so young. "Gone," he said. "Disappeared before I caught up with him. Damn, he was fast!"

Geena stood, accepting Domenic's help. He held her right hand and forearm, soft yet firm, and his was a comforting presence. *Am I so damn needy?* she thought, but this wasn't about being needy. There was something terribly wrong with Nico, and a friend was exactly what she wanted.

"We'll get you to a hospital," Domenic said.

"No, I'm fine," she said, wincing slightly as the act of standing twinged her wound.

"You need stitches," Domenic said softly. "And that cut will need cleaning. There's no saying where he got that knife from. Is there?"

Geena nodded slowly, because he was right. No saying at all. She remembered those flashes of vision she'd had as Nico had approached the Biblioteca, and then that stronger, harsher flashback to a time long gone, when a man called Zanco Volpe had stood outside this very building, watching Il Conte Rosso emerge having just . . .

Just what? Had she really seen some twisted memory of the Count just after he had overseen the slaughter of two of the Council of Ten? But it felt much more than a memory. She could remember the smell of old Venice in the air, not so dissimilar to how it smelled now, and the raw feel of the city as it was back then, younger and more vital with possibilities. But until she could find Nico, comfort him, and find out exactly what was happening, it was difficult to know exactly what to make of what she had seen.

"Okay," she said. "Hospital. But . . ." She looked around at the array of equipment, the laptops even now displaying flashes of murky images as Sabrina and the two divers made their way back up, and the shocked, pale faces all looking her way.

"We'll take care of things here, won't we?" Tonio asked, glancing at Finch.

"Of course," Finch said. "Plenty of time to carry on over the next few days. If you still want to . . . ?" He glanced back and forth between Tonio and Geena, and she felt the weight of responsibility pressing down on her. Even though Nico was not her fault, this was her project, and he was her lover. No one was making her feel responsible but herself, but that did not make it any easier.

"Of course we still want to," Geena said, and Finch visibly relaxed. "And Howard, thank you for helping me." She nodded at the bloodied handkerchief.

"You can keep it," he said straight-faced. "And I hope Nico . . ." He trailed off, because he had only started saying what no one else there could. Nico had crossed a very serious line, and whatever his problems, the relationship between him and everyone there had changed forever.

"I'm going to help him," she said. Finch blinked in surprise. Domenic's hand on her right arm squeezed. "That wasn't Nico. Not the Nico I know, anyway." Ramus averted his eyes—embarrassed?—but it had gone too far for her to be abashed now. "Something's upset him, made him the way he was when he came in here. Didn't you see, Domenic?"

"I saw Nico, but not as I've ever seen him before."

"Ramus?" Geena asked.

Ramus shrugged. He was the youngest of them all, but sometimes she thought he was also the most brilliant. She'd sensed his startling intellect battling with the need to be young and have fun, and sometimes there was an intensity to his gaze that spoke of colossal internal conflicts.

"He only looked like Nico," Ramus said. A chill ran down Geena's spine. A stab of pain sang in from the slash across her left arm.

"I think he's been asking for my help since he fell that first time in the chamber," she said, "and I've failed him. But no more."

"Geena, a day or two. Whatever you need," Tonio said, though she could tell that he didn't really want her to take time off, not now. Petrarch's library was one of the greatest finds ever during his time at the university, and perhaps one of the greatest in Venice over the last few decades. There was a mountain of material that needed cataloging, preserving, and analyzing, and the BBC interest would likely be only the beginning. Tonio would soon be flooded with requests from scholars all over the world who wished to come and view the collection, so it was more vital than ever that the head of the project be present. But she also knew that he was not a man to offer something like that lightly, and he meant what he said.

She nodded her thanks, and then the wail of the water ambulance reached them from outside.

"Come on," Domenic said. "Let's hurry. Hospital first, and *then* the police. I'm not happy with you being held up here any longer than necessary. That cut needs seeing to." They left the library together, and stepping out into the piazza, Geena glanced around nervously. Ramus had said that Nico was gone, but she could not help worrying. *If Domenic hadn't pulled me aside* . . . But no. Even if he hadn't acted quickly, Nico's blade would have done no more.

Because he'd been fighting. Something had him—that was obvious from the fragmented flashes she was receiving from him, tortured and strange and sometimes just *so far away*. And after seeing his face as he lunged at her, she was convinced. *He'd* attacked *her*, but he was the one who needed help.

People watched as Domenic held her arm and steered her toward the dock. Tourists stared, a few took pictures, and a young girl continued licking her ice cream as she stared at Geena's bloody arm. Geena smiled at her, but the girl's expression did not change. She never had understood kids. One day, she had hoped, she and Nico would have one themselves and learn together. But where did that dream stand now?

The ambulance was just bobbing against the jetty, and two paramedics jumped out and dashed across to her. While they assessed her and Domenic answered their questions, Geena tried to relax, soaking in the sunshine after being in the cool of the library, breathing in the familiar mixed scents that were uniquely Venice. And she opened her mind to Nico.

I'm here, and I'm going to help. There were no visions, no flashes of contact from Nico, wherever he was now, but that no longer worried her. She'd find him again, when he was ready to be found. For now she had to relax, and think, and use her time being stitched up to plan what she should do next.

When he opened his eyes, history stared back at him. He groaned and turned his head, and immediately recognized something different. He'd *intended* turning his head, and his body had obeyed. Something had changed.

Nico looked around, trying to keep as still as possible, as passive as he could be, because he did not want Volpe to know he was here and awake. Whatever flashback this turned out to be—he'd only recently witnessed Tonetti, Il Conte Rosso, emerging from the Biblioteca after having overseen the slaughter of the two traitors in the Council—it seemed that he had time to prepare for it.

He was lying in the corner of a small courtyard. A stone fountain stood in the center with gentle whispers of water rising in three low arcs. Plant pots surrounded the fountain's base, overflowing with colorful and lush plants—roses in one, exquisite orchids in another, and what seemed to be abundant herbs in several more. In the far corner stood a much larger pot from which sprouted an ornamental orange tree. A staircase climbed one courtyard wall, stepped with an intricate cast-iron balustrade around which a climbing rose twined. The walls were painted a faded orange that had blistered in the heat, flakes of paintwork scattered across the ground like dried skin. The courtyard was silent and still, but for the incessant buzzing of bees. The doors and windows opening out onto it seemed innocuous, hiding no shadows that did not belong.

Where and when am I? Nico wondered. Perhaps Il Conte Rosso would emerge from the door in the far wall at any moment, ready to reveal a new betrayal. Or maybe it would be another of the Council of Ten with whom Volpe would plot, or a Doge facing expulsion or death, or some other man or woman around whom Volpe would manufacture one of his elaborate schemes.

As he glanced to his left and saw the bag lying beside him, and spotted the thing that had half fallen from the bag's open mouth, he heard the ticking. He thought it was his breathing—even though he believed he'd stopped breathing, because the mummified hand seemed to have one finger hooked up and back, beckoning him with it into the bag. Then he gasped in a full breath and realized that the sound came from elsewhere.

A soldier's hand, he thought, and he remembered grasping the old dry thing in his warm hand, still bloodied from the nails he'd bent back whilst smashing the ossuary open. The book was also in there, along with . . .

With . . .

His watch was ticking, a distant sound so familiar that he only heard it now, when he paid attention. *His* watch on *his* hand, not Volpe's.

"This is all me," Nico said, sitting up and taking a closer look around the courtyard. There was certainly nothing there to age it specifically, either as modern day or five hundred years old. Nothing but his watch—a Police timekeeper that Geena had bought him for his birthday the year before.

Then he looked up and saw the plane trail across the sky.

We're going to find out exactly what happened, Geena said, and he saw her coming closer as he fell toward her. And it *had* been a fall— Volpe throwing himself toward the woman even as Nico tried to hold back. That he remembered for sure. Sitting in that humid courtyard his right hand clasped around nothing, but in his memory he felt the smooth wooden handle of the knife he'd been holding at the time.

"Oh no," he groaned. He looked down at his hand and saw the blood there, dried and peeling like the paint on the walls around him. "No, no, no . . ." He grabbed the bag and spilled its contents over the dusty ground. *The Book of the Nameless*, which Volpe had steered him to retrieve from the church's bell tower; the gruesome hand; and a knife, its blade and handle still smeared with the dried blood of the love of his life.

"Geena—" he started, and then Volpe rose within him.

Can't a man rest?

"You . . . you made me . . ."

I made you help me, that is all.

Geena, Nico thought, closing his eyes and trying to recall what exactly had happened.

"Come here, sweetness," he growled, and Volpe drew back again, giving Nico room to scream and snap his eyes open.

"Bastard!" he shouted. But he'd caught a glimpse of what had happened. Volpe had allowed that at least, and in the glimpse he saw Domenic pulling Geena back, and his knife blade slipping across her shoulder, shallow enough to cause no lasting damage, but deep enough—

The blood of a loved one, Volpe said. *And now that we're both rested, there's one more item we need before we can perform the ceremony.*

"The seal of the city," Nico said, standing because Volpe commanded him to.

They must be kept out, Volpe whispered, almost to himself, and for the first time Nico heard concern in that old remnant's voice. *They* will *be kept out.* Nico walked up the staircase, grasping the hot iron balustrade and enjoying the sensation of being in charge. *Only so long as you do as I command*, Volpe said. *I'm content in that at least. I'll edge you toward the seal, but I'm always here watching, Nico. Always ready to snap forward and make your muscles and flesh my own.*

"Haven't you done that already?" Nico asked bitterly.

Oh no. No. Laughter in his mind, a dry chuckle like old bones being juggled in a bag. *Nowhere near.*

◈

They put in five stitches and dressed her wound, insisting on a tetanus shot before letting her go. Domenic stayed with her all the time, protesting when the nurses told him he could not remain in the treatment room. "She was attacked," he said, and they relented grudgingly.

As she finished the dressing, the nurse—large, round, and sour-faced—kept glancing at Geena.

"Are you feeling okay?" she asked.

"Hmm? Yes. Fine."

"You look pale." The nurse was more focused now, looking into Geena's eyes, casually touching her cheek and holding her hand. *Checking for cold sweats*, Geena thought, but if she told the nurse what was really bothering her and what had really happened, it would be another kind of hospital she'd be admitted to.

"Just a little shaken up," Geena said. "It's not every day I get stabbed."

"You're sure?" Domenic asked. He'd been sitting so silently beside the treatment trolley that she'd almost forgotten he was there.

"Yeah." The whole time the nurse had been working—cleaning the cut, applying antibiotic ointment, stitching—Geena had been sensing Nico's presence. But this was unlike any time before. Sometimes he'd intentionally probe for her, casting delicious sensation-hints or sharing his mood. Other times she'd be able to pick up on his excitement or anger without him deliberately trying to "touch" her. But this felt . . . distracted. She could definitely sense him out there, but there was not so much power to the psychic transmissions as before. She was certain that this was not due to distance. He was in Venice, and close by. But what she did pick up was an overwhelming sense of fear.

Nico was struggling to fight against whatever had him. She sensed the ripples of that fight, like the echoes of distant battle, and felt the terror underlying every breath he took. If only she could send back calm, soothing thoughts, and promise him that she was coming to help.

Because she was. Really, there was no longer any alternative, and no other way she could go. The waiting was over.

"So she'll need to rest the arm for a while?" Domenic asked.

"A little, yes," the nurse said. "No reason she has to take to her sick bed completely, though. Er . . ."

"Yes?" Geena asked.

"I'm guessing you've reported this to the police?" she asked with the air of someone used to seeing such injuries.

"They were called," Domenic said. "They'll probably be waiting outside now."

"Very good," the nurse said, nodding to herself as she left. "Feel free to wait here a while, if you're still feeling a bit woozy."

"I'm not," Geena said, but the nurse glanced back and gave her a motherly smile, as if she hadn't heard.

"Maybe you should do as she—" Domenic started.

"Damn it, Domenic, I'm fine!" Geena struggled to keep her voice low, aware that there were people in several other treatment cubicles.

"Well, apologies for noticing your boyfriend attacked you with a knife." He stood beside the bed and glanced through the curtain, looking both ways along the corridor. "They'll be here soon. You'd better decide how straight you're going to be about Nico."

"How . . . ?" But she knew what he meant. There was no way she could lie about this and, she suspected, no way he'd let her. After she spoke with the law, Nico would become a suspect in a serious assault. Armed and dangerous. It was up to her whether he became a suspect for anything else.

I'm coming to help you, Nico.

"They'll need to know everything," Domenic said softly.

"I know." She sighed. "This has just thrown me so much."

"Thrown all of us. What the hell happened down there?"

For a second, realizing that Domenic was canny enough to connect this all with that first foray into the Chamber of Ten, Geena almost slipped and told him everything. It would take a while, she knew, and a good while longer for him to even come close to believing. But so much strange and frightening stuff had happened that she was starting to doubt some of her own reactions to all of this. Domenic's was a fine mind, and it would be relatively uninvolved. Perhaps a fresh approach could shed light where there were shadows.

But he would never believe her. It would be hard enough persuading him that Nico could touch her with his mind . . . and as for everything else she had been seeing, those flashes of vision from the past and what they might mean . . . Well, even she was having trouble coming to terms with them.

I banged my head down there, too, she thought. *And I was speaking the same language as Nico.*

"I just don't know," she said. "Maybe it was as simple as Nico knocking his head. Maybe he's still concussed."

"Maybe," Domenic said, but he sounded far from convinced.

Geena winced, looking down at her arm. Domenic's brow furrowed with concern.

"Damn, I'm so thirsty," she said.

"I'll get you a drink. I could do with a coffee myself. Something cold for you?"

"Wine?" she joked. It was still early, barely noon, but a glass of wine would have been quite welcome just then.

"I'm sure the hospital vending machine has plenty," he said, smiling as he slipped through the curtains.

"I'm sorry, Domenic," Geena whispered to herself, counting to ten in her head to make sure he'd gone.

Then she stepped from the bed and felt around with her feet. For a beat, she was terrified that Domenic had taken her shoes, but when she leaned forward and checked under the bed, there they were. As she straightened, she closed her eyes and bit her lip to try to stop herself from fainting. Sitting up, fisting sheets in both hands, she breathed deeply and waited for it to pass. *That was from the pain*, she thought. *The needle. I've always been afraid of needles. That wasn't him.*

The faint passed and she worked her feet into the shoes. The bustle of a hospital went on around her—subdued conversation, the rattle of a trolley being pushed somewhere, nurses' laughter, a soft snoring from somewhere close by. If she played this right she'd walk out unnoticed, just another stranger in the eyes of people who saw so many.

Taking a final deep breath, she parted the curtains and stepped into the corridor between treatment cubicles. A male nurse nodded at her as he passed by, a covered toilet pan in one hand. She glanced over her shoulder to make sure he wasn't looking back, and saw the back of Domenic's head. He was talking to the grim-faced nurse who'd stitched her, gesticulating gently as he tried to explain something, and she almost went to him. *He's so concerned, I can't just—*

But she could. She *had* to. Because just then two policemen appeared, quizzing the nurse and listening as Domenic provided some of their answers.

I have maybe ten seconds, Geena thought, and she turned away, put her head down, and walked. At the end of the emergency treatment ward, she took the first door to the left, slipping through into a lobby with three lifts, and doors leading to a staircase. She took the stairs and headed down, letting the door close quietly behind her. They would be at her cubicle by now, and Domenic would know that she'd given him the slip.

"Sorry, Dom," she said again, hoping they would not rush after her. Really, was there any need to? She hoped not. She'd not committed a crime, she was no risk to anyone, and—

But Domenic thought that Nico was a risk to her. He'd never just let her run.

So once she reached the ground floor and exited the doors out onto a busy street, run is exactly what she did.

CHAPTER 9

OUT OF BREATH, SWEATING, SITTING IN THE SHADOWY interior of a popular tourist café in the square behind Palazzo Cavalli-Franchetti, Geena realized that she needed a plan. It was all very well abandoning herself to the ebb and flow of the city, but without knowing what to do next she was as lost as Nico. His presence still tingled at the base of her neck, but there was no true contact. Whatever happened next was up to her. And she had to think quickly.

She ordered a cappuccino simply because sitting there without drinking or eating would attract attention. Others were having lunch around her, and she knew she ought to do the same—get some food into her—but the idea of eating anything just then did not appeal to her at all.

Her arm still hurt, but the nurse had done a good job on the dressing. If only she had a clean blouse; the one she wore had blood spattered on the short left sleeve and down her side, and she could do little to hide it. Add to that the damp patches of sweat from her headlong run through the city, and the fact that she'd not had a shower for some time, and she was starting to feel as if everyone was looking at her.

But she had cash in her pocket, and she was deep in the most tourist-friendly area of Venice. A drink, shop for new clothes, and all the while she could try to figure out what the hell to do next.

Slowly she calmed, catching her breath, watching the tourists and other visitors to the city with a calm detachment. None of them had any real idea about the amazing place they were visiting. She had only been in Venice for a few years, but already she had come to learn that the city was an incredibly Byzantine place, whose various histories crossed paths, merged, and collided with stunning complexity. The city's past was clouded in mystery, and part of her work was to try to delve beneath the present to discover these hidden histories. But sometimes the present was impenetrable. The people she saw here passed doorways behind which pivotal murders might have taken place, or important children have been conceived. They photographed canal bridges and gondoliers, little knowing that Venice's true story lay in architecture rarely seen, in people untouched by the tourist dollar, or buried away below the oily waves. She'd never looked down on tourists, because she knew that they came here for enjoyment and learning, and did the city much good. But she had always believed that only a small percentage absorbed the true allure of Venice. Sometimes she thought it was because subconsciously they did not wish to. It was an old city, and anywhere with history this ancient and complex had unknown ghosts.

And they were happy. They laughed over their coffees and pastries, referring to guidebooks as they planned the rest of their afternoons and evenings. She felt detached, and filling the void between them was her burgeoning knowledge of this city's shady past. If only she did not know this place so well.

"Another cappuccino?" the waitress asked, and Geena shook her head.

"No, I need to be somewhere, thanks." The waitress nodded, glanced at Geena's bloody blouse, then moved on to another table.

Geena stood and left a tip. Emerging once again into the late afternoon sunlight, she glanced around to make sure there was no one watching her. If Domenic found her now he'd be angry, but she was her own woman. He was a good friend, but she couldn't afford to have him looking over her shoulder if she truly wanted to help Nico. He knew so little of what was going on, and though she had already considered telling him, she could not trust that he'd be willing to find out more.

"Where are you, Nico?" she muttered. Still without a plan, she went to buy something to wear that wouldn't be so conspicuous.

The vision hit her as she was paying for the new clothes. She'd bought a plain white blouse that she could use afterward in meetings, and sensible trousers with deep pockets for carrying knick-knacks . . . but when the image crashed in, such considerations—to do with normal life in the mundane world—felt foolish. She gripped the counter, waving away the shop attendant's concerned flustering, and closed her eyes.

"Drink of water?" she managed to say, and was aware of the young woman dashing through curtains into the shop's rear.

Geena gasped and leaned against the counter, hairs on the back of her neck bristling, because this was not Nico. Not entirely. It was *him*.

He has most of what he needs now, and the next item—the last—should be the easiest to procure. If only this fool would do as instructed without questioning . . . but really, he does not mind. It is good to be back and see what has changed. Much of it is incredible—boats that move without oars; carriages that shift without horses, on wheels that whisper rather than clatter; lamps without oil, flickering boxes casting images behind barely shut curtains; and strange devices casting smoke-trails across the sky. But what amazes him more are the many things that have all but remained the same. Such as this place . . .

He's floating toward the rear of Venice's old Town Hall, the Palazzo

Cavalli, in a water taxi—in the vision, Geena recognizes it because she and Nico have made half jokes about getting married there. The canal is busy, and several people glance nervously his way, as if a chill has passed over them. He alights and approaches the building's rear entrance. People in suits come and go, a group of attractive women sits on the steps being photographed, a gaggle of children shouts and cheers and their guardians look flustered and tired. He stops, looking up at the great building, and for a moment seeing it as it was back then. The façade's colors are sharper, cleaner, newer. Gone are the tourists and those dreaming of marriage, and it is the Town Hall again, home to important decisions and policy making for the State . . . except that's not quite the truth. Most of that takes place back at the Doge's Palace, and this place is more a disseminator of decisions.

Be good, *the man thinks, and then the feeling is so much more familiar, because this is Nico. He's scared and tired, confused and muddled, and she cannot for a moment believe that he is letting her see this on purpose. This is spillage, his signal leaking because his emotions and consciousness are shredded, and she must take advantage of every moment that he cannot hold himself in.*

He walks toward Palazzo Cavalli looking down at his feet, and for the first time she notices the bags he's carrying. She has never noticed them before. One has a string-tied top, and looks heavy. The other is a briefcase, and inside—

The tools I don't know how to use, the keys I've never tried, and that knife, that knife—

She gasps and the vision blurs. He looks up at the building again and starts climbing the five steps, and then like the sun slowly setting, the vision fades out until there is nothing.

"Madam?" the shop assistant says, and Geena can tell from her tone that she's tried several times before.

"I'm fine, fine," she says. "Just the heat, you know? And I cut my arm building shelving at home, and . . ."

"Well, take a drink. Come through here and sit down."

Geena drank the proffered water gratefully, and followed the woman behind the counter and into a large storage area.

I need to get to Palazzo Cavalli!

"Actually," Geena said, "if I could change into my new clothes back here, I'd be grateful."

"Of course," the young woman said, a moment of suspicion and doubt raising her tone. "I'll be behind the counter."

And maybe she'll call the cops just because of that bloody blouse. Geena knew she didn't have much time. An urgency pressed her, a hot ball in her chest, and it wasn't only the woman's reaction. She thought perhaps she had a very real chance of finding Nico . . . but she had to move.

Geena changed quickly and thought of what she'd just seen. Her skin was crawling. It had never been like that before. She had been looking through Nico's eyes but with Volpe's thoughts, and it had felt like invading and being invaded at the same time, a grotesque contrast to the beautiful sensation of when they made love. She felt dirty, and after stripping her blouse and trousers she rolled them up, tipped some water from the glass, and used them to wash herself as best she could. The nurse had cleaned away most of the blood, but the harder she rubbed the more she seemed to remove the traces of Volpe from her.

"Stupid!" she said, but it didn't feel stupid.

Nico had Volpe inside him, controlling him, and though she had spent a long time immersed in the past, she had never believed in ghosts.

"It's no ghost," she said. Preposterous. He'd banged his head and now he was suffering from delusions. Maybe his psychic gift made him susceptible to such flights of fancy. And perhaps in his delusion, it also made it possible to construct an alternate personality that would fool even her. She'd only known him for two years; who knew what he'd been through before they met?

At least now she knew one important thing: where he was. Palazzo Cavalli was less than a mile away, close to the Rialto Bridge, and if she hurried she might reach it before he left.

Or before he did whatever he had planned with those things in his bags. The tools, the keys . . . the knife.

Time seemed to press in around her, and Geena hurried from the shop through the rear door, opening and closing it as softly as possible. The terrible idea was growing that, unless she found him soon, Nico would end up hurting or killing someone else, or himself.

On her journey along the Grand Canal to Palazzo Cavalli, with the mid-afternoon sun a bright splash over the mainland, Geena kept her mind and heart open. The idea of seeing things through the eyes of Volpe again was abhorrent, but she had to accept that if she was to listen for Nico. Her distaste must be only a fraction of what he was going through, and her discomfort was nothing compared to his. That he was suffering badly was not in question. She only hoped that he could be brought back.

And just how does someone rid themselves of a ghost? she thought, but the idea was too obscure to conceive of any realistic answers. Maybe there were people who might be able to help. Or perhaps once she found him, she and Nico could resolve things together.

As the water taxi powered along she checked her cell phone. Five missed calls from Domenic, but nothing from Nico. Ramus had called as well and left a voice mail. She listened.

Hey Geena, hope you're feeling better. Er . . . Howard Finch was wondering what happens now. He's got his team out here and . . . er . . . well, Tonio was wondering, too. I guess today's out, but let one of us know if you'll be well enough to come back tomorrow. There was the sound of shuffling, then Ramus' voice again, quieter this time. *Sorry to bother you with this, really, but it's that fucking Finch. Sleep well.* Another pause, awkward and loaded. *He'll be fine.*

Damn it, she felt tears threatening. Ramus was a bright kid, and the fact that he could see past the obvious—understand that there might be something more to Nico slashing her than first appeared—comforted her. Geena glanced at her text messages. They were all from Domenic, and all said roughly the same thing:

Call me. I want to help. Amazing that he wasn't ready to give up on her after she had ditched him at the hospital. At the moment, she felt as though she did not deserve such friends. She pocketed her phone before the temptation to call grew too great.

Palazzo Cavalli was a popular place for weddings, Venice's old Town Hall now converted to little more than a tourist trap. Remarkably romantic—and with the Grand Canal and Rialto Bridge close by, it was busy all year round. So what the hell did Nico have to do there?

As the taxi bobbed against the jetty, she let herself wonder what she would do when she faced Nico again. She had never been afraid of him, and she could not entertain that idea now. But when Volpe was driving him . . . who knew what else he might do?

Maybe that old ghost would want to finish the job started at the Biblioteca.

She alighted from the taxi and felt solid ground beneath her feet once again. The sun glittered on the waterways, even as the afternoon shadows grew longer. The smell of cooking food hung heavy in the air, and from elsewhere on the Grand Canal she heard the excited chattering of travelers.

Even before she pressed against one of the main doors, she knew that she was too late. He had been here, but she had no sense of his presence at all. But then she pushed and found that the doors were locked, and her brow furrowed in confusion and concern. It couldn't be much later than three o'clock, but the office was closed, without even a scrawled message taped to the door to indicate a reason. Had Nico done something here that caused them to lock up tight?

And just what the hell would Nico want here? she thought. She sat for a while, looking out across the Grand Canal, trying to avoid the despair that threatened to well up within her. She had to help Nico—she might be the only one who could—and if that meant walking the city day and night until she found him, that was exactly what she'd do.

She felt her cell vibrate, checked the screen, saw that it was

Domenic again, and turned it off. The only person she wanted to hear from right now was Nico. And he didn't need a phone.

Volpe took charge once they were away from Palazzo Cavalli, but he let Nico see. It was as if he was taunting him with the ability to take over control of his body and functions at will, but if that was the case Nico could accept it. He'd rather that than be thrust down out of sight, deep into his own subconscious, where his thoughts did not even feel as real as dreams. Those blackouts were the worst, and he knew that so long as he did not fight too hard, Volpe would leave him be. He'd already used them to exert his authority.

Besides, Nico knew that there was no way he could escape. To begin with he'd been thinking of it as having an invasive presence in his own body, but now that had changed. Now he was a prisoner in his own body, and the invader was triumphant.

Zanco Volpe obviously had some definite goal in mind. He strode with purpose, the drawstring bag clasped tight in his right hand. He'd left the briefcase back in the building, its contents scattered across the floor of one of the old offices now that he had what he'd come for. He'd also left a hole in one of the plastered walls, and a space where something had been hidden away for so long. The office had closed early today for some reason, but that had made his job much simpler. No need to be quiet when the building was empty. He had broken in through a side door and managed to slip in and out without being seen. Volpe had admitted that there was magic in his ability to remain inconspicuous, a spell that caused people to look away or even change direction in order to avoid encountering him. It was subtle magic, he had explained, and not infallible—the monk on San Marco had proven that—but when he wished to go unnoticed, it aided his efforts.

The bag in Nico's hand contained *The Book of the Nameless*, the soldier's hand from the shattered ossuary on San Marco, the blade—still stained with Geena's blood—and now the old seal of the city: an ivory stamp once used by the Mayor to stamp his authority into the wax seals of official city documents. It had been mainly ceremonial even back then, used on official certificates and state documents that would either go on show, or which were ruled more by tradition and ritual than by current laws. Yet it seemed important, and when Nico had first laid his hands on it—after hacking at the plaster and digging once again—Volpe's sigh had been almost audible. He'd spun around in the room, searching the shadows for the shape he was certain must be there, thinking, *He's come out, he's manifested, and maybe that means I'm rid of him.*

But then Volpe had chuckled and touched him inside, needing no words to urge caution.

He boarded a water taxi, and Volpe told him where to go.

"Chiesa di San Rocco," Nico said, offering the driver an initial payment. "We need to be quick."

"I follow speed limits," the driver said.

Volpe leaned Nico forward, his voice low and filled with threat. "We need . . . to be . . . quick."

They were. Like the driver on their way out to San Marco, this man seemed keen to get Nico out of his taxi as fast as possible. The boat bumped against the jetty and Nico stepped lightly off, and almost before his feet were on dry ground the taxi was powering away, the driver's hair flying about like a nest of upset snakes.

Almost there, Volpe said in his mind, and Nico knew he was being spoken to. *When we arrive there's a ritual, and you will perform while I conduct. There's no alternative. I'll guide you, and you will obey, and they will be excluded from the city once more.*

"What if I don't want to help?" Nico said out loud, and a sunburnt couple glanced at him warily as they approached the water taxi jetty.

You keep testing me, Nico? Volpe asked. He kept walking, looking at the ground before him, and he was being steered. *You provoke me? It'll do you well not to. I have done ugly things when they were required, but I am not a cruel man. I don't* want *to hurt you—*

"Like you didn't want to hurt that man in the apartment?" Nico whispered. "Or that monk? What happened to him? I have no memory, but my hands are bruised and cut, and I feel sick to the stomach every time I think of him."

Not your concern, Volpe said impatiently. *What is your concern is the health of your own self, yes? The well-being of this body that your Geena loves so much?*

"Geena is—"

My insurance, if other persuasions are not compelling enough. Don't force my hand. Neither of us will benefit from that. And besides, all of this is your fault.

"I'm an archaeologist," he said. Other people glanced at him, but perhaps they thought he was speaking to someone on Bluetooth. He almost laughed. Maybe this was the Bluetooth of the future, contacting the past.

You're a meddling fool. Fate compelled you, I know, but it relied upon your bumbling—

"What do you mean fate compelled me?"

Venice has chosen my successor, as she always does. But they have all lived and died without inheriting the legacy, because my essence remains.

"What the fuck are you talking about?"

Nothing and everything. Fate or not, it wouldn't have come to this if you'd left the Chamber alone . . . Volpe trailed off, as if what he'd been about to say was too much.

"Your rancid heart was so powerful?" Nico asked, wincing as he feared Volpe's rage.

Only because I made it so, the old ghost said. *Now walk on, Nico. This way . . . that way . . .*

Soon they reached the church of San Rocco. Nico felt control slowly return to him, and he came to a standstill.

The fools, Volpe said. *Oh the fools . . .*

"What is it?" Nico asked. He had been here several times before, examining the relics of Saint Roch and trying to develop a time line for the church's construction and alterations. It was unremarkable, as churches in Venice went.

The heart of the city, Volpe said. *But like the bell, they have changed this also. It's a wonder the Exclusion did not fail long before now. No matter. The ritual will still work, only differently. Walk on. Inside. If they haven't torn the guts from the place, I know where there's somewhere quiet.*

Nico entered the church, sorry to be leaving the sunlight behind. He moved through to the nave and glanced around at the noted Tintoretto paintings that attracted more visitors than the building's relatively recent architecture. *St. Roch taken to Prison* was his favorite—an atmospheric piece exuding repression and unfairness.

Almost there, Volpe said, and Nico felt the urge to look down at his feet. The old flagstone floor was worn smooth by centuries of footsteps, and such sights never ceased to fascinate him. He wondered how many people had stepped where he now stood—thousands? millions?—and who they had been, and what their stories were. Places like this had power, and myriad ghosts.

He caught a glimpse of an old priest walking through an arched doorway into the back of the church, perhaps heading for the sacristy. A pair of old women were kneeling in prayer in the front pew, but otherwise the church was quiet and empty as Nico moved around a velvet rope—careful to avoid being seen—and through a side door, closing it behind him. Beyond the door were stairs that he imagined led up to a choir loft, and a tiny chapel area. In centuries past, the Venetian ruling class had once been provided private services here, but now this narrow wing of the church was mostly abandoned. For the moment, he was by himself.

Nico was walked to the dark corner beneath the stairs. He knelt when Volpe urged him to, wondering what he would find in the old bookcase before him. Then Volpe took gentle charge, pulling out a pile of old books and stacking them on the floor in a shower of dust. When there was room he pressed sideways on one of the shelves, exerting pressure until the old wood creaked, then cracked. The shelf upright broke away. Books fell. Nico worried that someone would hear and come to investigate, but then recalled that there were only the two old women in the front of the church, and any sound from this forgotten corner of the building's history would be muffled, if it was audible to them at all.

Quietly, now, he thought.

And the efforts of his hands did grow more cautious. He felt Volpe eager and frantic in his mind, holding back and yet watching with glee. Soon many of the books were strewn across the floor behind the shelves, and Nico could see the gray stone of the church's bare walls.

The hole needs to be wider, Volpe commanded, and Nico could only do as he was told. As he prised the shelves away, Volpe was whispering, *They can't have changed this as well. Can't have. They wouldn't have been so stupid.*

And then Nico saw the first seam in the stonework, filled with crumbling mortar that powdered away at his touch, and Volpe said, *I hid it so well.*

He dug his fingers into the chalky mortar, quickly loosening one of the stone blocks. When he managed to shove the first block back into darkness—where it landed with a dull thump—Nico caught a whiff of something stale that inspired a rush of strange nostalgia, and he turned his face away trying to find clean air.

Volpe turned his head back and breathed in deeply. "Old air, and the smell of Venice as it should always be," he said aloud, sighing and breathing in again. Then he pulled back and returned Nico's body to him, saying, *I need to rest, and you need to get inside. I'll be watching. Light the braziers, but don't touch anything. This is a special place.*

"Special how?" Nico asked.

I told you . . . the heart of Venice.

Nico glanced over his shoulder at the arched doorway he had come through. The door was closed, but he still worried about being discovered. The priest would not remain in the sacristy all afternoon.

"What if someone comes while I'm in there?" he whispered in the gloom.

He could feel Volpe's exhaustion and his impatience, but then the old magician surged up inside of him again. Nico felt himself set adrift inside his own body, but he fought to remain aware, to continue to see out of his own eyes, and perhaps because Volpe was tired, he succeeded. His hands came up and clawed at the air, fingers contorted as if he were conducting some cruel symphony. He spit three times onto the dusty flagstones and used the toe of his shoe to scrape odd sigils in the dust.

The air in the room grew dense for a moment, the way it did just before a storm, and in that instant he blinked in surprise. The wall and bookcase looked exactly as it had when he had entered the room, intact and undisturbed. But then he inhaled deeply and the illusion vanished, so that he could see the opening in the wall clearly once again.

What have you done? Nico asked, though he spoke only in his mind.

A simple concealment, Volpe explained. *If anyone passes by, perhaps to ascend to the choir loft, they will see nothing out of order.*

And now I rest, Volpe added, but his words were only thoughts, as he retreated, fading back into Nico's mind. Nico could still feel his presence behind his eyes, like a parent overseeing its child's explorations. He started pushing at the next block.

No one disturbed him in his work, for which Nico was glad. If someone had come, he feared what might have happened. He would black out again for a while, and when he came to his fists would be bruised some more, his clothes more spattered with blood.

At last the hole was large enough to crawl inside. It took a nudge from Volpe to get him going, and he wormed his way through the hole and dropped to the floor. It was scattered with dust and grit and the crumbling remains of rat shit. He pulled the bag behind him, then the memory popped into his head that he'd bought matches the previous night as well as food and water. He had never smoked, but he knew whose idea it had been.

There were four metal braziers scattered around the room, filled with scraps of wood so dry that they ignited at the first touch of a match. Soon the room was illuminated, and Nico took a good look. He stepped back to the hole in the wall and sat on the pile of fallen blocks, enjoying being in control of his own body again—

But am I really in control? He's only leaving me alone because I'm doing what he wants. If I turned and tried climbing back through the hole with the bag—

You cannot! Volpe screamed in his mind, and Nico winced and clapped his hands over his ears. *This is important. This is urgent. Now do as I say, if you value your safety and sanity, and perhaps after that there may be chances to negotiate your freedom.*

Nico gasped and stood, swaying slightly as Volpe slipped away once again. When Volpe was to the fore it was like having terrible cramps, his muscles twisted and under the volition of someone else, and when control returned his limbs suffered from tingling pins and needles. *Freedom*, Nico thought, but he had no way at all of telling how sincere Volpe could be.

The chamber was unremarkable. Square, ten paces wide, the only items it contained were the burning braziers, the only architectural features the slightly vaulted ceiling and the hatchway he had just forced himself through. So what was there not to touch?

"The heart of Venice," Nico said, hoping for something from the spirit inside. But for now Volpe was silent, and Nico sat and waited for whatever came next.

This is important. This is urgent.

She had heard those words clear as day, drawled in the same not-Nico voice that had told her, *Come here, sweetness,* just before he'd slashed her shoulder. And whispered into the ear of her mind, they made the Venetian night more threatening, more dangerous, and a place where she knew Nico was once again being driven to do things he did not wish to or could not understand.

She had no idea where Nico was now. She'd left the Palazzo Cavalli soon after realizing she'd missed him, heading across the Grand Canal in the vain hope that she could pick up his trail again. She felt so lost in the city she had quickly grown to love, and several times around midnight she had tapped Domenic's number into her cell and hovered her finger over the call button. But she had resisted every time. She'd cast herself after Nico now, and this could only end when she found him. After that would come the investigation, the police interviews, Nico's assessment and possibly prosecution . . . but that was something to worry about in the future.

So she wandered, waiting for another flash that might tell her where Nico was now. She'd turned her cell off, but every now and then she switched it on again to check whether Nico had, by some miracle, tried to contact her. But the messages were all from Domenic, and the texts were also from him, along with one more from Ramus, and three from Finch. In his third text, Finch asked if she'd like to join him for dinner, and for an appalled moment she thought he was making a move on her. But her tiredness and worry were skewing her perception; it was a business meeting he requested, of course, though one carried out over a friendly dinner. Finch could feign concern for her and her wayward boyfriend—and in truth she thought he really did care, beneath that producer's veneer and distinctly British bluster—but for him, this visit to Venice was still very much a business concern.

She answered no messages, but she did send one to Domenic. *I'm fine, Dom. Thank you, and I'm sorry I ditched you. But I have to find Nico.* She knew how worried he'd be at that, and seconds after she'd sent it she realized how unfair it was putting him in such a position. But she thought she owed him some contact. And she wasn't about to lie.

She knew that Domenic would be looking, and he knew this city well. But she had the advantage of being truly lost.

Just after four o'clock, her wounded arm aching more now than ever before, she was sitting at a table toward the back of a great pizzeria she'd been to with Nico several times before. She had skipped lunch and needed to refuel. She'd eaten, and was making short work of a strong cup of coffee when someone passed by the window.

Many people had passed the restaurant window in the half hour she'd been inside, but something about this one had snagged her attention like a hook in her cheek. She felt drawn to it, standing and knocking her table so that coffee slopped over the lip of her cup. The figure was already gone.

Not for a moment did she think it was Nico. This person moved quickly, yet with a slight stoop, and there was nothing about the fleeting silhouette that she recognized. Yet she was drawn to the restaurant's front door, opening it and staring after whoever had passed. The street was empty, the canal running alongside silent for now but for the gentle lap of water against stone.

Looking into the emptiness, she shivered and knocked her wounded arm against the doorjamb.

"Would you like the bill?" the little waitress who'd been serving her asked. She was standing at Geena's elbow, perhaps afraid that Geena was about to leave without paying, or maybe just concerned.

"Yes, please," Geena said, still peering out the door. "The city's quiet today."

"It's a dreadful day," the waitress said.

Geena let the door close, keeping the air-conditioning inside, and turned to look at the waitress. "What do you mean?"

The young woman's eyes widened. "You haven't heard? Terrible stuff. An old building collapsed in Dorsoduro, just fell into the canal. Seven people were killed. They're saying there's some kind of tomb underneath."

"A tomb? What are you talking about?" Geena asked, more sharply than she'd intended.

The waitress shrugged. "All I know is what my customers tell me. I wish I could go home and watch the news."

Geena stared at her for a few seconds before the waitress shrugged again and went to fetch her bill, leaving her to wonder. Her archaeologist's mind went into overdrive. She wanted to know what building this was, how its foundations had been undermined enough for it to crumble into the canal, and—more than anything—if there really had been some kind of tomb revealed by its collapse. With her team busy at the Biblioteca, Tonio would send someone else on the university's behalf. The city council would want someone from

the department there, especially if there was some kind of archaeological value to the site. But if people had been killed, such concerns would hardly be the first things on anyone's mind.

And they can't be your concerns, she told herself. *It has to be someone else's job.*

Unless it was related to the madness that had begun when Nico
had shattered the stone jar at the center of the Chamber of Ten.
Could it really be coincidence that an ancient tomb had been discovered buried beneath a building in Venice only days after they
had found the Chamber of Ten and had its wall give way? She supposed it might be possible, but it didn't seem likely.

But if it was all connected, then how?

It occurred to her that Nico might be responsible for the building collapse, but she forced the thought away. How could one man
accomplish such a feat? She was letting her anxiety get the best of
her. The only way to get the answers she wanted, to find the truth,
was to track him down. Until she managed to do that, all of her
questions would have to be put on hold, along with whatever crisis
might be unfolding in Venice.

CHAPTER 10

It's a very precise confluence of forces, combined with a delicate placing of the physical. There are a thousand places where it can go wrong. But it must not go wrong."

He's talking to me, Nico thought, but he could not be sure. Volpe had come to the fore and taken complete control, relegating Nico once more to the periphery. Not quite as deep as that dark, hidden place where nothing was felt or known, but close enough for it to be a threat. *Challenge me now and I'll cast you down again*, the threat spoke, and while Nico simmered with restrained, useless rage, he had no wish to be blacked out again. So he watched and listened, and the more he saw and heard the more he felt lectured to.

He had moved the braziers to the four corners of the room, retreating briefly to the nave to retrieve some of the broken wood and making sure the fires were adequately fed. They gave that bare room a curious appearance, with pools of light at four corners and a more shadowy area in the center. It was as if the firelight could not quite reach that far. Outside, the sun would still be shining, but in here it felt like midnight. The flames were even and undisturbed, and the gentle spitting of burning wood was the only sound in the room, other than Volpe's occasional low, deep voice. Nico had stopped wondering how his own mouth, his own vocal cords, could make such a noise. But compared to the reality of what was happening, that was minor.

"*The Book of the Nameless* has always been the only true magical text," he went on. "Until the time I left this world that was true, and between then and now I have no reason to believe it has been usurped. I've seen wondrous things in my brief time walking the modern Venetian streets and canals, but nothing to convince me that magic is part of this place anymore. Magic has its own smell and taste, its own raft of senses, and Venice smells as it always did. This book, then, has the power, and from this book the new Exclusion shall be drawn."

What are you talking about? Nico asked.

"All in time," Volpe replied.

Despite his question, however, Nico knew some of this already. Volpe had used him to gather the materials needed to cast a spell of Exclusion, to keep his enemies out of Venice. But those enemies . . . they could not be the men Nico saw in Volpe's mind. Those men had been dead five hundred years and more.

Volpe knelt in the center of the room and placed the book on the ground before him, open to a page decorated with drawings, sigils, apparent formulae, and words that Nico could not read. Next he took the objects from the bag and placed them beside the book. Then he began to chant.

Nico drew back, repulsed by the strange words Volpe was spouting. He did not know them—they were in a language he had never heard before—but their cadences, their ebb and flow, carried a sickly weight of dread that he could not ignore. It was like hearing his own death pronouncement in another language, knowing the final meaning but not understanding the words used to reach it. His deep voice rose and fell in that small hidden chamber, and the firelight began to dance, as if his breath had disturbed the air of that place.

Before him, his shadow flitted across the book and the objects beside it. It jerked beside and behind him as well, a shadow cast four ways, and each shadow was moving to a different light.

"Grasp the hand of a dead soldier," Volpe said, "connecting the living with the dead and confirming that they are allied in this spell." He picked up the hand and clasped it as though in greeting.

Nico cried out, and Volpe gave it voice. He saw a flash of something too quick and remote to be memory, but it burned one scene indelibly onto his mind: an Italian woman leaning over him, tears collecting at the corners of her eyes. In one hand she held a bloodied cloth while the other was clasped around a small golden cross. Behind her, several more shapes. Family come to watch him die.

Volpe started chanting again and Nico returned to the present, terrified at what Volpe might be doing. But he had no control. He was so far back and down that he could only watch.

The chanting ended and Volpe placed the hand on the other side of the book, turning a page and dismissing it entirely. When he started reading from the next page he picked up the seal of the city—something that had likely put the official stamp on many important documents, an innocuous object that Nico knew had extreme value to the right people. He wondered what would become of it after this, and amazingly he felt a smile in his mind, because he thought of Geena then and how she'd be impressed that—

—*he is still thinking about his job.*

Geena reeled from the flash, staggering sideways and leaning against a wall. She recovered quickly, turning her head left and right, concentrating, trying to sense what direction the flash of words had come from. Keeping her mind open she stood straight again and looked along the nearest canal.

Words she does not know . . . an object clasped before her, it might be a stamp or seal of some sort, and when it's brought closer she sees that it is one of the old stamps of the city, Venice's coat of arms clearly visible on the raised underside, and then the hand—Nico's hand, she knows its look and touch so well—closes around the seal. He places it in the pages of a book open before him, touches some of the inscriptions on the right page, and—

She lost it. There almost solidly one second, gone the next, and not even any residual tingling on the back of her neck. But she was left staring across the canal at a wider waterway leading westward, and she had a very real sense that she needed to go that way. Had Nico urged her in that direction without consciously doing so? She did not know, and to question too much might be to implant doubt. A hundred yards along there was a footbridge, and she ran for it, her footsteps lonely in the night.

She glanced over her shoulder as she went, but only shadows followed.

Volpe read again for a moment, then started sketching shapes in the air with his left hand. Nico could feel his own arm and hand moving, his fingers flexing and twitching, but there was no sense at all of his controlling any of the movement. He was disassociated, an observer. It made him feel sick, but . . . fascinated as well.

Volpe continued sketching, and Nico tried to discern the shapes he was making in the air. They were formed of dancing shadow and flickering firelight, but they did not hold, and nothing was left behind. Volpe glanced down at the book again, and then Nico saw that some of the shapes echoed a series of sigils inked into the old paper.

Volpe picked up the seal again, licked its etched base, and stabbed it at the air. He did so five times, repeating the same phrase over and over, seemingly sealing his commitment with the darkness.

I hope I didn't hurt anyone getting that, Nico thought. *Not like that man in the apartment, and maybe that monk. I don't think there were blackouts in the Palazzo Cavalli, but . . . maybe they're so severe I can't even remember that they happened.*

"Quiet," Volpe said, his voice full of menace. Inside, Nico shut himself off for a moment, the psychic equivalent of closing his eyes and taking a breath. When he looked again he saw—

—the knife!

Geena gasped and went to her knees, looking behind her, ahead again, listening for approaching footsteps and wondering if Nico had lured her here just so that he could . . .

But no, she had more faith in him than that. Breathing hard, she stood again, hiding from the late afternoon sun in the shadows of a doorway. Clearing her mind, she tried to sense where that new sudden flash had come from. It had been fast, sharp, almost like the—

—knife, coming up toward his face with the dried smear of blood still on its blade, pressed to his mouth, stroked by his tongue, and even though it's Volpe doing this she can still feel the cold metal against her own tongue, and taste the stale tang of her own blood. She hears his voice again, deep and guttural, nothing like Nico has ever spoken before. There are flames, and shadows. The air is heavy. His excitement rises, a terrible thing, and the vision blurs as Nico draws back until—

She leaned against the cold stone jamb, breathing hard and yet more used to the transition from psychic flash to reality than she had been before. *They're in an old basement somewhere*, she thought, and she knew she had been heading in the right direction.

"Some weird ritual," she muttered. If she could reach him before the ritual was over, perhaps she could do something to help.

But she had to remember that he was still carrying the knife.

A small rowboat slid toward her along the canal. The old man rowing it offered her a grumbled greeting as she drew even with the boat.

"Lovely afternoon," he said.

"Hadn't noticed," Geena replied. He didn't respond to her rudeness, but neither did he stop rowing. *At least he knows where he's going*, she thought. The walkway ended, and she was faced with turning back or trying to continue along the canal herself. Water taxis were rare in these narrow canals, unless they were carrying travelers to and from hotels, and making her way out to one of the wider waterways would only waste time. But there were three row-boats tied alongside the canal.

Her skin tingled, and it was a very different feeling from Nico's touch. Eyes were upon her . . . or attention, at least. Someone was concentrating on her. Her skin grew cold, her spine ice-bound, and she hugged herself tight. Goosebumps speckled her arms and the fine hairs on her neck stood on end. Turning a full circle, squinting against the late afternoon sun, she tried to peer into gloomy alleys and shadowy corners. When the horrible feeling suddenly receded, it felt like a molester's hand stroking across her skin as he departed.

"Damn it," she said aloud, needing a noise to break the silence hanging heavy around her.

She looked up and around her at the buildings looming overhead, two- and three-story structures with the water as their foundation. Directly above her a second-floor set of French doors opened onto a small balcony. If anyone had been watching her from up there, they had gone back inside.

"Spooking myself," Geena said as she started unknotting the rope securing one of the dinghies. But she was not sure *what* had spooked her. She worked quickly, then bundled the line into the boat and stepped in. She unclasped the oars, placed them in their brackets, and pushed off from the canalside. No one shouted *Thief,* and if anyone did watch as she began rowing away, they were unconcerned.

Taking a huge breath to try and expunge her fears, she aimed the boat the way she thought she needed to go and, mind still open for more flashes from Nico, started rowing hard.

With Geena's blood wetted again, Volpe flicked the knife toward all four walls, chanting, "North, south, west, east." Specks of moisture flew, though they made no sound as they landed. Almost as if the air was absorbing the blood.

He turned several pages in *The Book of the Nameless*, still clasping hold of the knife in his other hand. Running his finger along lines of text, muttering. Nico thought Volpe had lost himself somewhere in the ritual.

"I know what comes next," Volpe said, answering the unasked question. "The words must be precise for the Expulsion and Repulsion to be renewed. Then the city will be closed off once more from the three bastard Doges."

Mad, Nico thought. *He must be—*

"Mad? Because they're so old, they're bound to be dead, of course. Is that what you mean?" Nico did not answer, and Volpe did not need one. "Dead, like me?"

You survived in spirit only, not in flesh, Nico thought. *Is that what you're saying? Somehow they've done the same thing?*

Volpe hesitated. Nico felt the uncertainty within him.

"I don't know," the old magician admitted.

What?

Volpe glanced around the chamber, surveyed the materials of the spell in progress in front of him, and Nico felt him grow impatient.

"Quickly, then," Volpe said. "And I'll save the rest for later. I preserved my essence because, without me, the Repulsion would break down. I knew the three of them, the damnable cousins, had each acquired enough of Akylis' magic to prolong their lives, and I intended to outlast them. When the last of them died, the spell that preserved my heart and spirit was meant to unravel, and then, at last, I could move on to the world beyond this life."

So, if your spell never unraveled—

"It means that at least one of them is still alive, these long centuries later," Volpe said. "But one or all three, it matters not. They can't be allowed to return to Venice. I should never have let them live, but I feared compromising my position in the government and the influence it granted to me. Had I simply killed them . . ."

But why keep them out? Nico asked. *What is it you fear?*

"Their hideous ambitions," Volpe replied. "Each of them, in his own time, fancied himself a magician of sorts. They were novices and fools, and they tapped into a power—an evil—that tainted them, turning their already monumental arrogance and greed into something monstrous."

This power . . . that's Akylis?

But Volpe's impatience had reached its breaking point.

"Enough," he said. "No more delays."

So Nico could only watch as Volpe began the final stage of a ritual designed to keep three six-hundred-year-old men from the city. He read from the book in that old language, punctuating the end of each sentence with a gentle stab of the knife at the air, north and south, west and east. He repeated the process twice more, then he set the knife down and settled back.

It's done? Nico thought, meaning it as a question for Volpe.

"Almost," Volpe said. "All that's needed now is . . ." He fell silent, perhaps concentrating, perhaps not wishing to give away the final ingredient to this strange ritual.

Then he held out his left hand, pressed the blade to his palm, and stroked it left to right.

Nico gasped. Blood flowed. He winced against the pain, but there was none.

"Ouch," Volpe said, then he chuckled. He flicked the knife again as he had before, but this time there was no chanting, and his actions had a casual grace. He fisted his hand, then wiped the dripping blood on his trousers. When Volpe glanced at the wound again, Nico saw that it was not too deep or long. The knife was sharp.

"And it's done," Volpe said, sighing, relaxing back on his haunches. His shoulders drooped and then the pain sang in Nico, the keen burning across the palm of his left hand. He wanted to scream, but Volpe still had his mouth.

Now will you leave me alone? Nico asked. Volpe raised his head, smiling . . . and then his smile froze into a grimace.

The air began to vibrate. Nico felt it through the body he did not control—a gentle murmur that grew in intensity and volume, setting the air shimmering like a heat-haze, shaking dust from the ceiling and shrinking the flames in the braziers.

"No!" Volpe said, and Nico had never heard such passion in that spirit's voice.

"What's happening?" Nico asked, and he spoke aloud. He looked down at his hand and lifted it; Volpe had let his control slip. In his other hand, Nico still clasped the knife that had slashed Geena's arm and his own palm, and he moved to throw it away. His muscles cramped, and it felt as if the bones of his arm had fused into glass. One wrong move and they would shatter.

"No!" Volpe roared. For a second his voice was as loud as the increasing disturbance in the chamber. He dragged Nico to his feet and took control again, complete control, and Nico was shoved deep like a body being stuffed down a well. "It's all wrong!" Volpe screamed, but this time the chaos around him was louder.

Still he let Nico see, and hear. Behind what was happening all around them in the chamber—the violence of an earthquake, with the echoes of something very different—Nico felt a simmering fury waiting to burst from the man who had stolen him away.

The fire in one of the braziers went out suddenly, and Nico thought of that buried chamber, the wall collapsing, and the stinking waters finding their way inside. But there was no water here, only dust and chaos. The air itself shook, bounced from wall to wall, a series of shock waves crossing and colliding, and Nico's teeth thrummed in his jaw. His hair stood on end as he turned to run for the door.

"It didn't work!" Volpe screamed. Nico froze again, muscles cramped, and he became a statue while everything around him seemed to move. "They're already *here!*"

Nico tried walking, and slowly the blazing pain in his limbs lessened. Its dilution matched the reduction in the violence around the room. Two braziers were out now, but the other two still guttered heroically, their flames soft and blue as if there were not enough oxygen in the air.

"What . . . happened?" Nico rasped, and then the fury he sensed exploded upon him, and from him.

"We were too late!" Volpe growled. And Nico found himself running at full speed, head down, toward the solid stone wall.

Geena moved through the city, guided by nothing discernable or definable. Leaving the stolen boat tied to a wooden jetty, she ducked through a rose-smothered archway and emerged into a small square. There were a few people here, milling around a restaurant busy with the early dinner crowd—Americans, mostly. Europeans ate much later. The diners spoke in strangely subdued tones, and she felt oddly unnerved by their presence. She skirted the square and hoped they did not see her. There was no fear that she would be recognized—the chance of her knowing anyone here was remote—but she felt involved in something so bizarre that the company of casual strangers seemed repellent. They would nod a greeting or comment on how warm it was, meals still heavy in their stomachs and eyes softened with wine, and somewhere Nico was in terrible danger. His life hung in the balance; she was certain of that. She might well be his only hope. Muttered platitudes had no place this day.

And still she sensed something following her. On the canal, she had paused in her paddling a dozen times—once to move aside as a water taxi chugged by, the rest simply to drift and listen. The dip and splash of the oars soon became soporific, but she needed to remain alert. She never heard anything behind her that indicated pursuit, nor did she see anything. And that convinced her more than anything that she *was* being followed, though not by anyone she could see. It felt as if someone remained just out of sight, always hidden behind the last turn in the canal.

She had checked her cell phone, floating in the middle of a narrow canal that was usually bustling during the day. Two more texts from Domenic, the last one over an hour before, and she guessed he'd given up for the day. No more voice mails. If he'd found her trail and was somehow following, surely he would try to call her, ask her to wait for him? Surely he'd let her know?

She left the square and headed along a narrow alleyway between buildings. At the first doorway she stopped and crouched down behind some rubbish bags. She smelled rotten food and musty clothes, heard the secretive rustlings of some of Venice's huge rat population, but no one entered the alley behind her.

"Nico?" she said softly, just in case. Speaking his name vocalized a truth she did not like—she was a little scared of him. It was a repulsive idea, because she was certain that he needed her now more than at any time in the past, but all this strangeness surrounded and came from him. Something he'd done down in that Chamber of Ten had initiated this—touching that urn, and the slick material it had contained—and though she could not find it in herself to lay blame, she did attach responsibility. She wanted to help him, but she was quietly terrified that he would not be willing, or able, to help himself.

No one followed her into the alley, and neither did she receive any more flashes from Nico. So she moved on, simply because remaining still no longer seemed a good idea.

She came to a canal with a narrow footpath along one side, where three people sat drinking outside a set of open French doors. She knew this to be a small hotel—there were many in this district, family-run places that spent most of the year filled with tourists who knew the better places to stay in Venice. She heard two American voices, and heavily accented English from a woman who might have been the owner. There was a small table between them, several wine bottles on its surface, and they each nursed a glass.

Geena passed by, trying to appear as nonchalant as possible but feeling conspicuous. As she drew level, the Italian woman said in English, "Have you heard about the Mayor?"

"What about him?" one of the American men asked.

"Dead!" the other American said, his voice slurring heavily. He lifted his glass and took a drink, and his companion glanced wearily at him.

Geena froze, wanting to eavesdrop but without getting caught. The Mayor was dead? Had he died in the collapse of the building in Dorsoduro? She patted her pockets as though searching for something.

"But how did he die?" the less obviously intoxicated American asked.

"Stabbed to death," the drunk man said, the seriousness quelling his drunkenness a little.

"In his house," the Italian woman said. "His wife and daughter found him just before dinner. Tragic."

Geena hurried quickly away, losing herself amidst the people bustling this way and that. *The Mayor, dead? Who would have done such a thing? Why?* Her mind was running, trying to decide if these were all pieces of a larger puzzle. Murder and disaster had struck Venice in a single day, and she could not help feeling as though chaos was spreading throughout the city. She looked at the faces of the people she passed and they all seemed troubled to her. Uneasy, as though they sensed dark forces working against them, just out of sight.

Or maybe you're just projecting, Geena thought, and managed a small smile. But what if she wasn't merely being self-indulgent? Could all of these things really be unrelated? Memories of the flashbacks she'd been following mixed and merged. Whatever Zanco Volpe had been—magician, murderer, manipulator—he had been first and foremost a politician, dedicated to the city he both loved and secretly controlled.

Stabbed to death, the man had said.

Though she fought against it, and ghastly though the idea was, she had little trouble imagining the knife in the hand of the man she loved; the hand now controlled by Zanco Volpe.

Volpe gave him back his nerves, but kept muscle and bone. He let him feel the pain that damage to his flesh caused, but retained mobility and impetus, exerting a terrible control that left Nico helpless in his agonies. It was a terrible, vengeful torture, and all the while Volpe kept shouting out the reason:

"You . . . slowed . . . me . . . down!"

He ran across the chamber again and struck another stone wall. The impact stole his vision, and he staggered back and fell.

"No!" Volpe said, hauling Nico to his feet again, wiping blood from his eyes so that he could launch himself at one of the flaming braziers. He tripped and went sprawling, pain biting in everywhere. Nico so wanted to scream, but Volpe had his mouth, using it to rant and rage.

"You made me late, you slowed me down, you let them get in!"

I let no one in, Nico thought, but he knew that was not quite true. He'd let Volpe in, and now the consequences of that mistake were mounting. *The Book of the Nameless* lay torn beneath him, the seal rolled across the floor, and close to his right hand lay the knife.

Volpe picked it up, and Nico screamed.

The scream was real. Volpe paused, holding the knife with its tip pointing toward Nico's right eye, inches away and invisible in the poor light. Volpe moved it closer, and Nico could sense it there, the cool sharp metal that was now smeared with a mixture of his and Geena's blood.

I've done nothing to you, he thought. *You've done it all to me.* But he tried to draw back, and thought as secretly as he could, *I love you, Geena, and I'm sorry, but the monster is going to kill me.*

Volpe stood, groaning as he took some of the pain he had bestowed. Nico felt a sense of wonder in the spirit, because he had not felt such pain for so long. It was almost liberating. His heart thudded, blood flowed, and as Volpe moved toward the small entrance hole into the chamber, Nico quietly assessed his injuries.

"I'm no monster," Volpe said, his tone betraying a sense of hurt.

Then give me back my life.

"I cannot. Not yet. Things have gone . . . wrong. There's danger to Venice. Its people and the city itself are in peril, and what I've been holding back for centuries might now—"

Might what? Nico thought. *How are you any different from them? They dabbled in dark magic? They were power-hungry bastards? So what? That describes you just as well. They're just like you!*

"No," Volpe said, "they're not."

What makes them so different?

He could feel Volpe's anger subsiding into grim determination.

"Listen well, Nicolo, and I will tell you."

For long minutes, the old magician whispered to him. Nico listened, first incredulous, then amazed, and finally terrified.

"I need rest," Volpe said, when he was through. "You need to find somewhere quiet, somewhere private, and rest yourself. I have injured you, and for that you have my apologies. But I can heal you. The longer we are joined together, the stronger the bond between us, and the greater control I have over my magic. While we both rest, your injuries will fade and your vigor will be restored, just as mine will be. I despise the thought of losing even a moment, but we must be at our best. We have a fight ahead of us."

"We?" Nico said, surprised at the sound of his voice. Volpe was already sinking down, and the pains across his body roared in like a fire bursting alight. Nico groaned and spit blood from mashed lips, and he hoped Volpe really could heal him.

You've no choice, Nico, from somewhere deep inside. *Venice needs you now, as much as it ever needed me. Now rest . . . and later, we will scheme.*

CHAPTER 11

STANDING BEFORE CHIESA DI SAN ROCCO, GEENA WAS UNSURE exactly what had brought her here. Since hearing about the Mayor's murder she had walked in a haze, the world around her seeming less real than the scenarios that came to life in her imagination. There were no more hints of something following her, but with her attention switched inward she probably wouldn't have noticed, anyway.

The church looked empty, and yet . . . there was something about it. An air of potential, or the sense that something momentous had just happened. Perhaps it was the silence that hung around the place, as if the walls themselves were shocked dumb.

"Nico?" she called. There was no trace of his presence, no inkling of the touch that had been fading in and out like a badly tuned radio. Her voice echoed only briefly then faded again to silence. She could hear sounds elsewhere in the city—the ever-present buzz of boat engines, wooden shutters clapping shut, and from somewhere distant the incongruous sounds of a party—but they only emphasized the silence. *I shouldn't even be here*, she thought, and then the church doorway opened.

She wanted to hide, but there was nothing close enough to hide behind.

When he emerged into the slanted sunlight on the top step, she heard something behind her, as though the night itself had gasped in disbelief. But she could focus only on Nico. She ran to him, mindless of the knife in his hand, forgetting everything that had happened save for losing him, and when he looked up he smiled with bloodied eyes.

"Nico!" She tried to yell but it came out as a whisper as she ran up the five steps. On the top step she paused, the sight of him stifling her joy. He looked terrible—face smeared with blood, lips gashed, one eye swollen shut, and he held his left side as if he'd cracked ribs. But in his good eye she saw only Nico—no one and nothing else.

"Sweet Geena," he said, and it was Nico's voice. She stepped to him and opened her arms, not even glancing at the knife he held in his outstretched right hand. But just as she moved in close, ready to rest her head against his shoulder and feel his heat, she saw his eyes open wide with shock and sensed something coming at her from behind.

She turned, her hand pressed against the small of his back. He moved in front of her and raised the knife. A figure streaked across the paved area in front of the church, a confusion of billowing darkness, and its footsteps had a peculiar pattern—*slap, thunk, slap, thunk.*

The man came to a halt before the steps, his sudden stillness more striking than the startling movement. He was dressed in a black cloak and hood, and as he raised his face, Geena felt terror clasping talons into her flesh. *He'll have no face, he'll be nobody . . .*

But it was only a man, his hair long and completely gray, his hands thin and fingers spindly. And when she saw his face—

I've seen this man before!

The way the left side drooped, left eye heavily lidded and mouth downturned—

—but it can't be him, it can't *be, because—*

She felt herself losing strength, her muscles relaxing, knees folding—

—*because that was six hundred years ago.*

Geena hit the ground but neither man seemed to notice. They only had eyes for each other.

"Pity," Giardino Caravello said. "I was certain you were Zanco Volpe."

One of the Doges, Nico thought, and he was certain that Volpe would rise then. But he did not, too exhausted from the ritual. Nico moved his left hand away from his ribs, and turned the knife in his right. He had complete control of his body.

"What are you talking about?" Nico said. *Act the fool and perhaps he'll leave. Plead ignorance, and this man who was banished from the city . . . almost six hundred years ago . . .*

"You know me?" the man asked. His voice was light and soft, belying the image he portrayed. When Nico had last seen him in Volpe's memory, he'd been dressed in stylish clothes, acting slighted as he boarded the boat to be taken from Venice forever. Now it seemed that even forever had limits.

My fault, Nico thought, and he felt Volpe's rotting heart slipping through his fingers all over again.

"No," Nico said, but he realized instantly that he could not lie to this man.

"Well . . ." The man shrugged. "If you don't know me, then you know Volpe." He mounted the steps, lurching up them as if one of his legs no longer worked properly.

"I don't know what you're talking about," Nico said. He glanced back at Geena, sitting on the ground and staring with her mouth wide open. *Up!* he thought, but there was no indication that she heard.

"The church has changed," Doge Caravello said. "It looks more elaborate than I recall. But I suppose time changes everything."

Volpe, Nico thought. *Volpe!* But the old spirit remained silent.

Caravello reached the top step, five paces from Nico, and there he paused. He looked Nico up and down, the good side of his mouth turning up in a smile that looked more like a sneer.

"Cut yourself shaving?" the ancient man asked. There would be no negotiating here, Nico knew. From everything he had witnessed of Volpe's memories of the city, he knew that those three banished Doges were Volpe's mortal enemies. Even through his broken and bloodied nose, he could smell violence in the air, and he moved a step to the right to stand between Caravello and Geena.

"Leave us alone, old man." *Volpe, hear this. Listen!*

"Old man?" Caravello asked with a gentle laugh. "If only you knew."

Nico remembered the canal turning red, Volpe's dismissal of this man who had once ruled Venice, the guards' nervousness, the Doge's pride as he was banished from the city he loved and which he had been making a play to rule completely—

Caravello read his face all too well.

"Oh, so you *do* know," the Doge said. He took one step closer and Nico raised the knife.

The old man laughed. It was a surprisingly light, high laugh, like a young girl's. He squinted and leaned closer, looking at Nico's face, his eyes, turning his head this way and that like a dog sniffing the air.

"I *did* think it was you, Zanco," he said, almost with regret. "But perhaps you really are gone for good. The others would be so pleased to hear it."

Nico bent his knees and dropped into a fighting pose, but he had not fought anyone since he was eleven years old. This was nothing like instinct. The manipulation was much more subtle than it had been before, and for the first time Nico gave himself entirely to the thing inside. He retained control but answered the hints, and far away he heard Volpe whisper, *Soon he will see the truth . . . and then he will attack.*

"Perhaps you opened up his old tomb," Caravello said. "We saw the news about the Chamber being found. I'd like to visit it myself,

but . . . fuck it. You know? Old times. The past is best left dead."
He was staring intently at Nico, watching for some hint that there
was more to him than first appeared.

"I don't know what you've been smoking, you crazy old fool,"
Nico said. "Now get out of here and mind your own business."

"My business?" Caravello asked. He was still scrutinizing
Nico—a discomforting experience. He took one step closer and
Nico smelled him for the first time. There was nothing normal
about his smell; he stank solely of age.

"He followed me," Geena whispered, and Caravello glanced her
way. Nico did not. He kept his eyes on the old man because—

Soon, Volpe whispered. *I can feel him gathering his senses, and we
must not let him win. This is the first, but it will not be the most difficult. Right now, we still have some element of surprise on our side,
because he's not quite sure.*

"Everything in Venice is my business," Caravello said softly.

The left side of his face barely moved, as if it had melted and
then set. The drooping muscles beneath that flesh might have been
the result of stroke or disease, but Nico caught a stray thought in
Volpe's mind and knew the truth. Caravello's ruined visage had
been caused by dark magic in the hands of an ambitious amateur.

He is an amateur no longer, Volpe whispered in Nico's mind.

The right side of Caravello's face was animated and filled with
confidence.

"Venice was mine," the Doge said. "And it will be again. A
united three are so much greater than one, Volpe. Do you hear?"

He jerked forward and Nico took a step back before Volpe took
control at last.

The ancient Doge sensed the change in him immediately.

"Ahh," Caravello sighed. "So it *is* you."

Volpe swung the knife. It hissed through the air inches from the
old man's face. Caravello slipped back to the top of the steps and
threw off his cloak, revealing two short swords stuck in his belt. As
he drew them, Volpe lunged, punching him in the face and sending him stumbling down the steps.

"What have you been doing all this time?" Caravello laughed, regaining his balance. He had the swords out now, and he spun them with amazing dexterity. "Hiding away? Keeping the city safe?"

"It worked," Volpe growled.

"Until now."

"A minor interruption," Volpe said, then he went at Caravello again.

Geena screamed. Nico heard her, but Volpe was fully in charge now, using Nico's fitness to compliment his experience. He ducked one sword swipe and went in low, punching at Caravello's crotch, missing, then stabbing with the knife. Caravello—upright, and with the advantage—kicked Volpe in the face. He should have screamed as his broken nose was crushed, but he had known much worse.

Nico gasped in surprise, his voice unheard.

"A *knife?*" Caravello said again, and he laughed. "Look at you, Volpe. Little more than a shade inhabiting a stranger's body." He circled Volpe, both of them tensed and ready for another attack. "And look at me. You know me, you old bastard. You've been dead all these centuries. Whereas *I* . . . I have advanced. Grown with the world. I've danced around this globe, Zanco, and seen things you cannot imagine. I've learned so much. But Venice has always been my home." He took in a deep breath. "It's *good* to be home."

"So where are the others?" Volpe asked.

Caravello sneered. "Not far at all. They'll be so envious that it was my hand that took your life." He kicked out, faster than Volpe had believed possible, and his foot struck cracked ribs. Volpe gasped, because even if he could withstand the pain, the pressure on his lungs was immense. He went down, coughing blood.

"You should have ignored the Council and killed me when you had the chance," Caravello said. He raised one sword, lowered the other, and came in for the kill.

Geena jumped from the third step and collided with Caravello, her shoulder striking his hip, hands clawing into his clothing as she fell. Unbalanced, he followed her down. One sword clattered to the ground, and Geena grunted as the man landed across her shoulders.

Volpe stood and darted forward, ignoring the crippling pain in his chest, and Nico heard the calm calculation in his mind: *While he kills the girl, I'll deal with him.*

No! Nico tried to scream, and with a supreme effort of will he pushed himself forward, knife lashing out. He feigned right and darted to the left, slicing across Caravello's stomach with the blade. It parted his shirt but did not draw blood.

Geena crawled to the steps and crouched, watching the fight, and tensed to jump again.

Left! Nico warned, and Volpe dropped to the left just in time to avoid a descending blade. He fell onto Caravello's arm, grabbed his wrist, and jerked down, feeling and hearing bone snap beneath his weight. The old man might have lived for those intervening centuries, but whatever dark magic he had employed to increase his longevity had done little to strengthen time-brittled bones.

Caravello screamed shrilly, and Volpe stood and pressed the tip of the knife beneath Caravello's chin.

The old Doge laughed. "A knife, Volpe? Do you really think—"

"A knife smeared with the blood of the new Oracle? Yes, I do think. The magic of Akylis cannot withstand the power of the city itself." And he pushed, pressing down on Caravello's head with one hand and shoving with all his might with the other, plunging the blade through the old man's throat and mouth cavity and into his brain. When he felt the gush of rancid blood around the knife's hilt he shoved the body aside and stepped back.

The Doge was trying to talk, but the knife held his mouth pinned shut. Volpe knelt before him—he wanted to be the last thing Caravello saw before he died. The corpse started to wither as though the centuries had begun to catch up to it.

Geena breathed hard, each exhalation a grunt building toward a scream.

"We have to leave here quickly and silently," Volpe growled, and he drew back again, giving Nico control. "I used what magic I could spare to turn attention away, so that we would not be interrupted. But I cannot sustain it."

Nico slumped before the still-twitching body of the old man, finding his strength. He could feel the slick blood on his hand now, and smell its rankness, like something left in a gutter to rot in the midday sun. Shocked at what had happened, still trying to come to terms with what it meant, he stood and turned toward Geena.

She was standing in the fading sunlight on the top of the steps, moving slowly sideways across the face of the church.

"You . . . killed . . . that man," she said.

"Volpe killed him," Nico said. "Geena, there's so much—"

"Caravello," she said. "He wore tights and a codpiece, and the canal was . . ."

"Red," Nico said, and he suddenly understood. "How much have you seen?"

"I have no idea," Geena said.

"We have to go. He told me . . . We have to leave now, before anyone can ask what happened here."

"What *did* happen here?" He could see that she was descending into shock. Her eyes were glazed and fixed on the dead man. But behind the shock, she was also struggling to comprehend what she had seen, fighting with reality.

"It's all real," he said.

"Yes," Geena said, nodding, and letting the tears come.

"Come on." Nico grabbed her arm, making sure he'd placed himself between her and Caravello's corpse. The old Doge was a sad bundle in the shadows, dead, and with Nico's fingerprints all over the knife jammed in his skull.

"Where to?" Geena asked.

"Anywhere but here." They were together again, and yet their world had changed almost beyond recognition. Whatever happened now, Nico was determined to protect Geena from the future.

"But first we have to hide the body."

While Geena kept watch to make sure their crime went unseen, Nico—or the man speaking with his voice—forced the door of an abandoned taverna just off the courtyard by the church. The windows were dark, all the chairs up on tables, and the old wood around the lock, softened by decades of damp, gave way easily.

"You saved my life," Nico said as he hurried back to help Geena lift the body.

"I saved Nico's life," she replied as she took the corpse by its feet. "I don't know who you are."

"Still denying? Still doubting?" he replied, hooking his hands under Caravello's arms.

"I just don't understand." She handed him Nico's phone. "But this is for Nico. I can't be out of touch with him again. I just can't."

They carried the body inside and set it on the floor behind the bar, then left swiftly, both of them glancing around nervously as Nico pulled the door tightly shut behind them.

The deed had been done largely in silence. Now, though, as they hurried away, Volpe spoke to her again, using Nico's mouth.

"Accept what you know, and what has happened. It's much easier than fighting. That way, what you don't understand—"

"I don't understand how you can be two people, and how what we did down in that chamber could lead to this. If you're even real, how could you have survived down there? Why did our opening the door cause the chamber to flood? Why were those ten Council members entombed there? How is it that you can speak enough modern Italian for me to understand you? Why did you do those things? Those terrible . . ."

Geena shook her head and stared at Nico, shivering. There was a stranger behind his eyes. Even though he was bruised and cut, she could still see it was not him. It was his hair and eyes, the mouth she had kissed so often, the hands that had caressed her and held her when she was upset or sad. But someone else watched her from inside.

He ducked into a café and steered her to a table. They did not speak again until they had ordered and the waitress had brought them coffee. Geena drank hers down. It burned her lips and tongue, but she didn't mind. She couldn't stop herself from shaking, and shock was settling in. Before today, she had never seen a person die.

"Thank you for saving my life," he said. Volpe.

Geena closed her eyes and remembered launching herself at that man with the two swords, and how the unreality of the scene had buffered her against the danger she was placing herself in. It had felt like a dream, so unreal that the action had seemed wholly logical and normal. The old man had been about to kill the person she loved, and there had been no hesitation at all. *But was that the only reason I did it?* she thought. *Probably not.*

She watched Nico stand. He didn't walk like Nico, and his voice was someone else's. *That's Zanco Volpe. A dead man.*

"I'm not without honor," Nico said in that other person's voice. Geena drank more coffee and turned away.

"I can't look when you're talking like that, and you still . . ."

"Look like Nico."

She nodded, setting the cup on the table and hugging her arms.

"Everything has changed," he said in his deep, unreal voice. It was like an echo from history. If a mummy could speak, it would sound like this.

"Let me speak to Nico," she said, realizing how ridiculous that sounded but unable to smile.

She heard a sigh, and then Nico's hands rested on hers.

"Geena," he said, with a tenderness that could only have been him—Nico speaking to her now, not Volpe. "You have to believe."

"I don't know *what* to believe," she confessed, keeping her voice low.

She glanced at the other people in the café, all of them seemingly content with their lives in that moment. The fading light of the end of a long summer day cast a golden glow just outside the windows.

"I've learned so much," Nico said. "It took me a while to believe Volpe, too, but now there's no alternative." He sounded almost happy. She heard his pain, and his fear, but . . .

"You sound pleased," she said.

"I am," Nico said. "Geena, I'm not insane, and neither are you."

She had seen Giardino Caravello over six hundred years before, boarding a boat and being driven from the city. She had seen him today, wielding two swords to kill Nico. She had pushed him over and started the final series of events that ended in his death.

"Please let him explain," Nico said. "I think he will . . . he says he will. I think he needs us now."

"Tell me one thing first, Nico," she said. She studied him so that hopefully she would see any lie in his eyes. "Did you kill the Mayor?"

First he was Nico, and then he changed. His eyes grew wider and darker.

"The Mayor has been murdered?" he said again in that deep, ancient voice. Then he closed his eyes and sat back in his chair. "That changes everything. They are moving even faster than I feared." He opened his eyes again and stared at her, and there was something compelling about him. The mystery, perhaps, or the power she knew he must hold . . .

The power *Zanco Volpe* must possess to do what he was doing now.

"Geena, Nico loves you, and I see that you have a good heart. If you'll hear me now, I'll do my best to explain why I need you. And why the future of Venice might well rest in your hands."

CHAPTER 12

You are a historian, are you not?" Volpe said.

Sitting there across from him, knowing it was him speaking through Nico, Geena studied him in fascination. Nico's face, yes, but the expressions were all wrong, and when Volpe came to the fore of Nico's mind—took him over like some puppeteer—his eyes had a perpetual squint that had never been there before. And his speech retained the flourishes of a Venetian dialect that no one had spoken for ages. Yet only flourishes, as though he had accessed Nico's mind to master modern Italian.

You're in shock, she told herself. *You're just focusing on details because you're trying not to scream.*

A thin smile parted her lips.

"Have I amused you?"

Geena felt her smile vanish. "Not in the least. You make me feel as if I might vomit at any moment."

Volpe looked—*Nico* looked—stung by this. His nostrils flared.

"I hardly think that's productive."

"What is productive? Murder?"

At this, those squinting eyes narrowed further. "It has its uses," he said, lowering his voice. "But you were there, Geena. I had no alternative. I saved all of our lives. Il Doge would have—"

Geena closed her eyes and held up a hand. "Stop."

He did. For several seconds she sat and listened to the sounds of the café, the Babel of tourist languages, the clink of spoons and cups, the creaking of the fan above their heads as it turned.

"Il Doge," she said quietly, and it was not a question. More an affirmation.

"Please, let's not spend any more time pretending that you do not believe what you saw with your own eyes, or inside your mind," Volpe said.

Geena studied him, and though the ancient Venetian had come entirely to the fore, occupying Nico's body to what she presumed was his full extent, she thought she saw a bit of Nico stirring in there as well.

Are you there? she thought, sending the question out into the ether.

And she felt a wash of love and worry in return that made her hand tremble as she lifted her coffee cup from the table. A bit of it splashed onto her lap, but it was not hot enough to burn.

We are both here, Nico replied.

She could sense the other in him. Volpe might not have Nico's ability, his touch, but their mental communication was no longer private. They had an audience. Whether or not Volpe could consciously utilize Nico's touch she did not know, nor did she have any desire to find out.

Volpe sighed and rolled his eyes. "Really, Geena, why do you keep running from the truth? I am here. I am real. You wanted to know what all of this is about, and I think it is only fair that I explain it to you. Your life has been irrevocably changed. You can accept that, and perhaps survive, or deny it and surely die."

She took a sip of coffee. Hand still shaking, she set the cup down. It was much too sweet, but the fault was her own. Four sugars. What the hell had she been thinking?

"I choose to live," she said.

Volpe smiled with Nico's mouth. If she had not known that mouth so intimately, it would almost have been convincing.

"Back to my question, then. You are a historian?"

"Archaeologist."

He waved the word away. "Yes, yes. A historian. Similar enough. I learned much of your work the first day and night after I returned, sharing this flesh with your lover."

Geena felt her face flush with embarrassment. Lover. She and Nico had made love that night and during sex, with him thrusting inside of her, she had sensed him become distant and cold and more aggressive, as though he did not seem like himself. Nausea roiled in her gut.

"Go on," she said, teeth snapping off the words.

Perhaps Volpe read her thoughts, though she did not feel Nico's touch. It might have been that he simply knew how to read people, to interpret their faces, for one corner of his mouth turned up in a momentary smirk, as though he knew exactly where her thoughts had led her. She hated him for that.

Rape? She might not be able to call it that, but the violation and loathing she felt were nonetheless fierce.

"I am the key to a thousand mysteries, the answer to a thousand riddles that you historians have encountered in your studies. Perhaps one day we will have opportunity for me to introduce you to all of the secrets of Venice and beyond, but for now—"

"I don't give a shit about Venice right now," Geena said. "Tell me about you and the Doges. Tell me what you've gotten us involved in."

His nostrils flared again and she felt a ripple of fury emanating from him, felt it through Nico. And then, in her mind, Nico's voice. *Volpe. Explain.*

Volpe smiled. "Fine. But speak to me in that tone again and, Nico's cooperation or not, I'll leave you to the Doges' mercies."

Geena felt all the blood rush from her face.

"You wouldn't dare. Or if you would, Nico wouldn't let you.

It's obvious that you can't control him completely. You need him, which means you need me. So get on with it. You're wasting time."

She signaled the waitress for a refill on her coffee.

"All right," Volpe said, breaking off a piece of biscotti. "But enough of your skepticism. Accept what is before you."

She nodded for him to go on.

"In the time of my youth, the Doge ruled Venice, but he did not have absolute power. Beneath him was the Council of Ten, and beneath them the Senate. Often the Ten exerted a great deal of influence over both Doge and Senate, so any man who could control the Council of Ten could chart the course for Venice himself."

"And you were that man," Geena said. She had seen much of this in the visions she had shared with Nico, which she now knew were flashes of Volpe's memory connected with parts of the city.

Volpe's smile sent an icy shiver down her back.

"I was. For many years of beauty and enlightenment, far beyond the standard human life span, I controlled the Ten. They saw me as their most trusted advisor, and in that role I manipulated them to my own ends, and through them the Doges as well. From time to time, a Doge would discover his own ambition and attempt to assert his power. Those who could not be controlled were ruined. But over the time of my influence, there were three whose ambitions were greater, and darker, than any of the others, ruthless men whose desires reached far beyond the limits of Venice, and who would have sacrificed anything to fulfill those desires."

"And you stood in their way," Geena said.

"Each of them ordered my assassination, at least once," Volpe said. "They failed, of course."

Geena took this in, sipping at a glass of water the waitress had brought. "Caravello," she said. "Aretino. Foscari."

Volpe blinked Nico's eyes in surprise. "Your link with Nico is stronger than I realized. You have plucked these names from his thoughts?"

She shook her head. "It doesn't work like that. He broadcasts and I receive. We are . . . open to each other. Yes, there's a link with me that he doesn't have with anyone else, as far as I know, but it's Nico who has the ability. Nico who is different."

Volpe nodded thoughtfully. "Just so. I believe he sensed me."

"What do you mean?"

He sipped his coffee and Geena wondered what it tasted like to him. If he liked the things that Nico liked because Nico's taste buds had acclimated to certain things, or if Volpe's ancient predispositions would carry over, despite the fact that he resided in a body not his own.

"The Chamber of Ten," Volpe said.

Geena flinched in surprise. "That's what I called it."

"And where did you derive that name? From your own imagination, or from your link with Nico? From his mind, and through his, from mine? That is what we all called it, myself and the Council, a place where we could meet in secret, unknown to the Doge and to the Senate."

The archaeologist in Geena came to the fore. "And Petrarch?"

"When the poet wanted to move his library from Venice, I persuaded him to change his mind and arranged for Petrarch's collection to be moved to the hidden room you and your people discovered beneath the Biblioteca. I could not allow him to remove certain arcane texts from the city."

"Magic, you mean?"

Volpe nodded. "Spellcraft. Call it what you like."

"You admit that you ruled Venice through deceit and manipulation. How were these three men, elevated to the position of Doge, any less worthy to guide the city than you were?"

"They cared nothing for Venice, only for themselves, and for their family," Volpe replied, lifting his chin and glaring at her imperiously. "To them, the people of Venice were pawns. Grist for the mill of their ambition. I had only the good of the city in mind."

Geena scratched at the back of her left hand. "Oh, of course," she replied archly. "You were the hero of the people."

"No, never that. I served them in secrecy, content to see the fruits of my labors in the rise of Venetian power and grandeur. But you mean to ask what the difference is between myself and these three corrupt men, if our goals were the same."

Geena sipped at her coffee. "Of course that's what I'm asking. You wanted Venice for yourself, just as they did. You're obviously ruthless. You manipulated and deceived and murdered to keep your power. Why are they any worse—"

"Because I was *chosen*," Volpe said.

Great, Geena thought. *A psychotic ghost with a Messiah complex.*

"Chosen how, exactly?"

Volpe sighed. Staring at him, she could barely see Nico in that face now.

"In your studies as an archaeologist, surely you must have encountered stories of the Oracles of the Great Cities of the World."

Geena had been about to lift her coffee cup again, but now she set it down, studying him closely. Volpe had said something before about an Oracle, but things had been happening so fast it had barely registered.

"You don't mean the Oracle of Delphi?"

"One of many."

She was about to tell him she had no idea what he was talking about when a memory rose up. While cataloging the earliest of the books they had retrieved from Plutarch's library, she had skimmed through a volume whose Latin title translated roughly to *The Souls of Cities*. Her Latin was very spotty, but she'd picked up a few sentences here and there that had made her think of a 14th-century French manuscript she had read during a dig in the ruins of a monastery in Talloires. It had included references to a woman who was considered the Oracle of Paris, who knew all of the secrets and the history of the city and who, it was believed, channeled its soul through her body. Collette something. She had offered wise counsel to nobles and commoners alike.

"Maybe I know what you're talking about," Geena admitted, "but only a little. The great cities of the world are, what, supposed to choose someone as their defender—"

"If need be, a defender," Volpe interrupted. "But more truly, a voice. I am the Oracle of Venice and I have been for a very, very long time, including all of the centuries my heart remained in the Chamber of Ten. My heart and the city's heart beat together. I know all of its secrets, its ancient history. Ruthless, perhaps, but I have done what was required of me.

"I used spellcraft to keep myself youthful, to remain strong, long past the limits of ordinary men," he went on. "But I was not immortal and, in time—long after I had banished the three cunning Doges—my health began to fail. I knew that I would die."

His voice trembled suddenly with remembered anguish. Though she felt only mistrust and even revulsion for him, he wore Nico's face, and she hated seeing that pain in the features of the man she loved.

"You wanted to continue to protect Venice even after your death," Geena said. "Venice would have chosen another Oracle, but you didn't want to trust that the next would be as capable as you were. Whatever the spell was that you used to banish the three Doges, it was tied to you, physically. Somehow—and you must have had help from members of the Council—you managed to preserve your heart, in order to keep the spell from ever breaking. But when we found the Chamber—"

Volpe's eyes flared with admiration. "I see why Nico is so profoundly in love with you. A formidable mind."

"You said Nico must have sensed you," Geena went on. "You meant down in the Chamber. I think you're right. Once we were inside, he was . . . not himself. When he dropped the urn—"

"He broke the spell," Volpe agreed, scratching at his forearm. "I attempted to restore the spell, gathering the elements necessary—"

"Including my blood."

Volpe glanced at her arm and nodded. "Regrettably. But it would have been worth it, had the spell worked."

"Why didn't it?"

"Caravello was already here, in Venice. The spell cannot keep someone from entering the city if they are already here. Given what Caravello said, we must assume Foscari and Aretino have returned as well."

Things clicked into place in Geena's mind, a memory surfacing.

"When Caravello came after us, you said that knife had the blood of the 'new Oracle' on it . . ."

Volpe's gaze flickered, and she saw danger in his eyes. But she pushed onward.

"But you cut me with that knife. Are you saying—"

He held up Nico's hand to show her a slice on the palm, already healing. "It had Nico's blood as well as yours. His mental power—what you call his 'touch'—may have guided him to me, but I believe there were other forces at work as well. I believe that Venice called to him. The city always chooses. Even throughout my long rest it chose successors, but it had no need of them as long as I endured. I believe that Nico is to be the new Oracle."

This was insane. Total madness. Her life had become a nightmare.

"You *believe?* Don't you know?" she asked.

Volpe traced his fingers along the rim of his coffee cup, not meeting her eyes. Hiding something. "Not yet. But the truth will reveal itself to all of us soon enough."

Geena knew if she pushed he would only shut her out. Whatever secrets he was hiding, she and Nico would learn them all eventually.

"You're arrogant as hell, but that doesn't make you right," she said. "You talk about the ambitions of these three Doges—and I don't understand how they're still alive—in such generalities. They're ruthless, but you've admitted you're just as ruthless. Even if you are this Oracle, I don't see how that makes you the good guy in all of this."

Volpe smiled, one corner of Nico's mouth lifting in something on the verge of a sneer. His eyes darkened with grim memory.

"I understand, Geena," the old magician said. He pushed his coffee cup aside and leaned closer to her, lowering his voice. "You want me to tell you that the Doges were evil, so you can feel better about helping me kill Caravello. So you can *trust* me. Well, let me assure you that you *cannot* trust me. If I must choose between your life and the preservation of my city, I will choose Venice. I must choose Venice. But evil? I can tell you about evil.

"In a time before the history of Venice had begun to be written, most of the tribes of the Earth had those amongst them who were different. Magicians, shaman, even gods—call them what you want. They were like us, but they weren't completely human. Some of the texts I've read claim that they were the offspring of demons who'd mated with humans, others the half-breed children of angels. I don't know the answer, only that these were the true magicians, who did not simply tap into the arcane energies of the world the way that I do, but who had that power innately within themselves.

"The Old Magicians were neither good nor evil, or they were not meant to be. They had wisdom and power and often kept themselves at a certain distance from the tribes with whom they lived, and from one another. Rarely would there be two of them together. Perhaps they were more like shepherds than anything else.

"They were immortal, inasmuch as their lives were longer than an ordinary man could imagine, and they could heal themselves of all but the most grievous wounds. They could die. In time, they all did. But to those around them they surely seemed immortal."

The waitress came and refilled Geena's cup and Volpe paused, staring at the woman, letting her see his irritation at the interruption. She didn't offer him a refill before she darted away, shooting them both a withering glance.

Despite the warmth lingering from the long summer day, Geena felt a chill deep enough that she warmed her hands on the cup.

"Even if I accepted this . . ." She almost called it a fairy tale, but stopped herself. There were enough ancient texts that referred, even if only tangentially, to magicians and gods, healers and shaman—and oracles, for that matter—that she could not brush it off so easily. Not after what she had experienced today. And she could not forget the visions she had shared, the parts of the past she had experienced through Nico's connection to Volpe.

"What do these Old Magicians have to do with the Doges?" she asked. "Are you saying that's why they're still alive? They're part of this ancient race?"

Volpe sneered, and this time there was no trace of a smile in it.

"It would be their fondest wish, but no. Not all of the Old Magicians remained so aloof and objective. There are many stories of them becoming corrupted, and among those, one of the ugliest tales is that of Akylis."

She nodded. "I've heard that name. Through Nico. I asked one of my colleagues about it and he mentioned Aquileia."

"Founded by Akylis," Volpe confirmed. "Or, at least, by his followers. Those who survived their worship of him. He began to see ordinary people as pets and playthings and he made himself a god amongst them."

He waved a hand in the air as though to brush his words away. "None of this matters. It is only history, and we must concern ourselves with the present. Akylis has been dead for millennia. The surviving Doges must be our concern."

Geena stared at him. "You're confusing the hell out of me."

Volpe leaned forward, locking eyes with her. For a moment she thought she could see Nico surfacing, but then his eyes narrowed and the old magician frowned, perhaps gathering his thoughts.

"Every city has a soul, a collective spirit of hopes and desires and needs that, in time, takes on a certain awareness. The Oracle is chosen by the city itself, and the bond between them is intimate and complete. You have been working to preserve the history of Venice, but I have it all inside of me, all its memories, from the magical to the mundane. The moment I became the Oracle of Venice, my mind was flooded with all that knowledge, but one thing stood out amongst the others. Before the city was truly born, when the only people here were fishermen who lived in crude huts in the marsh, a rare gathering of Old Magicians took place. It was a funeral, of sorts. They dug deep into what is now San Marco, more than one hundred feet down, casting spells to accomplish what men could not, holding back the water. At the bottom of this well, they built a dolmen—a tomb of standing stones—and there they lay to rest the remains of Akylis. He had become so corrupt, so evil, that these nearly immortal beings—usually above ordinary emotion—felt ashamed.

"They buried him there, and in time Venice rose above him. Akylis is dead. There is no awareness remaining in him. But his evil survives beneath the city, captured like the rancid gases inside a bloated, decaying corpse. Over the ages, many of those who have dabbled in magic in this city have touched this evil and been tainted by it, and throughout all of those many centuries it has been the duty of the Oracle to protect the city from those dark magicians. Only the Oracle can brush up against the evil trapped in the Well of Akylis without being tainted."

Geena sipped at her coffee, but did not take her eyes off Volpe. As he spoke, his voice almost mesmerizing, she had begun to really see him in that face, though the features were Nico's.

"That's what happened to the Doges," she said. "They delved into magic—"

"Their hearts were already dark with greed," Volpe said. "But, yes, they were tainted. It began with Caravello. Even before he became Doge he had already set his schemes in motion, sending cousins and uncles out of Venice, to the other great cities of the Mediterranean, with instructions to wheedle themselves into positions of influence. The family did the same, of course, in Venice. There were murders and blood sacrifices. But I heard every whisper of their conspiracy. Caravello wanted more than to be Doge of Venice. He wanted his family to take all of Europe, and perhaps beyond, one enchantment, one ritual, one murder at a time. And if that kind of black magic took the blood sacrifice of every man, woman, and child in Venice, he minded not at all, so long as his family continued its reign."

"Fuck's sake, why didn't you just kill him?" Geena asked, then blinked in surprise at the savagery of the sentiment.

"We fought a war of influence," Volpe said. "I did have some members of the family quietly arrested and secretly executed. But I couldn't kill the Doge without losing control of Venice. I needed to be in the position to protect the city, because even after I arranged to have the Council ban Caravello, I knew that the family would not surrender entirely. The war continued. I managed to keep them out of power for nearly two decades before Aretino became Doge. Even then I watched carefully, uncertain how far he would take it. But he followed the plan that Caravello had set in motion, becoming a minor magician himself, tapping into the evil power of Akylis, and I had to arrange for him to be driven from the city as well.

"Foscari was the last. Over the years after his banishment, I arranged for nearly every relative I could find to be killed. By then I had taken complete control of the Council of Ten and arranged to have them build an enormous crypt beneath a new school being erected in Dorsoduro. My influence did not reach beyond Venice, so there was nothing I could do about those outside the city. But I protected my—"

Geena held up a hand. "Wait. Stop."

Shaken from the reverie of memory, Volpe narrowed his eyes further. "What is it?"

Mind reeling, Geena took a breath to clear her head, trying to remember exactly what the waitress had told her at the pizzeria earlier in the day.

"A building collapsed today in Dorsoduro. A bunch of people were killed. Supposedly they found a massive tomb hidden beneath it."

Volpe stared at her, then turned away with a snarl of disgust. "I should have known."

"What?"

"I should have felt it," Volpe said. He looked out the window at the fading daylight. "I am less than alive, but more than dead. Not a ghost, but not a man. When you told me the Mayor had been murdered, it upset me that I had not already felt it. I am the Oracle of Venice. The soul of the city is bonded to my own. But since my awakening, now that I am also bonded to Nico, my connection to the city is muffled and unfocused. I should be able to feel them."

"Because you're the Oracle," Geena said, and it wasn't a question.

Volpe nodded thoughtfully. "They knew enough magic even when I banished them to hide their precise locations from me, but not their presence in the city. Perhaps now that Nico and I have begun to . . . accommodate each other, my rapport with the city will grow clearer.

"I never imagined that they had leached enough of the magic from Akylis' essence to keep themselves alive for this long, but perhaps the three of them worked together to reinforce what they had absorbed and what they had learned of magic. But now that they are back in Venice, they are already tapping into that evil repository beneath the city. They will sap all of the magic from it that they can. By killing Caravello though, we have bought ourselves some time."

Geena leaned back in her chair. "Time to do what? I mean, what is it that they're planning?"

"They will throw the city government into disarray, try to reclaim their old family properties—those still standing—and set old schemes in motion. The murder of the Mayor is a part of that, making the city council argue amongst themselves over who is really in charge of Venice. The destruction of that building in Dorsoduro incites chaos, draws the eyes of the city's authorities away from whatever else they might be doing in the shadows. There will be other assassinations. Already they will be moving lackeys and pawns into positions of influence."

"But what about the tombs of their relatives? Why would they expose the resting places of so many members of their family?" Geena asked.

"Perhaps simply to give the city something else to focus on, another distraction. Perhaps because they don't want their dead to be forgotten."

Something didn't sound right to Geena. "So they're just starting from scratch?" she said. "If what they wanted was to spread their influence across the Mediterranean, how will they accomplish that when all of their relatives have been dead for centuries?"

Volpe frowned, obviously troubled. "I don't know. But I am quite sure that we'll have the answer soon enough."

As she spoke, she scratched at the back of her hand again, and this time she winced and looked down to see a purplish-red sore.

What the hell? she thought. And then fear rippled through her and she looked up, thinking that somehow Volpe had done this to her, infected her with something. But when she saw the look in his eyes as he stared at the discolored, swollen blotch on her hand, she knew she was wrong. He knew what it was, but he hadn't done it.

"What?" she asked, her voice a rasp. "What is it?"

Her throat had been dry and a bit raw, but now as she swallowed, it actually hurt. She coughed softly into her fist.

Volpe looked down at his forearm. Where he'd been idly scratching, there were several of those sores.

"Bastard," Volpe sneered, but in his eyes—Nico's eyes—she saw fear.

"Tell me!" she snapped, too loud, drawing the attention of the other people in the little café. Twin girls eating lemon granita looked up at her. The barista fixing iced cappuccinos behind the counter gave an eye-roll and a shake of her head that showed her feelings about Americans.

Geena took in the entire scene in a single moment. But then Volpe was standing, his chair sliding back. He put his spoon into his coffee cup and followed it with Geena's, then stuffed both of their napkins into his pocket and shot her a hard look.

"Take your cup," he said, fury making his voice shake.

She wanted to ask why, but her imagination had already begun to supply answers that made her want to collapse into a fetal ball or scream or run or all of those things. In her entire life, she did not think she had ever stolen anything, but as Volpe swept past her she lifted her cup from the table and followed him out.

"Signora!" the barista yelled.

Geena heard a ruckus behind her, realized it must be the barista or a waitress coming after them, and ran through the open café door. With Volpe beside her, she fled along the alley and onto a stone bridge spanning a narrow canal. A shout came from behind, but they ran on.

Volpe coughed and she glanced at him to find that he had pulled Nico's shirt up to cover his mouth and nose. Her chest burned with the effort of running—exertion that should not have troubled her at all—and she felt her own cough building. She cleared her throat.

"Cover your mouth!" Volpe barked.

Breathless, shivering, they darted down an alley on the right, then took the first jog to the left and ducked into a doorway. For a long minute they only stood there, still covering their mouths, but soon it became clear that the barista had abandoned the pursuit.

Volpe stepped away from the recessed doorway. "Come."

"Where are we going?"

"Back to Caravello's corpse."

"But what if the police—"

"We've got to reach it before they do. Before anyone else is exposed."

Icy dread filled her. "Exposed to what?"

Nico's eyes narrowed, but then his expression softened and she saw that Volpe had retreated deeper into his mind, letting Nico come to the fore again. He faltered a moment, turning to stare at her, then glancing at the cup and spoons in his hand. He squeezed his eyes shut and then nodded decisively.

"Nico?" she said.

"Hurry, Geena. He can still save us."

"From what?"

Nico's face went slack, his gaze numb as he reached up to scratch his arm and then dropped his hand, picking up his pace.

"Contagion. Plague. Call it what you like. We've been infected, and we've got the plague, and we've got to stop it before it spreads."

They stood on the opposite side of the courtyard from Chiesa di San Rocco, watching warily for some sign that the murder of Giardino Caravello had been discovered. In the fading light of day, she could make out the blood that stained the cobblestones near the stairs. A spattered, broken trail led through the alley beside the church and up to the side door of the small taverna whose owner had abandoned it after the last flood.

"No police yet," Geena said quietly.

"So no one saw us," Nico replied, and coughed softly into his shirt.

The little church square was still quiet. One old woman swept the steps of a small ladies' clothing shop. They waited until she had gone back inside before starting across the courtyard.

"I just had the ugliest thought," Geena said. "What if a cat licked it? Or . . . or rats? That's how it all starts, right?"

"Whatever this contagion might be, it's not going to follow any rules," Nico replied. "Volpe has retreated now. It exhausts him, taking control." He coughed, a wet rattle in his throat. "But I gleaned enough from him to know that this isn't any ordinary sickness. It's some kind of dark magic, some kind of booby trap or fail-safe that Caravello had running through his veins."

"But it's been barely an hour," Geena said. "Not even plague kills that fast."

Nico glanced anxiously at her. "We just have to pray. Otherwise . . ."

He let that hang in the air between them. Neither of them wanted to think about "otherwise." They hurried over the cobblestones, Geena feeling a prickling on the back of her neck that might have been a result of her rising fever but felt like the eyes of hidden observers. She shook it off as paranoia. The feeling had none of the skin-crawling urgency and certainty that she had felt when Caravello had been stalking her. But how strange she thought the two of them must look, covering their faces and carrying coffee cups in their hands . . .

"What now?" she muttered as they approached the bloodstains . . .

. . . and felt Nico touch her mind. His fear blazed brightly, along with a fierce love for her. He was more frightened of losing her than he was of dying himself, and the raw intensity of that love nearly brought her to tears. God, why had this happened to them? They had been so happy.

And will be again, Nico thought, sending the words to her.

Lowering the shirt from over her mouth, Geena glanced around the church square. *You believe that?*

I have to.

She nodded, turning to him. "We need Volpe."

The old Venetian, the magician—whatever he was—had retreated into Nico's mind. The question of what exactly he was lingered in Geena's thoughts and she had seen it in Nico's as well. If there were such things as ghosts, that was one thing, but Volpe was obviously something else. To possess the body of a man five hundred years after your own death . . . Volpe had power. But exerting it exhausted him, and he had been silent in Nico's mind since they had fled the café. Geena had no sense of him in there. He had left Nico with a firm impression of what must be done, but they needed Volpe now.

Nico nodded. He took a deep breath and closed his eyes. Whatever Nico did to attempt to summon Volpe, Geena heard nothing in her own mind. But then Nico gave a sharp intake of breath that became a hacking cough and he brought a hand to his mouth to cover it. And when he lowered his hand, his expression had changed again. She knew she was looking at Zanco Volpe, hiding behind Nico's face. And Volpe looked tired.

"Are we being watched?" Volpe asked wearily.

Geena shook her head. "I don't think so. What can you do? We can't just leave the blood out here if it's infected."

"No," Volpe agreed. "We can't."

He began to turn, but then shifted his gaze back to her. Geena did not have to ask what he was looking at. New sores had appeared on her arms and legs and one on her left cheek. More had erupted on Nico's flesh as well.

"It's moving so quickly," Volpe said.

"Too quickly for us to . . . to have a chance?" Geena asked. She had been about to say "survive," but couldn't bring herself to use the word.

"This is insidious magic," Volpe said. "Caravello's blood exposed us to this infection. I could almost admire it—the assured destruction of whoever might be responsible for your own murder—but this won't only kill us. This is a hex-plague. Thousands could die, and all out of spite."

For the first time, Geena understood the loyalty Volpe had to his city. The old magician could be cruel and brutal in his efforts to preserve and protect Venice, and his arrogance was monumental. But she no longer doubted that the Doges were the enemy here. They were putrid creatures. Only a truly evil man could conceive of such an abhorrent act as Caravello's fail-safe contagion.

Volpe handed her his coffee cup and their two spoons but otherwise ignored her. He glanced around once, then thrust his arms downward, palms open and fingers splayed as though he were warming his hands over a fire. His fingers contorted, sketching odd symbols in the air, and he whispered something she could not hear.

The bloodstained cobblestones burst into flame. Geena gasped and stepped back as fire raced along the spilled blood and flashed up from each of the splotches they had left behind when moving the Doge's corpse to the abandoned taverna. It lasted only an instant, not much longer than the fire from the hand of some stage magician—a parlor trick.

But what Volpe had done was no parlor trick. The cobblestones were not scorched at all, but they were clean—cleaner, perhaps, than they had been in generations—and no trace remained of the blood of Giardino Caravello and the sickness it carried.

Nico staggered coming through the side door of the taverna. "So fast," he muttered.

Geena followed him in. He watched her close the door and said a silent prayer that no one had seen them. But his prayers weren't only for their benefit. If the police came and caught them before the work they needed to do here had been completed, all of Venice might be in danger. All of Venice, and far beyond.

She winced in pain as she coughed, and Nico felt her pain as his own. He tried to soothe her with his mind, but it was of no use. He could let her feel the depth of his love for her, the fullness of his heart, but he could not hide his own fear.

Geena's thoughts were clear. *We just need to focus. Please. If there's any chance to save ourselves, we have to hurry.*

Nico nodded. Together they slid a table against the door to prevent anyone else from coming in. The broken lock would be easily discovered, but at least this would gain them seconds in which to attempt escape, or finish the task at hand.

With Geena so close, he could not avoid looking at the purplish-red swelling under her neck and the wet, leaking sores on her face. He bit his lip and forced himself to focus.

Caravello's body lay behind the bar, just as they had left it. The bloody trail on the floor had vanished, cleansed by the fire Volpe had summoned, but the corpse remained. Now, though, the flesh was pustulent and raw, and the dead Doge's throat had swollen massively and turned black. They set the coffee cups and spoons and napkins on the floor beside the body.

"I don't understand," Geena said. "If the Doges want Venice, why would Caravello do this, knowing it might kill everyone in the city?"

"I don't know," Nico said. "Maybe it's a side effect of accessing Akylis' power? His evil? They're contaminated."

"Maybe," Geena said. "Or maybe he didn't even trust his cousins. Maybe the fail-safe was so the other Doges couldn't betray him. We don't even know if the others are also carrying it."

Nico started to reply, but choked on a cough, which turned into a hoarse, seal-like bark that bent him double. When at last he caught his breath, he spat blood onto the floor.

Geena stared at him. "Nico, your eyes."

He reached up to touch them and his fingers came away wet, not with tears but blood. Geena reached a hand toward his face. Nico felt his legs weaken and he collapsed to his knees, blackness swirling in his peripheral vision.

Volpe, he thought, turning his focus inward. The ancient presence remained, but diminished. Nico could barely feel Volpe's awareness within him. *We're going to die if you don't wake up and do something. And what of you? Will you die without a host?*

Nico felt Volpe stirring, felt him rush upward, stepping forward to take control once again. But even as he did, he sensed barriers in place now between his mind and the old magician's. Once again, Volpe was hiding something.

❖

Geena saw it happen. Still on his knees, Nico sagged further, his head lolling onto his chest. Then his head snapped up, eyes narrowed, and though the fear remained it was no longer Nico's fear, but Volpe's. The shape of the mouth was different, and the merciless curl of the lip had returned.

Volpe looked up at her. Then he reached out for a nearby chair and used it to pull himself to his feet.

"Get me a knife. And hurry."

Chills racked her body, cold sweat dripping down her back and between her breasts, but Geena did as he asked. The kitchen had been stripped of most of its valuable equipment, but a drawer near the sink in back held a handful of old knives and wooden spoons and a ladle. She grabbed one of the knives and stumbled away from the counter, accidentally pulling out the drawer, which crashed to the floor. Geena barely noticed as she staggered back through the door into the restaurant proper.

Light fixtures were dark. Ceiling fans did not turn. Dust covered the room. Over the stale smell of old beer, she could smell the stink of rotting flesh and knew the smell came from her own body as much as Caravello's.

How did I come to this? she thought. *None of this is . . .*

Real? Possible? She shoved away the denials. The life she had known had felt strong and vibrant to her, but in truth it had been fragile and ephemeral. She had to tell herself that it could be reclaimed; that it waited for her, just out of reach. But if she ever hoped to have that life back, she and Nico first had to live, and she would do whatever was necessary to make certain of that. To protect him, above all.

Nico—no, Volpe—pulled out a chair and sat down, the legs scraping on the dusty wooden floor.

The knife, he thought.

She swayed to a halt, brought up short. *Get the fuck out of my head.*

He could use Nico's ability after all. Or perhaps he and Nico were working together for now.

We are, Nico said, reading her thoughts. *We have to.*

Geena erupted in a fit of coughing, but in its midst she managed to give Volpe the dulled blade. He took her hand and sliced the blade across her palm. She tried to scream but only coughed hard, black spots swimming at the corners of her eyes.

"Bastard," she said, clutching her bleeding fist against her chest.

But then an image rose in her mind, of the Council of Ten slicing their own palms as part of some spell of Volpe's, and she knew this was magic. Blood magic.

Volpe held up his own hand, Nico's hand, and cut the palm, blood running down the blade of the knife. He held his fist above the splash of Geena's blood already on the floorboards. For a moment he seemed to sag again, his eyelids drooping, and she thought he might pass out. His breath rattled with phlegm.

"Wake up!" he said, and it was Nico's voice, Nico's panicked gaze.

Replaced immediately by Volpe, blinking and shaking himself. He looked at Geena. "Paper? An old tablecloth? Did you see anything in the kitchen?"

She shook her head and hugged herself, shivering with the chill of her fever. Pain had begun to make a fist in her gut, and she knew that to speak would be to give it voice.

"Behind the bar, then. A rag. A napkin. Anything?"

"Maybe," she managed to say.

Geena tried to rise and her legs went out from under her and she sprawled on the floor, little trickles of their blood spreading toward her, where her cheek lay on the coolness of the wood.

"I'll find something," Volpe said. "I need his eyes, anyway."

"His . . . eyes . . . ?"

"They saw us in health. All the better to restore us, having those images."

Taking a guttural, rasping breath, he staggered to his feet and stalked across the room. She watched him go to the bar and vanish behind it. When the noises began—wet, squelching sounds—she closed her eyes, but that only made it worse, made the sounds clearer and her imagination more vivid.

She gagged, managed to keep herself from throwing up, but then began to cough. Blood and bile filled her mouth and she spit it onto the floor, but the coughing continued until the black spots at the edges of her field of vision darkened and spread, and then the whole world tilted and . . .

. . . *How long?* she thought as she opened her eyes. She knew she'd been out, but for how long? If Nico heard her thoughts—or Volpe, for that matter—neither of them replied.

She tried to lift her head and the darkness swept in again and she was . . .

. . . blinking . . . *careful this time.* What did she hear? Murmuring, so softly, like whispered sins coming from inside a confessional.

Taking a deep breath, she opened her eyes wide and gave herself a second to focus. Nico sat cross-legged on the floor perhaps four feet from her, on the other side of the blood he—no, Volpe—had taken from both of them. She blinked, studying his face. She knew it intimately, had traced the lines of that face with her fingers and her lips, had gazed into those eyes and thrown herself open to the man.

Tears of blood streaked Nico's face. The disease, taking its toll.

But it wasn't Nico. Exhausted as he must be, Volpe did not want to die for eternity. With horrible tenacity, he seemed to be hanging on inside of Nico, propping up the body around him like a boy in his father's old suit. The body seemed to be shrinking in upon itself. The blotches on his throat had gone black now and spread, and his neck had bloated hideously.

A bar rag lay spread out on the floor in front of him and with one blood-wetted finger, he dabbed and scrawled something she could not see from this angle.

"What is your name?" Volpe gasped. "The name you were born with?"

Though she was confused and curious, she did not have the strength to ask why he needed to know.

"Geena Louise . . . Hodge."

Volpe nodded. "Geena Louise Hodge. Nicolo Tomasino Lombardi."

He dipped his finger in the blood again and again, smearing the cloth. A gelatinous mush quivered in the midst of the spilled blood, and it took her a moment to understand that these were Caravello's eyes.

She hadn't the strength to vomit.

The murmuring, the whispers, were coming from Nico's lips, and it took her a moment to realize that Volpe was chanting some sort of rite. Spellcraft, she remembered he called it. Meant to heal them.

But the darkness encroached again. She fought to stay conscious.

Nico, she thought, an abyss of sorrow opening up to swallow her. *I think I'm going to die now.*

His reply was weak, but he was there. *We live or die as one.*

"Quiet, you fools," Volpe growled. He took a rattling breath and continued his strange song.

Geena saw the rats before she heard the skittering of their claws upon the wood. They skittered toward Volpe as though dragged upon strings. When they reached him, they waited, quivering and squealing but frozen in place.

"What are you doing?" Geena asked, coughing. "Did you call them?"

"Our lives are fading," Volpe rasped. "If we're to survive . . . we have to steal life from elsewhere."

When he had finished scrawling on the bar rag, he reached out a shaking hand and picked up one of the rats. It did not scratch or bite; it gave no resistance save those screams. Volpe placed it in the bloody mess on the floor, pressed the point of the knife to its belly, and slit it open.

Geena closed her eyes and drifted again . . .

. . . disoriented, eyes fluttering open, she saw that the second rat was already dead. Small mercies; she had not had to witness it. The smell of blood filled her nostrils and she felt it sticky on her cheek. It had trickled along the wood and pooled beneath her head.

Volpe sat unmoving, slumped down upon himself. If not for the phlegmy rattling in his throat, she would have thought he had died.

Dying, Geena thought. *The three of us are dying.*

Even as despair overcame her and bloody tears began to clot her eyes, she saw Nico's body twitch. One of them—she no longer knew if it was Nico or Volpe—raised his head. He lifted up the bar rag and began the chant again, though now it was little more than a low gurgle. She could see the rag now, arcane letters and strange sigils scrawled in blood upon it.

He dropped it onto the mess on the floor and blood began to soak into the fabric.

"I will not die," he snarled, even as he slid onto his side, blood pouring from his ears and nostrils. He choked, coughed, and then reached out a hand, holding his palm open above the cloth and the words and the death he had carefully prepared.

As before in the courtyard, it all burst into flame, an instantaneous eruption of fire that consumed the entire mess. The blood that had trickled toward her ignited, flames leaping up and racing toward the pool of blood beneath her face.

Geena tried to scream through her ragged, swollen throat, and a wave of pain crashed through her.

Then, once again, the darkness took her.

CHAPTER 13

THE SMELL HIT HER BEFORE SHE WAS EVEN FULLY AWAKE—A rancid stew of odors, of blood and death and illness. Geena recoiled as she drew herself up to a sitting position, her face and hair tacky with blood, her clothes stinking of disease. She glanced around the abandoned taverna in the golden gloom cast by street lamps outside and saw Nico lying six feet away.

"Nico?"

Her head throbbed dully as she rose to her feet, surprised to find she had the strength to stand. She reached up to touch her throat and found the pain had vanished, along with the swelling. Dried blood crusted on her face and around her ears and had stained her shirt, but when she experimented tentatively with clearing her throat, she found it clear.

"No way," she whispered to herself in English.

Grinning in spite of the stench, she stepped around the bloody, scorched spot on the floor where Volpe had done his spell. Geena went to her knees beside Nico's body and shook him.

"Wake up."

He lolled his head with her jostling and she saw that the black swelling of his throat had vanished completely. Like her, Nico had dark bloodstains soaked into his shirt and traces where blood had run from his nose and eyes and ears. Whatever Volpe had done, he had made it just in time.

Nico opened his right eye just a slit before blinking and opening both of them. He ran a hand over his face and wetted his lips with his tongue like a drunk waking from a bender.

"What . . . what time is it?" he asked.

"I'm not sure. I just woke up myself, but . . . It's night."

She let the words trail off. They had been unconscious in here for hours. Volpe might have removed all evidence of the murder of Caravello out in the church square, but she still felt as though it had been a miracle that no one had discovered them. Luck and timing.

"God, the smell," he said, wrinkling his nose in disgust.

Geena laughed.

Nico stared at her. "What, in any of this, is funny?"

She dropped to the floor, taking both of his hands in hers. "You're you."

Nico blinked, glanced around curiously as though waiting for Volpe to usurp his control of his body again. When nothing happened he ran a hand through his hair and turned to smile at her.

"So it would appear." He took a deep breath, his smile faltering. *He's still in here, though. Aren't you, Volpe?*

Geena held her breath, listening for a reply. Nico had shared the thought with her purposefully and they both waited for Volpe to acknowledge it. When nothing happened, she let herself hope for a moment before Nico brushed it off with a wave of his hand.

"He's still here. I feel him. Resting. But for now, I'm me."

When she had first woken, Geena had been slightly disoriented. Now she began to recall the details of the ritual Volpe had conducted. There had been rats and death and chanting and blood. She glanced down at the palm he had sliced open and blinked in astonishment before looking up at Nico.

He actually healed us, she thought.

Nico nodded grimly. *He needs us.*

"He needs *you*," she said aloud.

"As a host. But he knows that if anything happens to you, I'll fight him."

"But that fire," Geena said. *I thought we were both dead.*

"No. It was cleansing flame, the same as he used out on the cobblestones. It purifies, but only burns what it is intended to burn."

"It would have been nice if he had warned me," she said, though she knew that in the condition they had both been in, it would have been difficult for Volpe to say anything to her at all.

Nausea twisted through her stomach when she thought about how close they had come to death, and the feeling of the sickness clenched inside her. For as long as she lived she would never forget the panic and helplessness of the disease that had ravaged her and brought her to the brink of death in a matter of hours.

"We can't stay here," Nico said. "We've been lucky so far—"

"Lucky?"

"Perhaps not. Even so, every moment we remain here, we are tempting fate. Eventually someone will notice the broken lock on the side door, or pass near enough to the building to smell the stink of Caravello's remains."

Geena shuddered. The stench made her stomach churn, but she doubted anyone passing by would smell it, at least not yet. Much as she wanted to get away from that stink, she knew they had to clean up first.

"Look at me," she said. "Look at yourself. The owner of the building will have turned the water off. There may be enough in the toilet tanks to wash the blood from our faces, but our clothes are stained. We have to be careful not to be seen like this."

Nico glanced at the side door and the table they—well, she and Volpe—had bumped up against it. Even if she did not feel the worry coming off him, she would have seen it in his eyes.

"What about Caravello? Do we just leave the body here?"

They both looked at the bar, knowing the Doge's corpse lay behind it. *His eyes . . .* Geena thought. Nico glanced away, responding neither in thought nor word. She could feel that he shared her revulsion, but he also would not condemn Volpe for defiling the corpse, since it had saved their lives.

"He might not be as evil as the Doges, but he's not your friend," she said sharply.

Nico glanced up. "I know that."

"Do you?"

"After what he's done to my life? To our lives?"

She hesitated, then nodded, feeling the truth in his heart. This was the closest they would come to an argument. They knew each other too well for the kinds of misunderstandings that disrupted many relationships.

Cleansing fire, Nico thought, and she saw an image in her mind of the building going up in flames.

Geena stared at him, unnerved. "Isn't that a little excessive? It's just the body we need to get rid of."

Nico went to the window and looked out. "We should get rid of any evidence we were ever here."

"Without a body, it's only trespassing," she said. "Let's not add arson to our crimes."

Nico hesitated, then nodded in agreement. They wouldn't burn the building, but they did need to destroy Caravello's corpse to erase any trace of contagion. Geena glanced over at the bar again, imagining the eyeless corpse hidden behind it, perhaps still tainted with the plague.

There would have to be fire.

You cannot stay together.

Nico stood outside the taverna's bathroom, keeping the door propped open to let the lamplight beyond the windows filter in while Geena used a swatch torn from an old apron they had found in the kitchen to wash the blood from her face. She dipped the rag into the toilet tank and swabbed at her cheeks and her throat, careful not to streak the porcelain. There was no way for them to clean up after themselves entirely, but they were trying to be as careful as possible.

He loved to watch her move. Even now, filthy as they were, he took great pleasure in the arch of her back and the swell of her breasts beneath her shirt.

Geena turned to smile at him, hearing or sensing his thoughts. Nico had created such a powerful connection between them that sometimes he could not hide his thoughts from her even if he wanted to.

"He's awake, isn't he?" she asked.

Nico nodded. "For the past few minutes. He is not very strong yet, but he is here, yes."

"He's right, you know," she said, dropping the rag into the toilet tank.

"About what?" Nico asked. He had cleaned himself up already.

"He said we can't stay together. He's right." She replaced the top of the tank and stepped out of the bathroom to join him. "I hate it as much as you do, but if we're ever going to get Volpe out of our lives, we have to help him figure out if the other Doges are here and what they're planning. You and he will have to work together. He'll have ideas about what to do next. But there are things I can find out that you can't, starting with the building collapse in Dorsoduro and the tomb under it. Obviously the Doges have figured out that it's where Volpe put their dead relatives, but why knock the building down? Just to expose the tomb? To make sure those deaths are not forgotten? Or is there more to it?"

Nico hesitated, then nodded. He pulled her into an embrace, kissed her temple, and then stepped back to regard her grimly.

"Whatever you can learn will help," Nico said. "But as far as I'm concerned, you have something more important to do. I want to have a life for us to go back to when this is all over. You need to do whatever it takes to make sure it isn't in ruins. You've got to check in with Tonio, look in on the Biblioteca project. Don't cut the strings that connect us to our lives or I fear we'll be swept away."

Geena kissed him softly. "I won't let that happen."

"Good," Nico said. "But if the other Doges are here, and Caravello found you, they may be able to as well. You have to be very careful. You shouldn't go back to your apartment."

Geena frowned as she considered this, then shook her head.

"No," she said. "If Caravello followed me, it was from the Biblioteca. It was the project that brought him there, the shattering of Volpe's heart and the opening of the Chamber of Ten. We don't have any reason to think that he knew where I lived. Never mind that this is all happening so quickly. It doesn't make sense to think Aretino and Foscari would know anything about me, if the other two are even here."

Nico did not like it, but he could see she would not be dissuaded.

"If you see or even sense anyone following you or anything out of place at your apartment, tell Tonio and Domenic and the others the whole story. They might not believe you, but they'll keep you safe for a time. Long enough to finish this, I hope."

"Where will you go?" she asked.

"I suppose we'll keep moving," he said, feeling Volpe waking up further, growing restless inside of him. "Make sure you have your cell phone. Call me if you learn anything, and I'll do the same. But if, for any reason, we can't reach each other, we will meet on the north side of Rialto Bridge tomorrow night at eleven."

"Agreed."

"Meanwhile, be careful." Nico reached out and cupped her cheek in his hand, then bent to kiss her softly, ignoring the lingering stink of disease on her breath, just as she must be doing in return.

I wish you could just come with me, Nico thought.

Geena touched his hand and gently pulled it away. "I can't. We need to know what's happening with that tomb. And you're right. By now Tonio will be furious with me. I need to get myself out of hot water and try to smooth things over for you, too."

"Is that even possible? As far as the rest of the team is concerned, I stabbed you."

"Let me worry about that," she said, walking over to a window. "Besides, I'm more concerned about the fact that they reported the attack. If we want to have a future in this city, I've got to start with the police."

Caravello's corpse burned like the newspaper Geena's father had always used to start fires when she was a girl, crumbling up the movie section or the real estate pages and shoving them under the logs before setting them alight. They'd caught quickly, the edges flaring orange and red with rising flames, and then they would ignite with crackling, hungry fire.

Her heart pounded as she watched the flames burn away the ancient Venetian's clothing and flesh as if it were nothing more than yellowed papyrus.

"We've got to go," she said, reaching out to tug on Nico's wrist. "Someone will see."

But in the darkness the fire cast dancing shadows on his face and she could see in that smile and those narrowed, furtive eyes that Nico was absent again, and Volpe had taken over.

"Cleansing fire," he whispered.

She squeezed his wrist. "If we're caught—"

Volpe shot her a dark look that reminded her that should they be discovered here, it would not be them who were in danger, but whoever had the misfortune to attempt to interfere.

"We won't be caught," Volpe assured her.

"If they *are* already in Venice, Foscari and Aretino will be looking for Caravello by now," Geena reminded him. "What if they've tracked him here? What if they're out there in the square right now, waiting for us?"

The old magician turned and glared at her with Nico's eyes, then looked at the side door through which they had originally entered. With a wave of his hand, not even looking at the corpse, he doused the flames. The fire crackled and popped and burned down to cinders in the space of seconds, and all that remained of Caravello were black ashes.

"This way," Volpe said, leading her through the kitchen.

"Afraid?" Geena asked, both genuinely curious and taunting.

At the thick metal door at the back of the kitchen, he spun to sneer at her. "Of what would happen to my city if they should catch me unprepared, if they should destroy me? Of course I am."

Volpe passed a hand in front of the lock and she heard it click as the deadbolt drew back. The man would never need a key to any door. He glanced out into the narrow space between the taverna and the darkened bookstore next door.

"And so should you be," he said, and then he slipped out.

Geena followed, pulling the door quietly shut behind her. To the right, the canal ran by, but Volpe hurried along the alley to the left, pausing to make sure they weren't being watched.

"Why?" she whispered as she caught up to him. "Because you're the lesser of two evils?"

"The Doges would control every breath taken by the people of this city. They would corrupt and kill and enslave. There would be a great deal of blood; the Mayor is only the beginning. And while they might do all of this in secrecy, people would still be dead. Those whose hearts continued to beat would live only at the whim of these devils. And they would spread their cruelty and influence across Europe and beyond. Am I the lesser of two evils? I am the Oracle of Venice. The rest is for you to decide. If it helps you to focus, though, consider this: as long as this is *my* city, you get to live."

Volpe stepped out onto the cobblestoned street and walked north, ambling along as if he had not a care in the world. The time had come for them to part ways, but Geena stared after him for several seconds before turning south and heading for home, shuddering as those final words echoed in her mind.

Geena stood beside a narrow canal and tried to breathe through her mouth to avoid inhaling the stink from the water. All of the smaller waterways in Venice were rank with human waste and gasoline spill-off from the thousands of small boats that plied her canals, but various factors mitigated the smell. The tides swept in twice a day to attempt a cleansing they never quite managed. The breeze and the temperature also played a part, but there were some places in the city that seemed to stink ferociously no matter what the variables.

From the darkness just beyond the reach of a lamppost, she stared at the grimy, deteriorating façade of one of the city's police stations. The stink here was especially strong, and the irony attached to that observation did not escape her. The Italian government and all associated authorities were so rife with corruption that people had long ago accepted the fact as immutable. Payoffs to the right officials in sufficient amounts could achieve almost any desired result. And yet in Geena's experience, day-to-day business in Venice proceeded in the same fashion as that of other cities. The police kept the peace and tried to protect the public to the best of their ability. Of course, it would have been much simpler if the Venice police never did their jobs at all.

Going in, she thought, unsure if Nico could hear her, or even where he might be now. They had parted ways nearly two hours ago, and she could no longer sense his touch at all. Either he had traveled far from her, or he was purposefully keeping himself hidden. Or Volpe was. It was probably a smart decision, but that did nothing to take the sting out of it.

She crossed the dingy stone bridge that led to an alley that ran between the police station and a small hotel that seemed to have frozen in time during the 1950s. Small boats moored at the canal door of the police station and, as she passed, two uniformed officers came out onto the landing and dropped down into one of them, grim-faced and tired-looking.

Geena took a deep breath and went in through the alley door, which for civilians would be the main door, she supposed. The foyer had old benches with cracked leather seats and a thick barrier of glass or plastic—bulletproof, no doubt, and perhaps explosive-resistant as well—separating her from the two officers who sat on the other side, both of them with phones clutched against their ears, snapping off instructions.

Deeper inside the building she could see cubicle dividers and desks, but other than the two men in the front she saw only a handful of people. A woman peered at a computer screen, madly typing away at the keyboard, and two men in suits talked quietly in the back, worried expressions on their faces.

"Excuse me," Geena said in Italian.

The two cops on their phones ignored her, barking in rapid-fire Italian, reporting the location of various officers and detectives and, in some cases, ordering their deployment to other locations.

Geena took a breath and waited patiently. For perhaps the hundredth time since waking on the floor of that abandoned taverna, she took mental stock of her condition. When she had left there she had rushed back to her apartment, taking a water taxi, too impatient to wait for the bus across the canal. In a taxi there was only the driver to see her bloodstained shirt and smell the lingering odor of sickness on her.

She had showered quickly but thoroughly, and afterward she had stared at herself in the mirror over the sink. The slash on her palm had healed, yes, but so had the wound from where Volpe had stabbed her shoulder. It ached in a hollow, distant fashion, the way her left knee sometimes did in the winter, but there was no longer a wound there, nor any mark at all. Even the small scar on her chin—earned at the age of two from a fall on brick steps—had vanished. The magic that Volpe had worked to purge them of the contagion had apparently done much more.

"Excuse me," Geena said again, her tone sharper.

This time both cops glanced up at her, though more in irritation than assistance. One of them actually turned away from her to continue his conversation. Geena had pulled her hair back into a ponytail and put on a clean white crenellated top and black Capri pants, trying to look presentable, but though she spoke Italian, all they saw when they looked at her was an American. No matter how fluent she might be, they heard it in her voice, saw it in her face.

"I'm not a tourist," she muttered, almost to herself.

The officer still facing her arched an eyebrow in apparent amusement. He had gray hair and thick, wiry eyebrows and a ruddy face flushed from a lifetime of alcoholic indulgence, but when he hung up the phone and looked at her, he had a certain charm.

"How can I help you, Signorina?"

"I wanted to clear up a misunderstanding," she said. "A crazy thing happened. One of my colleagues has been accused of assaulting me—well, stabbing me, actually—and I would like to speak with someone about giving a statement."

The officer's eyes had widened when she mentioned stabbing, and now he gazed at her dubiously. One of those thick eyebrows arched upward, but the phone rang before he could speak and he held up a finger to indicate she should wait while he answered it.

He gave curt replies to the phone inquiries, something about a press conference in the morning, and when he hung up, the phone rang again almost immediately. This time he ignored it, muttering something to the younger, black-haired officer, whose only reply was an arrogant glance.

"You don't look like you've been stabbed," said the officer. He stood up to get a better look at her and she could read his name tag: Pendolari.

"That's what I'm trying to say. I wasn't."

"But someone filed a police report saying you were?" Officer Pendolari asked. "Why would anyone do that?"

Geena hoped her sheepish smile was convincing. "My colleague and I are . . . involved. We had an altercation in front of some co-workers. They're not very pleased with him and I'm sure they think they are helping me by trying to get him in trouble—"

"They could get in trouble for filing a false police report," Officer Pendolari said, wiry brows knitting.

"Oh no. I wouldn't want that. I just . . . I'd like the whole thing to go away."

The phone kept ringing. Past the cubicles in back she could see two men in suits, detectives or ranking officers, perhaps, leaning over the woman who had sat back from her computer to show them something. They must have had a lead on a case, for one started shouting orders immediately and the other snatched up the phone from the woman's desk.

"Listen, what's your name?"

"Geena Hodge."

Pendolari spread his arms wide to indicate the nearly empty police station and the hectic pace of the night.

"When I have a chance, Geena, I'll see what I can find and I'll make a note that you came in. Someone may want to talk to you, but do not be surprised if you never hear a word about it. You must know that the Mayor's been murdered—"

"Of course. I'd heard—"

"Between that and the disaster in Dorsoduro, well, you can imagine what it's like for us right now. If no one is pressing charges against this man, I suspect it will go away, just as you hope."

The dark-haired officer slammed down his phone at last and picked up the other, his displeasure evident.

Pendolari smiled apologetically. "And now . . ."

Geena nodded, gesturing toward the phones. "Yes, yes, of course. And thank you."

She hurried back out into the night, wondering if the Venice police would have bothered to follow up on her stabbing even if she hadn't just gone in and lied to them. The Mayor's murder and that building collapse would be getting worldwide media coverage and the higher-ups would be worried about their jobs and the image of the department. If she could persuade Tonio not to press charges against Nico, maybe it really would just go away, and there would be one less thing for them to worry about if they ever got their lives back.

With every police officer in Venice trying to solve the Mayor's murder, a little bloodletting at the Biblioteca would be the last thing they wanted to focus on, particularly if the supposed victim denied it had ever happened.

You could do almost anything in Venice this week and they'd barely notice, she thought as she crossed back over the crumbling stone bridge. Halfway across, she faltered, glancing back at the police station and wondering just how true that might be, and how much the theory would be tested.

She needed to talk to Tonio and find out what she could about the tomb in Dorsoduro, never mind doing as Nico had asked and making sure they both had a life to return to when this was all over. And maybe whatever she learned about the building collapse would be moot. A part of her—a willingly naïve part—hoped that it would all be over by the time she and Nico reconnected, that Volpe would have found the other two Doges and . . . *killed them, don't hide from it.* . . before they were reunited.

Geena just had to hold her life and their shared world together until then.

Are you sure this is a good idea? Nico thought, peering into his own mind, trying to get a sense of what Volpe had planned. All the old magician had said was that they would be searching for Foscari and Aretino, the other two Doges he had banished from Venice.

There are other ways to search, but it would be foolish not to begin with a more direct approach, Volpe whispered in his mind.

"Direct approach?" Nico asked. "If they're waiting for me, we might both be killed by your 'direct approach.' "

Though for the moment he had control over his own body, he could feel Volpe smile inside.

Then you should make at least an attempt at stealth, don't you think?

They had achieved a kind of fluidity in their sharing of Nico's body, an intuitive flow of thought and control. Nico gave Volpe the cooperation he desired so that the magician could rest—playing puppeteer with Nico's body exhausted him—and in return, Volpe would keep him and Geena alive, and leave them be as soon as he had destroyed Aretino and Foscari.

Nico would have expected it to be difficult to cede command of his own flesh to an outside force, but found it simple enough to retreat within himself. It was an almost meditative state. He did not like the intrusion, the constant presence of Volpe there in his mind, observing his thoughts and actions, but he could endure it.

He paused in front of a small restaurant, raised voices coming from within. A cheer rose up and he wondered what had caused it, a rush of loneliness filling him. He and Domenic had often crowded into this bar with dozens of others to watch soccer games on the television hanging above the bar. Were they cheering a goal in there now, or some feat of alcoholic indulgence? The situation with Volpe and the Doges had to be dealt with, but in some ways he thought Geena's mission the more vital. Without her, the life he had led before descending into the Chamber of Ten would be forever out of his reach.

Do not even think about her, Volpe said in his thoughts.

Nico clenched his fists in anger, but he had no one to hit. The magician was right. They did not know the extent of the Doges' spellcraft, so for the moment it was better if he did not reach out to Geena with his thoughts. Still, it made him all the lonelier.

Stealth? he thought.

It might be wise.

All right, then.

Nico hesitated. His apartment was not far from here, two blocks up and through a narrow alley into a hidden garden courtyard that almost made up for the shabbiness of the musty old building. But that would be the approach that anyone else would take, so he backtracked past the restaurant—leaving the noise of the bar behind—and turned onto a street whose broken gutters slanted down just enough to let rainwater and whatever else flooded into them run the three blocks to the lagoon.

Past a small pharmacy, its green and white light burning though the place was dark, he hugged close to the buildings and watched every doorway and street corner for signs of hidden observers. A small trattoria had been defaced with an obscenity scrawled on the stone wall beside the glass door.

He darted into a side alley that ran for blocks behind the buildings. The stink of piss and garbage had seeped into the brick and cobblestones. Rats scurried behind a row of dented trash cans. Some damn fool had parked a motorcycle behind the service doors of a small apartment building, heavy chains around the tires and looped to a grate in the street.

Where are you going? Volpe wondered.

Nico ignored him. *Why the stealth?* he asked instead. *Isn't there a spell you can use to find them? If they can sense you—*

Were I still alive I could have found them by touching the ground or a stone in any wall and thinking about them. But my bond with the city is frayed. For the moment, at least.

Are you sure they're not just hiding, somehow? Nico asked. *You've been dead for centuries while they've been out there together, learning more magic. They managed to pool the power they leached from Akylis enough to keep themselves alive this long. Is it really impossible they've found a way to make themselves invisible to you?*

A ripple of unease went through Volpe. The old magician did not like the question.

I do not know the extent of their magic, Volpe replied. *But that is why we have come here. They would have investigated the Chamber of Ten to discover what happened to disrupt the spell of Exclusion, to see if anything remained of me there. Caravello, or one of his lackeys, focused on Geena. Perhaps they sensed her connection to you, and thus to me. If they have traced my essence from the Chamber, they may have followed it here, or located you because of your work at the Biblioteca. They will want to make certain I am out of their way forever. And if they have a way to sense the location of the next Oracle, that might bring them here as well.*

All right. I'm convinced it's worth a shot, Nico thought. *But do you really think I'm the next Oracle?*

I don't think it was only your mind-touch that led you to me. And with a magician as powerful as Caravello—imbued with the evil of Akylis . . . the blood of the Oracle is one of the only things that could have killed him.

How do you know that?

Nico felt Volpe hesitate a moment before forging on.

Do you think that I never felt the dark power lingering down in the well of Akylis? When I first sensed it down there beneath the city, I tapped into that magic.

What?

It did not corrupt me, but it would have if I had been anyone else. That's why I could not allow other magicians to remain in Venice. The soul of the city is in me, Nico. You must understand that, especially if you are to be the Oracle yourself. And Venice is more powerful than Akylis. The soul of the city resists Akylis' evil influence.

Nico frowned. *So the blood of the Oracle does what? Disrupts the magic keeping them alive?*

Precisely. The soul of the city is bonded to mine, and apparently to yours as well.

Geena's blood was on the knife, too.

For long seconds, Volpe's voice was silent inside Nico's mind. He could feel the magician there, and knew Volpe was troubled, but not the source of that unease.

I've thought about that, he said at last. *But there is another possibility. On rare occasions, a city might choose twins or lovers to share the weight of its secrets and its history.*

Wait, you mean Geena and I might both have been chosen?

I sensed something in both of you the moment you entered the Chamber of Ten, Volpe admitted. *Your mind-touch, that gift, makes you more sensitive to ethereal powers, but the bond of love between you and Geena . . . there is precedent.*

This isn't just a guess, is it? Nico thought. *I can feel it in your mind. You believe we've both been chosen.*

I do.

I hope you're wrong. I don't want this.

The city chooses the Oracle, not the other way around.

The words weighing on him, Nico reached a wider part of the alley, where moonlight splashed in between the tops of buildings. He hewed close to the rear of a stone structure that had once been a school but was now being gutted and transformed into apartments. The demolition phase had ended but new construction had yet to begin, so the place looked as if a bomb had exploded inside, crumbling the walls and blowing out doors and windows.

A crane sat silent and dark behind the shell of the old school and Nico slipped into its shadow, glanced around to be sure he had gone unobserved, then darted through the arched entry, rubble shifting underfoot.

So this direct approach you're talking about, Nico thought, *you just want to let them find us? If you don't know the extent of their magic, you cannot be certain you can overcome them.*

No, I cannot, Volpe agreed. *Which is the reason for our stealth.*

Nico continued onward, moving quickly and quietly through the skeletal building to the staircase. He took the steps two at a time, ascending to the third floor, then he crossed the empty space to what had once been a window.

Beyond the gaping hole where the window had been was a stone balcony, and beyond the balcony a tower of metal scaffolding the workers had erected weeks ago. Crouched low, he crossed the balcony and climbed over onto a wooden platform on the scaffolding, and from there he could see across a narrow gap—only five or six feet—into the tall French doors of his own balcony.

Hidden from the moonlight by the upper levels of the scaffolding, he knelt and studied every available glimpse into his apartment. Only shadows lurked within. His home seemed a gray limbo of a place, silently awaiting his return. After five minutes on the scaffolding, he opened his mouth to say as much to Volpe, but before he could get the words out, he saw a shape separate itself from the darker shadows within and move across his apartment before settling again into a corner of the living room that would be out of sight of anyone who might foolishly come through the door.

"Jesus," Nico whispered.

Hush, Volpe thought, coming forward to seize control again. A passenger in his own mind, Nico could read Volpe's thoughts for the moment at least. The magician could see better in the dark, and a look at those windows from Volpe's perspective showed Nico there were two men inside. Reaching out with his mind, he could feel them—

No! Volpe cried in his thoughts.

What? Nico demanded, feeling the magician's panic.

Volpe shook his head. *Never mind. Whoever those men are—lackeys and cutthroats, I would imagine—the Doges are not with them.*

So what do we do? Nico asked.

Volpe grinned darkly and shuffled back to the edge of the balcony. He rose to his feet, ran to the edge of the scaffolding, and hurled himself through the night, twenty-five feet above the stinking alley below.

In his mind, Nico screamed.

CHAPTER 14

VOLPE SAILED ACROSS THE GAP BETWEEN BUILDINGS. AT THE last moment, he feared he would not clear the top of Nico's balcony and began to thrash in the air, lifting his feet. He made it by an inch. His feet touched the balcony but momentum hurtled him forward and he brought his arms up to shield his face—Nico's face—as he crashed through the French doors.

Wood splintered, glass shattered, and Volpe heard Nico screaming inside of him. Glass shards sliced his shoulders and arms and stabbed his thighs as he stumbled forward, but he managed to keep his footing.

There were two men inside the apartment, one in the kitchen and one sitting on the edge of the sofa. Murderous thugs but not seasoned killers; he could see that instantly, and it confirmed a suspicion—the Doges had not had time to enlist more competent help.

The pale man on the sofa stood, but Volpe had rested well and the fool might as well have been moving in slow motion. The one in the kitchen swore in some Slavic tongue as he slid a knife from a hidden sheath, even as the other fumbled behind his back, reaching under his jacket for a weapon.

Gun! Nico cried in Volpe's thoughts, and instantly the magician saw in Nico's mind what such a weapon could do.

Volpe dropped, snatched up a long sliver of broken glass, and darted at the pale man. Even as the gun came up, he swung the glass dagger and slashed open the gunman's throat. Blood sprayed in an arc, splashing Volpe's face, and the dying man pulled the trigger twice. The weapon had been silenced, the shots making only a muffled pop. One bullet went wide but the other punched through his shoulder, spinning him around in a spatter of crimson.

Volpe continued the spin, shot his hand out, and pulled the gun from the pale man even as he collapsed to the floor. He tore the weapon free, feeling in Nico's thoughts for how it was to be held, and then he pointed it at the Slavic killer even as the man rushed him with a long, wickedly gleaming blade.

The Slav faltered, arrogance and bloodlust battling logic in his brain.

What are you doing? Nico shouted in Volpe's head.

What must be done! Now be silent.

Volpe faced the Slav covered in blood, only some of it his own. The bullet hole seared his flesh with pain, but already it was diminishing, closing. Nico knew he had not suffered from earlier wounds as much as he would have because of the magic coursing through Volpe's spirit, and the magician's connection to the soul of the city. But it had taken powerful ritual magic to purge his and Geena's bodies of the plague, and heal all their other injuries. He wondered why it had become so simple and immediate now . . . but even as he wondered, he found the answer in the touch of Volpe's mind, could see the truth. The bond they were sharing— two spirits in one body, like the bond that Volpe shared with the city—had strengthened. The old magician's power was building back to its true strength.

"Listen carefully," Volpe told the Slav. "You still live because I needed one of you alive and your companion posed a more immediate threat. There are things I wish to know. Things that you will tell me."

The Slav scowled and spat on the floor between them.

Volpe inhaled sharply. "You are very stupid."

He thrust out his free hand and twisted his fingers in the air as though gripping the reins of a horse. To Volpe, the Slav seemed no less an animal, a beast to be controlled.

The thug straightened abruptly, arms flailing. Awareness lit up his eyes with panic as he recognized that he no longer controlled his own body, and he tried to fight. Eyes narrowed, snarling with the effort, he brought his knife around in front of him and took two staggering steps forward, murder in his eyes.

Nico whispered in Volpe's mind. *Is this magic?*

What do you think? Volpe thought.

But how is it done?

Volpe scowled. He had no time to explain himself to Nico. The young archaeologist had left his mind open to exploration several times and Volpe had learned a great deal about the modern world from him, among other things. But in order to fulfill his own plans, he needed Nico's cooperation, which included silence when necessary. And so he reached out to Nico in his mind, let barriers fall that he had erected in ages past. Nico—and through him, Geena—had glimpsed many of Volpe's memories already, but now he let Nico into the landscape of his mind and gave him free rein to explore . . . almost everywhere.

Nico is a boy, perhaps twelve years of age, on the night he waits in the corridor outside of the maid's chamber in his father's house. The woman speaks Italian perfectly but there is the hint of Arabia in her voice, and her almond eyes and coffee skin suggest such lineage. Her lips are full and sensuous, her body ripe beneath her draped clothing, and she has been the object of the boy's desire since the first stirring of his cock.

Tonight she cries out in a throaty rasp, hoarse with lust, and he has come to spy upon her. But as he peers through the keyhole, watching her serviced by an Athenian sailor whose thickly muscled body is slicked with sweat, his own maddening lust turns to fear and shock. The sailor hurts her, strikes her, begins to choke her, and she slashes his face with her fingernails, fighting against him.

The sailor bleeds and laughs and begins to pummel her face with every thrust.

After the fifth blow, somehow she seems to transcend the pain. Through the keyhole, Nico can see her eyes glittering with hatred in the candlelight, her teeth bared. He sees her arms drop back as though in surrender, but she is not surrendering. She twists her fingers until her hands appear to be huge spiders weaving their webs, and she rasps words in some guttural Arabic tongue.

The sailor lifts off of her as though the hand of God has snatched him from the bed. He flails, dangling above her, cursing her as a witch in his native tongue. Her chanting continues and the Athenian begins to twitch, batting at his glistening skin in fear, slapping as though killing insects. Nico has not mastered much of the Greek language, but he understands enough to know the sailor sees spiders on his flesh, digging holes, laying eggs. The man slaps and claws at his face, digging deep furrows in his cheeks, then he plunges fingers into his eye sockets and rips both eyes out, screaming that the spiders are still digging.

The nude woman, body still flushed with arousal, crawls from the bed, corded muscles standing out in her neck as though she herself is holding the sailor off the ground. Then, with a gesture, she lets him fall and he collapses to the bed, turning as though to search for her with those empty, gore-rimmed eye sockets.

Nico never sees where she finds the knife, but it is there. She reaches out and grips the sailor's sex in one hand, then brings the blade down swiftly. While he is screaming, she cuts his throat.

Nico cannot breathe. He cannot identify what he feels at the sight of this horror—the heart-stopping magnificence of the maid's nakedness, the violence, the blood. But he understands that the Athenian thought her vulnerable, thought himself her better, and that the maid has proven that an error.

She holds her hands out, palms turned downward above the dying man, and chants briefly. Fire leaps from the corpse and the floor and the bed, rages brightly for several seconds and sends a wave of heat blasting through the keyhole. Then, as abruptly as it began, the fire is gone and only charred ash remains. The maid picks up the bedclothes and shakes them out, and he sees that they are not burned at all.

The maid has only to sweep away the ash and the only sign of the Athenian ever being there will be the unfulfilled dampness of her sex and the marks of his hands upon her throat, and both will fade.

He should go, sneak back to his room and pretend that he has seen nothing. He could, and she would never know. But he cannot.

As if his actions are no longer his own, he rises, lifts a hand, and raps on the door. The house is empty other than the two of them. No one else has heard the screams. No one else is coming. And she will know that it can only be him at the door. Still, long seconds pass.

When the door creaks open she is clad in a thin robe and she studies him with a ravenous curiosity as he enters the room. And then she smiles.

"Zanco, what did you see?" she asks.

"Nothing," Nico lies.

By her bedside is a small silver mirror. She picks it up and holds it so that he can see his reflection. The skin around his right eye is burned a bright red in the shape of a keyhole.

She smiles.

Nico feels his heart thundering in his chest and wonders if she can hear it. His prick is rampant, straining against his clothing. His lower lip quivers and he cannot meet her gaze, but then he forces his fear away and lifts his eyes.

"Teach me," he says, and he does not stammer.

He is asking so many things with those two words, and she seems to understand them all. She releases the catch on her robe and it glides down her copper skin to pool at her feet.

And the magic, and the power, begin.

But he is not Nico. He is Zanco Volpe. And Nico knows he will learn his lessons well.

Tremors shook the Slav's body. The knife in his right hand shook most of all. Volpe turned his back on the man, walked to Nico's coffee table, and set down the dead thug's gun. The bullet wound in his shoulder had healed almost completely, but it gave an unpleasant tug as he reached down to turn a chair toward the Slav and sat in it, the blood on his clothes and hands soaking into the fabric.

"Now," Volpe said, "I have questions. You will provide answers."

The Slav's upper lip quivered as though he wanted to muster up another gob of phlegm to show his disdain for this suggestion, but he could not manage even that. Volpe had him.

How old are you? Nico asked, inside his head.

Quiet, Volpe said. *Sit and learn. I have opened the doors of my mind to you. If we must share this body—*

My body!

—then I will be a gracious host. You wish to understand spellcraft and ritual, but you must educate yourself. I have business to attend to. All of Venice is in peril.

Volpe could feel the doubt in Nico's thoughts.

Your control of the city is in peril, not the city itself, Nico thought.

Volpe ground his teeth in irritation. Nico's presence within this flesh had to be tolerated for now, but it had begun to wear on him.

We shall see. Now be silent.

"Bassssstaarrrrrd . . ." the Slav managed to slur.

"Ah, you want to talk now?" Volpe said, leaning forward in the chair. "Excellent. I'll give you the freedom to speak. Take a look at your friend there on the floor."

He gestured at the corpse—at the pouting gash in the pale man's throat and the way the dead eyes gazed lifelessly at the ceiling.

"Now, then," Volpe continued, "who sent you here and what were your instructions?"

"Go fuck yourself," the Slav growled.

Volpe sighed in unfeigned impatience, then clenched his right hand into a fist and raised it up. The Slav lifted his long, wicked-edged blade. He stared at it, Volpe all but forgotten.

"No. No, no," the Slav said, face contorting as he struggled to regain control.

At a gesture from Volpe, he drove the knife down into his thigh. He opened his mouth to scream, but Volpe gave a twist of his left hand, like the turn of a lock, and stole his voice. Blood sluiced from the wound. Tears sprang to the Slav's eyes and beads of sweat formed on his forehead.

This is wrong, Nico protested in his mind. *It's torture.*

Volpe had felt him examining old memories, turning them over like the pages in some grimoire. But now the events unfolding in his living room had gotten Nico's attention.

Yes, it's torture. But he has chosen it. Now, hush.

"No screaming," Volpe cautioned. He unlocked the Slav's voice and gave a nod. "Answer the question."

The Slav gritted his teeth, squeezed his eyes closed, and opened them again. The hatred in them had returned, but fear lingered as well.

"A man named Foscari," the Slav said in that guttural snarl of an accent. "Like the university. An alias, obviously."

"No," Volpe replied.

The Slav looked confused. With the twitch of a finger, Volpe made him raise the knife again and the fear returned to his eyes. After that, the words spilled out of him.

"I got word to meet at the Hotel Atlantico, that the money would be good. There were others there, too. Some I recognized. Others like me, professionals. Foscari came in with another, an older man with a long white beard tied in a knot. They were both . . . formidable. The other one—Foscari called him Pietro—never spoke; Foscari gave the orders, split us all up, and gave us our assignments. There were targets to follow, people to find—"

"People to kill?" Volpe asked.

The Slav resisted, his lips closed in a thin line.

Volpe made him stab himself in the meat of his left arm. To his credit, the man grunted in rage and pain but did not try to scream. He glared at his tormentor, breathing in and out through bared teeth.

"People to kill," the Slav repeated.

"The Mayor?"

The Slav blinked in surprise, but he no longer resisted. A hateful smile spread across his face. "To begin with. There were others. Financial people. The owner of an old palazzo in Dorsoduro. Minor officials in the city government. Some are still breathing, but not for long."

You were right, Nico thought. *They're moving in, disrupting everything so they can take advantage of the chaos. What will they do now, put people under their influence in positions of power?*

Of course, Volpe replied. *They will be buying homes—perhaps even the homes they once owned. Investing. Taking control. Killing those who refuse to assist them. But it's only the beginning. I've seen in your mind what you think of the government you have now. Those men are saints compared to the Doges. And with the magic they have accumulated, and the evil of Akylis surging through them, making them even more powerful, in time they will have the world, if they want it.*

"Were you here to kill Nico Lombardi?" Volpe asked.

The Slav blinked in surprise. His eyes saw Nico Lombardi sitting before him, speaking of himself in the third person. He could not see that another lurked inside the human shell that housed Nico's mind and spirit.

"No," the Slav said. "Foscari has had people watching your project at the library in San Marco since yesterday, talking to employees there. But none of the group has a kill order on you. It was all just observe and report—until tonight, that is. They didn't say we couldn't hurt you, even break you a little, but tonight we were supposed to bring you in alive. You and your girlfriend, Dr. Hodge." He sneered into a smile as he said it. "Wait until she meets the sick bastards they sent after her."

Geena! Nico shouted in Volpe's mind. For a moment, their thoughts were merged and Volpe caught glimpses of his own past, of spells he had cast and murders he had orchestrated, of women he had loved and arcane objects he had stolen.

Volpe had to tear his thoughts free of Nico's.

"We've got to get to her!" Nico snapped, and only when the words came from his mouth did Volpe realize the young man had resumed control of his body for a moment.

Volpe pushed him back down even as the Slav staggered forward, released from the puppet strings that had held him. A flicker of confusion crossed the killer's face at his target's bizarre outburst, but then the Slav grinned.

"Worry about yourself," he said, lunging with the knife.

Then his wounded leg gave out and he stumbled, crashing into the base of the chair as Volpe twisted up and out of the way, rolling off the armrest. His heart—Nico's heart—beat wildly at the thought of how close the blade had come, and what Nico had almost cost him.

"Piece of shit," Volpe snapped, and he thrust both hands out, muttering a spell and gaining control of the killer again.

The Slav lurched up from the floor, dangling from invisible strings. He had dropped the knife but now, at a gesture from Volpe, he knelt and retrieved it from a smear of his own blood, then stood again.

What are you doing? Nico demanded. *Didn't you hear him? They're going after Geena. Let me out, you fucker. I have to get to her. We have to warn her. Christ, they may already have her.*

We don't need her—

But you need me! Nico raged.

For now, Volpe thought, and raised his eyes to stare at the Slav again.

"You said you were supposed to bring us in," Volpe said, lip curling in disgust. "In *where?*"

The Slav hesitated, for this was the moment when he knew he would have to die. Either his target would kill him in this very room, or his employer would do so the moment that his betrayal had been discovered. Volpe saw all of this in his eyes.

"I am a fair man," Volpe said. "I can see that you perceive no chance of survival, but I can offer you that chance."

"How?" the Slav growled.

Volpe grinned. "I will have an answer to my final question, even if it means forcing you to carve your flesh into pieces and eat them. I will not allow you to die without giving me my answer. But if you simply tell me, I make you a promise. I will kill the two men who hired you, so that they can never punish you for your weakness."

The word "weakness" filled the Slav with momentary fury, but then he sagged upon the invisible strings from which he hung. A moment's thought, and then he nodded.

"The hotel. The Atlantico."

Slowly, Volpe shook his head. "No."

The Slav flinched. "I swear. Those were our orders!"

"I don't doubt it," Volpe said. "But Foscari and Aretino would never linger long in a hotel. Too many variables." He thought a moment. "Where is this palazzo in Dorsoduro?"

The answer made Volpe smile.

All right, Nico. Find her, if you like. I'll leave you to it. But be wary. If they haven't caught her already, they will be on her soon, and I will not allow myself to be taken by the Doges, no matter what my freedom costs you.

The magician retreated to the back of Nico's mind, surrendering control of the body. But not before he forced the Slav to stab himself in the heart, and gave Nico a word of advice.

Never give a man a second chance to kill you.

Geena had kept her cell phone silenced the entire time she had been with Nico, but all along she had felt the vibrations as calls and texts had come in. When she left him to go home and clean herself up, she had been too busy unraveling the confused tangle of her thoughts to worry about those messages. On the way to the police station she had finally taken the time to skim through them—texts from Tonio and Domenic and Sabrina. Ramus hadn't called or texted, but they had never had that kind of relationship.

Now, leaving the police station, she felt a kind of aimlessness that unnerved her. Tomorrow would be another day. She would talk to Tonio, go to the Biblioteca, lay the groundwork for reclaiming her life once Nico had exorcised himself of the spirit of Zanco Volpe.

Just thinking about it made her tremble. The world had seemed so structured and rational to her only days ago. There had been rules.

There are rules, she thought. *You just never knew the real ones.*

Volpe. Geena just wanted to be rid of him and everything associated with him. If the Doges truly were as evil as he claimed and were conspiring to spread their influence far and wide, then of course they needed to be stopped. But if Volpe was the lesser of two evils, that did not make him some kind of hero. However noble his motives, he was still a ruthless, brutal man, and Geena trusted him not at all. It seemed very clear that she and Nico were nothing more than useful tools as far as Volpe was concerned, and she feared what might happen if he no longer needed them.

She had to find some way to get an advantage over him, to shift the balance of power between them, just in case. It had been in the back of her thoughts all night, and an idea had begun to coalesce, but it would require more contemplation.

Crossing a canal, Geena stopped on the bridge to watch a gondolier ply the filthy water below. A middle-aged couple sat in the prow of the gondola, snuggling close in a romantic haze, oblivious to the dirty water, the rats scuttling along building ledges, and the dark, malignant powers beginning to wage war in the city around them. She envied them for their blissful ignorance, and hated them for it at the same time.

The gondolier poled toward a blind corner ahead and shouted out to any of his brethren who might be approaching from the other angle. A reply echoed off the stone façades of the buildings around them and the gondolier maneuvered his charges to one side, steadying the gondola as another made the corner ahead, a trio of college-aged girls on board.

The gondoliers greeted one another with a cheerful camaraderie, and it hurt Geena's heart to see their smiles. Suddenly she could not bear to be alone tonight, could not put off the restoration of her life until the sunrise. How could she sleep at all, alone in her apartment, knowing that Nico was out there with that insidious, conniving magician holding the reins on his soul?

Awash in moonlight, ignoring people who passed her on the bridge and the gondolas now retreating in either direction, she pulled out her phone and stood there listening to the thirteen voice messages that her friends had left her. Even Finch had called twice purely out of concern rather than business, despite the fact that they'd only known each other for a few days.

Tonio wanted her in his office first thing in the morning. His tone was difficult to read, but she knew the conversation would be grim. Yet she welcomed it. Her whole life was crumbling around her and she needed to take action to prevent it from falling apart completely. And whatever was going on in the tomb revealed in Dorsoduro, Tonio would surely know all about it.

There were three new messages from Domenic. He and the rest of the team had gone to a small café in San Polo called Il Bacio where they sometimes gathered, and he said they were all hoping she would join them if she felt up to it. Geena doubted that they were all that enthusiastic about her company tonight, but she believed Domenic was sincere, and the lure of human companionship was powerful. And perhaps she wouldn't have to wait until morning to ask about the hidden Foscari tomb.

Gripping the phone in her hand like some kind of talisman—a connection to normalcy—she left the bridge and canal behind and started off through alleys and courtyards. In the years she had spent in Venice, some areas of its complex labyrinth had become very familiar to her and she tried not to stray into sections she did not know well. Tonight she navigated the maze purely by instinct. Il Bacio was just a few minutes walk from the Rialto Bridge and she made her way in that direction.

The phone felt solid and real in her hand, but she needed more than that. It was late, but not so late that a ringing phone would alarm anyone. At the risk of waking his children or irritating his wife, she dialed Tonio. Her toe caught on a loose cobblestone and she stumbled but did not fall, cursing softly.

"Geena? Are you all right?" Tonio answered. He'd heard her swear, which was not the way she'd hoped to begin the conversation.

"I am," she said. "I really am. I'm sorry to call you so late, but I didn't want to leave it until morning."

"So you intend to come back to work tomorrow?"

Geena hesitated. "I . . . of course I do. This is my project. I should be there."

"And there's nowhere I would rather you be," Tonio replied gently. "But you were attacked by your . . . assistant. You were stabbed. You should take time to—"

"Tonio, please, just listen."

A brief silence, and then: "All right."

"I've just been to the police. I'm not going to press charges against Nico—"

"But he stabbed you with a knife!" Tonio said, incredulous. "I know you love him, Geena, but he could have killed you."

"No. There's . . . there's more to it than that. It's difficult to explain. Anyway, the knife barely drew blood. There's barely a mark. I won't even have a scar."

"Geena, he *stabbed* you."

She stopped in the middle of a courtyard where cobblestones were cracked and uneven, the only light aside from the moon coming from an old iron lantern hanging beside the door to a long building that had once been a convent but now contained apartments. If the lantern had run on oil instead of electricity, she might have thought herself in another of Volpe's memories.

"I know," she said quietly. "But I promise you there's more to it."

"But you can't tell me what it is."

She smiled softly to herself, but it faded instantly. "It's . . . difficult."

Tonio sighed. "You love him."

It wasn't a question.

"And because you love him," he continued, "I won't press charges on behalf of the university. But he no longer has a job here. You understand that, yes? The liability if we were to continue to employ him and there was some further incident of violence would be enormous. But more than that, I won't have him here. It would seem as if I were condoning his behavior."

Geena swallowed hard. "I understand. And thank you."

"You should get as far away from him as you can," Tonio continued. "I fear for you."

I fear for myself, Geena wanted to say, but she could not. Tonio would misinterpret her words.

"You're a good man," she told him.

"Rest tonight," Tonio replied. "Regain your focus. Come in late tomorrow if you need the time, but do come in. Not because we need you, though we do, but for your own sake. This is the biggest moment of your career, Geena. I would hate to see you let it slip out of your hands."

Il Bacio buzzed with the sounds of humanity. Voices were punctuated by laughter and the clinking of glasses and music that came from small speakers overhead and seemed to rise and fall on the dips and swells of conversation. Geena weaved through the busy café with an easy familiarity, tension already easing out of her shoulders. This dose of normality could not erase the madness of the past few days, the horrors of what she had seen and endured just since morning, but it could help her shut it all out for an hour, and she needed that respite.

She spotted Sabrina first, sitting close with another young woman, who Geena recognized as a student at the university but could not name. The two of them whispered to each other in a way that could only be thought of as intimate, and their eyes sparkled in what might have been mischief or flirtation. Geena arched an eyebrow, but neither option troubled her. Sabrina intrigued her and had proven herself a loyal employee, but they weren't really friends. There were doubtless many things they did not know about each other.

Three tables had been dragged together, and the group was much larger than Geena had anticipated. There were graduate students, several undergrads, lovers and friends and spouses, and even Sandro Pustizzi, a history professor from Ca'Foscari. Coffee cups and wineglasses festooned the table, along with silver trays that had borne many pizzas, most of which had been devoured by now. No matter how long she lived in Italy, she would never get used to how late the Italians often ate their meals.

A waitress bumped her, skillfully managing not to dump the tray of drinks in her hand, and they danced away from each other in the swirl of movement in the café. When Geena looked at the table again, Ramus had already jumped up from the table and was rushing toward her with a broad smile on his face, his skin flushed from too much wine.

"Dr. Hodge! I'm so glad you came!" he said, glancing at her shoulder. "Are you all right?"

Geena nodded, wondering what Ramus would say if he could see her unmarred skin. She had worn a thin cotton top, but fortunately it hid the absence of a wound.

"A claret wouldn't go amiss," she said.

This seemed all the confirmation Ramus needed of her physical and mental well-being, and he went in search of a drink.

That left Geena standing alone and awkward a few feet from the table, but by now perhaps a third of those gathered there had turned to notice her arrival. Sabrina waved, some people whispered to their immediate companions—gossip about her, no doubt—but Domenic stared at her with a relief that made her swell with gratitude that she had such a friend.

He dragged an empty chair from another table and slid it in beside him just as she approached, and he gestured for her to sit. Thankful, she sank into the chair and then, before either of them had spoken a word, she sighed and leaned on his shoulder.

"I'm so glad you called me," she said, sitting up and turning to face him.

"I'm glad you *came*," Domenic replied. "You need to be around sane people for a while."

Geena surprised herself by laughing, and Domenic joined her.

"You look all right, considering," he said. "What's going on? Did you talk to Tonio? Have you seen Nico since . . ."

The questions stalled as Geena held up a hand. "Please, let's not talk about it. Just tell me about the project. Where are we?"

Domenic warmed to the subject immediately, happy to provide her with a distraction.

"You'll never believe it," he said excitedly. "After you and I left—after all the drama and the bloodletting—Sabrina and our divers and the BBC team were documenting everything down in the Chamber when some men from the city engineer's office showed up with enormous pumps and hoses and said they'd finished shoring up the canal wall."

Geena stared at him. "You're not serious? That quickly?"

"That's what *I* said. There's obviously more work to be done out there, but they've filled the hole, at least temporarily. The BBC must have put a ton of money into it, both on the table and under it, to make it happen that fast."

"I guess," Geena said, but she wasn't so sure. Finch's people had money, all right, but graft and corruption were nothing new in Italian government. How much money would it have taken to get the local authorities moving so swiftly? Was there enough money in the world?

Or were the Doges somehow involved? She tried to think of a reason they might use their influence in that fashion, why they might want access to the Chamber of Ten, but nothing occurred to her.

Maybe you're just being paranoid. These guys aren't pulling the strings on everything. She was so tired and confused.

"We got the pumps running right away," Domenic was saying.

"How long, do you think, until the chamber's dry?"

"Maybe forever. Whatever kept it dry—which Sabrina found no sign of, by the way—it isn't working now. The pumps have probably already drained what flooded in, but there's still going to be groundwater. Once the canal wall is permanently repaired we'll know more, but my guess is a drainage system might need to be installed long-term."

Geena let that sink in. Right now, as they sat there talking, the Chamber of Ten might be accessible. Who knew how much damage it had sustained? The broken wall, of course, and one of the obelisks had cracked. And then there was the urn . . .

"Domenic, there's something I need you to do for me," she said. "Now. Tonight."

He nodded. "Of course. Anything."

Geena spoke quickly and quietly, so that only Domenic could hear her over the din of the café. If he thought her request strange he showed no sign of it, only agreed to do as she asked.

"Now, tell me about this horrible thing in Dorsoduro," she said. "What is this crypt they've discovered?"

"Awful, isn't it?" Domenic said. "You saw it on the news?"

"Heard it from a waitress in a café, actually."

"That's what I love about Venice. We get our news over coffee." Domenic smiled and then nodded toward a young guy who was one of the graduate students. "Luciano was over there today."

Domenic got the grad student's attention and made the introductions, though given his field of study, Luciano was well aware of Dr. Geena Hodge. It would have been almost impossible to be an archaeology student in Venice and not be familiar with her.

"Lu, Dr. Hodge was just asking about the tomb in Dorsoduro."

Luciano nodded enthusiastically, as though being allowed to visit the site had been the best gift he had ever received.

"Dr. Schiavo sent a group of us down to observe," Luciano said.

"The city council wanted us there as consultants, or something. I've never seen anything like it, Dr. Hodge. Most of the building slid into the canal. No one seemed sure why. There was talk of explosives, but I overheard policemen saying there was no sign of anything like that. But if it hadn't collapsed, the tomb wouldn't have been discovered right away. It's a mass grave, really. The building had a subchamber, probably 16th century. It's similar in some ways to Petrarch's library, but its only purpose was for burial. From what we could tell based on an initial evaluation, there's not a single marking to indicate the identity of any of the entombed dead. Don't you think that's bizarre?"

Geena nodded to urge him on. "Very peculiar. And what about the tomb? Was it intact?"

Luciano had been excited to tell her his story, building up to something, but now his excitement left him in a single exhalation and he looked at her oddly.

"What have you heard?"

"Nothing. That's why I'm asking. Why?"

He gave a small shrug. "It's just weird that you would ask, considering."

"Considering what?"

"I received a call just before I came over here," Luciano said. "A couple of my classmates went down there tonight with a camera and a lighting rig to begin documenting the inside of the tomb so they would have photographs of what the site looked like before they started disturbing things tomorrow. The area around the building had been blocked off and the workers had gone home for the day. But there should have been at least a handful of police on guard, for safety if nothing else. Yet no one tried to stop them when they arrived with the equipment, or approached to ask them what they were doing. They called Dr. Schiavo and he called the police, who said there were officers posted there, but whatever their orders were, those police were nowhere to be found. My friends went inside the tomb—"

"It had been violated," Geena said, a sick feeling spreading through her belly.

"Yes," Luciano said, nodding emphatically. "I was just telling the others about it before you arrived. But it's worse than that. The tomb is empty, Dr. Hodge. All of the bodies have been stolen!"

Geena stared at him, feeling vaguely nauseous.

"Disgusting, isn't it?" Domenic said, sipping his drink. "Grave-robbers in the 21st century. In Venice! Who would do such a thing?"

Geena knew the answer. She might not trust Volpe, but he couldn't possibly have moved all of those bodies, unless he had used magic to make them simply vanish, and she had a difficult time imagining that. She felt sure that the surviving Doges had been behind the removal of their relatives' remains. To her, the question was not who had stolen the withered remains, but why. To give them a proper burial?

She shivered, hoping it would turn out to be something that simple, but certain it would not.

In her pocket, her cell phone vibrated. She frowned, wondering for a moment if it was Tonio calling her back. Then her pulse quickened as she realized it might be Nico. Pulling out her phone, she barely saw Ramus place her glass of red wine on the table before her.

Nico.

"Hello?" she said, cupping a hand over her left ear to block out the café noise.

"Where are you?" he snapped, and she couldn't be sure if it was Nico or Volpe asking the question.

"Il Bacio. With Domenic and Sabrina and Ramus and a bunch of other people," she said.

"Good. Stay there with them. Don't even go to the bathroom. I'm on my way right now. Please don't go anywhere until I reach you." He was breathing hard, so she now realized he must be running.

"Why? What's happened? What's wrong?" she asked, panic rising, turning to gaze at the people around her. Professor Pustizzi and two of his graduate students were watching her with obvious disdain.

"Is that Nico?" Domenic asked.

He frowned angrily and reached for the phone, but she twisted away from him.

"What's going on?" she demanded.

"They've got people working for them," Nico said, short of breath. "They've been watching us. And not just us—the whole team from the Biblioteca project. If you're all there, there are probably at least half a dozen inside and outside the café who are there to watch you. And they'll be after you, Geena. They've been watching up until now, but tonight they have orders to capture you. Just stay right where you are until I get there. Volpe can help."

She clicked the phone shut and looked around. Sick fear twisted in her gut and radiated throughout her body. She wanted to scream but could not. Volpe? He was supposed to help? Volpe had been the start of all of this. He was a cancer inside Nico's body, and she was supposed to trust him?

Domenic tried to talk to her but she could barely hear his voice. She knew she should try to appear calm but realized she was failing badly. As she picked up her glass of wine, her hand shook so hard that some of it spilled over the rim and down along the stem. She glanced around the café, searching for anyone who might be watching their table, watching her.

The man by the bar stood alone, his back to them, his eyes dark in the reflection of the mirror behind the counter. A thin man with a well-groomed goatee was sitting with a beautiful icy blond woman, neither of them speaking as they sipped coffee. The blond woman glanced at Geena, who averted her eyes, and immediately spotted the African man sitting at a small table near the front door with a book in his hand, though he didn't have enough light to read.

Were they watching? Were these people killers in service to the Doges? Were there others? A terrible feeling came over her and she glanced around the table, at the pretty girl who reached out to push a lock of Sabrina's hair aside, smiling at the two people with Professor Pustizzi, whom Geena assumed to be grad students. She had thought she recognized most of these people, but even if they were familiar, some were complete strangers.

Her chair scraped back and then tipped over, clacking to the floor as she stood.

"Dr. Hodge?" Ramus asked, frowning at the wine as though it might somehow be to blame.

"Geena, what is it?" Domenic asked.

"I can't be responsible," she said, knowing he wouldn't understand. How could she explain that she could not live with any of them getting hurt because they were a part of her team, because they were her friends?

Nico had told her to stay put, but she could not bring violence on these people.

"Whatever happens, just do what I asked," she said, staring at him. "Will you, please? Promise me."

Domenic nodded. "I do. I promise. If you promise to tell me why whenever this—whatever this is—is over."

She kissed his cheek and whispered a thank you, then started moving toward the door. On cue, the icy blond and her goateed lover stood and, without looking at her, started on a path to intercept. The black man near the door closed his book without marking the page, and then she knew it was all true, that they were really there for her.

She ran, rushing through the crowd, bumping chairs and spilling drinks, nearly plowing into a waiter. The door was in sight. If Nico had been close, he might be here any minute. She could elude them long enough for Volpe to help.

The door loomed ahead. The black man reached for her arm but she shook him off as she grabbed the door and yanked it open.

A man filled the doorway, blocking her path to the street. His white beard had been knotted beneath his chin and his startling green eyes froze her where she stood.

She knew him at a glance. Pietro Aretino.

"Good evening, Dr. Hodge," he said. "We need to talk."

Then he grabbed her by the hair and dragged her out into the moonlight.

CHAPTER 15

Nico's breath was harsh, muscles weak, limbs shaking as he ran as fast and hard as he could toward his true love. He tried to send her reassuring sensations, but it seemed that he could only concentrate on one thing at a time. *I'm coming, Geena*, he thought, and he barreled into a couple emerging from a restaurant, stumbling and tripping over the man's feet. He grunted as he fell, rose again, and ran on without looking back, the woman's shouts pursuing him as echoes and threats.

He concentrated purely on running, because getting there in time was more important than telling Geena he was on his way. He'd folded his cell and slipped it into his pocket and he dreaded hearing it ring again. That would mean they had her.

But as he turned the corner into the small square where Il Bacio sat, the noises he heard told him that he'd been a fool to hope for anything else.

Help me, he thought to Volpe, and without waiting for an answer he ran at the struggling shapes.

At first he could not see Geena. There was a knot of figures at the café's main door, and behind them in the square stood several more men and women, armed, tensed, squatting slightly as they watched the commotion. *More hired thugs*, Nico thought, and two of them turned at the sound of his approach. He was waiting for Volpe to rise up, waiting to feel his hands claw at the air as they scratched out arcane sigils to shove the thugs aside, flip them on their heads, or send them crashing backward through windows. But though he felt Volpe close behind him now—pressing against his eyes and senses like a child eager to see outside—the magician's attention was focused elsewhere.

The man was tall and thin, and something long glinted in his hand. The woman was shorter, with a terrible burn marring the left side of her face. Her hands were full with something Nico could not make out, and he hit her first.

Surprise was on his side. They'd been watching the struggle in front of and inside the café, not expecting an attack from behind, and he felt a grim satisfaction when the woman opened her eyes wide, his shoulder striking her chin and shoving her backward across a slew of tables and chairs. Bottles smashed, and the woman cried out as she skidded across a carpet of broken glass.

Nico was already ducking. He'd never been a fighter, but perhaps Volpe was steering him subtly now, for he heard the swish of something passing just above his head. When he looked up, the tall man was already swinging the knife back, repeating its arc, except lower this time, its vicious blade held flat, ready to slash across Nico's eyes.

Nico lashed out with his right hand and closed it around the man's unprotected genitals. As he twisted and pulled, he had a flash memory of a sweat-sheened naked woman slicing through a man's erection somewhere so long ago, and inside he felt Volpe laugh.

The man screamed and dropped the knife. Nico rose quickly and brought an elbow up beneath his chin, then pushed him aside and went for the doorway.

Volpe quickly came to the fore and stilled him, and for a second Nico railed against this intrusion. His blood was up, his rage burning bright, as he saw Geena thrashing and struggling in the grip of an old, old man. He wanted to go to her, help those others who were already trying to help, but then he realized why Volpe had stopped him in his tracks. The old man was Pietro Aretino, one of the three Doges, and on his face was the calm certainty of success.

Time seemed to slow. Aretino turned to look at Nico, grinning a grotesque smile as he twisted Geena's hair harder in his clenched fist. All around them, the struggling continued at full speed, but these two men simply stared at each other. Nico was aware of Domenic standing in the open doorway, trying to reach past Geena toward Aretino, while a black man bashed at the side of Domenic's head with a closed fist. Behind Domenic, in the chaos of the café, Nico thought he saw Ramus fighting with a blond woman, fists flailing, sharper things whispering at the heavy air.

"Volpe," the old man said in a heavy, guttural voice, and then Nico was flung back into the flow of things. He darted toward Aretino, his eyes on Geena. *His arm*, he thought. *I'll go for his arm. It looks old enough to snap at the first breath of wind and—*

Something struck him across the stomach. He bent forward and exhaled, pivoting over the extended leg even as it bent back and kicked in again. He was ready the second time—Volpe was there, quickening his reactions with a touch of something that felt sickeningly unnatural—and he caught his attacker's foot and twisted.

The man had a neat goatee and slicked-back hair, and resembled a lawyer more than a killer. He might have come from any one of a hundred countries. But his skills were refined, his eyes cold and calm, and as Nico twisted, the man jumped and span with the twist. As he spun, his other leg caught Nico across the back of the head, and he went sprawling.

"Volpe, for fuck's sake," Nico whispered, rolling just as a foot skimmed across the cobbles toward his face. It struck his shoulder instead and he turned away and became entangled in other legs, feeling bodies falling around and onto him and searching all the time for Geena, hearing her strangled gasps as that old bastard twisted her hair even more. He was about to call out to her when he felt his body starting to burn.

Nico was on his feet instantly, and Volpe raised his hands. He muttered a few words, clawed his right hand in the air a couple of feet in front of the bearded man's face, then clenched his fist.

The man grabbed the sides of his head and screeched as he went to his knees.

Domenic and the black man were fighting in the doorway, but both seemed to have paused at the sound of goatee-man's screams. Domenic was wide-eyed and disbelieving, the man he was fighting bleeding from a gash above his right eye. *Never thought Dom had it in him.* But when Domenic looked at him there was no trace of goodwill in his glance, and he looked quickly away to where the old man had started dragging Geena away.

Through the shattered door Nico caught sight of the confusion in the café: chairs and tables overturned, patrons backing away, waiters and waitresses retreating behind the small bar, one of them talking frantically on the phone. And Ramus on his knees before the blond woman, hands raised to ward off the blows raining down on him.

Then Nico's attention was torn away as Volpe went after Geena.

"Leave her, old man," Volpe said, and if there was a hex in his words they did not affect Aretino at all. The white-haired man only laughed as he pulled Geena harder. He was walking backward, dragging her by her hair. She'd raised both hands to clasp at his wrists, lessening the strain, but still it must have been agony. She saw Nico at last, but in her eyes he saw the reflection of Volpe.

"I won't be as easy as Caravello," Aretino said. "He always was a dandy, too concerned with his appearance to—"

Volpe grabbed at the air, hauling himself forward. Nico heard a thud, like the sound barrier being broken somewhere close by, and everyone around the café grunted. He muttered three words and coughed, pressing his hands toward Aretino, and Nico thought, *Watch out for Geena.*

"I'll do my best," Volpe said, "But the city only needs one of you."

Aretino frowned slightly and took a stumbled step back. Then he laughed.

"Time has lessened you, Volpe, buried away like a dead rat." He turned to leave, casually calling his people to him.

"Nico!" Domenic shouted.

Nico felt Volpe's temporary exhaustion after his magical efforts. He turned slightly and looked at Domenic, wanting to tell him everything that was happening. Domenic was standing before the café with both hands raised, gripping a man who was no longer there. The black man followed Volpe now, as did the man and woman Nico had tackled moments before. The goateed man rocked back and forth on his knees, holding the sides of his head. Blood trickled from his ears.

"Domenic," Nico began, and then he saw the blond woman emerging from the café. "Look out!"

Domenic turned and leaned back, just avoiding the knife that slashed at his throat.

The woman grinned as she walked on. Her knife dripped blood. Nico looked for Domenic's wound, but then he remembered the woman raining blows down on Ramus, and—

Volpe took him again, roaring in rage. *In this fight, I cannot be fighting you!* He took in several huge breaths. Nico felt the potential building in his body, and then Volpe shouted, "Aretino!"

Windows shattered in the café's frontage, and Aretino turned. The black man stood beside him, and the blond woman paused a few steps away. In their eyes Nico saw a restrained fear the likes of which he had never seen before. *They're slaves in his thrall,* he thought, and he sensed Volpe's agreement.

"So, the mouse roars," Aretino said. Geena squirmed beneath his hand, kneeling now that he'd come to a standstill. She was crying silently. Nico tried to send calming thoughts, but Volpe was at the fore now, allowing him to see but denying him any influence.

"You'll fail," Volpe said. "Caravello died badly."

"And you're looking good for plague survivors," Aretino said.

"All these years, you think you've been getting stronger," Volpe countered, and Nico could feel him stalling for time, building his magical potential again for one last, momentous attack. *Mind Geena*, he thought, but he wasn't sure that Volpe was even listening. "But you've simply been fading away. Whatever evil you've bled out of Akylis' lingering power can't change that. Existence isn't living, Aretino. The day I banished you from the city you died, and your stink has been worsening ever since. You've been waiting for so long, and for what?"

"For your own stink to subside, Volpe," Aretino said, the first signs of annoyance clouding his glare. Geena squirmed in his hand, and he gave a cruel tug on her hair.

Bastard! Nico thought, but he was powerless.

"I was always stronger than you," Volpe said, "but it's not only about strength."

"No?" the old man asked, and Nico thought, *He's the one stalling. Volpe. Volpe!* But Volpe went on, building his power inside, teasing it to the fore, and even when Nico felt that his whole body was burning with the need to vent the magical energy gathered there, still Volpe continued speaking.

"It's about passion," he said. "The difference between the two of us is that I have always *loved* this city, and you have simply coveted it."

From inside the café came the sound of someone crying out in terror and grief, and Nico recognized Sabrina's voice. *Ramus*, he thought, but he could not turn around. He could do nothing but watch, and listen.

Aretino's smile widened.

"I may have been down for a long time," Volpe said, "but I have been aware of every step the city itself has taken. I am the Oracle."

Aretino laughed then. It was a cutting sound, dismissive and triumphant at the same time. "Do you think we haven't also moved with the times? We've outlasted you, Volpe. And soon we'll have all of Akylis' power in our hands. We will be as powerful as the Old Magicians, like gods in the eyes of men." And then he glanced past Volpe at someone behind him.

Turn! Nico thought, just as Volpe swiveled to see what the old man had been looking at. Beyond the tall man with the knife, and the shorter woman casually picking glass shards from her hands, a shadow manifested from beyond the café.

Francesco Foscari.

He lifted a gun and shot Volpe in the chest.

Nico cried out, Volpe faded back, and the pain came. Both men were subsumed beneath the storm of loosened, uncontrolled magic.

As agony dragged Nico into unconsciousness, the screaming began.

Geena could hardly breathe. It wasn't the fear, because that had settled and set a fire in her chest that would not go away. And it was not from concern for herself, because if Aretino had wanted her dead, he would have killed her by now. Her breathlessness came from seeing the man she loved shot in the chest and crumple to the ground, and then the terror of what came next.

Geena had never been in a hurricane, so she had no real concept of what it would feel like to live through one. But her cousin had been in New Orleans when Katrina hit, spending a semester studying history at Tulane on a student exchange program, and she'd once spent a long drunken evening telling Geena about it. She'd actually been one of the lucky ones, evacuated soon after the hurricane and never going back, but the thing that had struck her—and, she claimed, changed her forever—was the feeling of utter hopelessness beneath the brutal, indifferent powers of nature. It wasn't that the wind could tear down buildings and the rain could bruise your skin, it was that this unbelievable power expended itself without reason, conscience, or concern. *You heard the term 'a fart in a hurricane'?* she'd said. *I don't laugh when I hear that anymore.*

Watching what happened after Nico fell made Geena feel a little like that, and the only comforting factor was that she felt Aretino's shock as well.

Even before Nico hit the ground, the whole atmosphere of that small square changed. The violence was still there—the smell of blood, a heaviness like impending lightning—but the air suddenly seemed to come alive, gusting and spinning, twirling in miniature whirlwinds that caught up dust and litter and lifted it skyward. Geena saw flashes of fire here and there—cool blue flames that danced for brief instants before being extinguished again.

The patrons in the café pulled back from the shattered doors and windows, and the building's lights fluttered and went out. She heard that scream again—Sabrina, calling Ramus' name—and in her heart she knew what that meant. *I didn't get out quick enough*, she thought, and she wondered whether Volpe had let Nico call her as soon as he wanted to, or whether there had been a pause—a stutter in time long enough for him to get here just as one of the Doges came to take her . . .

Someone else started screaming, and the man whose ears had been bleeding stood with flames enveloping his head—real flames, blackening skin and sizzling hair. Smoke and steam were whipped away from his twisted face by the sudden storm.

Nico's body twisted on the ground, curling in on itself even as his hands reached out and clawed at the air. Any time his hands shifted position or his fingers clenched, someone else screamed. The tall man flailed at some invisible thing buzzing around his head. The blond woman slashed at her own legs, screaming in pain and bafflement each time the knife performed another sweep. And Geena watched Domenic stumble back with his hands held out, as if warding off the invisible thing that shoved him through the café's already-shattered window.

Aretino pulled her away, and staggering across the square came the other ancient Doge, Foscari. He was aiming his gun at the writhing shape on the ground and frowning, obviously unable to shoot again. The Doge tugged hard on Geena's hair, sending a sheen of pain across her scalp.

"Finish him!" Foscari shouted. The Doges' hired thugs were backing away from Nico—all but the bleeding woman—their hands raised to defend themselves against the strange storm whipping around the square. At Foscari's words, however, they paused. The fear Geena glimpsed on their faces was real. She wondered what they had seen done to those who chose not to obey the Doges.

The tall knifeman stalked in toward Nico.

Aretino pulled Geena backward across the cobbles, her feet scrabbling for purchase to prevent herself from being dragged purely by the hair. She knew that shouting and screaming at the old bastard would be useless, but she did so, anyway. She was leaving her friends behind, with Ramus perhaps dead or mortally wounded and the man she loved with a bullet in his chest.

The knifeman drew his arm back close to Nico . . . and the first flame sputtered to life in his hair. He batted at his head, looking around, knife hand still raised, and several more flames sprung up along his left arm. He dropped the knife to slap at them and the fires spread. First to his hands, then across his chest and stomach as he wiped them there, napalm-sticky. The man shouted. Others around him drew back as the look on his face went from confused to terrified, and as he opened his mouth to scream, Geena saw flames licking across his teeth. Silhouetted against his blazing clothes and hair she spied Nico's hands clawing at the air, drawing unknown shapes, and she knew that Volpe was saving them both. But as she watched he fell back again, hands resting, and the chaotic storm erupted around the burning man.

Foscari drew close and she caught the shared look between the Doges—confusion, and maybe even fear. Then Foscari grabbed her feet and lifted, and together the two Doges carried her away from the square and into darkness, leaving their hired thugs behind. The glow and screams of the burning man faded away, and Geena closed her eyes and tried to sense Nico.

He was silent. But for now she held on to the sight of him moving on the ground, and Volpe casting spells, and perhaps that would give her strength to survive whatever was to come.

❖

He knew that Geena had gone, but he could not give chase. Commanding his body to rise, Nico found that he could not move. He wasn't sure why. Perhaps it was Volpe remaining in control, but that usual sense of being wielded like a marionette was absent, and he could not sense or hear Volpe's voice or thoughts. He could turn his head and watch the chaos around the square, and when the burning man fell at last and continued to spit and sizzle, Nico could feel the flames' heat all down his left side. Maybe that meant he wasn't paralyzed after all . . . but he had no idea how these things worked.

He shot me in the chest!

He could not move far enough to see the wound, so he tried lifting his hand to examine what damage had been done. Neither arm obeyed the command. He rolled his head sideways and looked at the café and the riot of people there, and one of them was Domenic. He stood staring at Nico, blood on his face and spattered across his white silk shirt. Always so smart, Domenic. Never a ladies' man, though he could have been, and Nico had always sensed the soft spot he had for Geena. He'd never said anything, of course, because friendship was worth more than that. Now the silver-haired man stared across a calming scene at his wounded friend, and when the shouting inside the café became louder he turned and pushed through the broken doorway.

Domenic, Nico tried to say, but he did not have the strength. And then he heard someone shouting Ramus' name over and over again, and he feared what had happened. He'd seen death today, but only of people he did not know. And other than his terror for Geena, he'd barely considered the nightmare of this coming home to roost.

Sit up! Volpe's voice commanded, and Nico felt himself sitting. He sighed and groaned, feeling blood running across his chest and stomach.

"Heal it," Nico said, and his voice had changed. Weaker than before, and there was a wet sighing effect behind it as well.

The shoulder was easy, Volpe said. *The heart is more delicate.*

Shot in the heart?

Close enough. Now listen to me, Nico. We've helped each other a lot today, and—

"You've used me," Nico rasped. "You haven't helped me."

I allowed you to come and save your girlfriend.

"Only because you knew they would be here."

Stop your sniveling! You're dying, and unless you do exactly what I say, you'll likely be dead before they torture her to death. Aretino always favored younger boys, but Foscari was a ladies' man, and he preferred it when they didn't welcome his advances. You hear me, boy?

Nico groaned and closed his eyes. Dizziness threatened, and for an instant the pain in his chest grew huge and mind-numbing, snapping his eyes open with shock. He caught his breath to scream, but Volpe sighed it out again.

"I can shield you from the worst of it," he croaked, "but you have to leave here now. There are people dead, and you've been shot. We can't afford the time it would take to deal with the police."

Nico glanced sidelong at the burning man. The Doges' other thugs had fled, doubtless already wondering what madness they had become involved in.

"Ramus." Nico stood, wincing against the expected pain but feeling only a distant numbness. He heard Volpe's voice, but the old ghost seemed to be mumbling words Nico could not quite make out. *He's just doing his magic*, he thought, but it did not feel like that at all. Though shielded from the pain of a terrible wound, control was his once again.

"Which way?" Nico asked. And in that one question he realized his dependence on this thing in his body.

North.

Nico had seen the Doges taking Geena west. That way called him but, even though Volpe had drawn back again, mumbling, fuming, he knew that he had to follow the magician's lead. So

north he went, leaving the square by a small rose-encrusted archway that led to a short alley, emerging onto a narrow jetty. Several boats were tied there, and Nico chose one, starting the motor
and steering away from the chaos behind him. He could smell the
stench of burning meat on his clothes, see Foscari aiming the hand-
gun at his chest and pulling the trigger, feel the heavy blankness at
the heart of him where Volpe was struggling to keep the agony at
bay. *Is that why his mumblings seem so mad?* he wondered. *Because
he's taking on all that pain himself?*

There was no answer from Volpe, and no sign that he had heard.
So Nico guided the dinghy north along the old city canals, passing
across the Grand Canal and then entering the shadows once again.
He thought of Ramus, certain that his friend was dead. He thought
of Domenic staring at him writhing on the ground, then choos-
ing to reenter the café to help his other friends. And he thought of
Geena.

Soon, Volpe whispered in his mind. And Nico knew that old
ghost was still there.

San Michele, Volpe said when Nico left the lights of Venice behind.
The waters of the lagoon were calm, and for that he was glad. There
were few lights on the cemetery island.

"What's in San Michele?" he asked. He'd been there only recently,
retrieving the soldier's hand for the ritual that had been so wasteful.
He only hoped that Volpe was not wasting time again now.

Just go, Volpe said. He sounded weak and distracted. Nico had
examined the bullet wound in his chest once, and he had no wish
to look again. The exit wound on his back must be even worse. But
even in that brief glance he'd seen signs that the healing was com-
mencing: drying blood, smoothed skin around the ragged wound,
and a puffiness to the flesh that had more to do with fresh growth
than bruising. Inside, he knew, the damage must be immense. *The
heart is more delicate*, Volpe had said, and Nico had a flash of some-

thing that might have been memory: holding the slick remnants from that smashed urn in his hands as water surged around his feet.

He blinked and changed course slightly.

As larger waves began to slap against the boat's hull, Nico was shocked by a series of images that flashed across his mind, each one accompanied by the fresh impact of a wave:

A circle of men, each of them grim-faced as if attending a wake, each of them holding a small, curved knife in one hand and in the other—

A ceiling painted in extravagant colors, intricate symbols and sigils intertwining, and each spread of the color red still drips—

Chanting that terrifies, in words he does not know, its rising and falling cadences seeming to penetrate to the heart of him and—

Nico cried out, leaning against the tiller as the images snapped away. He probed after them, because he knew they needed to be seen. Timing the impacts of wave against wood with his own psychic surges, he reached into what he knew were Volpe's memories. The old magician was struggling, and Nico so wanted to know more:

A hand rises and then comes down slowly, the knife glinting, the bare flesh of his chest speckled with spots of perspiration . . . only, the knife and hand are a woman's head, hair long and luscious, and she closes her lips around the head of his cock and looks up at him, smiling.

Nico shook the image away and probed deeper.

Hands rise and fall, twelve of them in quick succession, and then the first hand returns with a different knife, penetrating deep into his chest and . . . and the woman's rump rises and falls, and he can see himself buried deep, and he has seen her before with a knife in one hand and a soldier's member in the other. She turns and looks at him over her shoulder, eyes hooded and mouth open, still moving.

"No!" Nico shouted. His voice winged across the water and echoed from the boundary wall of San Michele, now drawing very close. Volpe was trying to hide that memory from him, flooding him with other memories to distract him. But Nico had a grip now, and he was clasping onto those flashes that felt so real. His claws remained in the past, and he groaned with effort as he began to reel it in.

He sensed Volpe's anger, but he was wounded. He felt the raw rage brewing deep inside, and knew there would be consequences . . . but this was something he needed to know.

"If you truly want my help to save this city," he said, "then you have to let me see."

When he did see, it was not because of a weakening of Volpe's opposition. It was because, for a short time, Nico was stronger.

The men have finished painting the necessary wards and sigils on the chamber's ceiling, and two of them have removed the wooden bench they used to reach that far. Each has a bloodied cloth bound tight around his left hand, and Nico knows that their palms are slashed and sore. But these men do not betray their pain. Their faces are grim and spotted with droplets of their own blood. The ceiling drips, and when Nico looks down he sees the droplets splashed across his bare body.

Volpe's torso is withered and old. Skin hangs from his frame, his ribs protrude even when he's lying down, and there's a grayness to him that not even this subterranean place should impart. Nico is merely a witness here, yet when his arm raises and he draws his finger through blood splashes, it feels as though he is giving the command.

"Here," Volpe's voice says, "and here." He has drawn two intersecting lines across his breast, skin wrinkling and stretching to follow his finger.

"Zanco, there must be another way," a man says, and Il Conte Rossi steps into view. He is bloodied again now, the cloth around his hand dripping blood as if he has cut himself deepest.

"There is no other way," Volpe says. "My spirit is strong but my flesh is weak, and we must not let that spirit rot away with this flesh." He motions Il Conte to him and lowers his voice. "I'm trusting you to complete this ritual, when the others might shy away."

"I'm not sure I—"

Nico's hand flashes out. He claws his fingers into the man's robe and pulls him even closer, and he sees Il Conte turn his face away from the rotten smell of his breath. "I have been dying for a long time. What you do here today is of little significance to me, but vital for the city. You understand? This time is over, a new time is to begin. And it's imperative that those three bastards are not allowed to even look upon this city again without fire scorching their eyes."

The standing man nods. He understands.

"Vital!" Nico says. Volpe's voice, Volpe's grasp, and Volpe's final moments. Because then Il Conte stands back and motions the other men around him, and together they raise their knives.

This time when they bring their blades down into Nico's stomach and chest, the view does not change afterward. Il Conte steps in and carves at the ruptured flesh, cracking ribs, ripping the chest cavity open, his face set grim and lips tight.

And all the while, Nico is muttering words that he has heard before.

Il Conte finally pulls Nico's heart free, and there is no pain. The heart continues to beat, and even as the man slashes away the final connecting arteries, the muscle looks strong and healthy.

But the Chamber bleeds. Blood flows from the ceiling, and Nico hears the men's feet splashing in fluid that is too thick to be water. One of them brings an urn that Nico has seen before, and as Il Conte lowers the heart inside, his vision begins to blur.

But he sees the Red Count's final gestures over the urn, and he remembers them. From the hands of another member of the Council of Ten, he takes the severed hand of a soldier, dips its fingers into Volpe's blood, and uses it to run a symbolic seal around the urn's lid.

Nico feels his body swaying and shifting as vision fades, sounds drift out, and then against all expectations the pain comes in, and—

It was immense.

Nico screamed. The boat nudged against a wooden jetty. Volpe rose in him again, and before Nico was shoved way down into his own injured body, he felt the old ghost's rage.

Leave alone what is not yours! Volpe roared, and then Nico knew nothing.

CHAPTER 16

THE ONLY REASON THE BASTARD HAD LET GO OF HER HAIR was that it made it easier to walk.

They'd already passed two groups of people who had protested at his treatment of her, and both times Aretino had merely glanced at Foscari. The first time, the other Doge had chosen one of the complaining men and beaten him, flooring him quickly and then stomping on his knees until Geena heard the sickening crunch of bones and the heavy silence of shock. The second time, Foscari had only approached the two young couples and they'd seen something in his eyes that made them flee. Such casual violence was nauseating, made her sick to her soul. But it also made her realize that these two men—if indeed men they still were—were totally in charge.

Aretino walked ahead, his old man's body moving with confidence. The white knotted beard and shriveled face were misleading. When he'd let go of her hair at last, he had not even instructed her to follow, but she knew if she did not she would suffer. Besides, Foscari was behind her. Close behind. Sometimes she swore she could feel his breath on the back of her neck, and she had felt his hand brush casually across her ass several times. *And if I turn and punch him in the fucking nose?* she thought. She had no wish to find out. Aretino had said they needed to talk, but he had not said she needed her knees unbroken to do so.

She was terrified. That evening she had been stupid enough to believe that she could find a few hours away from this madness—from Nico and his crazy ghost, the deaths she had witnessed, and the fact that she'd been infected by some black magic plague less than twelve hours ago. Repair the foundations of the existence she and Nico had together, in the hope that they would be able to reconstruct the walls of their life when this whole bizarre mes was over. Now she saw how foolish she had been. And perhaps blind. Maybe *she* had been driven a little mad by what had happened, and though she had a mind that she thought was open and willing to explore, the certainty of what was happening might have been too much for her to handle.

But that was nothing compared to this.

She'd seen Nico burn a man to death by looking at him, and . . .

And Ramus.

She sobbed once and slowed down. Foscari walked into her—on purpose, she was sure—and grabbed her upper arms.

"You shouldn't keep Aretino waiting," he whispered, hot breath in her ear. She shrugged him off and walked on.

Hope. She had to cling to that. Nico had been shot, but it was Volpe who possessed him—a magician who had returned from a five-hundred-year limbo to cast his influence across the city once again. Nico had been moving on the ground even with a bullet hole through him, painting those weird signs against the Venetian night to protect himself against the Doges' hired help, and surely that meant that Volpe was shielding him from the effects of the wound? Could he do that?

Hope. Prisoner of two old men who should have died half a millennium before, she had little else.

She tried to keep track of where they were taking her, but their route quickly became confused. After several years here she thought she had a good understanding of the city's geography, but Aretino led them along alleyways she had never seen, into courtyards that might have changed little since he had been banished from the city, and she could only follow.

Before long, any thought of making a break for it had gone. If she did run and somehow escape Foscari's grasp, she would have to sprint to lose him in this warren of alleys and shadows, narrow bridges and small cobbled squares, and she'd just as likely emerge onto a dead-end before a canal. No, she needed a plan. She already had the sense that Aretino was the one with the power, and Foscari the more physical of the two. To escape them both, she'd need a plan that covered all angles.

"Ahh, my old Venice at last," Aretino said, and Geena shivered. It was as if speaking of the city he'd once loved and coveted brought its oldest places alive around him, shoving them back through centuries to a time that these men had called home. It was a foolish notion, but as they walked between buildings that leaned so close together that they almost seemed to touch, walls dripping with clematis and climbing roses, Geena desperately looked for signs of the present. Who knew what powers these men had? If they could defeat time by living to this unbelievable age, perhaps they could manipulate and mold it to their liking.

How will he find me? she thought, imagining Nico even now scouring the streets and canals for her with Volpe's help. *If they take me back to their time, will he see me represented on some buried fresco? Find my bones in an old tomb he might uncover years from now? How will he even know it's me?* She had never felt so disassociated from her surroundings, an intruder in the city she had grown to love.

Aretino paused and glanced back at her, smiling as if he knew exactly what she was thinking. "This might interest you."

"Nothing you do or say can interest me," she countered, but his wrinkled smile didn't slip, so she added, "Fucker."

Aretino shrugged. "Maybe I'm wrong. We know so little about you, really, but what we have learned in the short time we've been aware of your existence—the short time we've known of that traitor Volpe's tenacity and his hold on the one you love—leads me to believe you exist in the past."

He was listening to my thoughts! she thought. But no, it was merely Aretino's manner of speaking. She knew what having her thoughts and mind read felt like.

She did not reply. Foscari moved in close again and she pressed her lips tightly together, resisting the inclination to step away from him. He did not touch her, but he was so close that she could feel the heat of his body.

"It doesn't matter," Aretino said, waving one hand dismissively. "When we reach our destination, I'll tell you what you must do to preserve the life of the one you love, and also your own." He turned and slipped through a short alley, and Geena followed. They emerged on the other side onto a narrow path beside a canal, and she sighed with relief. One of the windows across the canal flickered with that blank silvery light that could only be a television, brightness rising and fading again as the picture changed. And from another window, she heard the shrill ringing of a phone, and then a brusque man's voice answered.

They were still in the present. Her imagination must have been working overtime.

It was minutes later when Aretino opened an old door set in the façade of a building Geena had never seen before, that their journey back in time really began.

"What is this place?" Geena asked, instantly hating herself for vocalizing her astonishment.

They had walked through an empty, dilapidated room to a door set in the wall at the far side, plastered and painted over many times. Foscari had used a heavy knife to trace the line of the door— his knife strokes fast, strong, and unerringly accurate—and then Aretino had shoved it open. A breath of musty air, a staircase heading down, thirteen steps . . . and then this.

"Just an old house," Aretino said, dismissing a hoard of artwork that was probably close to priceless. Paintings lay stacked against one wall, and the lead canvas on one pile looked like something Masaccio might have created. Exquisite old furniture was piled against another wall, along with sculptures in various states of completion, one of which looked like a brass pulpit created by Donatello. On a huge table lay hundreds of scattered sheets of paper and canvas, stored carelessly and in no discernable order, and Geena glimpsed the unmistakable cogs and lines of a da Vinci. Gasping, trying not to reveal her amazement, she followed Aretino through the room.

He was smiling. She could feel that even before he turned around.

"Interested?" he asked.

She did not answer. She didn't want to give him the satisfaction. But she could not keep her eyes on him—she kept glancing to the left and right, thinking how much her friends and colleagues would give to spend some time in this room. Domenic would love the paintings, Tonio would be hugging some of the incredible sculptures she saw, and Ramus . . .

Ramus never had been able to contain his enthusiasm. He'd possessed a love and fascination for old art that belied his young age. The last she'd seen of him was as that blond woman had been stabbing him, the murderous attack only fleetingly visible from the square outside the café. An attack at the Doges' behest.

"Don't you want to know how?" Aretino asked.

"Fuck you."

He raised his eyebrows—gray slugs over eyes that should no longer sparkle. "Manners have certainly fled since we were last here, don't you think, Francesco?"

Foscari, still behind Geena, placed a hand on her shoulder. He squeezed lightly, released, and squeezed again. She couldn't help thinking that he was kneading her. It filled her with disgust, but she pretended he wasn't there.

"You want to tell me what a wonderful thief you were when you were alive?" Geena asked.

"Not quite," Aretino said, frowning slightly. "A collector. And a cautious one, at that."

"So when you were *alive*, you liked collecting?" Geena could see that she was getting to him. The old bastard's eyes had changed infinitesimally, shedding a hint of smugness and taking on irritation. But if the best she could do was to irritate him . . . well, so be it.

"Few people have seen any of these pieces since I was sent from the city by your Volpe," Aretino said softly.

"He's not *my* Volpe!"

"And yet you and he have copulated."

"No!" Geena said, but when she glanced away from the Doge and back again she saw the smugness had returned.

"There are many places in the city like this," he said, sweeping his hand around the basement. Its walls were dry, without any signs of damp, and she thought again of the Chamber of Ten. That place had been hidden away for so long, there was no reason now to doubt what the Doge was saying. "Not all are filled with such riches. One has a small table upon which rests a book that would change the world. Others, my old belongings. One place so close to the Doge's palace that the same air circulates through its rooms has a single sealed box." He paused and raised an eyebrow expectantly.

"What's inside?" Geena asked.

Aretino smiled, lifted one hand, and before he could speak Geena snapped, "You're just a dead thing!"

The impact was sharp and sudden, yet not unexpected. Foscari's fist was hard with knuckles knotted. Geena fell. She preferred being punched than molested, though, and as she sat up she looked at the Doge, exuding hatred.

"Watch your tongue, Dr. Hodge," Aretino said. "My cousin does not like women who speak out of turn."

Geena felt a sickening laugh gurgle in her throat. "All of this . . . just to get your *things* back?"

"Not at all," Aretino said. Smiling, he glanced around the room. "Don't misunderstand; there are many pieces of our history that we are very pleased to be able to reacquire. Things that are right-fully ours. But there is only one thing in all of Venice that we truly needed."

"Access to the tomb of Akylis," Geena said.

Foscari stared at her in fury. Aretino arched his eyebrows in sur-prise and then smiled in approval.

"It appears that Volpe has shared more with you than we had imagined," Aretino said.

He must have seen the surprise on her own face when she real-ized that Volpe had been telling the truth all along.

"Ah, you doubted him," Aretino said. "As well you should."

"Why do you even need Akylis' magic?" Geena demanded. "You've lived six hundred years. If you have enough power for that, what more magic do you need?"

Aretino's dancing eyes grew cold and still. "We have spent five centuries *surviving*, when we should have been *ruling*. Volpe tried to end us, tried to exterminate our entire bloodline, but all he did was postpone the inevitable. Now our family will rise, and with the dark power Akylis left behind, we will cover the world. We will be the new gods and Venice the new Olympus."

Geena looked into those eyes and saw madness staring back.

"But they're all dead," she whispered. "You have no family left. Just the two of you. Are you going to send thugs and assassins out into the rest of the world to try to take over? Even with Akylis' magic—"

"Don't be stupid," Foscari snarled at her, darting in close enough that she felt his spittle on her cheek. "We have family. Volpe took them from us, just as he took all of this—" He spread his arms wide, indicating the treasures in the room. "And all of Venice. But like the rest of it . . . we have taken them back."

Geena felt all the blood draining from her face. *The tomb*, she thought. *The bodies.* How many Foscari cousins, uncles, distant relatives had Volpe had killed and buried in that crypt under the building in Dorsoduro? A hundred? Two hundred?

The Doges had stolen them back.

"With the magic you're taking from Akylis' burial well . . ." she began, the truth striking her at last. "You're going to raise them from the dead."

She tried to imagine it—two hundred Caravellos, Aretinos, and Foscaris resurrected and restored to life, filled with the dark power of Akylis and sent out into the world to conspire and manipulate, to magically influence governments and corporations, all to draw the reins tight on the entire globe and put them in the hands of the Doges.

"This is a waste of time," Foscari growled. "Show her, Pietro, and then let me show her what *I* have for her."

"You hear that?" Aretino said. "Francesco wants to rape you. You're just his type, too. I doubt you'd submit without a fight."

Geena did not satisfy either man with an answer. Instead she examined her left hand where she'd grazed it as she fell, and brushed droplets of blood from another deep scratch across one elbow.

"Bring her!" Aretino said, and Geena knew instantly that their game was over. Foscari grabbed her beneath the arms and lifted— his strength was impressive for someone over five hundred years old—and hefted her upright, half pushing, half carrying her after Aretino. They passed items of priceless art and antiquity, and though she struggled to remain composed, Geena could not help her amazement.

They opened another door that had also been sealed shut and descended another flight of stairs. Geena knew that they were well below the waterline now, and she wondered whether whatever had held the waters back from the Chamber of Ten also worked here. From the vague memories of Volpe's that she'd seen and sensed, these Doges were mere dabblers in magic when they were banished, not master practitioners like him.

She was curious, but she did not want to ask.

At the foot of this new staircase was a small chamber, hacked from the ground without any aesthetic consideration. Its walls were uneven, ceiling and floor rough, and it was barely ten feet across. At its center stood a small wooden stool. On the stool was a sealed clay container. The container bore no marks or decoration, and the clay looked delicate.

"This," Aretino said, gently touching the urn, "is our protection."

"I'm really not interested—" Geena began, and Foscari thumped her in the kidneys. She went down to her knees, biting back a groan but closing her eyes as the pain tore through her torso. *Bastard bastard bastard!* she thought. She remembered Volpe jamming his knife under Caravello's chin and up into his brain, and she so wished she had a blade.

"Just tell her and get it over with," Foscari said, his voice heavy with something other than anger. "Then I'll have her before we send her back."

Geena's eyes snapped open. Aretino glanced from her to the Doge standing behind her, but she could not read his expression. *He's in charge*, she thought. *A word from him and . . .*

"It's delicate," he said, touching the urn again. "It has to be. When the waters pour through and these walls come down, it has to break. Even if it doesn't, its salt seal will dissolve over time and release what's inside. But the sort of revenge I'd want . . . I'd need it to be quick."

"So what's in there?" Geena asked.

"Something you've had already."

Plague. She shuddered, remembering the magical contagion that had nearly killed her and Nico, the sores and the blood and the certainty that her lungs would flood and her throat would swell until she died.

"While Volpe has been guarding this city from a place of rest, the three of us have been busy. We couldn't return home for five hundred years because of that interfering bastard, but that hasn't meant that we have lost all influence over people within the city, nor have we been unable to send people in and bring them out as desired. Volpe slept, and we were building. Volpe rested, and we worked. All we needed was the magic of Akylis to bring our plans to fruition. Now we have it. And if anything happens to us, the city dies."

Geena understood. Some form of magic held the water from this chamber, just as it had in the Chamber of Ten. By sending clumsy magicians from the city instead of killing them, Volpe had given them time to mature, learn their craft, and plot their eventual revenge. He'd been weak, too concerned with the opinions of the Council of Ten to take proper care of the city he professed to love. By ridding it of its potential dictators, he created Venice's greatest enemies.

"There are other places," Foscari said. "Seven, all told. The spell that holds the waters out will only endure as long as at least one of us survives. If all three of us are killed—the two of us, now that Caravello is dead—the walls come down, the urns shatter, and the plague is released."

Foscari seemed afraid that Geena had remembered the way here. He wanted to make sure she knew there were other such plague rooms. *Which means there must be a way to stop this!* she thought, *To undo all of it. Otherwise he wouldn't have needed to tell me that.*

"So while Volpe slept, you've been catching up on James Bond movies," she said. "And now that I know your diabolical plan, I suppose you're going to kill me."

"Not at all," Aretino said. "Actually, we're going to release you. You will have until dawn to bring Volpe to us, or we will kill the city."

"You're bluffing," she said, heart missing a beat. "You love this city. You'd never—"

"We do love the city," Aretino said, and Foscari leaned in close behind her again, his hands slipping around to her breasts, wet mouth against her neck.

"But only because it is home to us, to our family, going back fifteen hundred years," Foscari said. "The rest of the people of Venice mean nothing to us. Once they're dead and gone, we'd still have the city itself. Scoured clean. Simple enough to start anew."

"But we don't wish for that," Aretino said. There was a hint of reprimand in his voice, and Foscari moved back. Geena wanted to wipe the places where he had touched, but she crossed her arms instead.

"I'll do it," she said, looking at the clay urn. She did not have to feign her fear, nor her disgust at the choice they had given her. "But I can't bring him here. He'd never believe that I'd found this place on my own."

"We don't want you to bring him here," Aretino said. "You'll bring him to the Chamber of Ten. At dawn, we will meet there, and there will be an end to this."

Geena pretended to think on this, looking down at the Doge's feet, frowning. If Aretino had not suggested the Chamber of Ten, she would have done it herself. It could work to her advantage, if she was very persuasive and very lucky. *Will there be time . . . will Volpe listen . . . will he believe me . . . And did Domenic do as I asked?*

"The Chamber of Ten," she said softly. "Why there?"

"You think yourself so clever," Foscari said. "I'm certain you'll figure it out."

"The Chamber," Aretino said, eyes widening, smile growing, and a small ripple of doubt went through Geena. *Have I really done the right thing?* But it was too late to back out now. "The Chamber, by dawn."

Behind her, Geena heard Foscari's breath growing more rapid. She stared at Aretino without blinking. He nodded slowly, then drew a small shape in the air before her with his unnaturally long index finger. The shape seemed to hang suspended for a few seconds, like a smoke ring that slowly dissipated. She blinked, swayed a little, frowned.

"Away from here," Aretino said to her at last. "Quickly. But if there is any deceit on your part, any schemes, think better of it. We have been alive—*truly* alive, woman—for long enough to outsmart anything your feeble mind might conjure. And Foscari's attentions will be only your first punishment."

Dismissed, Geena had no desire to linger a moment longer. She turned and pushed past Foscari, up the stairs and through the room holding the priceless treasures. Denying the temptation to stop and examine them, she climbed the next staircase to the bare room above. She still felt strange, and it was only when she exited the building onto the canal path that she began to realize what was wrong. But by then she could not stop. She walked without appreciating direction, passing through alleys she instantly forgot, crossing bridges she thought she had never seen before and would never be able to identify. Direction meant nothing, and struggle though she did, she could not construct a map of where she was or where she had been in her mind. She paused and turned around, going back the way she had come, but every square, courtyard, alley, and canalside walk was unknown to her, all of them blending into one.

So she kept walking through the night until the time came when she no longer tried to recall where she had been, but rather craved something familiar.

The first touch of Nico's mind on hers made her cry out with joy.

When Nico regained consciousness, he was surrounded by the dead. The room, lit by several weak candles that all seemed to be sputtering their last, was filled with skeletons. They were piled on shelves carved into the walls, one on top of the other like firewood stacked against the winter. They were propped in alcoves several deep, held in place like collected insects by long pikes driven through rib cages; he could not tell whether they'd been pinned there before or after death. In one far corner there was a pile of skulls, and all of them bore signs of trauma to their pale domes. Other bones scattered the floor, tangled with shreds of rotten clothing. Candlelight shifted here and there, and the shadows cast into skulls' eyes blinked at him, arm bones moved, and clawed fingers clasped at the floor as they tried to pull themselves closer.

None of that shocked him. What *did* shock him was the weight in his chest. It felt as though his heart had been ripped out—

—Il Conte hacking away, breaking, reaching in—

—and replaced with a lead weight. When he breathed he hardly felt his chest move, and his lungs were burning.

What has he done to me now? Nico thought, and he wondered how many of these skeletons were made by Volpe's bidding.

I've healed you, fool, Volpe's voice said.

Nico looked down at his chest. He was shirtless, and the place where he'd been shot—just to the left of his sternum, an inch higher than his nipple—was a mass of heavy purple, green, and yellow bruising. He touched himself there with his right hand, running his fingertips across his puffy skin in search of the bullet hole. But it was not there.

A hair's breadth closer to your heart and you would have bled to death, Volpe said.

"And you?" But the old magician did not answer that. "So where are we?" Nico asked, but already the memories were coming back at him, punching in with each fresh revelation—Ramus' death, Foscari shooting him gleefully in the chest, Geena being taken by that bastard Aretino—and Volpe did not answer straightaway.

It was easier to cure the wound when you were unconscious. Magic's influence can be . . . indelicate sometimes. And the heart is most delicate. *It took a while, but you're well now.* I'm well. *Now we both need rest.*

"But they took Geena," Nico said.

They won't hurt her. Not yet.

"How can you be sure?"

Because they want me, and you and I are inextricably bound.

"So they'll use her as bait," Nico said coldly.

Of course.

"You sound tired," Nico said, and Volpe did not reply. He was still there—Nico could feel him, looming in his mind like a shadow in blazing sunlight—but he was musing, his silence loaded with something important.

Nico sighed and closed his eyes. This would have been a great find for any archaeologist, and some vague part of him hoped that he'd discover where they were and remember it. But such considerations seemed like part of a life he no longer knew. Here he was surrounded by bones bearing evidence of violent deaths, and he felt calm. Not quite at home, but settled. He breathed in deeply and smelled dust.

You sought memories that were not your own, Volpe thought. Nico had never heard such caution in that voice. *You . . . forced your way in.*

Nico opened his eyes and sat up. He had full control of his body, and he looked around to confirm that, lifting one hand, then the other. He felt righteous rage building inside him, and knew that Volpe would feel it as well. He stood. The chamber's ceiling was low and brushed his head, and whilst standing he seemed to look down on all the bones and skulls, viewing them as if from the position of a conquering warrior.

Those were not your things to know, Volpe continued. *Magic is a dangerous thing, and does not bestow itself upon just anyone.* There was a hesitancy to his voice now, and Nico was enjoying the feeling of subtle power it gave him. Volpe did not sound afraid, not quite . . . but the things Nico had seen were obviously precious to him. The memories were still clear, though disjointed.

What do you expect me to do about it?

"I expect you to forget," Volpe said.

Nico lashed out. He kicked at a skull, and it shattered beneath his boot, bone shards ricocheting around the room. He turned on the spot, looking for something else to hit or kick, and it was only as his anger bubbled over that he realized, *There's no door to this place.*

"I forced *my* way in?" he shouted. "Then what the fuck did *you* do to *me*? Serves you right. How do *you* like it?" He stalked across the chamber and stomped on a pile of skeletons, feeling a wave of queasiness as they cracked and crumbled beneath his boot. His chest felt heavy and hot, but he could not describe it exactly as pain, more the memory of pain having been there. Right then, he might have welcomed its return.

Volpe held back and let Nico expend his anger. It did not take very long. He turned from the bones he had broken and knelt again in the center of the chamber, shaking, sweating, and thinking of those knives plunging into Volpe's torso over and over again. Each shred of memory brought a stab of pain in his own chest, and he wondered whether Volpe could transmit to him exactly what it had felt like. Probably. He was the old magician's mannequin, and though this burst of fury felt good, he was sure that Volpe could stop it at any moment.

"Once the remaining two are put down, you'll be rid of me," Volpe said. Nico felt those bloodied memories drawn away, and he frowned as he tried to hold on to them. "They are the threat right now," the magician continued, the sound of his voice surprising Nico. He'd not sensed the takeover, and now it felt natural speaking as Volpe.

I don't want any of this, Nico thought.

"We're in a place I haven't been to for a long time," Volpe said, as if answering a question. Control of Nico's body remained with him, and he relaxed back onto his haunches as Volpe spoke. He could not deny his interest. "Even years before I died, I had no cause to come here. We're deep beneath my family tomb on San Michele, in the buried ruin of the church that once stood here. This place houses the remains of those who wronged my family and friends over the decades and centuries."

Popular family, Nico said, looking around and trying to guess how many were entombed down here. There were too many to count.

"When you're at the forefront of progress, there are always those keen to hold you back." Volpe took subtle control and pointed at the stacked skeletons, and those pinned against the walls. "Some were brought here dead, this was simply a place to dispose of them." Then he indicated bones scattered across the floor, not all of them as a result of Nico's brief show of anger. "Others were put here alive."

Nico could barely comprehend the fate of those thrown in here still alive, dying in a darkness full of rotting cadavers. *So why bring me here now?* he asked.

"Recuperation," Volpe said. "The gunshot damaged more than I can touch right away. You feel well because I'm holding back the pain. I'm accepting it myself."

The hesitant voice, Nico thought. *The caution. It's because he's in pain. And . . . afraid of the Doges?*

"No," Volpe said. "Cautious. They know the city, but never knew this place. I believe the Doges are hidden in a mansion in Dorsoduro. That's where they will have Geena. For either of us to get what we want, we will have to kill them both. But before we can face them, you must heal. While fighting them, I cannot also take on your pain. And it would be crippling to you."

Nico touched his chest again and felt Volpe withdraw. His skin felt warm, but the heavy weight inside his chest gave out no real sensations. He almost thanked Volpe, but felt little real gratitude.

"How long do we have to wait?" he asked.

Awhile, Volpe said, and he was fading further away.

"Where's the door?" Nico asked. He was looking around the chamber again, trying to perceive squared edges in the uneven shadows. But all he sensed from Volpe was a smile, and then nothing.

So he sat down for a while and rested, closing his eyes, breathing calmly and smelling age and candle wax, and the dust of broken bones. And when he thought Volpe was deep enough and far enough away, Nico opened his mind and perception and thought, *Geena, I'm alive, and I'll guide you in.*

CHAPTER 17

GEENA DESPERATELY WANTED TO GO TO HIM. *I'LL GUIDE YOU in,* Nico had whispered into her mind, and every part of her wanted to surrender to that guidance. In his thoughts she felt pain and sorrow, and she wished that she could be in his arms, taking and giving the comfort their intimacy would provide.

If they were very lucky, and her courage did not fail her, perhaps they would know that comfort again. But now was not the time. Enemies still lurked all around them, working in shadows to wreak havoc upon their lives. But even that was selfish thinking; more hung in the balance than just the lives of two lovers. Plague and ancient hatreds had come to Venice on wings of greed.

All of it needed to be expunged and, somehow, the fates had conspired to make Geena Hodge the only one able to do that. If she acted now, and swiftly, and as mercilessly as her enemies.

She felt Nico's psychic touch, the flutter of his thoughts caressing hers, and she wanted to melt into him. She chose ice instead, freezing emotion out in order to preserve it.

Geena? Nico whispered in her mind.

I'm here, but I can't come to you. They set me free but only to find you. The contagion is in Foscari and Aretino, just as it was in Car-avello. And they have more, secreted away in chambers even Volpe doesn't know about. If they can't have Venice, no one will. If we don't do as they demand, they'll scour the place of life and start over.

She felt his thoughts recoil.

They've given us a choice, she continued. *I bring them Volpe by dawn or everyone in the city dies. So you have to come to me, Nico. You and Volpe have to meet me in the Chamber of Ten an hour before dawn.*

But Volpe—

He loves this city. He'll come, and he'll try to kill them. But if all three of them are dead, the plague in those chambers will be released, so he's got to come up with some other way to stop them.

Geena felt his confusion. *But what are you going to do between now and then?* he asked.

Prepare, she replied. *Whatever you do, don't trust him. When this is over—*

She did not finish the thought, but she knew that Nico would feel it and understand her fear. Perhaps Volpe would sense it as well, but perhaps not. She was not sure how much of their communication he could understand, if it had to be concrete thoughts or if just feelings were enough. But Nico would know, he would feel her suspicion and mistrust of Volpe. The magician had promised to leave them alone, to depart Nico's body when all of this was over, but Geena no longer believed him, if she ever had. His hubris had made him preserve his heart and his spirit for centuries so that he could remain the Oracle of Venice long past the time someone else ought to have inherited the role. He saw himself as the only one capable of protecting his city, and would not surrender that responsibility for anything.

To be the Oracle, he needed a body.

I'll be all right, Nico thought, the words a salve to her troubled soul. But words were not enough.

Geena could not risk letting him see more of what was in her mind. *I'll see you an hour before dawn. Until then, don't search for me. Don't reach out. We'll make it through this, honey, and we'll be together again, just the two of us.*

She felt his concern and his love and his fear for her, but just before the connection between them was severed, what Geena felt more than anything was his trust, and that gave her the strength to go on.

Nico sagged back against the stone wall of the catacombs beneath the Volpe family crypt, feeling the absence of Geena in his mind like the urgent nothingness of a missing limb. The shadows were fluttering moths in the dim, jittery candlelight. More than anything, the place felt dry, all of the moisture drawn from the bones of the dead long ago.

As though stepping out from the dark recesses of his mind, Volpe slunk forward. *What do you suppose she's up to?*

"You were listening in," Nico said. "You know as much as I do."

Or did he? He knew that Volpe had heard the thoughts he and Geena had exchanged, but how much more had he been able to understand?

You are her first priority—

"I was. But if your old friends are telling the truth—"

Caravello carried the plague in his blood, under his control, like a weapon. We must assume they are telling the truth.

Nico winced, both from the lingering ache of his healed-over wound and from the strange glee he felt coming from Volpe.

"You're happy about this?"

We were going to have to face the two prodigals regardless, but I could not have chosen a better location. It was the locus of my power and influence for all these many years.

"But they must know that, and they still plan to attack you there."

They want access to the well.

Nico froze. "The well? You mean where Akylis' tomb is buried?"

The Old Magician's remains were never buried, Volpe said, the tone—even in Nico's mind—like that of an adult correcting an errant child. *The well was dug, the dolmen erected around the corpse, and then the well was capped. There is no awareness there, nothing lingering of Akylis' mind. But as his body liquefied, the magic and evil remained. All that power, down there at the bottom of the well. Though it had been capped, when I built the Chamber of Ten, I sealed it with magic of my own and a new stone cap.*

An image flashed across Nico's mind and he realized he had seen the well cap. He had been too distracted when they had first entered the Chamber, too absorbed with the power emanating from the urn where Volpe had preserved his heart. But when he and Geena and the rest of the team had watched the footage Sabrina had shot, he had seen the granite disk set into the floor of the Chamber.

"Why do they need to open it?" Nico asked. "You said they're already leaching Akylis' power."

Don't you see? They want to bathe *in it, to absorb it all at once. It would probably kill them, but I can't risk the possibility that it won't, never mind the potential that Akylis' evil, unleashed from the well, could taint the hearts and spirits of all of the people of Venice. I can't allow it.*

"But we're still going to meet them there?"

Are you suggesting we ignore this summons? That we leave your woman and all of the people of my city to die?

"Of course not! But it's obvious they're not afraid of you."

They will be. They'll never unseal the well. I won't allow it. Besides, they don't know what awaits them in the Chamber of Ten.

"And what's that?"

The past.

Nico felt Volpe shifting inside of him and he felt himself expanding the way he did when he drew a deep breath, lungs filling with air. But this wasn't air—the empty spaces in his body and mind were being filled up with the spirit of Zanco Volpe. A flash of panic sparked inside of him and he thought of the impressions he had gotten from Geena, her certainty that Volpe intended to betray him and take over his body . . .

"What are you doing?" Nico asked.

Making myself comfortable, Volpe replied. *We will have to work together as never before if we are to survive to see the dawn.*

"We?" Had Volpe not heard his thoughts and doubts?

How could I not know of your suspicions? I would fear the same if our situations were reversed.

"All right. So how do I know I can trust you?"

You have no choice.

Nico felt a chill that had nothing to do with the bones around him. Or perhaps it did . . . were these not the remains of generations of those foolish enough to make enemies of the Volpe clan?

We are in swift waters now, Nico, and we have little influence over where they will finally cast us ashore. The magician's presence and even his inner voice diminished. *We have several hours before we must depart for this rendezvous and the best use of that time for both of us is to rest and heal. Sleep now. Soon you and your love will be reunited.*

Even as Volpe's magic clouded his mind and dragged him down into a healing slumber, his suspicions were at work.

"For how long?" he whispered.

But the magician's only reply was oblivion.

Geena stood again in the courtyard of the church of San Rocco, paranoia creeping like spiders along her arms and up the back of her neck. The taverna where she and Volpe had burned the corpse of the Doge Caravello remained dark and undisturbed.

The façade of the church had an appealing plainness to it, and its windows were just as dark as the shops. It seemed to be waiting for her, offering a sanctuary she only wished she could claim.

The shops were dark, only a rare light visible in the windows of the apartments above them. Surely no one would be awake now, and yet she could not dispel the fear that even now she was observed. It was not the feeling that prickled her skin, not the certainty she had felt when Caravello had been stalking her.

She took a deep breath and began walking again, not across the courtyard—that would have been foolish—but retracing the same roundabout route that she and Volpe had used to depart the taverna earlier in the day. If things went as she hoped, being observed approaching the church would not be a problem. But if she had to improvise, if there was damage done, she did not want anyone to be able to say that they saw her there.

Is this my life now? I'm a criminal?

The thought upset her, but only for a moment. The old rules no longer applied—if they ever really had.

Geena worked her way around to the side of the church. Even the moonlight did not reach into that narrow alley between buildings. At the back of the building, another structure was attached. An arched doorway recessed into the stone marked the entrance to the rectory. She raised her fist and hammered on the door to the priest's residence.

The noise echoed off the walls, amplified in that enclosed space, and she left off seconds after she began, waiting to see if her pounding would bring anyone to the door. Again she pounded on the door and this time she kept it up, hammering away for ten or twenty seconds, pausing, then starting up again. The second time she paused she heard the scrape of metal on metal from inside, followed by the clank of a deadbolt being thrown back.

She froze, swallowing hard, as the heavy wooden door swung inward and a thin, white-haired priest peered out at her.

"What are you doing, coming here at this hour? Who are you?" the priest demanded, anger crackling in his imperious tone.

But Geena would not be intimidated.

"Do you believe in magic, Father?" she asked.

The priest practically sneered, about to slam the door in her face.

"Please, Father. The whole city is in danger," she said, and when he hesitated she forged ahead. "Someone broke into the church earlier today. You won't have noticed yet, but I swear to you, you've been vandalized. Something's been hidden here, and if you don't let me in, people are going to die."

Uncertainty rippled across his face. "Come in, then, and we'll call the police together."

Geena did not move. "There's nothing they can do. Look in my eyes, Father, and decide what you see. But if you don't help me, when the sun comes up tomorrow every man, woman, and child in Venice will begin to cough and choke and bleed, and they'll die in the thousands. Maybe I asked you the wrong question. Maybe 'magic' is too fanciful a word for you. So tell me, Father, do you believe in evil?"

The confusion in his eyes gave her hope. He studied her, searching her face for some fragment of truth, and his anger gave way to fear and concern.

"What's your name?" he asked.

"Dr. Geena Hodge. I'm an archaeologist in the employ of Ca'Foscari University."

"And does your employer know what you're up to tonight, in the small hours of the morning?"

She shook her head. "No one knows."

The priest stared a moment, eyes narrowed, and then he stepped back, swinging the door wide.

"Come in, Dr. Hodge. It seems you have little time. We'd best not keep evil waiting."

He let her in and closed the door behind her, sliding the deadbolt. A small statue of the Virgin Mary stood upon a pedestal against the wall opposite the door, but otherwise the entryway was as utilitarian as the exterior of the building. In the dim gray light, which filtered down to them from a room farther along the hall, she studied the face of the priest as he turned to her. His eyes were alight with interest instead of anger now, and he seemed years younger than he had when he'd first opened the door.

"Come along," he said, and led her toward a door she realized must lead from the rectory into the church.

Geena followed him through the door into a back room of the church, which was lined with wooden cabinets. A big desk sat in one corner, and she was surprised by the clutter—microphone and music stands, two chairs in need of repair, stacks of old missals, the priest's vestments hanging in an open closet. This disarray humanized him, and that troubled her. She wanted faith and strength, and a certain mysticism.

He gestured to a chair, as if they had all the time in the world. Geena glanced at a clock on the wall—1:17 a.m.

"Go on," the priest said. "Tell me your story. Dawn is a long way off yet."

Geena shook her head. "I'm sorry, Father—"

"Father Alberto."

"I can't afford for you to simply humor me." She glanced around the room. "If you let me show you where the vandalism took place, you'll see soon enough that there are powers at work here you've yet to consider."

The old priest hesitated, and then sighed.

"Lead the way."

"Wait," she said. "Do you have a lantern or a candle or something?"

He gave her an odd look, then walked over to open one of the cabinets. Reaching in, he produced a heavy-duty flashlight.

"I know you must spend a lot of time living in the past, Dr. Hodge, but it's the 21st century."

"So it is," Geena said sheepishly as he handed it to her. "I've been losing track lately."

Father Alberto led her out into the vast hall of the church and past the altar. From there, Geena saw the door to the small royal chapel, and she started toward it. The priest turned on a single light switch, a few bulbs providing only wan illumination in the vastness of the church. Her own footfalls seemed too loud on the flagstones as they passed the Tintoretto paintings for which the church's nave was famous, and then she led him through the door into the royal chapel.

Although she knew the damage had been done, it still took her a few seconds of concentration, staring at the bookshelf under the stairs, before she could see through the spell of concealment that Volpe had cast. The spell could not withstand the scrutiny of someone who expected something other than the illusion. Books had been stacked and scattered on the floor near the wreckage of what had once been an ornate bookshelf. Broken boards leaned against the stone wall.

"How did I not see this before?" the priest asked.

Geena turned and looked at him in surprise. "You can see it now?"

"What do you mean? Of course I can see it."

Now that she had drawn his attention to it, the spell of concealment could not hide the vandalism from the priest. She narrowed her eyes, stepping right up to the ruined bookshelf.

"Is there a hole in the wall back there?" Father Alberto asked. "It's too dark for me to make out, but . . . there is, isn't there?"

"There is," she agreed, reaching out to touch the rough, broken edge of the stones that had been pulled out of the wall.

Inside of that opening, a small door hung partially open, and she pushed it inward.

"I'll be damned," the old priest muttered.

Geena could not help smiling at him. "I certainly hope not, Father," she said, and then she clambered through the opening. "Now I think it's your turn to follow me."

She clicked on the flashlight and they descended together into a small square chamber Geena had seen before only through the dreamlike lens provided by Nico's touch. The braziers in the corners were dark and cold and the room's shadows seemed to resist being dispelled by the flashlight's wide beam, but soon enough she located bloody sigils inscribed upon the flagstone floor and a cloth bag that she recognized as belonging to Nico.

Father Alberto could not tear his gaze from the markings on the floor, even when she set the flashlight down and knelt to open the bag.

"The Devil's work," he said.

"Not *the* Devil, but *a* devil, most certainly."

Geena shone the light into the bag. She thought about how much to reveal to the priest, but she knew that if she wanted his help she would need to shock him. So she took out the ivory seal once used on the city's official documents and set it on the floor. Then she withdrew the dry and dessicated hand of a dead man and set that down as well.

Father Alberto whispered a blessing as he crossed himself.

"Explain this to me, Dr. Hodge. What it means and how you knew it was here."

"It will have to be quick, Father."

"All the better," he said.

She sat back on the flagstones, the flashlight in her hands, and the tale spilled from her like a ghost story told late at night at summer camp. The flashlight must have contributed to that impression for her, but there was more to it than that. Those stories always felt to her both real and unreal at the same time, and so did the turns her life had taken these past days.

When she had finished, she did not wait for him to reply, afraid that in spite of the evidence she had just shown him and his belief in powers beyond the understanding of humanity, he would think that she had somehow staged it all. Before he could say a word, she reached into the bag again and withdrew the grimoire that Volpe had so coveted. He had left it here for safekeeping, hidden behind a glamour until he could retrieve it, but he had not counted on her having seen it all.

Seen the book. Seen the ritual.

The cover felt unnaturally warm and damp under her touch and the book weighed more than it seemed it should.

"This is *Le Livre de l'Inconnu—The Book of the Nameless*—and though its name is French, I've seen for myself that the incantations and other writings inside are not in that language, or at least not all of them are. It contains a great many impossible things that are nevertheless true."

She held the book in her palm and let it fall open where it

would. Geena had seen it with textbooks and cookbooks and even
well-read hardcover novels . . . after a certain amount of use, a book
will fall open to its most frequently used pages. But when *Le Livre
de l'Inconnu* spread its pages, she did not recognize the words and
symbols there.

Geena closed her eyes. Time was wasting. Fortune had been
with her thus far tonight and she had thought her luck would continue. She opened her eyes and began to turn the pages, but nothing looked familiar. How far had he been into the book? She tried
to remember and realized that the ritual Volpe had used had been
from little more than a third of the way through its thickness. She
paged backward in the book, training the flashlight beam on the
hideous things uncovered there—images and words she only half
understood and did not want fully revealed to her.

Father Alberto had come around behind her now, reading over
her shoulder, and several times she heard him mutter in revulsion
or horror.

"This is real?" he whispered at one point. "You're certain?"

"Are you asking about the authenticity of the book or the magic
in it?"

"Both, I suppose."

Geena glanced over her shoulder at him. "I'm sorry, Father. But
both are very real."

He reached into his pants pocket and withdrew a rosary, which
he wrapped around his fingers and then brought up to his lips, kiss-
ing the beads once before clutching them against his chest.

And then she found the pages.

"Here," she said, pointing. "Most of this looks like an antiquated
Latin to me—"

"You can't read Latin? I thought you were an archaeologist."

"I can make out some of it, but only some. I'm not a linguist,
and the one I'd normally bring onto a project—"

"All right, all right," Father Alberto said, waving her argument
away. "You're right. It's an archaic Latin . . . or some of it is. Part of
it is in Greek."

She caught her breath. "Then you *can* read it?"

"I can translate it, if that's what you're asking. I can tell you what it says."

Geena shook her head, staring down at the pages.

"No. I don't care what it says. I don't want you to translate it." She looked up at the old priest. "It's an incantation, Father. I want you to teach me how to speak the words."

In the hour before dawn, the night was blue.

Nico wanted to run through St. Mark's Square beneath the indigo sky, but Volpe held him back as if he were on a leash. He slipped through the deeper shadows of the arcade at the western end of the square and then in the lee of the buildings on the south side. Volpe had taken control for a minute, just long enough to cast a spell that gathered the darkness around him like a cloak, and then retreated.

The magician wanted to conserve his strength. There were attacks and betrayals to come, and they both knew it.

The humid air clung to him along with the dark. No breeze stirred the errant bits of rubbish strewn around the square. The basilica loomed against the sky, the stars fading with the oncoming dawn, and Nico's heart pounded fiercely in his chest as though trying to escape the cage of his bones and flesh. He longed to reach out with his mind and touch Geena's thoughts, but she had warned him against doing so.

The temptation to turn and run was great. He would never have done so—it would have doomed Geena and all of Venice—but even if he'd tried, his puppeteer would have yanked the strings and put him right back on course.

Watch for them, Volpe snapped.

"I'm watching," Nico whispered.

He spotted the first of the Doges' thugs on the steps of the basilica—a slim man in a gray suit who made no attempt to hide himself. He stood with the confidence of a Western gunfighter but, cloaked in shadow, Nico passed by without notice. There were others as well, in front of the Doge's Palace and the Biblioteca itself. Two men leaned against the striped poles at the edge of the canal, where gondolas bobbed in the water, tied up for the night. As Nico approached the door of the library he saw a lovely blond woman standing in the trees at the beginning of the small park that separated the Biblioteca from the canal.

"They're already here," Nico whispered. "They must be waiting for us inside."

No. These are their eyes. If they were already here, I would feel them.

"Like you felt them before, when they fucking shot me?"

Spellcraft marks the soul like bloodstained hands, and each mark is different. I have always been sensitive to such things. Now that I have encountered their magic, they could not hide themselves from me . . . not this nearby.

Nico no longer knew what to believe and what not to believe. But even if Volpe was telling the truth, he had to wonder if one or both of the Doges might be just as sensitive—if they would know when Volpe was near.

They are fools, always more concerned with the tactile than the spiritual.

"They've managed to survive hundreds of years and become much more than arcane dabblers, enough to get you hiding in crypts and nursing bullet wounds. Not bad for fools."

You're wasting time.

Nico flashed on Geena, got a momentary touch of her mind. Though she had told him to keep his thoughts to himself, this close it was impossible not to feel her. *Like Volpe and the Doges*, he thought.

He could feel Volpe's amusement at the idea, and a fresh wave of determination filled him.

Fueled by frustration and anger, wanting morning to come and put an end to all of his uncertainty, he glanced around again at the killers Foscari and Aretino had put in place as sentries. The Doges weren't here now, but there was less than an hour before dawn and they would arrive soon enough. Perhaps the moment Nico opened the door to the Biblioteca—surely one of the thugs would witness it—the lunatic wizards would rush to take them like hunters hearing the trap closing around their prey.

So be it.

As project manager, Geena had a key to the Biblioteca. Volpe could have unlocked it with a wave of his hand, but that was unnecessary. Nico grabbed the door handle and it swung open easily. He stepped inside and closed it swiftly behind him, moving immediately across the foyer. Exit signs glowed red along corridors to either side, and dim, subtle lighting kept the library from darkness even overnight.

Had the killers seen him? Almost certainly, and he doubted the Doges would wait for dawn. He rushed along the long hall that led into the back room where they had found the hidden doorway down to Petrarch's library. The lights should have been off there, but Geena had turned them on. Long black tubes snaked up through the open door, humming softly. They must have pumped the millions of gallons of water out of the flooded chambers, right out the door, across the small park, and into the canal. But they had left the pumps in place, still working, constantly draining the water that continued to seep in.

He went through the yawing stone door and started down the steps into the ancient librarian's hiding place. Those long, fat tubes were tucked against the wall and he was careful not to stumble over them. The lights that Nico and the other members of the team had strung flickered brighter and then brighter still when he reached the bottom step, as though new power surged into them. The place smelled of damp and rot, but the stones were dry.

Debris had been scraped against one wall, the wreckage left by the flood.

The pumps were huge, humming things, their tubes snaking in both directions—up the stairs to the Biblioteca and through the door that led down into the Chamber of Ten. When Geena had told him they were to meet here, Nico had wondered how the university had arranged for the wall of the canal to be shored up and the Chamber pumped out so quickly. But now that he knew what the Doges wanted with the Chamber—that they needed to get to the well of Akylis—he knew it had not been Tonio Schiavo's influence that had inspired such Herculean efforts.

The memory of discovering this door and the chamber below remained fresh in Nico's mind. He could still feel the strange chill he had felt when descending with Geena and the rest of the team, and his mesmerized fascination with the urn at the center of the room. The power of the spell Volpe had used to keep the Chamber safe and keep the Doges out of Venice had made him feel almost drunk. And the lure . . . Volpe's consciousness might have been shut down, but his essence had somehow woken at Nico's arrival.

I woke him, Nico thought.

And you dropped the urn, Volpe replied. *You finally understand. All of this is happening because of you.*

"Bullshit," Nico said. He had not used deceit and intrigue and threats to control Venice, murdered members of the Council just to keep his power, and banished the Doges.

No. I'm more convinced than ever that you and Geena were meant to be there. The city called you. I have been the Oracle of Venice for half a millennium. I would serve her forever if I could, but I think she has chosen the both of you.

"We don't want the job," Nico said. "We just want to be done with this. I want my body back."

Volpe did not reply, and yet again Nico had the impression the magician was shielding his thoughts, hiding something.

He went through the door that led down to the Chamber of Ten. The light from Petrarch's library reached half a dozen steps into his descent and, below, electric lantern light shone through the place where there had been a stone door engraved with the Roman numeral X, but there was a stretch of darkness in between and he put his fingers on the cold, damp walls to guide him as he continued downward.

Whispers drifted up to him. He could not make out the words. Volpe did.

The idiot. What is she doing? Turn around, damn you! Go back up!

"Who? I thought you said they weren't here yet?"

It's not the Doges. It's your damned woman, meddling with dark rites she hasn't the power to—

"Geena?" Nico called, continuing toward the light at the bottom of the stairs.

Turn around! Volpe shouted in his mind.

Nico felt the magician surging forward within him, taking control of his limbs. His arms were tugged, his body twisted, and the puppeteer inside of him began to turn on the stairs.

No! Nico fought him, thinking only of Geena, trusting her, knowing that whatever she had planned it meant he had to bring Volpe to the Chamber of Ten as she'd asked.

For just a second, he wrested control of his body back. Then Volpe shunted him out again, but now he was off balance. His foot slipped on a step and he fell in a tangle of arms and legs, spilling down the stone stairs and then sprawling through the vacant doorway into the inch or so of water that covered the floor.

He'd struck his head. Disoriented, Volpe tried to get Nico's body off the ground, drawing his knees up beneath him. The whispers had risen to a determined incantation and Volpe looked over to see Geena kneeling nearby, using a chunk of the broken wall as a table. A lantern stood upon it, illuminating the sigils she had scrawled on the rock, and other things as well. Nico saw them now and understood—the hand of a soldier, the seal of the master of the city, *The Book of the Nameless*, and a long knife.

Her eyes were wide, her hair wild, beads of sweat on her forehead. She launched herself toward him like a madwoman, the blade glittering in the lantern light. Fear crashed over Nico, but it was not his own.

"No, you stupid bitch, you—"

Geena kicked him onto his side. He tried to raise his hands to defend himself, tried to scramble away, but she was too fast, too savage. The blade hacked into the meat of his forearm, blood spattering the thin layer of water.

Instantly she retreated, racing to the book and lantern and the ritual symbols she had drawn on the broken stone. She looked at the open pages and started in with the incantation again. Nico struggled within Volpe—he had wrested control once and knew he must be able to do it again—but the bastard was too strong.

You fool! Volpe thought. *You let her see the entire ritual through your eyes.*

You'd never have given me back my body. You'd never have left us alone.

That remains to be seen, Volpe replied.

Trapped within his own body, Nico could not even cry out as Geena used the knife on her own palm. Seconds later she began to flick her wrist, spattering blood off of the knife in a complex pattern around the Chamber. The lantern light flickered.

Volpe began to laugh, rising slowly to his feet.

Geena looked up in panic.

What are you going to do? Nico thought.

Volpe let the pain of the knife wound through and Nico groaned, but the bastard did not give up control of the flesh.

"Dear Geena," Volpe said. "You're adorable, really. You had me worried for a moment. I thought you might actually know what you're doing."

Geena glared at him, fearless and full of venom. "You think I don't know what you're talking about? The Repulsion and Expulsion ritual only works if the banished is already outside the city. You've got to be out before I can keep you out. But guess what, Zanco? You *are* outside the city. Last night, I had my friend Domenic scrape what was left of your black heart—all that's left of your dead husk—off the floor. He's removed it from Venice."

Defiantly she stood and flicked the knife three times more, thrice repeating the last words of the incantation.

Volpe let his shoulders slump, let his eyelids flutter.

"Nico?" Geena asked, and the hope in her voice broke his heart. She dropped the knife and rushed toward him.

No. No, stop! Nico shouted. He raged against Volpe, clawed at the magician's very soul, forced himself upward, and took control just long enough to work his own lips, his own tongue.

". . . didn't . . . work . . . still here . . ." he slurred.

Geena staggered to a halt, confusion in her eyes. Volpe dropped the act and reached out to grab her by the throat. He slapped her hard enough that the sound echoed off the walls of the Chamber of Ten, off the three stone columns in the center of the room, off those ten obelisks that housed the remains of the men who had been loyal to Volpe and who had murdered him at his own behest.

"My heart may no longer be in Venice, but I am still here," Volpe snarled. "I'm right here in front of you. If you understood the first thing about spellcraft, you might have managed to bind my soul to my heart and then your foolish gambit would have worked. Why the Spirit of Venezia chose the two of you to be its next Oracles is baffling to me."

Oracles. The two of us?

Geena tried to speak, tried to claw at the fingers cutting off her air, but she couldn't get the words out.

Nico was the one who answered: *Volpe thinks the city has chosen us both, that we're both Oracles.*

You will be one day, but only if you live, Volpe replied. *Now listen to me, young fools. You were never in any danger from me.* He shoved Geena away and she splashed to the floor, gasping.

"I hope you have a better plan for dealing with Foscari and Aretino, Dr. Hodge, because they're nearly here."

A soft, chuffing laughter filled the Chamber and the lantern light flickered in time with it. Volpe and Geena both spun around and Nico saw the Doges and their hired killers stepping into the Chamber.

" 'Nearly'?" Aretino asked. "You're slipping, Volpe."

Foscari licked his lips, glancing from Geena to Nico and back. "A lovers' quarrel. And we're just in time. Please don't let us interrupt. We'll happily watch you murder each other."

Wearing Nico's body, Volpe glanced at Geena. Something passed between them—*among* them, all three.

Geena smiled. "It can wait until the two of you are as dead as Caravello."

"You'd betray us?" Foscari asked, feigning insult.

"I kept my part of the bargain," she said. "I brought you Volpe."

"Yes, thank you," Aretino said, nodding to her in gratitude. Then he glanced at his hired killers—the slim man in his gray suit and the blond woman were in front—and gestured at her with a flourish of his hand.

"My friends, if you'd be so kind. Kill her."

CHAPTER 18

I HAD TO TRY, GEENA THOUGHT.

Nico's reply did not come in words but in an outpouring of anguished love. As she stared at the two mad Doges and their hired killers, at cold eyes and gun barrels, she knew that she was about to die. Aretino and the depraved Foscari had not waited for dawn. Her only regret was that Nico would die with her, and that he would die with Volpe still inside of him. She'd tried to drive the magician out, thinking it was her only chance to free the man she loved, the only opportunity to prevent Volpe from claiming his body forever.

The Doges had to be stopped, but she'd told herself that she and Nico could do it. They'd already killed one of the ancient lunatics. It could be done. She'd been taking huge risks, flying by the seat of her pants, relying on hope and the way fate seemed to have been running her way . . . as if the city itself was on their side. And if Volpe was right, and she and Nico were meant to become the new Oracles of Venice, maybe it had been. But now her luck had run out.

She hadn't expected so many guns.

"My friends, if you'd be so kind," Aretino said. "Kill her."

Nico moved to block the killers' aim—or was it Volpe, wearing Nico's body? Would the magician do that for her? Surely not, and yet . . .

He stood straighter, his head slightly cocked, and she knew that if she could have seen his face his features would have changed in that subtle way that told her who looked out from those eyes at any given moment. He had fooled her once, but this was no performance. This was Zanco Volpe.

The Doges knew it, too. Geena could see it in their eyes.

"You were fools to come back," Volpe said, speaking with Nico's lips, protecting her. "I will never allow you to uncap the well. Akylis' evil has caused enough strife in my city. Venice will be tainted no further."

Foscari laughed. "We've been waiting for this moment, Volpe. Now it has finally come, do you think there is anything that would have kept us away?"

The killers paused a moment, glancing back and forth between Aretino and Volpe, unsure.

Geena cast a glance at the granite disk set into the floor perhaps twenty feet away from her. She had risked so much. If her risk led to the release of that evil, to the fate that the Doges had in store for Venice and the world, she would never forgive herself.

But once exposed to the full power of Akylis' evil, would she even care? The thought made her sick.

Aretino shook his head almost sadly. "Honestly, Zanco. You've been out of the world for centuries. You're nothing but a ghost."

"I am far more than a ghost," Volpe snapped.

Geena glanced around quickly and spotted the bloodstained knife on the stone floor. She measured the distance in her mind, wondering if she could reach it and make it to cover behind an obelisk before bullets cut her down. But there was no way. It would be suicide.

"Venice is ours," Foscari said, preening. "The fullness of Akylis' power will be ours. Whatever power you had is nothing to us now. If you still had a shred of your true power, you would not have allowed me to wound that shell you're wearing."

"You shot me because I had no experience with guns," Volpe said. "I did not understand them. I do now."

"You bled. This time I'll cut you into pieces."

"Then do it. Until you do, I am still the Oracle of Venice. Her soul is under my protection."

Aretino blinked slowly, a predator just coming awake. He glanced at the man in the gray suit, then down at his gun. His left eye twitched with anger.

"Didn't I tell you to kill the woman?"

The man in the gray suit nodded toward Volpe. "He's in the way."

Aretino glared at him in disgust and the gray suit got the message. He and the blond woman started forward again, eyeing Volpe warily. Geena's breath quickened, pulse racing as she cursed. The knife lay perhaps ten feet to her left. She had no choice.

No, Nico said in her mind. *Volpe, you keep her alive.*

She just tried to kill me.

"You're already dead, you son of a bitch," Geena whispered to his back. *You had your friends cut out your heart.*

Gray suit and the blond aimed their guns at Volpe's skull as they began to edge around him. Four other thugs stood with the Doges, awaiting the opportunity to kill someone.

Tears began to well in her eyes and she grew furious with herself for letting these monsters see her cry.

I love you, Nico. You were the best thing about living.

Volpe flinched as he overheard this thought. He turned his head just enough so that she could see the thin smile on his face. He lifted his left hand, clutched into a fist, and whispered a single word—it might have been *"araignées,"* French for *spiders*—and popped open his hand as though releasing something from his grasp.

Gray suit and the blond cried out in unison, dropping their guns as they reached up to claw at their faces.

"No!" Aretino barked, and raised both hands, beginning a guttural chant.

Volpe took a step toward the Doges and brought both hands together in a single clap that echoed off the stone walls. As if struck by a sudden gale, the Doges and their lackeys were blown backward, limbs flailing as they hit the floor with a splash.

Find cover! Nico shouted in her thoughts.

Geena had already started running. The blond and the man in the gray suit had collapsed to the ground and were having some kind of seizures, still tearing at their faces.

"They're in here!" the man in the gray suit screamed. "The spiders are inside my head!"

Geena bent to snatch up the knife as she ran by, then sprinted for the three columns at the center of the Chamber of Ten. Any of the obelisks would have hidden her, but from in there she might be able to defend herself, to survive precious seconds or minutes— long enough for Volpe to kill the Doges and their hired help. Until now, casting spells had drained him. The lack of a body of his own had weakened his magic. But something had obviously happened, because now the Doges seemed outmatched.

She darted between two of the stone columns, took cover, and peered back out at the magicians.

Just in time to see Volpe fall to his knees in the inch of water, too weak to raise a hand in his own defense, or in hers.

"Is that the best you can do these days?" Foscari said, wiping at a bloody scrape on his face as he stood.

Aretino rose stiffly, hatred burning in his eyes. "You know, Francesco, I think that might have exhausted our old friend. I think that might well be the last spell he will ever cast."

Get up! Geena thought. *Goddamn you, get up!*

As if in reply, Volpe snapped his head back and grinned wildly at the Doges. "Just waiting for you to catch your breath," he said. "I want to make this last."

Brave words. Cruel words. But only a ruse. From the darkness of the three columns, Geena saw his face in the flickering lantern light and the features had changed again. Volpe had burned himself out and retreated back into Nico's mind, leaving Nico himself to face the Doges, pretending to be Volpe.

"Come, then," Nico said, trying his best to mimic Volpe's arrogant sneer. "Do your worst."

"Oh, we will," Foscari promised, licking his lips.

What are you doing? Geena cried in her mind.

Venice chose us as her Oracles—

We're not the Oracles yet!

And maybe we never will be, Nico replied. *But we were chosen. We can't let them win.*

Geena felt the weight of the knife in her hand. She tightened her grip on the handle and looked down at the blade, dark with her blood and with Nico's. They only had Volpe's word on it, and she did not trust the old magician at all, but somehow she knew that much was true.

Grim-faced, she narrowed her eyes and peered out into the Chamber of Ten, raising the knife.

Nico held his hands in front of him, fingers hooked into claws as though any second he might sketch a spell on the air. He had experienced Volpe's casting of such enchantments before and prayed he looked convincing enough to make the Doges wary. Aretino's eyes gleamed with hatred and ambition, but Foscari seemed excited only by the prospect of causing pain.

No time to lie down on the job, he thought, trying to jostle Volpe. *If they kill me, we'll both be dead! Come on, do something!*

But the magician had diminished somehow, fallen down deep inside of him like a light at the bottom of a well. He had managed the appearance of strength, but those two spells had drained him. Nico felt him stirring, but only weakly.

I can't fight them, Volpe said. *The Chamber is filled with residue from my magic, but I can barely draw on it. Without physical form—*

You've got physical form! Me!

It isn't the same. I need a foundation to provide leverage. Volpe did not explain further, but an image flashed through Nico's mind and he understood at last what the magician meant. Without his own body, casting spells was like trying to lift something heavy while swimming in deep water.

Foscari began to chant in a language Nico did not even recognize—something ancient and ugly—and the Doge's grin widened. Aretino gestured for their hired killers to hang back. Nico felt his mask of courage begin to slip and Aretino must have noticed something amiss, for he narrowed his eyes and took a step forward.

Then he laughed softly, holding up a hand.

"Wait, Francesco. It's over."

Foscari pulled up and glared at him liked a dog rounding on his master. "What do you mean, 'over'?"

"That's not Volpe talking to us. It's the boy, Lombardi. Volpe's blown out his own candle already," Aretino said, smiling at Nico. "Isn't that right, Nico?"

Nico wanted to smash the old bastard's skull against the stone floor until his brains leaked out. *Boy?* He tried not to change his expression, tried to hold on to Volpe's sneer.

Are you hearing this? Volpe, fucking do something!

You've got to surrender.

They're not here for prisoners!

To me, Volpe said, his inner voice stronger. *It's the only way. Give yourself over to me willingly, let us merge completely. It may be confusing, it may only make it more difficult to fight, but it's possible it will truly join us and I will be able to use your body fully as my own, and wield the most powerful spells without collapsing.*

Nico stared in horror at Aretino's fading smile and the growing delight on Foscari's face.

"Get the girl," Aretino said.

"Allow me," Foscari said, giving their lackeys a savage glance that made even those hardened killers fall back.

How can I trust you? How do I know I'll get my body back?

Even I don't know if you'll get your body back. This merging could be permanent. But choose quickly, or the choice will be taken from you.

It was no choice at all. He saw Foscari striding toward the three columns at the center of the Chamber, caught a glimpse of Geena huddled there, knife glinting in her hand, and he knew.

"Do it, you bastard!" he shouted.

Aretino flinched in surprise. Thinking Nico had been talking to him, Foscari turned to leer at him.

Take a deep breath and then let it out. When you inhale again, let it be with an invitation in your heart. Let me fill the spaces in you.

Just hurry, Nico thought.

And he did as Volpe asked. Closed his eyes. Deep breath in, let it out, another breath, let it out. It felt to him as if he were growing, as though when he opened his eyes he ought to be a giant. But when he did look, he had not changed physically. Inside, though . . . he bristled with vigor, alert to the slightest sound or shift in the texture of shadows in the Chamber. He could see skeins of light like spiderwebs throughout the room—gold and silver, green and red and black, purple as a bruise, pink as a woman's secret flesh.

Volpe did not like to call it magic because it did not come from within him. But the power—the magic—it was there, all around them, and if he could only reach out and touch those skeins, weave them together with the right gestures, the right words, he could bend the world to his whim.

Nico had never been so terrified or so aroused.

"Hello again, Pietro," Volpe said with Nico's mouth. *Or is that me?* It was impossible now to know where he ended and Volpe began. They were one.

Aretino swore. He lifted his hands, about to cast a spell. A whip-thin gunman behind him sensed the change, saw it all happening, raised his weapon, and pulled the trigger.

Water, Volpe thought.

Even as the sound of the gunshot erupted in the Chamber, Nico twitched a finger, throat working a subaudible grunt that was in itself a spell so ingrained in Volpe that it required nothing more.

The bullets splashed against him, dampening his clothes where they struck, nothing but water now.

Foscari turned at the gunshot's echo and threw up his hands, beginning a spell. Nico held up both hands, whispered words he had never learned, and the spells slid harmlessly away from him.

"This city is under our protection," Nico said. "And this Chamber . . . this is mine, laid with magical traps five hundred years ago. Fools, indeed."

Foscari roared and ran at him, drawing a dagger laden with curses.

Nico dropped to one knee, slapped his open palms on the stone floor, and shouted two words to trigger a spell Volpe had cast half a millennium ago.

"Expergefactum amicitiae!"

A tremor ran through the Chamber, a groan from deep beneath the city, and dust rained down from the ceiling. One of the obelisks had shattered during the flood, and now the rest of them cracked, lines running through the identical Roman numeral X engraved upon each one, and split open. Arms thrust out, knocking black stone aside, and the Council of Ten emerged from their tombs draped in crumbling robes and flaps of withered skin.

In amongst the three columns, Geena began to scream.

The Doges' hired killers swore and shouted and opened fire. A thick-necked brute bolted for the stairs. Aretino and Foscari began to cast spells. One of the dead men ignited in flames that blackened the ceiling and spread to the robes of another.

But the dead were swift. They were not slowed by bullets. In seconds they were breaking bones and tearing flesh, and the Chamber resounded with the screams of killers as the Doges' thugs were slaughtered. Several of the Ten grabbed Foscari. The Doge held one by the face and it decayed in seconds, withered flesh sloughing off of bones as its age caught up with it, and then turning to dust.

Nico strode toward Aretino. He thrust out a hand, muttered a spell from *The Book of the Nameless*, and Aretino lifted off the floor and crashed into the ceiling, breaking bones and caving in the left side of his face.

But the Doge had studied well in his centuries of wandering. He rasped the initial words of a spell to drive out an invasive spirit, and Nico felt as though he were being torn apart.

Fight it! Volpe screamed in his thoughts. *Without me, he'll destroy you.*

Nico fought, but as pain ripped into him, he feared that he was now so inextricably bound to Volpe that separation would kill them both.

Geena felt it happening, heard Nico scream inside of her head, and she saw what needed to be done.

Bring him down! she shouted in her mind, praying Nico or Volpe would hear her thoughts through the haze of their pain. *Drop him!*

With a roar of pain, Nico slashed his hands through the air and—as though he had cut the strings holding the Doge aloft—Aretino plummeted to the floor, crying out as the impact jarred broken bones. Snarling, sodden with canal water, he reached up to carve another spell from the air, but then two of the dead Ten attacked him. Geena had seen them waiting for the opportunity. From inside its tattered robes, one of them drew a long ritual dagger and hacked it down with inhuman strength, severing Aretino's hand at the wrist.

Blood sprayed the two dead men.

Nico reeled backward and fell to his knees, but she felt the pain subside within him. For better or worse, he and Volpe were still joined.

A cry of fury erupted nearby and she twisted around to see Foscari struggling with a cluster of the Ten. He screamed words in some guttural tongue, some ancient Babel language she would never learn, and grabbed one of them by the throat. Like the other he had destroyed, it began to unravel and collapse in upon itself.

But the rest had his arms then, twisting them behind him, trying to keep him from touching any more of them.

Foscari threw them off, staggering, wheeling across the floor to crash into the stone column right in front of her. His face had been clawed and beaten, cheek gashed to the bone, and his left arm was torn and bloody.

As he started to push away from the column, he saw her there in the dark.

"Bitch! I'll have your eyes for this!"

Another dead man tugged him backward. Knife in hand, Geena followed him out. The blade felt heavy in her grasp, but the weight of consequence—what would happen if she did not stop this man—was far heavier.

Foscari laughed at the sight of the knife. "You can't be stupid enough to think that will kill me."

One of the Ten got a fistful of his hair, began to drag his head back. Another of the dead caught his arm. With a muttered curse, Foscari tried to strike back, but by then Geena was already moving.

He tore free, whipped his fist around and caught her with a skull-rattling backhand, but the dead man still held him by the hair. Blood dripped down her chin, her lip swollen and split, but she barely felt it as she lunged at him. Her free hand caught his wrist, held it back, and she swept the knife around in an arc that sliced cleanly through his throat. Blood sprayed her face and clothes; it stung her eyes as she blinked it away.

Choking on his own blood, Foscari gurgled laughter.

"Damn you, stop fucking laughing!" she screamed.

". . . plague . . ." he croaked, wheezed, pointed to her. ". . . dead."

Clutching a hand over his throat, sealing the wound, he sneered as he stumbled toward her. She thought of the sickness that had ravaged her and Nico after they'd killed Caravello and the spell Volpe had done to cure them, and she wondered if it had an expiration date.

"I'll be fine," she said with a confidence she did not feel. She held up the knife. "But you won't."

Foscari's eyes narrowed with sudden alarm. He fell to one knee. Then, furious with his sudden weakness, forced himself to rise again. But he moved slowly now, reaching for her with a trembling hand.

"This blade is stained with the blood of the chosen Oracles of Venice," she said. "The city endures, but you're not as immortal as you like to think."

With a choking, wordless rage, Foscari lunged for her. Cruelty and lust still tinged his gaze, even as he began to die, and she knew he was intent upon taking her with him into death.

Geena stabbed him in the chest, putting all of her weight behind the blade, pulling him in close like a lover, and twisting. Foscari stiffened and then crumpled into her embrace. She could have laid him gently upon the ground, but he did not deserve her tenderness. She recoiled from his diseased blood and his filthy touch—just tugged the knife out and let him slump wetly to the floor.

The plague. If she was going to get sick again, how soon would she begin to cough? How quickly would the sores appear?

Finish him!

The words were Volpe's, echoing in her mind. She'd heard little of Nico's thoughts in the past two minutes, but had felt his fear and fury and pain. Now she spun, thinking for a moment that Volpe had been talking to her, that he didn't realize Foscari was already dead.

But the words weren't for her.

Four of the withered dead, the last remnants of Volpe's loyal Council of Ten, were holding Pietro Aretino pinned against the wall. One of his hands had been hacked off and the other broken and bloodied, meaning that spells that required the use of his hands were out of the question. He began to chant something, still trying to stay alive.

"I said, finish him!" Nico shouted in Volpe's voice. Or the other way around. There was little distinction now between one and the other.

Nico stood only a few feet from Aretino and began to claw his fingers at the air, summoning a spell that would end the life of the last Doge.

"No!" Geena screamed, running toward him, but they didn't seem to hear her.

Nico, stop!

He hesitated, glanced over at her. Through the rapport they shared she could sense Volpe trying to finish the job. Geena slammed into Nico, knocking him to the ground, straddling him there and staring down into his eyes.

"The plague jars!" she shouted. "Didn't you listen? If all three of them die, the waters will flood in and smash the jars and the plague will take all of Venice."

Anger had clouded the minds of both men who lived in that body, but now the eyes cleared. She could not tell who gazed out at her from within, but she saw that reason had returned, and she exhaled.

"That's all right," Nico and Volpe said, in one voice. "I have a better idea."

❖

The dead Ten—those Foscari had not destroyed—restrained Aretino while the magician, this strange combination of Nico and Volpe, silenced the old Doge with a spell. He could not speak enchantments, could not warp the air without fingers.

Eyes wide with the terror he would have gladly brought to others, Aretino struggled uselessly as the dead men began a chant that sounded more like creaking hinges than voices. They cut the papery skin on their palms and held their hands forward, but only chalky dust fell to vanish in the water on the floor. When Nico sliced his palm open, true blood flowed and pooled and swirled in the water with that dust, and the ritual gathered its power.

So much remained to be done. With the Doge's life essence preserved just as Volpe's had been, his heart still alive and still beating, the spells that had been woven around the plague jars and the chambers where they had been hidden would be maintained. She and Nico would have to find every single one of those chambers and destroy the plague jars with the cleansing flame Volpe would teach them how to use. It would take time, but Geena was beginning to realize that they would have that time. Time to learn. Time to love.

But only if Volpe kept his word.

When Nico—and Volpe, always Volpe—stepped in to drive their knives into Aretino's chest and carve out his heart, Geena couldn't watch any longer. She bolted for the stairs, knowing as she did that she had seen the Chamber of Ten for the last time.

Aren't you going to say good-bye? Volpe whispered in her mind.

He had promised to leave Nico, to let his spirit pass into the next world and leave Venice to a new generation of Oracles, but she still did not trust him. How could she? The question followed her up the stairs into Petrarch's library, and then up into the Biblioteca, and finally out into golden morning of the city that had chosen her and Nico to be the keepers of its soul and its secrets.

Venice. *La Serenissima.*

The Most Serene.

CHAPTER 19

THE SUN SHONE BRIGHT ON THE DAY THEY BURIED HIM.

She sailed to San Michele in a water taxi with Tonio, Domenic, Sabrina, and several other lecturers and students from the university. It was the first time she had seen them all since the melee that had ended in Ramus' death. She'd arrived at the jetty moments before the water taxi, and stood behind them for a while, staring at their shadows. Today, they were as darkly attired as the shadows themselves, all visions in black. Domenic had seen her first, raising an eyebrow as he glanced back over his shoulder, and when they boarded the taxi the others offered her nods, or smiles, or awkward combinations of the two. Only Tonio had seemed unfazed by her appearance. He had granted her two weeks' sick leave, on the proviso that upon her return she spend some time explaining. He knew, of course, that in the meantime she was helping the police with their inquiries.

She had a week left in which to construct her watertight story. It was more than long enough. She hoped that Nico would be there for that week to help her.

She had not seen Nico in five days, but she had always sensed him close. It was nothing like those usual sensations she picked up from him, because he was no longer himself. He was Nico and Volpe, Volpe and Nico—the merging of a 15th century magician with a 21st century academic. He was a stranger that she recognized, and today was the day she hoped everything would change. To face a new beginning, first she needed an ending.

Aren't you going to say good-bye? Volpe had whispered. Perhaps he had remained in Nico waiting for just that.

The boat hit a small wave and Geena swayed, shifting her foot to regain balance. A hand held her elbow, strong and firm, and she glanced sidelong at Domenic. He smiled sadly, and in his eyes she saw something that she clung to, storing away for future reference in case the future became too harsh: the ability to understand. When she'd asked him to gather the soaked remains of Volpe's heart and transport them out of Venice, he had not questioned her request, strange though it had been. She was beginning to suspect that perhaps he loved her, but it was more than that. Domenic could see past the normal and into the incredible, and maybe in his mind the line between the two had always been blurred.

"How are you?" he asked. A simple question with so many answers.

"I'm bearing up," she said.

"And Nico?"

She shrugged, because she didn't know. Nico's future was not yet defined. If Volpe kept his word, today would be the day. But she could barely let herself hope.

"Well, it's a shame about him and the university," Domenic said softly. The sound of the boat's engine and its hull striking the low waves covered his voice, so that only Geena could hear. "He's a clever guy."

"He is," Geena said. "He'll find his own way."

"So . . ." Domenic said. He still had a hold on her elbow, and she found herself comforted by his contact. Domenic was strong and firm, and there was no ambiguity about him. "So, that other thing? Those . . . remains I moved out for you? How did all that work out?"

It didn't, Geena needed to say, *because the old magician's spirit it belonged to lied, and he's tenacious, and after we'd killed the Doges and those other people he promised to go and* . . . But she could tell him nothing of that, of course. Not now. Maybe later.

"It worked out fine," she said, and the boat nudged against the jetty.

Ramus' coffin was already on San Michele, and there were hundreds of mourners milling around the entrance to the cemetery as they awaited notice that the service was about to begin. Geena saw many students and lecturers she knew from the university, and plenty more she did not. Ramus' family was also there—a large group of adults and children keeping close together like an island in the sea of mourners. There was much crying, and little laughter. That more than anything made Geena sad, and brought on her first tears of the day. Ramus deserved much better than this. If he'd been killed in a cave-in while on a dig, or the collapse of an ancient building he was studying, perhaps the mood here, though heavy at the tragic death of someone so young, might have also been lifted to celebrate the fact that he'd died doing what he loved.

But he had been stabbed to death in a café by a mysterious assailant. He'd bled out on the floor waiting for paramedics to arrive, with Sabrina holding his hands and Domenic struggling to stem the bleeding from his many wounds. That was no way for such a bright light to be extinguished.

Geena walked close to Domenic, looking out for Nico. She knew he would be here, because they'd arranged it. They had spoken that morning, mind to mind. They no longer had any need for phones.

"Quite a turnout," Domenic said.

"He deserves it."

"What happened, Geena?" he asked, quietly again. Behind Domenic, Tonio glanced at her, and she wondered if he'd heard. She smiled over Domenic's shoulder and her boss smiled back, but there was a distance in his expression that had nothing to do with today's funeral. She knew that he would never fully trust her again. The ongoing investigation into the Mayor's murder had been linked by the police to the fight at the café, and Ramus' death. And one of the abiding mysteries of that evening revolved around Geena. Who had the men been who'd dragged her away? So far, she'd stuck with the insistence that she didn't know. But Tonio was not stupid.

"Domenic, one day soon we can talk," she said, and she stepped forward to hug him tight.

"And that book you want locked away at the university?"

"A very old book about forgotten magic. It's got to be kept secure and it deserves to be studied. But I need full access, at any time."

She felt him tense, sensed his confusion, and then she felt the moment that Domenic started trusting her again.

"But is it over?" he asked.

"Yes," she said, and she thought, *For everyone but me.* At that, he returned her hug. It felt good.

Moments before the service began she sensed Nico nearby. *I'm here*, he said in her mind, *and I have it.*

Won't you stand with me?

I'm not sure that's for the best. She listened for Nico's true voice, and Volpe's slurring of his meaning, but heard neither. He was speaking with her plain and simple.

But—she began.

Here, he said. And she felt his hand in hers. *Just because we're not standing side by side doesn't mean we can't be together.*

Geena sobbed, once, and as well as Nico's hand in hers, she felt Domenic's comforting touch on her shoulder.

After the service came the burial, and she was surprised to find Howard Finch positioning himself to her left. He gave her a soft smile, which she returned, and then they stood in silence while Geena's student and friend was buried. The crowd of mourners was so large that many people found themselves standing on or beside other graves, careful to avoid the gravestones, peering from behind larger tombs, and filling the narrow pathways that crisscrossed this part of the island. The markers here were basic and mostly new;

older remains were stored in metal ossuaries and kept in elaborate tombs elsewhere on the island. Even here, Ramus' mortal remains would not be at rest for some time. Geena only hoped that his spirit was becalmed, wherever it might be now. As a young woman, she'd always had doubts about such things, even though her life was committed to tracing communications of the past with the present. Now she was much more of a believer.

As the burial ended and the crowd slowly began to disperse, she felt Nico's influence leaving. *I'll be waiting*, he said, and she told him she'd be there soon.

"Dr. Hodge, I'm so sorry for your loss," Finch said at last. "He was a bright lad. Terrible. Tragic." He took a handkerchief from his pocket and mopped at his forehead, obviously uncomfortable in the suit. The sun was blazing. Geena wondered when it was that she'd got used to such heat.

"Thanks, Howard. And please, call me Geena."

"Geena," he said, nodding. "Well."

"Well?"

He grimaced at her, shrugged, and she knew he had to talk business. Of course. "Tonio tells me you'll be back at work in a week, and—"

"Sooner," she said. "I'll be back in two days."

"Good. Good. And . . . after everything, I was still hoping we might be able to . . . work together?"

"Even though the Chamber is flooded again?"

Finch shrugged, mopping at his brow. He was losing his fight against sweat. "I still have some resources at my disposal," he said.

"I don't know," Geena said, looking away, thinking of that granite disk, the cap on the well of Akylis. "The Chamber of Ten is dangerous. Surely you can use what footage you've already got, and focus the rest on the books themselves? Sabrina is a whiz with the camera. There'll be footage of the books being examined, and plenty of time for interviews down the line."

"I don't have that much time."

"All the more reason to just go with what you've got."

During the several days since those events down in the Chamber, Nico had gently filled her in on what had happened. He'd never once asked her why she had fled—he didn't have to, because the fear had been rich and hot in his own mind as well—but he had insisted on letting her know what happened afterward. *In case,* he had said, and she'd known what he meant. In case Volpe stays for good.

Strange that it was Volpe also saying that.

After the deaths had come the cleansing fire. The contagion in the Doges was wiped out, and Volpe had also used it to consume evidence of the conflict. Aretino and Foscari were dust, and their hired thugs were melted and charred away to nothing. And then, on his way out of the Chamber and Petrarch's library, Nico had turned off the pumps.

By the time the Chamber was pumped out again, the broken obelisks and scattered remains of the Council of Ten would be blamed on the water surge.

"This needs to be done gently, and with respect," Geena said. "We marched in there too quickly. We need to study and catalog, not storm in like we own the place."

"But you do," Finch said, confused. "Or at least, the city council does."

"The building, yes. But not the past. That's a strange place, and no one owns it. So . . . perhaps in a few weeks, I can call you and invite you back over. You can view our footage then, yes? You'll be able to use a great deal of what we've already got. As for the documentary . . . Petrarch's library is a collection of thoughts and ideas and stories on paper, not the room they were stored in."

She could see that he was angry, but he was also at a funeral. There could be no raised voices here, and in truth she thought he'd respect her wishes. A lot had happened that he did not understand—that no one understood, other than her and Nico—and she sensed an underlying desire in this man to leave. Once he moved on to the next project, he would do his best to forget this one.

"Tonio has my contact details," Finch said.

"He does. Thank you, Howard."

He smiled, not unpleasantly, and walked away.

"Are you coming back with us?" Domenic asked.

"No," Geena said. "Nico's here. I haven't seen him in a few days, and we have things to discuss."

Domenic looked only momentarily startled. He was sharp enough not to ask if she thought she'd be all right with Nico. *I saw him shot*, he'd said to her two days before, talking about that attack when Ramus had been killed.

You saw the bullet hit him?

No, but . . .

He was terrified, Domenic. More scared than all of us there. The gun fired and he fell.

Who the hell were those men?

We don't know. The police have been asking me that for the last twenty-four hours. They think they were linked to the ones who murdered the Mayor, but . . . in reality, no one knows. All I can think is they want something from the library.

That had given Domenic pause. *Or from the Chamber below.*

The Chamber? There's nothing down there but dust.

Now that I moved that thing out of the city for you, yes.

Thieves, perhaps, Geena had said. *You know as well as I do some of those books are priceless.*

There was added security at the university and the Biblioteca now, and Geena knew her future held more interviews with the police. They continued to search the city for men who were dead and gone to dust, using pictures sketched from her own memory. It had been unsettling, looking at artists' impressions of Aretino and Foscari.

"I'll see you soon," Domenic said.

"Count on it." She smiled as he left, and then Geena wended her way through the crowd of black-dressed mourners, toward Nico.

And there, hopefully, she would find the man she loved.

❖

Nico stood beneath an olive tree planted just to the side of a wide path. Sunlight dappled his head and cast the shadows of a hundred leaves across his arms and hands, and the thing he was holding there against his chest. The urn was old and looked delicate, but Geena knew that it was sealed by more than wax and blood. Magic held this container tighter than Nico's hands.

He watched her as she approached, smiling, and she smiled back. She could feel the tingle of pleasure that seeing her gave him. But even as she drew close she could not see his eyes—the shadows here were deeper than she'd thought, the tree canopy heavier—and as he spoke, she knew that Volpe was still there.

"It's all coming to an end," he said.

"Yes."

"You sound sad. You were hoping I'd be gone?"

"I was hoping you'd keep your word."

Nico stepped forward and his eyes were not quite his own. And yet, she did see parts of Nico there. The care for her, the confusion, and his undeniable youth struggling with the aged thing settled within him.

"And I intend to," Volpe said. "But it's not quite that simple. There's this to finish." He lifted the urn, shook it slightly with a dry laugh. "And then . . . one more thing."

"Only one more?" she asked. She so wanted to go to him, hug him, feel his warmth, but she could only ever embrace him again when he was purely Nico. It was cruel to shun her lover over something beyond his control, but she had to think of herself as well. She had to think about her safety. Her sanity.

"Only one more," he said. "I promise." He turned and walked away, glancing back to see if she was following.

After a pause in the shade of that tree, she was.

❖

Geena was not shocked or surprised at the skeletons. Over the past few days, conversing in her mind, Nico had told her where this had to end. Aretino's heart had been contained and in Nico's possession ever since the Chamber, but it needed to be hidden away where no one would ever find it. The Volpe crypt on San Michele was the one place left in Venice that was still governed by dregs of the magician's magic. Concealment spells had not been disturbed, shielding hexes were still strong and in place, and this might as well have been a hole in the ground of another planet. As far as anyone in Venice was concerned, this place did not exist.

And located where it was, on an island where invasive archaeology had ceased long ago, it never would.

The journey down had been strange, passing through doorways that looked like blank walls to Geena, and along a short corridor whose atmosphere had felt thick and heavy as molasses. And emerging into the underground room, waiting at the doorway while Nico went around and lit a dozen candles, the true turmoil of Volpe's family history came to light.

"So all these were your enemies?" she asked, and Volpe smiled.

"A man without enemies has lived an unremarkable life."

"Nice outlook."

"It's almost over," Nico said. "Can't you feel that, Geena?"

She wasn't sure. She felt a change coming, for certain, and she knew it was more than simply putting what had happened with the Doges—and poor Ramus—behind them. Ramus' death would echo for a long time, because the police investigation would be a part of their lives for months to come. But there was something else beyond that, a feeling embedded in the roots and heart of the city.

"I don't know," Geena said. "I know that something new is about to begin."

"That, too," Nico said. He came close, and looked into her eyes for the first time since meeting beneath the tree. Even lit by candles, she knew his eyes were different. She'd seen them last as she fled that chamber of death and blood, and they looked exactly the same now. Volpe was still in residence alongside Nico, merged with him and, perhaps, subsuming him a little.

He would deny that, of course. And this was why she knew she could never live with him like this.

"Not long," he said.

"Good-bye," Geena said.

Volpe chuckled, a deep guttural laugh that could never belong to Nico. And yet there was a lightness to it she had not heard in his voice before.

"A sense of humor is good," he said. "And, perhaps, something I should have tried to develop more in myself."

"Nico laughs."

"And I will again." Nico moved away and finished lighting the candles. The soft light shone yellow from old bones, and he shoved a few scattered skeletons aside as he walked across the room. Skulls stared at Geena, eye sockets dancing with shadowy amusement. She wondered who they had been, and whether they had thought themselves good.

"Good and bad," Nico said, reading her mind. "We have to learn that sometimes neither matters. Where the city is concerned, such human foibles are petty and meaningless compared to its survival. This is such an important place. There are other cities around the world with their own Oracles, and each one is important in its own right. But Venice is a jewel in a pile of coal. You understand?"

"I understand that's the way you think."

Nico smiled, shrugged. "Perhaps I am biased." He picked up the urn from where he had placed it close to the door and moved to a pile of skeletons mounded against one wall. "Will you help?"

Geena surprised herself by helping Nico lift the bones aside. They worked well together, shifting the skeletons quickly, though she tried to ignore the cool chalky feel of them and the way they clicked tonelessly together as they touched. When there were only two skeletons left against the wall, Nico nestled the urn in one of their rib cages. Then, without pause, he started piling the others back on top.

"No final spell or last words?" Geena asked as she helped.

"For him, no."

"But for you?"

Nico was panting by the time he'd finished stacking the bones, and he wiped his hands across his front. Sweat speckled his forehead and upper lip. He smiled.

"For me," he said. "And as for me, so for you. I'm going to keep my promise, though you suspected I would not, because it's my time to move on. The city chose me, and the city has chosen again. You and Nico. And who am I to question the will of a city?"

"You're Zanco Volpe," she said. "A powerful magician."

"I'm a breath in a hurricane," he said.

"So what do we do?"

"We accept the will of the city," Volpe said. "In doing that, I will leave this flesh and rest in an object that must then be broken to release me fully."

"Everything's broken down here," Geena said, looking around at the piles of bones and skulls.

"It's the fresh breaking that matters," he said. "Symbolic." He walked slowly around the subterranean room, and then paused, kneeling before a pile of skulls and drawing one out. "Ahh, Gualtiero," he said, running his finger across a ragged rent in the skull's dome.

"Who's that?" Geena asked, but Volpe did not reply. He remained kneeling for a while, and Geena opened her mind to his memories. But there were none. She felt Nico holding back, too, and realized with shock that he was granting Volpe some measure of space and respect. That was the first time she believed that the old magician meant to keep his word.

After a few more moments of reminiscence, Volpe stood and returned to Geena. He sat on the floor before her and motioned her to follow suit.

"Welcome the city's choice," he said, "you and Nico both. Open your minds to its influence. Breathe deeply, and when you take your third breath you will become what I have been for so long. Oracles."

"And you?"

He nodded down at the skull. "Trapped, for a fleeting moment, before the shattering that grants me release."

Geena was shaking. Volpe had threatened and abused her and Nico, but he had also saved their lives more than once. He had not *chosen* Nico in which to commit the acts he had performed. Accident and fate had brought them together. And now, close to having her own love back with her, whole and unblemished, she felt a curious sadness.

"Oh, I could have stayed," Volpe said softly, and he smiled—an ugly expression. Perhaps he'd never had much cause for it.

"Thank you," Geena said. She closed her eyes and caught a momentary stab of surprise from Nico—or from Volpe, perhaps—and then they held hands and started breathing together.

She breathed in once, deeply, and Nico did the same. She smelled the dust of old bones.

On the second breath, Geena felt a staggering attention focusing on her, as if everyone in Venice had stopped what they were doing and were thinking of her, and her alone. She gasped and tasted Nico's expelled breath as well, heard his own gasp, and squeezed back when he clasped her hands.

They breathed in together for the third time.

Her beating heart settled. Calmness descended. She felt Nico shaking, just for a second, but enough to force her eyes open. Looking down at the skull on the ground between them she saw nothing different. She held on while Nico calmed more slowly than she had, his shoulders slumping, and he seemed to lessen before her, shrinking down into something . . .

Into something she knew. He was becoming Nico again, and the realization struck her that, over the past few days, Volpe had changed her lover so much. *Can he ever really recover from that?* she wondered, squeezing his hands. *Can he ever be himself again?*

She stood and Nico stood with her, his eyes still squeezed shut. She raised one foot and brought it down on the skull, the old fractures snapping under the impact, bone fragments and teeth scattering around her feet.

The room gasped. Nico's eyes snapped open, and they were fixed directly on Geena. Shock froze the moment for them both. In her mind, and through the unique link she had with Nico, she felt a widening of perception, and an expansion of knowledge. She knew the city like never before—its shape and quirks, its people and places, those that lived good lives, and those not so good—and for a moment she and Nico felt as if the city was inside them, not the other way around.

We are both the new Oracles, she thought, and she heard that idea echoed in Nico's voice.

She paused for a measureless instant before stepping in close and hugging him to her. Breathing him in. Holding him tight.

CHRISTOPHER GOLDEN is the *New York Times*–bestselling, Bram Stoker Award–winning author of such novels as *Ararat*, *Snowblind*, *Of Saints and Shadows*, and *The Pandora Room*. With Mike Mignola, he is the co-creator of two cult favorite comic book series, Baltimore and Joe Golem: Occult Detective. As an editor, he has worked on the short story anthologies *Seize the Night*, *Dark Cities*, and *The New Dead*, among others, and he has also written and co-written comic books, video games, screenplays, and a network television pilot. His original novels have been published in more than fifteen languages in countries around the world.

Please visit him at **www.christophergolden.com**.

TIM LEBBON is a *New York Times*–bestselling author of more than forty novels. Recent books include *The Folded Land*, *Relics*, *The Family Man*, *The Silence*, and the Rage War trilogy of Alien/Predator novels. He has won four British Fantasy Awards, a Bram Stoker Award, and a Scribe Award. The movie of his story *Pay the Ghost*, starring Nicolas Cage, was released Hallowe'en 2015. *The Silence*, starring Stanley Tucci and Kiernan Shipka, is due for release in 2018. Several other movie projects are in development in the US and UK.

Find out more about Tim at his websites:
www.timlebbon.net and **www.noreela.com**.

CPSIA information can be obtained
at www.ICGtesting.com
Printed in the USA
BVHW072240041118
531763BV00001B/1/P

9 781635 763935